About the Authors

Nina Singh lives just outside Boston, USA, with her husband, children, and a very rumbunctious Yorkie. After several years in the corporate world she finally followed the advice of family and friends to 'give the writing a go, already'. She's oh-so-happy she did. When not at her keyboard she likes to spend time on the tennis court or golf course. Or immersed in a good read.

Leanne Banks is a *New York Times* bestselling author with over sixty books to her credit. A book lover and romance fan from even before she learned to read, Leanne has always treasured the way that books allow us to go to new places and experience the lives of wonderful characters. Always ready for a trip to the beach, Leanne lives in Virginia with her family and her Pomeranian muse.

Award-winning author **Jennifer Faye** pens fun contemporary romances. With more than a million books sold, she's internationally published with books translated into more than a dozen languages and her work has been optioned for film. Now living her dream, she resides with her very patient husband and Writer Kitty. When she's not plotting out her next romance, you can find her with a mug of tea and a book. Learn more at jenniferfaye.com

D1330319

A Royal Christmas

NINA SINGH

LEANNE BANKS

JENNIFER FAYE

MILLS & BOON

First Published in Great Britain 2022
By Mills & Boon, an imprint of HarperCollins*Publishers* Ltd
1 London Bridge Street, London, SE1 9GF
www.harpercollins.co.uk

HarperCollins*Publishers*
1st Floor, Watermarque Building,
Ringsend Road, Dublin 4, Ireland

ISBN: 978-0-263-31787-9

MIX
Paper | Supporting
responsible forestry
FSC™ C007454
www.fsc.org

This book is produced from independently certified FSC™ paper to ensure responsible forest management.

For more information visit: www.harpercollins.co.uk/green

Printed and Bound in Spain using 100% Renewable electricity at
CPI Black Print, Barcelona

CHRISTMAS WITH
HER SECRET PRINCE

NINA SINGH

To my two very own princes.

And my two princesses.

CHAPTER ONE

PRINCE RAYHAN AL SAIBBI was not looking forward to his next meeting. In fact, he was dreading it. After all, it wasn't often he went against his father—the man who also happened to be king of Verdovia.

But it had to be done. This might very well be his last chance to exert any kind of control over his own life. Even if it was to be only a temporary respite. Fate had made him prince of Verdovia. And his honor-bound duty to that fate would come calling soon enough. He just wanted to try and bat it away one last time.

The sun shone bright and high over the majestic mountain range outside his window. A crisp blue stream meandered along its base. The pleasant sunny day meant his father would most likely be enjoying his breakfast on the patio off the four-seasons room in the east wing.

Rayhan found his father sitting at the far end of the table. Piles of papers and a sleek new laptop were mixed in with various plates of fruits and pastries. A twinge of guilt hit Rayhan as he approached. The king never stopped working. For that matter, neither did the queen, his mother. A fact that needed to be addressed after the events of the past year. Part of the reason Rayhan was in his current predicament.

This conversation wasn't going to be easy. His father

had been king for a long time. He was used to making the rules and expected everyone to follow them. Particularly when it came to his son.

But these days the king wasn't thinking entirely straight. Motivated by an alarming health scare Rayhan's mother had experienced a few months back and prompted by the troublesome maneuverings of a disagreeable council member, his father had decided that the royal family needed to strengthen and reaffirm their stability. Unfortunately, he'd also decided that Rayhan would be the primary vehicle to cement that stability.

His father motioned for him to be seated when he saw Rayhan approach.

"Thank you for seeing me, Father. I know how busy you are."

His father nodded. "It sounded urgent based on your messages. What can I assist you with, son? Dare I hope you're closer to making a decision?"

"I am. Just not in the way you might assume."

Rayhan focused his gaze on his father's face. A face that could very well be an older version of his own. Dark olive skin with high cheekbones and ebony eyes.

"I don't understand," his father began. "You were going to spend some time with the ladies in consideration. Then you were to make a choice."

Rayhan nodded. "I've spent time with all three of them, correct. They're all lovely ladies, Father. Very accomplished—all of them stunning and impressive in their own unique way. You have chosen well."

"They come from three of the most notable and prominent families of our land. You marrying a prominent daughter of Verdovia will go far to address our current problems."

"Like I said, you have chosen well."

The king studied him. "Then what appears to be the issue?"

Where to start? First of all, he wasn't ready to be wedded to any of the ladies in question. In fact, he wasn't ready to be wedded at all.

But he had a responsibility. Both to his family and to the kingdom.

"Perhaps I shall choose for you," the king suggested, his annoyance clear as the crisp morning air outside. "You know how important this is. And how urgent. Councilman Riza is preparing a resolution as we speak to propose studying the efficacy and necessity of the royal family's very existence."

"You know it won't go anywhere. He's just stirring chaos."

"I despise chaos." His father blew out a deep breath. "All the more reason to put this plan into action, son."

The *plan* his father referred to meant the end of Rayhan's life as he knew it. "It just seems such an archaic and outdated method. A bachelor prince choosing from qualified ladies to serve as his queen when he eventually ascends the throne."

His father shrugged. "Arranged marriages are quite common around the world. Particularly for a young man of your standing. Global alliances are regularly formed through marriage vows. It's how your mother and I wedded, as you know. These ladies I have chosen are very well-known and popular in the kingdom."

Rayhan couldn't argue the point. There was the talented prima ballerina who had stolen the people's hearts when she'd first appeared on stage several years ago. Then there was the humanitarian who'd made the recent influx of refugees and their plight her driving cause. And finally, a councilman's beautiful daughter, who also happened to be an international fashion model.

Amazing ladies. All of whom seemed to be approaching the king's proposition more as a career opportunity than anything else. Which in blatant terms was technically correct. Of course, the people didn't know that fact. They just believed their crown prince to be linked to three different ladies, and rumors abounded that he would propose to one of them within weeks. A well-calculated palace publicity stunt.

"As far as being outdated," the king continued, "have you seen the most popular show in America these days? It involves an eligible bachelor choosing from among several willing ladies. By giving them weekly roses, of all things." His father barked out a laugh at the idea.

"But this isn't some reality show," Rayhan argued. "This is my life."

"Nevertheless, a royal wedding will distract from this foolishness of Riza's."

Rayhan couldn't very well argue that point either. The whole kingdom was even now in the frenzied midst of preparing for the wedding of the half century, everyone anxious to see which young lady the prince would choose for himself. Combined with the festivities of the holiday season, the level of excitement and celebration throughout the land was almost palpable.

And Rayhan was about to go and douse it all like a wet blanket over a warming fire.

Bah humbug.

Well, so be it. This was his life they were talking about. He wanted to claim one last bit of it. He wouldn't take no for an answer. Not this time. But this was a new experience for him. Rayhan had never actually willingly gone against the king's wishes before. Not for something this important anyway.

"Well, I've come to a different decision," he told his father. Rayhan made sure to look him straight in the eye as he continued, "I've decided to wait."

The king blinked. Several times. Rapidly. "I beg your pardon?"

"I'd like to hold off. I'm not ready to choose a fiancée. Not just yet."

"You can only postpone for so long, son. The kingdom is waiting for a royal wedding... We have announced your intention to marry. And then there's your mother."

Rayhan felt a pang of guilt through his chest at the mention of the queen. She'd given them all quite a scare last year. "Mother is fine now."

"Still, she needs to slow down. I won't have her health jeopardized again. Someone needs to help take over some of the queen's regular duties. Your sisters are much too young."

"All I'm asking for is some time, Father. Perhaps we can come to a compromise."

The king leaned toward him, his arms resting on the table. At least he was listening. "What sort of compromise did you have in mind?"

Rayhan cleared his throat and began to tell him.

"Honestly, Mel. If you handle that invitation any more, it's going to turn into ash in your hands."

Melinda Osmon startled as her elderly, matronly employer walked by the counter where she sat waiting for her shift to begin. The older woman was right. This had to be at least the fifth or sixth time Mel had taken the stationery out simply to stare at it since it had arrived in her mailbox several days ago.

The Honorable Mayor and Mrs. Spellman request
the pleasure of your presence…

"You caught me," Mel replied, swiftly wiping the
moisture off her cheeks.

"Just send in your reply already," Greta added, her
back turned to her as she poured coffee for the customer
sitting at the end of the counter. The full breakfast crowd
wasn't due in for another twenty minutes or so. "Then
figure out what you're going to wear."

Melinda swallowed past the lump in her throat before
attempting an answer. "Greta, you know I can't go this
year. It's just not worth the abject humiliation."

Greta turned to her so fast that some of the coffee
splashed out of her coffeepot. "Come again? What in the
world do you have to be humiliated about?"

Not this again. Greta didn't seem to understand, nor
did she want to. How about the fact that Mel hadn't yet
moved on? Unlike her ex-husband. The ex-husband who
would be at the same party with his fashionable, svelte
and beautiful new fiancée. "Well, for one thing, I'd be
going solo. That's humiliating enough in itself."

Greta jutted out her chin and snapped her gum loudly.
"And why is that? You're not the one who behaved
shamefully and had the affair. That scoundrel you were
married to should be the one feeling too ashamed to show
his face at some fancy-schmancy party you both used to
attend every year when you were man and wife."

Mel cringed at the unfiltered description.

"Now, you listen to me, young lady—"

Luckily, another customer cleared his throat just then,
clearly impatient for a hit of caffeine. Greta humphed and
turned away to pour. Mel knew the reprieve would be
short-lived. Greta had very strong opinions about how

Mel should move along into the next chapter of her life. She also had very strong opinions about Mel's ex. To say the older woman was outraged on Mel's behalf was to put it mildly. In fact, the only person who might be even angrier was Greta's even older sister, Frannie. Not that Mel wasn't pretty outraged herself. A lot of good that did for her, though. Strong emotions were not going to get her a plus-one to the mayor's Christmas soiree. And she certainly was nowhere near ready to face the speculation and whispery gossip that was sure to greet her if she set foot in that ballroom alone.

"She's right, you know," Frannie announced, sliding into the seat next to Mel. The two sisters owned the Bean Pot Diner on Marine Street in the heart of South Boston. The only place that would hire her when she'd found herself broke, alone and suddenly separated. "I hate to admit when that blabbermouth is right but she sure is about this. You should go to that party and enjoy yourself. Show that no-good, cheating charlatan that you don't give a damn what he thinks."

"I don't think I have it in me, Frannie. Just to show up and then have to stare at Eric and his fiancée having the time of their lives, while I'll be sitting there all alone."

"I definitely don't think you should do that."

Well, that was a sudden change of position, Melinda thought, eyeing her friend. "So you agree I shouldn't go?"

"No, that's not what I said. I think you should go, look ravishing and then confront him about all he put you through. Then demand that he return your money."

Melinda sighed. She should have seen that argument coming. "First of all, I gave him that money." Foolishly. The hard-earned money that her dear parents had left her after their deaths. It was supposed to have been an investment in Eric's future. Their future. She had gladly handed it to him to help him get through dental school. Then it was supposed to be her turn to make some kind of investment in herself while he supported her. Instead, he'd left her for his perky, athletic dental assistant. His much younger, barely-out-of-school dental assistant. And now they happily cared for teeth together during the day, while planning an extravagant wedding in their off-hours. "I gave it to him with no strings attached."

"And you should take him to court to get some of it back!" Frannie slapped her palm against the counter. Greta sashayed back over to where the two of them sat.

"That's right," Greta declared. "You should go to that damn party looking pretty as a fashion model. Then demand he pay you back. Every last cent. Or you'll see him in front of a judge."

Mel sighed and bit down on the words that were forming on her tongue. As much as she longed to tell the two women to mind their own business, Mel just couldn't bring herself to do it. They'd been beyond kind to her when she'd needed it the most. Not to mention, they were the closest thing to family Mel could count since her divorce a year ago.

"How? I barely have the money for court fees. Let alone any to hire an attorney."

"Then start with the party," Greta declared as her sister nodded enthusiastically. "At the very least, ruin his evening. Show him what he's missing out on."

Nothing like a couple of opinionated matrons doubleteaming you.

Mel let out an unamused laugh. "As if. I don't even have a dress to wear. I sold all my fancier clothes just to make rent that first month."

Greta waved a hand in dismissal. "So buy another one. I tell you, if I had your figure and that great dark hair of yours, I'd be out shopping right now. Women like you can find even the highest-end clothing on sale."

Mel ignored the compliment. "I can't even afford the stuff on sale these days, Greta."

"So take an advance on your paycheck," Frannie offered from across the counter. "We know you're good for it."

Mel felt the immediate sting of tears. These women had taken her in when she'd needed friendship and support the most. She'd never be able to repay their kindness. She certainly had no desire to take advantage of it. "I can't ask you to do that for me, ladies."

"Nonsense," they both said in unison.

"You'd be doing it for us," Greta added.

"For you?"

"Sure. Let two old bats like us live vicariously through you. Go to that ball and then come back and tell us all about it."

Frannie nodded in agreement. "That's right. Especially the part about that no-good scoundrel begging you for forgiveness after he takes one look at ya."

Mel smiled in spite of herself. These two certainly knew how to cook up a good fantasy. Eric had left her high and dry and never looked back even once. As far as fantasies went, she was more likely to turn a frog into a prince than receive any kind of apology from her ex-husband.

"I don't think that's going to happen anytime soon." Or ever. Mel reached down to tighten the laces of her comfortable white tennis shoes. She had a very long shift ahead of her, starting with the breakfast crowd and ending with the early-evening dinner guests.

"You won't know unless you go to this ball."

She couldn't even tell which of the ladies had thrown

that out. Mel sighed and straightened to look at them both. Her bosses might look like gentle, sweet elderly ladies, complete with white hair done up in buns, but they could be relentless once they set their minds to something.

"All right. I give."

They both squealed with delight. "Then it's settled," Frannie declared and clasped her hands in front of her chest.

Mel held a hand up. "Not so fast. I haven't agreed to go just yet."

Greta's smile faded. "Come again?"

"How about a deal?"

"What kind of deal?"

"I'll go out after my shift and look for a dress." Though how she would summon the energy after such a long day was a mystery. But she was getting the feeling she'd hear about this all day unless she threw her two bosses some kind of bone. "If, and only if, I come across a dress that's both affordable and appropriate, I'll reconsider going."

Frannie opened her mouth, clearly about to protest. Mel cut her off.

"It's my only offer. Take it or leave it."

"Fine," they both said in unison before turning away. Mel stood just as the bell for the next order up rang from the kitchen. She had a long day ahead of her and it was only just starting. She was a waitress now. Not the young bride of an up-and-coming urban dentist who attended fancy holiday balls and went shopping for extravagant ball gowns. That might have been her reality once, but it had been short-lived.

Little did the Perlman sisters know, she had told them something of a fib just now when making that deal. She had no expectation that she'd find any kind of dress that would merit attending that party in a week.

The chances were slim to zero.

His driver-slash-security-guard—who also happened to be a dear childhood friend—was very unhappy with him at the moment. Rayhan ignored the scowl of the other man as he watched the streets of downtown Boston outside his passenger-side window. Every shop front had been decorated with garlands and glittery Christmas decorations. Bright lights were strung on everything from the lamp poles to shop windows. Let his friend scowl away, Rayhan thought. He was going to go ahead and enjoy the scenery. But when Saleh took yet another turn a little too fast and sharp, he found he'd had enough. Saleh was acting downright childish.

To top it off, they appeared to be lost. Saleh had refused to admit he needed the assistance of the navigation system and now they appeared to be nowhere near their destination.

"You know you didn't have to come," Rayhan reminded the other man. "You volunteered, remember?"

Saleh grunted. "I clearly wasn't thinking straight. Why are we here, again? At this particular time, no less."

"You know this."

"I know you're delaying the inevitable."

He was right, of course. Not that Rayhan was going to admit it out loud. "I still have a bit of time to live my life as I see fit."

"And you decided you needed to do part of that in Boston?"

Rayhan shrugged, resuming his perusal of the outside scenery. "That was completely coincidental. My father's been eyeing property out here for months now. Perfect opportunity for me to come find a prime location and seal the deal."

"Yes, so you say. It's a way to... How do the Americans say it? To kill two birds with one stone?"

"Precisely."

"So why couldn't you have come out here with the new soon-to-be-princess after your engagement?"

Rayhan pinched the bridge of his nose. "I just needed to get away before it all gets out of control, Saleh. I don't expect you to understand."

Not many people would, Rayhan thought. Particularly not his friend, who had married the grade-school sweetheart he'd been in love with since their teen years. Unlike Rayhan, Saleh didn't have to answer to nor appease a whole country when it came to his choice of bride.

Rayhan continued, "Everywhere I turn in Verdovia, I'm reminded of the upcoming ceremonies. Everyone is completely preoccupied with who the heir will choose to marry, what the wedding will be like. Yada yada. There are odds being placed in every one of our island casinos on everything from the identity of the next queen to what flavor icing will adorn the royal wedding cake."

Saleh came to a sudden halt at a red light, a wide grin spread across his face.

"What?" Rayhan asked.

"I placed my wager on the vanilla buttercream."

"I see. That's good to know." He made a mental note to go with anything but the vanilla buttercream when the time came. If he had any say on the matter, that was. Between his mother and the princess-to-be, he'd likely have very little sway in such decisions. No doubt his shrewd friend had made his bet based on the very same assumption.

"I don't understand why you refuse to simply embrace

your fate, my friend. You're the heir of one of the most powerful men in the world. With that comes the opportunity to marry and gain a beautiful, accomplished lady to warm your bed. There are worse things in life."

Saleh overlooked the vast amount of responsibility that came with such a life. The stability and prosperity of a whole kingdom full of people would fall on Rayhan's shoulders as soon as he ascended. Even more so than it did now. Few people could understand the overwhelming prospect of such a position. As far as powerful, how much did any of that mean when even your choice of bride was influenced by the consideration of your position?

"How easy for you to say," he told Saleh just as the light turned green and they moved forward. "You found a beautiful woman who you somehow tricked into thinking marrying you was a good idea."

Saleh laughed with good-natured humor. "The greatest accomplishment of my life."

Rayhan was about to answer when a screeching noise jolted both men to full alert. A cyclist veered toward their vehicle at an alarming speed. Saleh barely had time to turn the wheel in order to avoid a full-on collision. Unfortunately, the cyclist shifted direction at precisely the same time. Both he and their SUV were now heading the same way. Right toward a pedestrian. Saleh hit the brakes hard. Rayhan gripped the side bar, waiting for the inevitable impact. Fortunately for them, it never came.

The cyclist, however, kept going. And, unfortunately for the poor pedestrian woman, the bicycle ran straight into her, knocking her off her feet.

"Watch where you're going!" the rider shouted back over his shoulder, not even bothering to stop.

Rayhan immediately jumped out of the car. He ran

around to the front of the SUV and knelt down where the woman still lay by the sidewalk curb.

"Miss, are you all right?"

A pair of startled eyes met his. Very bright green eyes. They reminded him of the shimmering stream that lay outside his windows back home. Not that this was any sort of time to notice that kind of thing.

She blinked, rubbing a hand down a cheek that was rapidly bruising even as they spoke. Saleh appeared at his side.

"Is she okay?"

"I don't know. She's not really responding. Miss, are you all right?"

Her eyes grew wide as she looked at him. "You're lovely," she said in a low, raspy voice.

Dear heavens. The woman clearly had some kind of head injury. "We have to get you to a doctor."

Saleh swore beside him. "I'm so terribly sorry, miss. I was trying to avoid the bike and the cyclist was trying to avoid me but he turned right toward you—"

The woman was still staring at Rayhan. She didn't acknowledge Saleh nor his words at all.

He had a sudden urge to hold her, to comfort her. He wanted to wrap her in his arms, even though she was a complete stranger.

Rayhan reached for his cell phone. "I'll call for an ambulance."

The woman gave a shake of her head before he could dial. "No. I'm okay. Just a little shaken." She blinked some more and looked around. Her eyes seemed to regain some focus. Rayhan allowed himself a breath of relief. Maybe she'd be all right. Her next words brought that hopeful thought to a halt.

"My dress. Do you see it?"

Did she think somehow her clothes had been knocked off her upon impact? "You…uh…you are wearing it still."

Her gaze scanned the area where she'd fallen. "No. See, I found one. I didn't think I would. But I did. And it wasn't all that pricey."

Rayhan didn't need to hear any more. Unless she was addled to begin with, which could very well be a possibility, the lady had clearly suffered a blow to the head. To top it all off, they were blocking traffic and drawing a crowd. Kneeling closer to the woman sprawled in front of him, he lifted her gently into his arms and then stood. "Let's get you to a hospital."

"Oh!" she cried out as Rayhan walked back toward the SUV with her embraced against his chest.

Saleh was fast on his heels and opening the passenger door for them. "No, see, it's all right," she began to protest. "I don't need a doctor. Just that gown."

"We'll make sure to get you a dress," Rayhan reassured her, trying to tell her what she clearly needed to hear. Why was she so focused on clothing at a time like this? "Right after a doctor takes a look at you."

He gently deposited her in the back seat, then sat down next to her. "No, wait," she argued. "I don't need a doctor. I just want my dress."

But Saleh was already driving toward a hospital.

The woman took a panicked look out the window and then winced. The action must have hurt her injuries somehow. She touched a shaky finger to her cheek, which was now a dark purple, surrounded by red splotches.

Even in the messy state she was in, he couldn't help but notice how striking her features were. Dark, thick waves of black hair escaped the confines of some sort of complicated bun on top of her head. A long slender neck graced her slim shoulders. She was curvy—not quite what one would consider slim. Upon first glance, he would never consider someone like her his "type," so to speak. But he had to admit, he appreciated her rather unusual beauty.

That choice of words had him uncomfortably shifting in his seat. He stole a glance at her as she explored her facial injuries with shaky fingers.

Now her right eye had begun to swell as an angry, dark circular ring developed around it. Rayhan bit out a sharp curse. Here he was trying to enjoy what could very well be his last trip to the United States as a free man and he'd ended up hurting some poor woman on his first day here.

Perhaps Saleh was right. Maybe this whole trip had been a terrible idea. Maybe he should have just stayed home and accepted his fate.

There was at least one person who would be much better off right now if he had.

CHAPTER TWO

SHE WOULD HAVE been much better off if she'd just ignored that blasted invitation and thrown it away as soon as it arrived in her mailbox. She should have never even opened it and she definitely should have never even considered going to that godforsaken party. Her intuition had been right from the beginning. She no longer had any kind of business attending fancy balls and wearing glamorous gowns.

But no, she had to go and indulge two little old ladies, as well as her own silly whim. Look where that had got her—sitting on an exam table in a cold room at Mass General, with a couple of strange men out in the hallway.

Although they had to be the best-looking strangers she'd ever encountered. Particularly the one who had carried her to the car. She studied him now through the small window of her exam room door. He stood leaning against the wall, patiently waiting for the doctor to come examine her.

Even in her stunned shock while she lay sprawled by the side of the road, she hadn't been able to help but notice the man's striking good looks. Dark haired, with the barest shadow of a goatee, he looked like he could have stepped out of a cologne advertisement. Though there was no way he was some kind of male fashion model. He carried himself with much too much authority.

His eyes were dark as charcoal, his skin tone just on the darker side of dessert tan. Even before they'd spoken, she'd known he wasn't local.

His looks had taken her by surprise, or perhaps it had been the blow she'd suffered, but she distinctly remembered thinking he was lovely.

Which was a downright silly thought. A better description would be to say he looked dangerous.

Mel shook off the fanciful thoughts. She had other things to worry about besides the striking good looks of the man who had brought her here. They'd called the diner after she'd been processed. Presumably, either Greta or Frannie was on her way to join her at the hospital now. Mel felt a slight pang of guilt about one of them having to leave in the middle of closing up the diner for the night.

She would have frowned but it hurt too much. Her face had taken the brunt of the collision with the reckless cyclist, who, very rudely, had continued on his way. At least the two gentlemen out there hadn't left her alone and bleeding by the side of the road. Though now that meant she would be saddled with an ER bill she couldn't afford. Thinking about that expense, coupled with what she'd paid for the evening dress, had her eyes stinging with regret. In all the confusion and chaos right after the accident, her shopping bag had been left behind. Mel knew she should be grateful that the accident hadn't been worse, but she couldn't help but feel sorry for herself. Would she ever catch a break?

A sharp knock on the door was quickly followed by the entrance of a harried-looking doctor. He did a bit of a double take when he saw her face.

"Let's take a look at you, Miss Osmon."

The doctor wasted no time with his physical examination, then proceeded to ask her a series of questions—everything from the calendar date to what she'd had for breakfast. His unconcerned expression afterward told her she must have passed.

"I think you'll be just fine. Though quite sore for the next several weeks. You don't appear to be concussed. But someone will need to watch you for the next twenty-four hours or so. Just to be on the safe side." He motioned to the door. "Mind if I let your boyfriend in? He appears to be very concerned about you."

"Oh, he's not—they're just the—"

The doctor raised an eyebrow in question. "I apologize. He took care of the necessary paperwork and already settled the fees. I just assumed."

He had settled the bill? A nagging sense of discomfort blossomed in her chest. This stranger had paid for her care. She would have to figure out how to pay him back. Not that it would be easy.

The physician continued, "In any case, if he's the one who'll be watching you, he'll need to hear this."

"He won't be watching me. I have a friend—"

Before she got the last word out, Greta came barreling through the door, her springy gray hair still wrapped tight in a kitchen hairnet.

"Yowza," the older woman exclaimed as soon as her gaze landed on Mel's face. "You look like you went a couple rounds with a prizefighter. Or were ya fighting over a discounted item at The Basement? Their shoppers can be brutal!"

"Hi, Greta. Thanks for coming."

"Sure thing, kid. I took a cab over as soon as we heard. You doin' okay?" She'd left the door wide-open behind her. The two strangers hovered uncertainly out in the hallway, both of them giving her concerned looks.

Mel sighed. *What the heck? May as well make this a standing room–only crowd.* After all, they were nice enough to bring her in and take care of the processing while she was being examined. She motioned for them to come in. The taller, more handsome one stepped inside first. His friend followed close behind.

"The doctor says I'll be fine," she told them.

The doctor nodded. "I also said she needs to be monitored overnight. To make sure there are no signs of concussion or other trauma." He addressed the room in general before turning to Mel directly. "If you feel nauseous or dizzy, or if over-the-counter medications don't seem to be addressing the pain, you need to come back in. Understood?"

"Yes."

He turned to the others. "You need to watch for any sign of blacking out or loss of balance."

Greta nodded. As did the two men for some reason.

The doctor gave a quick wave before hastily walking out.

Mel smiled awkwardly at the two men. It occurred to her she didn't even know their names. "Um… I'm Mel."

They exchanged a glance between them. Then the taller one stepped forward. "I'm Ray. This is Sal." He motioned to his friend, who politely nodded.

More awkwardness ensued as all four of them stood silent.

"I'm Greta," the older woman suddenly and very loudly offered.

Both men said hello. Finally, Greta reached for Mel's arm. "C'mon, kiddo. Let's get you dressed. Then we'll call for a cab so we can get you home."

Ray stepped forward. "That won't be necessary. We'll take you anywhere you need to go."

Ray sighed with relief for what must have been the hundredth time as the old lady directed them to the front of a small eatery not far from where the accident had occurred. Thank goodness that Mel appeared to be all right. But she was sporting one devil of a shiner on her right eye and the whole side of her face looked a purple mess.

For some inexplicable reason, his mind kept referring to the moment he'd picked her up and carried her to the car. The softness of her as he'd held her, the way she'd smelled. Some delicate scent of flowers combined with a fruity shampoo he'd noticed when her head had been under his nose.

"This is our stop," Greta declared and reached for the door handle.

Ray immediately got out of the car to assist Mel out onto the street. After all, the older woman looked barely able to get herself moving. She'd actually dozed off twice during the short ride over. Ray hadn't missed how Mel had positioned herself to allow Greta to lean against her shoulder as she snored softly. Despite her injury. Nor how she'd gently nudged her friend awake as they approached their destination.

Who was taking care of whom in this scenario?

How in the world was this frail, seemingly exhausted older lady supposed to keep an eye on her injured friend all night?

Ray would never forgive himself if Mel had any kind of medical disaster in the middle of the night. Despite his reassurances, the doctor had made it clear she wasn't completely out of the woods just yet.

"My sister and I live in a flat above this diner, which

we own and manage," Greta informed him around a wide yawn as the three of them approached the door. She rummaged around in her oversize bag for several moments, only to come up empty.

"Dang it. I guess I left my keys behind when I rushed over to the hospital."

She reached for a panel by the side of the door and pressed a large button. A buzzer could be heard sounding upstairs. Several beats passed and…nothing.

Mel offered him a shy smile. Her black hair glistened like tinsel where the streetlight hit it. The neon light of the diner sign above them brought out the bright evergreen hue of her eyes. Well, the one that wasn't nearly swollen shut anyway. The poor woman probably couldn't wait to get upstairs and lie down.

Unfortunately, she would have to wait a bit longer. Several more moments passed. Greta pressed the button at least half a dozen more times. Ray wasn't any more reassured as they continued to wait.

Finally, after what seemed like an eternity, the sound of shuffling feet could be heard approaching as a shadow moved closer to the opposite side of the door. When it finally opened, they were greeted by a groggy, disheveled woman who was even older than Greta. She didn't even look fully awake yet.

It was settled. There was no way he could leave an injured woman with the likes of these two ladies. His conscience wouldn't allow it. Especially not when he was partly responsible for said injury to begin with.

"I'm glad that's over with." Saleh started the SUV as soon as Ray opened the passenger door and leaned into the vehicle. "Let's finally get to our hotel, then. I could use a long hot shower and a tall glass of something strong and aromatic." He reached for the gearshift before giving him a quizzical look. "Why aren't you getting in the car?"

"I've decided to stay here."

Saleh's eyes went wide with shock. "What?"

"I can't leave the young lady, Saleh. You should see the older sister who's supposed to watch Mel with Greta."

"You mean Greta's the younger one?"

"Believe it or not."

"Still. It's no longer our concern. We've done all we can. She'll be fine." He motioned with a tilt of his head for Rayhan to get in the car.

"I'm going to stay here and make sure of it. You go on ahead and check us into the hotel."

"You can't be serious. Are you forgetting who you are?"

Ray bit down on his impatience. Saleh was a trusted friend. But right now, he was the one close to forgetting who he was and whom he was addressing.

"Not in the least. I happen to be part of the reason that young lady is up there, sporting all sorts of cuts and bruises, as well as a potential head injury, which needs to be monitored. By someone who can actually keep an eye on her with some degree of competence."

"Your Highness, I understand all that. But staying here is not wise."

"Don't call me that, Saleh. You know better."

"I'm just trying to remind you of your position. Perhaps I should also remind you that this isn't an announced state visit. If these ladies were to find out who you are, it could leak to the rest of the world before morning. The resulting frenzy of press could easily result in an embarrassing media nightmare for the monarchy. Not to mention Verdovia as a whole."

"They won't find out."

Saleh huffed in exasperation. "How can you be sure?"

Ray ignored the question as he didn't really have any kind of adequate answer. "I've made up my mind," he said with finality.

"There's more to it. Isn't there, Rayhan?"

Ray knew exactly what his friend meant. The two had known each other their whole lives, since they were toddlers kicking around a sponge soccer ball in the royal courtyard. He wouldn't bother to deny what his friend had clearly observed.

"I saw the way you were looking at her," Saleh threw out as if issuing a challenge. "With much more than sympathy in your eyes. Admit it. There's more to it."

Ray only sighed. "Perhaps there is, my friend." He softly shut the car door.

Ray was asleep on Frannie and Greta's couch. Mel popped two anti-inflammatory pills into her mouth and then took a swig of water to swallow them down. Her borrowed nightgown felt snug against her hips. It belonged to Greta, who could accurately be described as having the figure of a very thin teenage boy. A description that didn't fit Mel in any way.

The feel of her nightwear wouldn't be the only thing bothering her tonight, Mel figured. The man lying in the other room only a few feet away would no doubt disrupt her sleep. Had she ever felt so aware of a man before? She honestly couldn't say, despite having been married. He had such a magnetism, she'd be hard-pressed to put its impact on her into words. Everything about him screamed class and breeding. From the impeccable and, no doubt, expensive tailored clothing to the SUV he and his friend were driving around in, Ray was clearly not lacking in resources. He was well-mannered and well-spoken. And judging by what he'd done earlier tonight, he was quite kindhearted.

Ray had feigned being too tired to travel with his friend to their hotel across town and had asked the Perlman sisters if he could crash on their couch instead. Mel wasn't buying it in the least. First of all, he didn't seem the type of man to lack stamina in any way. No, his true intention was painfully obvious. He'd taken one look at Frannie, studied Greta again and then perused Mel's battered face and decided he couldn't leave her in the care of the elderly sisters. None of them questioned it. Sure, Ray was barely more than a stranger, but he'd had ample opportunity if his motives were at all nefarious.

Besides, he hardly appeared to be a kidnapper. And he definitely wasn't likely to be a thief looking to take off with the Perlman sisters' ancient and cracked bone china.

No, he was just a gentleman who'd not only made sure to take care of her after she'd got hurt, he'd insisted on hanging around to keep an eye on her.

She crawled into the twin bed the Perlman sisters kept set up in their spare room and eyed the functional sleigh-bell ornament taken off the diner Christmas tree that Greta had handed her before going to bed. She was supposed to ring it to arouse their attention if she felt at all ill during the night. As if either sister had any chance of hearing it. Frannie hadn't even heard the much louder door buzzer earlier this evening. No wonder Ray had insisted on staying.

She felt oddly touched by his thoughtfulness. Not every man would have been so concerned.

She tried to imagine Eric going out of his way in such a fashion under similar circumstances. Simply to help a stranger. She couldn't picture it. No, Ray didn't seem at all like her ex. In fact, he was unlike any other man she'd ever met. And his looks! The man was heart-stoppingly handsome. She still didn't know where he was from, but based on his dark coloring and regal features, she would guess somewhere in the Mediterranean. Southern Italy perhaps. Maybe Greece. Or even somewhere in the Middle East.

Mel sighed again and snuggled deeper into her pillow. What did any of her speculation matter in the overall scheme of things? Men like Ray weren't the type a divorced waitress could count among her acquaintances. He would be nothing more than a flash of brightness that passed through her life for a brief moment in time. By this time next week, no doubt, he wouldn't give the likes of Melinda Osmon more than a lingering thought.

"So did she even find a dress?"

"I guess so. She says she lost the shopping bag 'cause of the accident, though."

"So no dress. I guess she definitely isn't going to the ball, then."

"Nope. Not without a dress. And not with that crazy shiner where her eye is."

What was it about this dress everyone kept talking about? Ray stirred and slowly opened his eyes. To his surprise it was morning already. He'd slept surprisingly well on the lumpy velvet-covered couch the sisters had offered him last night. Said sisters were currently talking much too loudly in the kitchen, which was off to the side of the apartment. Clearly, they didn't entertain overnight guests often.

His thoughts immediately shifted to Mel. How was she feeling? He'd slept more soundly than he'd expected to. What if she'd needed something in the middle of the night? He swiftly strode to the kitchen. "Has anyone checked on Mel yet?"

Both ladies halted midspeech to give him curious looks. "Well, good morning to you, too," Greta said with just a touch of grouchiness in her voice. Or maybe that was Frannie. In matching terry robes and thick glasses perched on the ends of their noses, they looked remarkably similar.

"I apologize. I just wondered about our patient."

The two women raised their eyebrows at him. "She's *our* patient now, huh?" one of the women asked.

Luckily, the other one spoke before Ray could summon an answer to that question. "She's sleeping soundly. I sneaked a peek at her as soon as I woke up. Breathing nice and even. Even has some color back in her face. Well, real color. Aside from the nasty purple bruise."

Ray felt the tension he wasn't aware he held slowly leave his chest and shoulders. One of the women pulled a chair out for him as another handed him a steaming cup of coffee. Both actions were done with a no-nonsense efficiency. Ray gratefully took the steaming cup and sat down.

The small flat was a far cry from the majestic expanse of the castle he called home, but the sheer homeliness and coziness of the setting served to put him in a comfortable state of ease, one that took him a bit by surprise. He spent most of his life in a harried state of rushing from one activity or responsibility to another. To be able to simply sit and enjoy a cup of coffee in a quaint New England kitchen was a novel experience. One he was enjoying more than he would have guessed.

"Damn shame about the dress," Greta or Frannie commented as she sat down across him, the other lady joining them a moment later after refreshing her mug.

He really needed one of them to somehow identify herself or he was bound to make an embarrassing slip before the morning was over about who was who.

"Can someone tell me what the deal is with this dress?" he asked.

"Mel was coming back from shopping when you and your friend knocked her on her keister," the sister right next to him answered.

"Frannie!" the other one exclaimed. Thank goodness. Now he just had to keep straight which was which once they stood. "That's no way to talk to our guest," she added.

Ray took a sip of his coffee, the guilt washing over him once more. Though technically they hadn't been the ones to actually run into Mel—the cyclist had done that—he couldn't help but feel that if Saleh had been paying better attention, Mel wouldn't be in the state she was in currently.

"She lost the shopping bag in all the confusion," Frannie supplied.

"I'm terribly sorry to hear that," Ray answered. "It must have been some dress. I'll have to find a way to compensate for Mel's losing it."

"It's more what she needed it for."

Ray found himself oddly curious. When was the last time he cared about why a woman needed an article of clothing? Never. The answer to that question was a resounding *never*.

"What did she need it for?"

"To stick it to that scoundrel husband of hers."

Ray found himself on the verge of sputtering out the coffee he'd just taken a sip of. Husband. Mel was married. It really wasn't any of his business. So why did he feel like someone had just landed a punch in the middle of his gut? He'd met the woman less than twelve hours ago for heaven's sake. Had barely spoken more than a few words to her.

"He's her ex-husband," Greta clarified. "But my sister's right about the scoundrel part."

"Oh?" Ray inquired. For the second time already this morning, he felt like a solid weight had been lifted off his shoulders. So she wasn't actually married currently. He cursed internally as he thought it. What bit of difference did it make where he was concerned?

"Yeah, he took all her money, then left her for some flirty flirt of a girl who works for him."

That did sound quite scoundrel-like. A pang of sympathy blossomed in his chest. No woman deserved that. What little he knew of Mel, she seemed like she wouldn't hurt another being if her life depended on it. She certainly didn't deserve such treatment.

"Before they got divorced, Mel and her ex were always invited to the mayor's annual charity holiday ball. The mayor's daughter is a college friend of both of theirs. This year that no-good ex of Mel's is taking his new lady. Word is, he proposed to her and they'll be attending as doctor and fiancée."

Frannie nodded as her sister spoke. "Yeah, we were trying to convince her to go anyway. 'Cause why should he have the satisfaction? But she had nothing to wear. We gave her an advance on her paycheck and told her to find the nicest dress she could afford."

Ray sat silent, taking all this in. Several points piqued his interest, not the least of which being just how much these ladies seemed to care for the young lady who worked for them. Mel was clearly more than a mere employee. She was family and so they were beyond outraged on her behalf.

The other thing was that she'd been trying to tell him right there on the sidewalk about how important the dress was, and he hadn't bothered to listen. He had just assumed that she'd hit her head and didn't know what she was talking about. He felt guilt wash over him anew.

"I still wish there was a way she could go." Greta shook her head with regret. "That awful man needs to know she don't give a damn about him and that she's still going to attend these events. With or without him."

A heavy silence settled over the room before Frannie broke it with a clap of her hands. "You know, I got a great idea," she declared to her sister with no small display of excitement.

"What's that?"

"I know she don't have anything to wear, but if she can figure that out, I think Ray here should take her." She flashed a brilliant smile in his direction.

Greta gasped in agreement, nodding vehemently. "Ooh, excellent idea. Why, he'd make for the perfect date!"

Frannie turned to him, a mischievous sparkle in her eyes. "It's the least you can do. You did knock her on her keister."

Greta nodded solemnly next to him.

This unexpected turn proved to take him off guard. Ray tried to muster what exactly to say. He was spared the effort.

Mel chose that moment to step into the room. It was clear she'd heard the bulk of the conversation. She looked far from pleased.

Mel pulled out a chair and tried to clamp down on her horror. She could hardly believe what she'd heard. As much as she loved the Perlman sisters, sometimes they went just a tad too far. In this case, they'd traveled miles. The last thing she wanted from any man, let alone a man the likes of Ray, was some kind of sympathy date. And she'd be sure to tell both the ladies that as soon as she got them alone.

For now, she had to try to hide her mortification from their overnight guest.

"How do you feel, dear?" Greta asked.

"Fine. Just fine."

"The swelling seems to be going down," Frannie supplied.

Mel merely nodded. She risked a glance at Ray from the corner of her eye. To his credit, he looked equally uncomfortable.

Frannie stood suddenly. "Well, the two of us should get downstairs and start prepping for the weekend diner crowd." She rubbed Mel's shoulder. "There's still fresh coffee in the pot. You obviously have the day off."

Mel started to argue, but Frannie held up a hand to stop her. Greta piped up from across the table. "Don't even think about it. You rest and concentrate on healing. We can handle the diner today."

Mel nodded reluctantly as the two sisters left the kitchen to go get ready for their morning. It was hard to stay aggravated with those two.

Except now she was alone with Ray. The awkwardness hung like thick, dense fog in the air. If she was smart, she would have walked away and pretended not to hear anything that was said.

Of all the…

What would possess Greta and Frannie to suggest such a thing? She couldn't imagine what Ray must be feeling. They had put him in such a sufferable position.

To her surprise, he broke the silence with an apology. "I'm so terribly sorry, Mel."

Great, he was apologizing for not taking her up on the sisters' offer. Well, that got her hackles up. She wasn't the one who had asked him to take her to the ball.

"There's no need to apologize," she said, perhaps a little too curtly. "I really had no intention of attending that party anyway. I hardly need a date for an event I'm not going to. Not that I would have necessarily said yes." Now, why had she felt compelled to add that last bit?

Ray's jaw fell open. "Oh, I meant. I just—I should have listened when you were trying to tell me about your dress. I didn't realize you'd dropped your parcel."

Mel suddenly realized her mistake. He was simply offering a general apology. He wasn't even referring to the ball. She felt the color drain from her face from the embarrassment. If she could, she would have sunk through the floor and into another dimension. Never to be seen or heard from again. Talk about flattering oneself.

She cleared her throat, eager to change the subject. Although this next conversation was going to be only slightly less cringeworthy. "I was going to mention this last night, but you ended up staying the night."

"Yes?"

"I know you paid for my hospital visit. I have every intention of paying you back." Here was the tough part. "I, um, will just need to mail it to you. It's a bit hard to reimburse you right at this moment."

He immediately shook his head. "You don't need to worry about that."

"I insist. Please just let me know where I can mail a check as soon as I get a chance."

"I won't accept it, Mel."

She crossed her arms in front of her chest. "You

don't understand. It's important to me that I pay back my debts." Unlike her ex-husband, she added silently.

He actually waved his hand in dismissal. "There really is no need."

No need? What part about her feeling uncomfortable about being indebted to him was he unable to comprehend? His next words gave her a clue.

"Given your circumstances, I don't want you to feel you owe me anything."

Mel felt the surge of ire prickle over her skin. She should have known. His meaning couldn't be clearer. Ray was no different than all the other wealthy people she'd known. Exactly like the ones who'd made her parents' lives so miserable.

"My circumstances? I certainly don't need your charity, if that's what you mean."

His eyes grew wide. "Of course not. I apologize. I meant no offense. I'm fluent, but English is my second language, after all. I simply meant that I feel responsible for you incurring the fees in the first place."

"But you weren't responsible. The cyclist was. And he's clearly not available, so the responsibility of my hospital bill is mine and mine alone."

He studied her through narrowed eyes. "Is it that important to you?"

"It is."

He gave her a slight nod of acquiescence. "Then I shall make sure to give you my contact information before I leave so that you can forward reimbursement at your convenience."

"Thank you."

Ray cleared his throat before continuing, "Also, if you'll allow me, I'd love to attend the Boston mayor's annual holiday ball as your escort."

CHAPTER THREE

MEL BLINKED AND gave her head a small shake, the action sending a pounding ache through her cheek straight up to her eye. In her shock, she'd forgotten how sore she was. But Ray had indeed just shocked her. Or maybe she hadn't actually heard him correctly. Maybe she really did have a serious head injury that was making her imagine things.

"I'm sorry. What did you just say?"

His lips curved into a small smile and Mel felt a knot tighten in the depths of her core. The man was sinfully handsome when he smiled. "I said I'd like to attend the ball with you."

She gently placed her coffee cup on the table in front of her. Oh, for heaven's sake. She couldn't wait to give Frannie and Greta a speaking-to. "You don't need to do that, Ray. You also didn't need to cover my expenses. And you didn't need to stay last night. You've done more than enough already. Is this because I insist on repaying you?" she asked. How much of a charity case did he think she was? Mel felt her anger rising once more.

But he shook his head. "Has nothing to do with that."

"The accident wasn't even your fault."

"This has nothing to do with the accident either."

"Of course it does. And I'm trying to tell you, you

don't need to feel that you have to make anything up to me. Again, the accident yesterday was not your fault."

He leaned closer to her over the table. "But you don't understand. It would actually be something of a quid pro quo to take me to this ball. You'd actually be the one doing me a favor."

Okay, that settled it. She knew she was hearing things. In fact, she was probably still back in Frannie and Greta's guest room, soundly asleep. This was all a strange dream. Or maybe she'd accidentally taken too many painkillers. There was no way this could actually be happening. There was absolutely nothing someone like Mel could offer a man such as Ray. The idea that accompanying her to the ball would be a favor to *him* was ridiculous.

"Come again?"

"Allow me to explain," Ray continued at her confused look. "I'm here on business on behalf of the king of Verdovia. He is looking to acquire some property in the Boston area. The type of people attending an event that the mayor is throwing are precisely the type of people I'd like to have direct contact with."

"So you're saying you actually want to go? To meet local business people?"

He nodded. "Precisely. And in the process, we can do the two-birds-killing."

She was beginning to suspect they both had some kind of brain trauma. Then his meaning dawned on her. He was misstating the typical American idiom.

"You mean kill two birds with one stone?"

He smiled again, wider this time, causing Mel's toes to curl in her slippers. "Correct. Though I never did understand that expression. Who wants to kill even one bird, let alone two?"

She had to agree.

"In any case, you help me meet some of these local business people, and I'll make sure you stick your ex-husband."

She couldn't help it. She had to laugh. This was all so surreal. It was like she was in a completely different reality than the one she'd woken up in yesterday morning. "You mean stick it to."

"That's right," he replied, responding to her laugh with one of his own.

For just a split second, she was tempted to say yes, that she'd do it. But then the ridiculousness of the whole idea made her pause. It was such a harebrained scheme. No one would believe Mel and someone like Ray were an actual couple. An unbidden image of the two of them dancing close, chest to chest, flashed in her mind. A curl of heat moved through the pit of her stomach before she squelched it. What a silly fantasy.

They clearly had nothing in common. Not that she would know with any real certainty, of course. She didn't know the man at all.

"What do you think?" Ray prompted.

"I think there's no way it would work. For one thing, we've barely met. You don't know a thing about me and I don't know a thing about you. I have no idea who you are. How would we even begin to explain why we're at such an event together?"

A sly twinkle appeared in his eye. "That's easy to fix. We should spend some time getting to know each other. Can I interest you in breakfast? I understand there's an excellent eating establishment very nearby. Right downstairs, as a matter of fact."

Greta seated them in a corner booth and handed him a large laminated menu. The giant smile on the older woman's face gave every bit the impression that she was beyond pleased at seeing the two of them at breakfast together. Though she did initially appear quite surprised.

Well, Ray had also surprised himself this morning. He'd had no idea that he'd intended to ask to take her to the mayor's ball until the words were actually leaving his mouth. Saleh would want to throttle him for such a foolish move. Oh, well, he'd worry about Saleh later. Ray's reasons were sound if one really thought about it. So he'd exaggerated his need to meet local business leaders, considering he already had the contacts in Boston that he needed. But Mel didn't know that or need to know that. And what harm would it do? What was so wrong about wanting to take her to the ball and hoping she'd have a good time there? Between the terrible accident yesterday and what he'd found out this morning about her past history, she could definitely use some fun, he figured. Even if it was only for a few hours.

Why he wanted to be the one to give that to her, he couldn't quite explain. He found himself wishing he'd met her under different circumstances, at a different time.

Right. He would have to be a completely different person for it to make an iota of difference. The reality was that he was the crown prince of Verdovia. He'd been groomed since birth to be beholden to rules and customs and to do what was best for the kingdom. He couldn't forget this trip was simply a temporary respite from all that.

This ball would give him a chance to do something different, out of the norm, if he attended as an associate of the royal family rather than as the prince. After all, wasn't that why he was in the United Sates? For one final adventure. This was a chance to attend a grand gala without all the pressures of being the Verdovian prince and heir to the throne.

He asked Mel to order for them both and she did so before Greta poured them some more coffee and then left their booth, her smile growing wider by the second.

"All right," Mel began once they were alone. "Tell me about yourself. Why don't you start with more about what you do for a living?"

Ray knew he had to tread carefully. He didn't want to lie to her, but he had to be careful to guard his true identity. Not only for his sake, but for hers, as well.

"You said something about acquiring real estate for the Verdovian royal family. Does that mean real estate is your main focus?" she asked.

Ray took a sip of his steamy beverage. He'd never had so much coffee in one sitting, but the Boston brew was strong and satisfying. "So to speak. I'm responsible for various duties in service of the king. He'd like to expand his American property holdings, particularly in metropolitan cities. He's been eyeing various high-end hotels in the Boston area. I volunteered to fly down here to scope out some prospects and perhaps make an agreement." Technically, he was telling her the complete truth.

Mel nodded. "I see. You're definitely a heavy hitter."

That wasn't an expression that made immediate sense to him. "You think I hit heavy?"

"Never mind. Do you have a family?"

"My parents and two younger sisters."

"What would you tell me about them?"

This part could get tricky if he wasn't careful. He hated being on the slim side of deceitful but what choice did he have? And in the overall scheme of things, what did it hurt that Mel didn't know he was a prince? In fact, he'd be glad to be able to forget the fact himself for just a brief moment in time.

"My father is a very busy man. Responsible for many people and lots of land. My mother is an accomplished musician who has studied the violin under some of Europe's masters and composes her own pieces."

Mel let out a low whistle. "Wow. That's quite a pedigree," she said in a near whisper. "How'd you end up picking such a high-profile career?"

He had to tread carefully answering that one. "It was chosen for me," he answered truthfully.

She lifted an eyebrow. "You mean the king chose you?"

He nodded. Again, it was the complete truth. "There were certain expectations made of me, being the only son of the family."

"Expectations?"

"Yes. It was a given that I would study business, that I would work in a career that led to the further wealth and prosperity of our island kingdom. Otherwise…"

The turn in conversation was throwing him off. Mel's questions brought up memories he hadn't given any consideration to in years.

She leaned farther toward him, over the table. "Otherwise what?"

He sighed, trying hard to clamp down on the years-old resentments that were suddenly resurfacing in a most unwelcome way. Mel stared at him with genuine curiosity shining in her eyes. He'd never discussed this aspect of his life with anyone before. Not really. No one had bothered to ask, because it was all such a moot point.

"Otherwise, it wasn't a career I would have chosen for myself. I was a bit of an athlete. Played striker during school and university. Got several recruitment offers from coaches at major football clubs. Though you would call it soccer here."

She blinked. "So wait. You turned down the opportunity of a lifetime because the king had other plans?"

Ray tapped the tip of his finger against the tabletop. "That about sums it up, yes."

She blew out a breath. "Wow. That's loyalty."

"Well, loyalty happens to be a quality that was hammered into me since birth."

"What about your sisters?" she asked him. "Are they held to such high standards, as well?"

Ray shook his head. "No. Being younger, they have the luxury of much fewer demands being made of them."

"Lucky for them. What are they like?"

"Well, both are quite trying. Completely unbearable brats," he told her. But he was unable to keep the tender smile off his face and his affection for his siblings out of his voice despite his words.

That earned him a small smile. "I'm guessing they're quite fortunate in having you as a brother." She sighed. "I don't have any siblings. I grew up an only child." Her tone suggested she was somewhat sad about the fact.

"That can have its advantages," he said, thinking of Saleh and the rather indulgent way the man's family treated him. "What of your parents?"

Mel looked away toward the small jukebox on the table, but not before he caught the small quiver in her chin. "I lost them about three years ago. They passed within months of each other."

"I'm so terribly sorry."

"Thank you for saying that."

"To lose them so close together must have been so difficult."

He couldn't help but reach for her hand across the table to comfort her. To his surprise and pleasure, she gripped his fingers, taking what he offered her.

"It was. My father got sick. There was nothing that could be done. It crushed my mom. She suffered a fatal cardiac event not long after." She let go of his fingers to brush away a tiny speck of a tear from the corner of her eye. "It was as if she couldn't go on without him. Her heart literally broke. They'd been together since they were teens."

Ray couldn't help but feel touched. To think of two people who had decided at such a young age that they cared for each other and stayed together throughout all those years. His own parents loved each other deeply, he knew. But their relationship had started out so ceremonial and preplanned. The same way his own marriage would begin.

The king and queen had worked hard to cultivate their affection into true love. He could only hope for as much for himself when the time came.

A realization dawned on him. Mel had been betrayed by the man she'd married within a couple of years of losing her parents. It was a wonder the woman could even smile or laugh.

He cleared his throat, trying to find a way to ask about her husband. But she was way ahead of him.

"You should probably know a little about my marriage."

"Aside from the knowledge that Frannie and Greta refer to him as 'that scoundrel,' you mean?"

This time the smile didn't quite reach her eyes. "I guess that would be one way to describe him."

"What happened?" He knew the man had left his wife for another woman. Somehow he'd also left Mel to fend for herself without much in the way of finances. He waited as Mel filled in some of the holes in the story.

She began slowly, softly, the hurt in her voice as clear as a Verdovian sunrise. "We met at school. At homecoming, our first year there. He was the most attentive and loving boyfriend. Very ambitious, knew from the beginning that he wanted to be a dentist. Husband material, you would think."

Ray simply waited as she spoke, not risking an interruption.

"When I lost my parents, I couldn't bear to live in their house. So I put it on the market. He invited me to live with him in his small apartment while he attended dental school. Eventually, he asked me to marry him. I'd just lost my whole family…"

She let the words trail off, but he could guess how the sentence might end. Mel had found herself suddenly alone, reeling from the pain of loss. A marriage proposal from the man she'd been seeing all through college had probably seemed like a gift.

"My folks' house netted a good amount in the sale. Plus they'd left me a modest yet impressive nest egg."

She drew in a shaky breath.

"Here's the part where I demonstrate my foolishness. Eric and I agreed that we would spend the money on his dentistry schooling after college graduation. That way we could start our lives together free of any school loans when he finished. I handed over all my savings and worked odd jobs here and there to cover any other costs while he attended classes and studied. When he was through, it was supposed to be my turn to continue on to a higher degree. I studied art history in my undergrad. Not a huge job market for those majors." She used one hand to motion around the restaurant. "Hence the waitressing gig. At the time, though, I was set on pursuing a teaching degree and maybe working as an elementary school art teacher. Once we had both achieved our dreams, I thought we would start a family." She said the last words on a wistful sigh.

Ray didn't need to hear the rest. What a foolish man her former husband was. Mel was quite a beautiful woman, even with the terrible degree of bruising on her face. Her injuries couldn't hide her strong, angular features, nor did they diminish the sparkling brightness of her jewel-green eyes.

From what he could tell, she was beautiful on the inside, too. She'd given herself fully to the man she'd made marriage vows to—albeit with some naïveté— to the point of generously granting him all the money she had. Only to be paid back with pure betrayal. Her friends obviously thought the world of her. To boot, she was a witty and engaging conversationalist. In fact, he wouldn't even be able to tell how long they'd been sitting in this booth, as time seemed to have stood still while they spoke.

"Frannie and Greta are sorely accurate in their description of this Eric, then. He must be a scoundrel and a complete fool to walk away from you."

Mel ducked her head shyly at the compliment, then tucked a strand of hair behind her ear. When she spoke again, she summoned a stronger tone. He hoped it was because his words had helped to bolster some of her confidence, even if only a little.

"I have to take some of the blame. I moved too quickly, was too anxious to be a member of a family again."

"I think you're being too hard on yourself."

"Enough of the sad details," she said. "Let's talk about other things."

"Such as?"

"What are your interests? Do you have any hobbies? What type of music do you like?"

She was trying valiantly to change the subject. He went along.

For the next several minutes, they talked about everything from each other's favorite music to the type of cuisine they each preferred. Even after their food arrived, the conversation remained fluid and constant. It made no sense, given the short amount of time spent in each other's company, but Ray was beginning to feel as if he knew the young lady across him better than most of the people in his regular orbit.

And he was impressed. Something about her pulled to him unlike anyone else he'd ever encountered. She had a pure authentic quality that he'd been hard-pressed to find throughout his lifetime. Most people didn't act like themselves around the crown prince of Verdovia. Ray could count on one hand all the people in his life he felt he truly knew deep down.

As he thought of Saleh, Ray's phone went off again in his pocket. That had to be at least the tenth time. If Mel was aware of the incessant buzzing of his phone, she didn't let on. And Ray didn't bother to reply to Saleh's repeated calls. He'd already left a voice message for him this morning, letting his friend know that he'd be further delayed.

Besides, he was enjoying Mel's company too much to break away simply for Saleh's sake. The other man could wait.

"So just to be sure we make this official." He extended his hand out to her after an extended lull in their lively conversation. "May I please have the pleasure of accompanying you to the mayor's annual holiday ball?"

She let out a small laugh. "You know what? Why not?"

Ray held a hand to his chest in mock offense. "Well,

that's certainly the least enthusiastic acceptance I've received from a lady. But I'll take it."

It surprised him how much he was looking forward to it. Even so, a twinge of guilt nagged at him for his duplicity. He'd give anything to completely come clean to Mel about who he was and what he was doing here in the city. Something shifted in his chest at the possibility of her finding out the truth and being disappointed in him. But he had no choice. He'd been groomed to do what was best for Verdovia and its people.

As Mel had phrased it earlier, though, the king had other plans for him.

CHAPTER FOUR

A LIGHT DUSTING of snow sprinkled the scenery outside the window by their table. Mel couldn't remember the last time she'd had such a lighthearted and fun conversation. Despite his classy demeanor, Ray had a way of putting her at ease. Plus, he seemed genuinely interested in what she had to say. He had to be a busy man, yet here he still sat as the morning grew later, happy to simply chat with her.

She motioned to Ray's plate. She'd been a little apprehensive ordering for him. He didn't strike her as the type who was used to diner cuisine. But he'd done a pretty nice job of clearing his plate. He must have liked it a little. "So, what did you think? I know baked beans first thing in the morning is an acquired taste. It's a Boston thing."

"Hence the name 'Boston Baked Beans'?"

"Correct."

"I definitely feel full. Not exactly a light meal."

She felt a flutter of disappointment in her stomach. Of course, she'd ordered the wrong thing. What did she know about what an international businessman would want for breakfast? She was completely out of her element around this man. And here she'd just agreed to attend a grand charity gala with him. Pretending she was his date. As if she could pull off such a thing.

"But it definitely—how do you Americans say it?—landed in the spot."

His mistake on the expression, along with a keen sense of relief, prompted a laugh out of her. "Hit the spot," she corrected.

"Yes, that's it. It definitely hit the spot."

His phone vibrated for the umpteenth time in his pocket. He'd been so good about not checking it, she was starting to feel guilty. He was here on a business trip, after all.

She also hadn't missed the lingering looks he'd received from all the female diner patrons, young and old alike. From the elderly ladies heading to their daily hair appointments to the young co-eds who attended the city's main university, located a shuttle ride away.

"I know you must have a lot to do. I probably shouldn't keep you much longer."

Ray sighed with clear resignation. "Unfortunately, there are some matters I should attend to." He started to reach for his pocket. "What do I owe for the breakfast?"

She held up a hand to stop him. "Please, employee privilege. It's on me."

"Are you sure? It's not going to come out of your wages or anything, is it?"

Not this again. It wasn't like she was a pauper. Just that she was trying to put some money away in order to finally get the advanced degree she'd always intended to study for. Before fate in the form of Eric Fuller had yanked that dream away from her.

"It so happens, Greta and Frannie consider free meals part of my employee package." Though she normally wouldn't have ordered this much food for herself over the course of a full week, let alone in one sitting. Something told her the two ladies didn't mind. Not judging by the immensely pleased smirks they kept sending in her direction when Ray wasn't looking.

"Well, thank you. I can't recall the last time I was treated to a meal by such a beautiful woman."

Whoa. This man was the very definition of *charming*. She had no doubt that had to be one doozy of a fib. Beautiful women probably cooked for him all the time.

"But you're right, I should probably be going."

She nodded and started to pile the empty plates in the center of the table. Waitress habit.

"Can I walk you back upstairs?" Ray asked.

She wanted to decline. Lord knew he'd spent enough time with her already. But a very vocal part of her didn't want this morning to end. "I'd like that," she found herself admitting.

He stood and offered her his arm. She gently put her hand in the crook of his elbow after he helped her out of the booth. With a small wave of thanks to her two bosses, they proceeded toward the side door, which led to the stairway to the apartment.

"So I'll call you tomorrow, then?" Ray asked. "To discuss further details for Saturday night?"

"That sounds good. And I'll work on finding a plan B for what my attire will be."

His mouth furrowed into a frown, causing deep lines to crease his forehead. "I'd forgotten about that. Again, I'm so terribly sorry for not paying more attention as you were telling me about your parcel."

She let out a small laugh. "It's okay. It wasn't exactly a situation conducive to listening."

"Still, I feel like a cad."

"It's all right," she reassured him. "I'm sure Frannie

and Greta won't mind if I do some rummaging in their closet. They might have something bordering on suitable."

He paused on the foot of the stairs right as she took the first step up. The difference in height brought them eye to eye, close enough that the scent of him tickled her nose, a woodsy, spicy scent as unique as he was.

"I'm afraid that won't do at all." His eyes looked genuinely troubled.

"It's all right. I'm very creative. And I'm a whiz with a sewing machine."

"That may be, but even creative geniuses need the necessary tools. Not to mention time. Something tells me you're not going to find anything appropriate in any closet up in that apartment." He pointed to the ceiling.

It wasn't like she had much choice. She'd already spent what little she could afford on the now-missing dress. All her closest friends had moved out of the New England area, so it wasn't as if she could borrow something. She was out of options. A jarring thought struck her. Could this be Ray's subtle way of trying to back out of taking her? But that made no sense. He was the one who had insisted on going in the first place. Could he have had a sudden change of heart?

"There's only one thing to do. I believe I owe you one formal ball gown, Miss Osmon. Are you up for some shopping? Perhaps tomorrow?"

Mel immediately shook her head. She absolutely could not accept such an offer. "I can't allow you to do that, Ray. Thank you, but no."

"Why not?"

She would think it was obvious. She couldn't allow herself to be this man's charity case. He'd done enough when he'd paid for her hospital bill, for goodness' sake.

A sum she still had to figure out how to pay back. Further indebting herself to Ray was absolutely out of the question. She opened her mouth to tell him so.

He cut her off before she could begin. "What if I said it was more for me?"

A sharp gasp tore out of her throat. He had to be joking. That notion was so ridiculous, she actually bit back a laugh. He didn't look like the type, but what did she know? Looks could be deceiving. And she certainly wasn't one to judge.

He responded with a bark of laughter. "I see I've given you the wrong impression. I meant it would be for me in that if I'm trying to make an impression at this event with various people, I would prefer to have my date dressed for the occasion."

That certainly made sense, but still, essentially he would be buying her a dress. She cleared her throat, tried to focus on saying the right words without sounding offended. He really couldn't be faulted for the way he viewed the world. Not with all the material privilege he'd been afforded. She understood that better now after the conversation they'd just had together. Lord, it was hard to concentrate when those deep dark eyes were staring at her so close and so intently.

"If it makes you feel better, the gown can become the property of the royal family eventually. The queen is always looking for donated items to be auctioned off for various charities. I'll have it shipped straight to her afterward. I can pretend I was considerate enough to purchase it for that very purpose."

That cracked her resolve somewhat. Essentially, she'd only be borrowing a dress from him. Or more accurately, from the royal family of Verdovia. That was a bit more palatable, she supposed. Especially if in the end it would result in a charitable donation to a worthy cause.

Or maybe she was merely falling for his easy charm and finding ways to justify all that Ray was saying. Simply because she just couldn't think straight, given the way he was looking at her.

Saleh was already outside, idling on the curb in the SUV by the time Ray reluctantly left the diner. His friend did not look happy.

Ray opened the passenger door only to be greeted by a sigh of exasperation. No, definitely not happy in the least.

"After yesterday, maybe I should drive," Ray said before entering the car, just to further agitate him.

It worked. "You have not been answering your phone," Saleh said through gritted teeth.

"I was busy. The ladies treated me to an authentic New England breakfast. You should try it."

Saleh pulled into the street. "If only I hadn't already eaten a gourmet meal of warm scones made from scratch and fresh fruit accompanied by freshly squeezed orange juice at my five-star hotel."

Ray shrugged. "To each his own. I'm happy I got to try something a little different." Who would have thought that there were parts of the world where people had baked beans for breakfast?

"Is breakfast the only thing you tried?" Saleh removed his hands from the steering wheel long enough to place air quotes on the last word.

"What you're alluding to is preposterous, my friend. I simply wanted to make sure the young lady was all right after the accident. Nothing more."

Saleh seemed satisfied with that answer. "Great. Now

that you've made sure, can we move on and forget all this unpleasantness of the accident?"

Ray shifted in his seat. "Well, not exactly."

Saleh's hands gripped the steering wheel so tightly, his knuckles whitened. "What exactly does 'not exactly' mean, my prince?"

"It means I may have made a commitment or two to Miss Osmon."

"Define these commitments, please."

"I'll be taking her shopping at some point."

"Shopping?"

"Yes. And, also, I'll be accompanying her to the Boston mayor's holiday charity ball on Saturday."

Saleh actually hit the brake, eliciting a loud honk from several cars behind them. "You will do what?"

"Perhaps I should indeed drive," Ray teased.

Saleh took a breath and then regained the appropriate speed. "If you don't mind my asking, what the hell has got into you?"

"I'm simply trying to enjoy Christmastime in Boston."

"There are countless ways you can do that, Prince Rayhan. Ways that don't involve risking embarrassment to Verdovia and the monarchy behind it."

"I've already committed. I fully intend to go."

"But why?" the other man asked, clearly at a loss. "Why would you ever risk your identity being discovered?"

Ray pinched the bridge of his nose. He didn't want to have to explain himself, not about this. The truth was he wasn't sure even how to explain it. "I'll be careful to avoid that, Saleh. I've decided the risk is worth it." Mel was worth it.

"I don't understand. Not even a little."

Ray sighed, searched for the perfect words. If he

couldn't confide in Saleh, there really was no one else on this earth he could confide in. He had to try. "I'm not sure how to put it into words, Saleh. I felt something when I lifted her into my arms after she was hurt. The way she clung to me, shivering in my embrace. And since this morning, the more time I've spent with her, the more I want to. You must understand that. You must have felt that way before."

Saleh bit the inside of his cheek. "My wife and I were seven when we met."

Okay. Maybe Saleh wasn't the person who would understand. But he had to see where Ray was coming from.

"I just don't understand how this all came about. How in the world did you end up agreeing to attend a charity ball of all things? You always complain about having to frequent such affairs back home."

"It's a long story."

"We have a bit of a drive still."

Ray tried to summon the words that would make his friend understand. "It's different back home. There I'm the crown prince. Everyone who approaches me has some ulterior motive." Most especially the ladies, be it a photo opportunity or something more involved. "Or there's some pressing financial or property matter." Ray halted midspiel. He was bordering on being perilously close to poor-little-rich-prince territory.

"So we could have hit a few clubs in the evening," Saleh responded. "I don't see how any of that leads you to your decision to take this Mel to a holiday ball."

Ray sighed. "Also, her ex-husband will be attending. A very nasty man. She had no one to go with. She wants to prove to him that she's content without him."

Saleh nodded slowly, taking it in. "I see. So she has feelings for her former spouse."

"What? No. No, she doesn't." At least Ray didn't think she did.

"Then why would she care about what he thinks?"

It was a possibility Ray hadn't considered. He felt himself clench his fists at his sides. The idea rankled more than he would have thought.

Saleh continued, "I urge you to be careful. This is simply to be a brief reprieve, coupled with a business transaction. Do not forget you still have a duty to fulfill upon your return."

Ray turned to stare out the window. Traffic had slowed down and a light dusting of snow filled the air.

"I haven't forgotten."

CHAPTER FIVE

MEL DIDN'T COME to Newbury Street often. By far one of the ritziest neighborhoods in downtown Boston, it housed some of the city's most premier shops and restaurants, not to mention prime real estate. Many of New England's sports stars owned condos or apartments along the street. High-end sports cars, everything from Lamborghinis to classic Bentleys rolled down the pavement. Being December, the street was currently lined with faux mini Christmas trees, and big red bows adorned the old-fashioned streetlights.

When she did come out this way, it certainly wasn't to visit the type of boutique that she and Ray were about to enter. The type of boutique that always had at least one limousine sitting out front. Today there were two. And one sleek black freshly waxed town car.

When Ray had suggested going shopping, she'd fully expected that they'd be heading to one of the major department stores in Cambridge or somewhere in Downtown Crossing.

Instead his friend Sal had picked her up and then dropped both her and Ray off here, at one of the most elite shops in New England. A place she'd only heard of. The sort of place where a well-heeled, well-manicured associate greeted you at the door and led you toward a sitting area while offering coffee and refreshments.

As soon as they sat down on the plush cushioned sofa and the saleslady walked away, Mel turned to Ray. "This is not what I had in mind. It's totally wrong. We shouldn't be here," she whispered.

Ray lifted one eyebrow. "Oh? There are a couple of other spots that were recommended to me. This was just the first one on the street. Would you like to continue on to one of those stores?"

He was totally missing the point. "No, that's not what I mean."

"Then I don't understand."

"Look at this place. It has to be beyond pricey. This is the sort of place queens and princesses buy their attire."

Ray's face grew tight. Great. She had no doubt insulted him. Obviously he could afford such extravagance or whoever his acquaintance was wouldn't have recommended this to him.

"Please do not worry about the expense," he told her. "We have an agreement, remember?"

"But this is too much. I doubt I'd be able to afford so much as a scarf from a place like this." She looked down at her worn jeans and scruffy boots. It's a wonder the saleslady hadn't taken one look at her and shown her the door. If Ray wasn't by her side, no doubt she would have done exactly that.

"It's a good thing we are not in the market for a scarf today."

"You know what I mean, Ray."

"I see." He rubbed his chin, studied her. "Well, now that we're here, let's see what's available. Don't forget, we are not actually buying you a dress. It will go up for bidding at one of the queen's auctions, remember?"

That was right. He had said that yesterday. When one considered it that way, under those conditions, it really didn't make sense for her to argue. Essentially, she was telling Ray how to spend his money and what to present to his queen. Who was she to do that? "I suppose it won't hurt to look."

As soon as she made the comment, the young lady who'd greeted them stepped back into the room.

"Miss, our designer has some items she would have you look at. Come right this way." With no small amount of trepidation, Mel followed her. She wasn't even sure quite how to act in a place like this. She certainly didn't feel dressed for the part. The slim, fashionable employee leading her down an elegant hall looked as if she'd walked straight off a fashion runway. Her tight-fitting pencil skirt and stiletto heels were more stylish than anything Mel owned.

The saleslady must have guessed at her nervousness. "Our designer is very nice. She'll love working with a figure such as yours. I'm sure there are several options that will look great on you."

Mel had the urge to give the other woman a hug. Her kind words were actually serving to settle her nerves, though not by much.

"Thank you."

"I think your boyfriend will be very pleased with the final choice."

"Oh, he's not my boyfriend. We're attending an event together. Just as friends. And I had nothing to wear because I lost my bag. It's why I have this black eye and all this bruising—" She forced herself to stop talking and to take a deep breath. Now she was just rambling. "I'm sorry. I'm not used to seeing a designer to shop for a dress. This is all so unreal." She probably shouldn't have added that last part. Now the poor lady was going to think she was addled in addition to being talkative.

The other woman turned to her with a smile. "Then I think you should pretend."

"I don't understand."

"Pretend you are used to it."

Mel gave her head a shake. "How do I do that?"

She shrugged an elegant shoulder. "Pretend you belong here, that you come here often. And pretend he is your boyfriend." She gave her a small wink before escorting her inside a large dressing room with wall-to-wall mirrors and a big standing rack off to the side. On it hung a dozen dazzling evening gowns that took her breath away. And even from a distance, she could see none of them had a price tag. This wasn't the type of place where tags were necessary. Customers who frequented a boutique like this one knew they could afford whatever the mystery price was.

"Deena will be in to see you in just a moment."

With that, the greeter turned on her high, thin heels and left. All in all, her suggestion wasn't a bad one. Why shouldn't Mel enjoy herself here? Something like this was never going to happen to her again. What if she really was here on one of her regular shopping trips? What if this wasn't a completely novel experience and she knew exactly what she was doing? There was nothing wrong with enjoying a little fantasy. Lord knew she could use a bit of it in her life these days.

And what if the charming, devilishly handsome man sitting in the other room, waiting for her, really was her boyfriend?

Ray stared at the spreadsheet full of figures on his tablet, but it was hard to focus. If someone had told him a week ago that he'd be sitting in a fashion boutique in the heart of Boston, waiting for a woman to pick a gown, he would have laughed out loud at the notion. Not that he was a stranger to being dragged out to shop. He did have two sisters and a mother, after all. In fact, one of his sisters had been the one to suggest this particular boutique. Those two knew the top fashion spots in most major cities. The only problem was, now he was being hounded via text and voice mail about why it was that he needed the recommendation in the first place. He could only hold them off for so long. He would have to come up with an adequate response. And soon.

He felt Mel enter the room more than he heard her. The air seemed to change around him. When he looked up and saw her, his breath caught in his throat. The slim tablet he held nearly slipped out of his hands. Even with a nasty purple bruise on her cheek, she was breathtakingly stunning in the red gown. The color seemed to bring out every one of her striking features to their full effect.

Mel took a hesitant step toward him. She gestured to her midsection, indicating the gown she wore. "I wanted to see what you thought of this one," she said shyly.

He couldn't seem to get his tongue to work. He'd spent his life around some of the most beautiful women in the world. Everything from actresses to fashion models to noble ladies with royal titles. Yet he couldn't recall ever being this dumbstruck by a single one of them. What did that say about his sorry state of affairs?

"Do you think it will work?" Mel asked.

Think? Who would be able to think at such a moment? She could only be described as a vision, perhaps something out of a romantic fairy-tale movie. The dress hugged her curves in all the right places before flaring out ever so slightly below her hips. Strapless, it showed off the elegant curve of her necks and shoulders. And the color. A deep, rich red that not many women would be able to wear without the hue completely washing them out. But it only served to bring out the dark blue hint of her hair and accent the emerald green of her eyes. The fabric held a sheer hint of sparkle wherever the light hit it just so.

Since when had he become the type of man who noticed how an article of clothing brought out a woman's coloring or features?

He'd never felt such an urge to whistle in appreciation. Hardly suitable behavior for someone in his position.

What the hell, no one here actually knew who he was. He whistled.

A smile spread across Mel's face. "Does that mean you like it?"

Someone cleared their throat before Ray could answer. Sweet heavens, he hadn't even noticed the other woman in the room with them. She had a long tape measure hanging from her neck and gave him a knowing smile.

"This one was the top choice," the woman said. "If you're okay with it, we can start the necessary alterations."

He was way more than okay with it. That dress belonged on Mel; there was no way they were walking out of here without it.

"I think it's perfect," he answered the designer, but his gaze was fixated on Mel's face as she spoke. Even with the angry purple bruising along her cheek and jaw and the black eye, she was absolutely stunning.

"Are you sure?" Mel asked. "If you'd like, I can show you some of the other ones."

Ray shook his head. He couldn't be more sure. "I have

no doubt you'll be the most beautiful woman to grace that ballroom with that dress."

Mel ducked her head, but not before he noticed the pink that blossomed across her cheeks. "Even with my black eye?"

"I've never seen anyone look so lovely while sporting one."

"I'll be in the dressing room when you're ready, miss," the designer offered before leaving them.

Ray found himself stepping closer to her. He gently rubbed his finger down her cheek, from the corner of her eye down to her chin. "Does it still hurt very much?"

She visibly shivered at his touch, but she didn't pull away. In fact, she turned her face ever so slightly into his caress. It would be so easy for him to lean in closer, to gently brush her lips with his. She smelled of jasmine and rose, an intoxicating mix of scents that reminded him of the grand gardens of his palatial home.

He'd been trying to deny it, but he'd been thinking about kissing her since having breakfast with her. Hell, maybe he'd been thinking about it much before that. He had no doubt she would respond if he did. It was clear on her face, by the quickening of her breathing, the flush in her cheeks.

The loud honk of a vehicle outside pulled him out of his musings and back to his senses. He couldn't forget how temporary all this was. In a few short days, he would return to Verdovia and to the future that awaited him. One full of duty and responsibility and that would include a woman he wasn't in love with.

Love. For all the earthly privileges he'd been granted by virtue of birth, he would never know the luxury of falling in love with the woman he was to marry. He just had to accept that. He couldn't get carried away with some kind of fantasy while here in the United States. And he absolutely could not lead Mel on romantically. He had nothing to offer her. Other than a fun night celebrating the holiday season, while also proving something to her ex. That was all this whole charade was about.

With great reluctance, he made himself step away.

"You should probably go get the dress fitted and altered. I'll go settle the charge."

It took her a moment to speak. When she did, her voice was shaky. "So I guess we're really doing this, huh?"

"What exactly are you referring to?"

"Going to the ball together. I mean, once the dress is purchased, there'll be no turning back, will there?"

Ray could only nod. He had a nagging suspicion that already there would be no turning back.

Not as far as he was concerned.

CHAPTER SIX

As far as transformations went, Mel figured she'd pulled off a major one. The image staring back at her in the mirror couldn't really be her. She hardly recognized the woman in the glass.

She was in Frannie and Greta's apartment. The two women had spent hours with her in order to get her ready. A lot of the time had been spent camouflaging the discolored bruising on her face. But the effect was amazing. These ladies knew how to use makeup to cover up flaws. Even upon close inspection, one would be hard-pressed to guess Mel had met the broadside of a set of steel handlebars only days before.

As far as soreness or pain, she was way too nervous to take any notice of it at the moment.

Her bosses had also helped do her hair in a classic updo at the crown of her head. Greta had found some sort of delicate silver strand that she'd discreetly woven around the curls. It only became visible when the light hit it just so. Exactly the way the silver accents in her dress did. Frannie had even managed to unearth some antique earrings that were studded with small diamond chips. They provided just enough sparkle to complement the overall look. All in all, the older women had done a notable job helping her prepare.

It was like having two fairy godmothers. Albeit very chatty ones. They'd both gone on incessantly about how beautiful Mel looked, how she should act flirty with Ray in order to get under Eric's skin and because they thought Ray was the type of man who definitely warranted flirtatious behavior. Mel had just stood silently, listening. The butterflies in her stomach were wreaking havoc and made it hard to just breathe, let alone form a coherent sentence.

She was trying desperately not to think about all the ways this night could turn into a complete disaster. Someone could easily ask a fairly innocuous question that neither Ray nor she had an adequate answer to. They'd never even discussed what story to tell about how they'd met or how long the two of them had known each other. The whole scenario was ripe for embarrassing mistakes. If Eric ever found out this was all some elaborate pretend date merely to prove to him that she'd moved on, he'd never let Mel live it down.

His fiancée would also have an absolute field day with the knowledge. Not to mention the utter embarrassment it would cause if her other acquaintances found out.

"I believe your ride is here," Frannie declared, peeking around the curtain to look outside.

Greta joined her sister at the window. She let out a shriek of appreciation. "It's a stretch."

"Not just any stretch," Frannie corrected. "A Bentley of some sort."

Greta gave her sister's arm a gentle shove. "Like *you* would know what a Bentway looks like."

"Bentley! And I know more than you, obviously."

The butterflies in Mel's stomach turned into warring pigeons. He was here. And he'd gone all out apparently, hiring a stretch limo. He so didn't need to do that. She'd never been quite so spoiled by someone before—certainly not by a man. If she wasn't careful, this could all easily go to her head. There would be no recovering from that. She had to remind herself throughout the night how unreal all of it was, how temporary and short-lived it would all be. Tomorrow morning, she'd go back to being Mel. The woman who had no real plans for her future, nothing really to look forward to until she managed to get back on her feet somehow. A task she had no clue how to accomplish just yet.

Taking a steadying breath, she rubbed her hand down her midsection.

"How do I look?"

The sisters turned to her and their faces simultaneously broke into wide grins. Was that a tear in Greta's eye?

"Like a princess."

The buzzer rang just then. "I guess I should head downstairs."

"I say you make him wait a bit," Frannie declared. "In the diner. It's not often our fine establishment gets a chance to entertain such an elegant, handsome gentleman in a well-tailored tuxedo."

"Not often?" Greta countered. "More like never."

That comment earned her a scowl from her sister. Mel slowly shook her head. "I think I should just get down there, before I lose all my nerve and back out completely." It was a very real possibility at this point. She wasn't sure she could actually go through with this. The more she thought about it, the more implausible it all seemed.

"Not a chance we would let you do that," both sisters said in unison with obvious fear that she actually might do such a thing.

Mel willed her pulse to steady. Slowly, she made her high-heeled feet move to the door. Without giving herself a chance to chicken out, she yanked it open to step out into the stairway. Only to come face-to-face with Ray.

"I hope you don't mind. The street door was open so I made my way upstairs." He handed her a single red rose. "It matches the color of your dress."

Mel opened her mouth to thank him but wasn't able to. Her mouth and tongue didn't seem to want to work. They'd gone dry at the sight of him. The dark fabric of his jacket brought out the jet-black of his hair and eyes. The way the man looked in a tuxedo could drive a girl to sin.

What had she got herself into?

The woman was a stunner. Ray assisted Mel into the limousine waiting at the curb as the driver held the door open for them. He had no doubt he'd be the most envied man at this soiree from the moment they entered. If he thought she'd looked beautiful in the shop, the completed product was enough to take his breath away. He would have to find a way to thank his sisters for recommending the boutique; they had certainly come through.

He had half a mind to ask the limo driver to turn around, take them to an intimate restaurant instead, where he could have Mel all to himself. And if that didn't make him a selfish cad, he didn't know what would. He had no right to her, none whatsoever. By this time tomorrow, he'd be walking out of her life for good. A pang of some strange sensation struck through his core at the thought. A sensation he didn't want to examine.

Within moments, they were pulling up to the front doors of the Boston World Trade Center grand auditorium. The aromatic fishy smell of Boston Harbor greeted them as soon as they exited the car. An attendee in a jolly elf hat and curly-toed shoes greeted them as they entered through the massive glass doors.

Mel suddenly stopped in her tracks, bringing them both to a halt.

"Is something the matter?" She'd gone slightly pale under the bright ceiling lights of the lobby. The notes of a bouncy rendition of "Jingle Bells" could be heard from the ballroom.

"I just need a moment before we walk in there."

"Take your time."

"I know this is no time to get cold feet," she began. "But I'm nervous about all that could go wrong."

He took her gently by the elbow and led her away from the main lobby, to a more private area by a large indoor decorative fountain. "I know it's not easy right now, but why don't you try to relax and maybe even have a good time?" She really did look very nervous.

"I'll try but... Maybe we should have rehearsed a few things."

"Rehearsed?"

"What if someone asks how we met? What will we say? Or how long we've known each other. We haven't talked about any of those things."

Ray took in the tight set of Mel's mouth, the nervous quivering of her chin. He should have been more sensitive to her possible concerns under these circumstances. He hadn't really given any of it much thought himself. As prince of Verdovia, he was used to being questioned and spoken to everywhere he went. As a result, he'd grown masterful at the art of delivering nonanswers. Of course, someone like Mel wouldn't be able to respond so easily.

He gave her elbow a reassuring squeeze. "I find that under situations like these, the closer one sticks to the truth, the better."

She blinked at him. "The truth? You want to tell them the truth?"

"That's right. Just not all of it. Not in its entirety."

"I'm gonna need an example of what you mean."

"Well, for instance, if someone asks how long we've known each other, we can tell them we've only met very recently and are still getting to know one another."

The tightness around her eyes lessened ever so slightly. "Huh. And if they ask for details?"

"Leave that part up to me. I'll be able to come up with something."

That earned him a grateful nod. "What if they ask about how we met?" She thought for a moment and then answered her own question. "I know, I can tell them I was knocked off my feet before I'd barely laid eyes on you."

He gave her a small laugh. "Excellent. See, you'll do fine." He offered her his arm and motioned with his head toward the ballroom entrance. When she took it, her grasp was tight and shaky. Mel was not a woman accustomed to even the slightest deception. But some of the tension along her jawline had visibly eased. Her lips were no longer trembling. Now, if he could just get her to smile, she might actually look like someone about to attend a party.

He slowly walked her to the ballroom. The decor inside had been fashioned to look like Santa's workshop in the North Pole. Large replicas of wooden toys adorned various spots in the room. A running toy train traveled along a circular track hanging from the ceiling. Several more staffers dressed up as elves greeted and mingled with the guests as they entered. Large leafy poinsettias served as centerpieces on each table.

"How about we start with some Christmas punch?" he asked Mel as he led her toward a long buffet table with a huge glass punch bowl in the center. On either side was a tower of glass flutes.

"I'd like that."

Ray poured hers first and handed her the glass of the bubbly drink. After grabbing a glass for himself, he lifted it in a toast. "Shall we toast to the evening as it's about to start?"

She tapped the rim of her glass to his. To his happy surprise, a small smile had finally graced her lips.

"I really don't know how to thank you for this, Ray. For all of it. The dress, the limo. That was above and beyond."

"It's my pleasure." It surprised him how true that statement was. They'd only just arrived and already he was having fun and enjoying all of it: the bouncy music, the fun decor. Her company.

"I wish there was some way I could really thank you. Aside from a diner meal, that is," she added, clearly disturbed. Ray had no doubt that even now she was racking her brain to come up with ways to "repay" him somehow. The concept was clearly very important to her.

He wanted to rub his fingers over her mouth, to soften the tight set of her lips with his touch. He wished there was a way to explain that she didn't owe him a thing. "Look at it this way, you're helping me to enjoy Boston during Christmastime. If it wasn't for you, Sal and I would just be wandering around, doing the same boring old touristy stuff I've done before."

Complete with a droll official tour guide and the promise of hours-long business meetings afterward. No, Ray much preferred the anonymity he was currently enjoying. Not to mention the delight of Mel's company.

"You have no idea how refreshing this all is," he told her.

Before Mel could respond, a grinning elf dressed all in green jumped in front of them. She held her hand whimsically above Mel's head. In her grasp was a small plant of some sort.

Mistletoe.

"You know what this means," the young lady said with a cheery laugh.

A sudden blush appeared on Mel's skin. She looked at him with question. "You needn't—" But he wasn't listening.

Ray didn't hesitate as he set his drink down and leaned closer to Mel. As if he could stop himself. What kind of gentleman would he be if he didn't kiss her under the mistletoe at a Christmas party?

They were no longer in a crowded ballroom. Mel's vision narrowed like a tunnel on the man across from her, the man leaning toward her. Ray was about to kiss her, and nothing else in the world existed. Nothing and no one. Just the two of them.

How would he taste? What would his lips feel like against hers?

The reality was so much more than anything she could have imagined. Ray's lips were firm against hers, yet he kept the kiss gentle, like a soft caress against her mouth. He ran his knuckles softly down her cheek as he kissed her. She reached for him, ran her free hand along his chest and up to his shoulder. In response, he deepened the kiss. The taste of him nearly overwhelmed her.

But it was over all too soon. When Ray pulled away, the look in his eyes almost knocked the breath from her. Desire. He wanted her; his gaze left no doubt. The knowledge had her off balance. He was looking at her like he was ready to carry her off to an empty room somewhere. Heaven help her, she would let him if he tried. She gulped in some much-needed air. The mistletoe-wielding elf had left, though neither one of them had even noticed the woman walk away. How long had they stood there kissing like a couple of hormonal teenagers?

"Mel." He said her name like a soft breeze, his breath still hot against her cheek. She found herself tilting her head toward him once more. As foolish as it was given where they were, she wanted him to kiss her again. Right here. Right now.

He didn't get a chance. A familiar baritone voice suddenly interrupted them.

"Melinda? Is that you?"

Her ex-husband stood less than a foot away, staring at her with his mouth agape. He looked quite surprised. And not at all happy. Neither did the woman standing next to him. Talley, his new fiancée.

"Eric, hello." Mel flashed a smile in Talley's direction. "Talley."

Eric unabashedly looked her up and down. "You look nice, Mel." It was a nice enough compliment, but the way he said it did not sound flattering in the least. His tone was one of surprise. Ray cleared his throat next to her.

"Excuse my manners," Mel began. "This is Ray Alsab. He's visiting Boston on business."

Talley was doing some perusing for herself as the men shook hands. She seemed to appreciate what she saw in Ray. But who wouldn't? The man looked like something out of *Billionaire Bachelors* magazine.

"Is that so?" Eric asked. "What kind of business would that be?"

"Real estate." Ray answered simply.

"Huh. What exactly do you do in real estate, Ray?"

Mel wanted to tell him that it was none of his business, and exactly where he could go with his questions. But Ray gave him a polite smile. "I work for the royal government of Verdovia. It's a small island nation in the Mediterranean, off the Greco-Turkish coast. His Majesty King Farood is looking to expand our US holdings, including in Boston. I've been charged with locating a suitable property and starting the negotiations on his behalf."

Eric's eyebrows rose up to near his hairline. He gave a quick shake of his head. "I'm sorry, how does someone in that line of work know Mel?"

The condescension in his voice was so thick, Mel wanted to throw her drink in Eric's face.

But her date merely chuckled. "We met purely by accident." Ray turned to her and gave her a conspiratorial wink, as if sharing a private joke only the two of them would understand. Her laughter in response was a genuine reaction. The masterful way Ray was handling her ex-husband was a talent to behold.

"We'll have to tell you about it sometime," he continued. He then took Mel's drink from her and set it on the table. "But right now, this lady owes me a dance. If you'll please excuse us."

Without waiting for a response, he gently took Mel by the hand and walked with her to the dance floor.

Talley's voice sounded loudly behind them. "I wouldn't mind a dance, Eric. Remember, you promised."

"Nicely done, sir," Mel giggled as she stepped into Ray's arms. The scent of his skin and the warmth of his breath against her cheek sent tiny bolts of lightning through her middle.

"He's still staring. At you. The way he looks at you…" He let his sentence trail off, his hand on her lower back as he led her across the dance floor.

Mel could hardly focus on the dance. She was still enjoying how he'd just handled Eric. But the grim set of Ray's lips and the hardness in his eyes left no question that he was upset. Interactions with her ex often had that effect on people.

"He's just arrogant. It's one of his defining traits."

He shook his head. "It's more than that. He looks at you like he still has some sort of claim," Ray bit out. "As if you still belong to him." His tone distinctly told her that he didn't like it. Not in the least.

Mel had never been much for dancing, but she could hold her own with the steps. Plus, she'd done her fair share of clubbing in her university days. Having Ray as her partner however was a whole new experience. She felt as if she was floating on clouds the way he moved her around the dance floor, perfectly in tune with whatever beat the current song carried.

"You're a man of many talents, aren't you? Quite the talented dancer."

He tilted his head to acknowledge her compliment. "I started taking lessons at a very young age. My parents were real sticklers about certain things they wanted me to be proficient at. It's expected of the pr—" He suddenly cut off whatever he was about to say.

Mel didn't bother to ask for clarification. Whatever the reason, he was the most fluid dance partner a woman could ask for. Whether classic ballroom dances or modern holiday music, he moved like a man who was comfortable with himself. As the kids who ate at the diner would say, the man had the rhythm and the moves.

The impact of the unpleasant encounter with Eric was slowly beginning to ebb, and she decided to throw herself into this experience fully. Remembering what the assistant in the store had told her helped. Sometimes it was all right just to pretend.

And it wasn't exactly difficult to do just that as she

leaned into his length once a slower song had begun to play. He was lean and fit, the hard muscles of his chest firm and hard against hers. It took all her will to resist leaning her head against his shoulder and wrapping her arms around his neck.

And she couldn't help where her mind kept circling back to: the way he'd kissed her. Dear heavens, if the man kissed like that while out in public in front of a crowd of partygoers, what was he like in private? Something told her that, if they hadn't come to their senses, the kiss might very well have lasted much longer, leading to a thrilling experience full of passion. Her mind went there, to a picture of the two of them. Alone. Locked in a tight embrace, his body up against hers. His hands slowly moving along her skin. A shiver ran all the way from her spine down to the soles of her feet.

Stop it!

That train of thought served no purpose. The man lived thousands of miles away, never mind the fact that he was part of a whole different world. Women like her didn't date millionaire businessmen. She had him for this one evening, and she'd make the most of it before he walked out of her life for good.

But someone had other plans. Eric approached from the side and tapped Ray on the shoulder. "May I cut in?"

Ray gave Mel a questioning look, making sure to catch her eye before answering. Mel gave him a slight nod. If she knew anything about her ex, he wasn't going to take no for an answer, not easily anyway. The last thing she wanted was some sort of scene, even a small one. Ray didn't deserve that. And neither did she.

"I'll just go refresh our glasses," Ray told her before letting her out of his arms and walking to the beverage table. "Come find me when you're ready."

Reluctantly, she stepped into the other man's embrace, though she made sure to keep as good a distance as possible. "This was one of your favorite Christmas carols," Eric commented as soon as Ray was out of earshot. "I remember very well."

He remembered wrong. The song currently in play was "Blue Christmas," one she wasn't even terribly fond of. He was confusing it with one she did like, "White Christmas." She didn't bother to correct him. She just wanted this dance to be over.

It was ironic really, how this evening was supposed to be about proving something to the man who currently held her in his arms. But right now, she didn't even want to give him a moment of her attention. In fact, all of her attention was currently fully focused on the dark, enigmatic man, waiting alone for her by the punch bowl. A giddy sense of pride washed over her at the thought. Authentic date or not, Ray was here with her. She could hardly wait to be dancing in his arms again.

Though judging by the looks several ladies were throwing in his direction, he might not be alone for long.

"So is he your boyfriend?" Eric asked with characteristic disregard for any semblance of propriety.

"We are getting to know each other," she answered curtly.

"Right. Is that what you were doing when we first walked in? It looked like you were getting to know his face with your lips."

That was more than enough. "Honestly, Eric. I don't see how it's any of your business. We are divorced, remember?"

He winced ever so slightly. "Don't be that way, Mel. You know I still care about you. I don't want to see you get hurt."

"That's rich. Coming from you."

Eric let out a low whistle. "Harsh. But fair. You've grown a bit...let's say *harder*, in the past several months."

"I've had to grow in all sorts of ways since we parted."

"Just be careful, all right. That's all I'm saying." He glanced in Ray's direction. "Where's he from anyway? Exactly? *Vanderlia* doesn't ring a bell."

"Verdovia," she corrected. "We haven't really had a chance to discuss it." A sudden disquieting feeling blossomed in her chest. She really didn't know much about Ray's homeland. Why hadn't she thought to ask him more about where he was from?

"Why does it even matter, Eric?"

He shrugged. "Just trying to discover some more about your friend." He let go of her just long enough to depict air quotes as he said the last word. "He who's here to investigate potential properties and begin negotiations," he uttered the sentence in an exaggerated mimic of Ray's accent. Mel felt a surge of fury bolt through her core like lightning. Even for Eric, it was beyond the pale. Boorish and bordering on straight elitism.

"Are you actually making fun of the way he speaks?"

"Maybe."

Tears suddenly stung in her eyes. More than outrage, she felt an utter feeling of waste. How could she have given so much to this man? She wasn't even thinking of the money. She was thinking of her heart, of the years of her youth. He'd made it so clear repeatedly that he hadn't deserved any part of her. How had she not seen who he really was? She'd been so hurt, beyond broken, when he'd betrayed her with another woman and then left. Now she had to wonder if he hadn't done her an immense favor.

She pulled herself out of his grasp and took a steadying breath, trying to quell the shaking that had suddenly overtaken her. "I think I'm ready to go back to Ray now. I hope you and Talley have a great time tonight."

Turning on her heel, she left him standing alone on the dance floor. She wouldn't give him anything more, not even another minute of her time.

"You look like you could use some air," Ray suggested before she'd even come to a stop at his side. The grim expression in her eyes and the tight set of her lips told him her interaction with her ex-husband hadn't been all that pleasant. Not that he was surprised. He didn't appear to be a pleasant man in any way.

Which begged the question, how had someone like Mel ever ended up married to him in the first place? He was more curious about the answer than he had a right to be.

She nodded. "It's quite uncanny how well you know me after just a few days."

The comment was thrown out quite casually. But it gave him pause. The truth was, he *had* begun to read her, to pick up on her subtle vibes, the unspoken communications she allowed. Right now, he knew she needed to get away for a few minutes. Out of this ballroom.

"But first—" She reached for the drink he held and downed it all at once.

"It went that well, huh?"

She linked her arm with his. "Let's go breathe some fishy Boston air."

Within moments they were outside, behind the building, both leaning on a cold metal railing, overlooking the harbor. She'd certainly been right about the fishy smell. He didn't mind. He'd grown up near the Mediterranean and Black Sea.

And the company he was with at least made the unpleasant stench worthwhile.

The air held a crisp chill but could be considered mild for this time of year. Still, he shrugged off his jacket and held it out to her.

She accepted with a grateful nod and hugged the fabric around her. She looked good wearing his coat.

Mel drew out a shaky breath as she stared out over the water. "Hard to believe I was ever that naive. To actually think he was good husband material."

"You trusted the wrong person, Mel. You're hardly the first person to do so." His words mocked him. After all, here he was leading her to trust *him*, as well. When he wasn't being straight with her about who he was, his very identity. The charade was beginning to tear him up inside. How much longer would he be able to keep up the pretense? Because the longer it went on, the guiltier he felt.

"I should have seen who he really was. I have no excuses. It was just so hard to be alone all of a sudden. All my friends have moved away since graduation. On to bigger and better things."

He couldn't help but reach for her hand; it fitted so easily into his. Her skin felt soft and smooth to the touch. "What about extended family?"

Her lips tightened. "There's no one I really keep in touch with. Neither did my parents. It's been that way for as long as I can remember."

"Oh?"

"My father had no one. Grew up in foster homes. Got into quite a bit of trouble with the law before he grew up and turned his life around."

"That sounds quite commendable of him."

"Yeah. You'd think so. But his background is the reason my mother was estranged from her family. She came from a long line of Boston Brahmin blue bloods, who didn't approve of her marriage. They thought my father was only after her for their money. They never did come around. Not even decades of my parents being happy and committed could change their minds. Decades where neither one asked for a single penny."

Her declaration went a long way to explain her feelings about the hospital fee payment. No wonder she'd insisted on paying him back. It also explained her pushback and insistence on donating the dress, rather than keeping it.

"I never met any of them," she continued. "Supposedly, I have a grandmother and a few cousins scattered across the country."

He gave her hand a gentle squeeze. "I believe it's their loss for not having met you," he said with sincerity. It sounded so trite, but he wholeheartedly meant it.

"Thank you, Ray. I mean it. Thank you for all you've done tonight. And I'm sorry. I realize you haven't even had a chance to do any of the networking you had planned."

"I find myself caring less and less about that," he admitted.

She tilted her head and looked at him directly. "But it was your main reason for wanting to come."

"Not any longer."

She sucked in a short breath but didn't get a chance to respond. A commotion of laughter and singing from the plaza behind them drew both their attention. Several male voices were butchering a rendition of "Holly Jolly Christmas."

Ray turned to watch as about a dozen dancing men

in Santa suits poured out of a party van and walked into one of the seafood restaurants.

He had to laugh at the sight. "You saw that, too, right? I haven't had too much of that champagne punch, have I?"

She gave him a playful smile and a sideways glance. "If it's the punch, then there's some strange ingredient in it that makes people see dancing Santas." She glanced at the jolly celebrators with a small laugh.

"Only in Boston, I guess."

She turned to face him directly. "You mentioned you wanted to experience the city, but not as a tourist. I may have an idea or two for you."

"Yeah? Consider me intrigued."

Ducking her chin, she hesitated before continuing, as if unsure. "If you have the time, I can show you some of the more interesting events and attractions. There's a lot to see and do this time of year."

He was more intrigued by the idea than he would have liked to admit. "Like my very own private tour guide?"

"Yes, it isn't much, but it would be a small thank-you on my behalf. For all that you've done to make this such a magical evening."

Ray knew he should turn her down, knew that accepting her offer would be the epitome of carelessness. Worse, he was being careless with someone who didn't deserve it in the least. Mel was still nursing her wounds from the way her marriage had dissolved and the heartless way her ex-husband had treated her. He couldn't risk damaging her heart any further by pursuing this charade any longer. This was supposed to be a onetime deal, just for one evening. To try to make up for the suffering and pain she'd endured after the accident he and Saleh had been indirectly responsible for.

But even as he made that argument to himself, he knew he couldn't turn down her offer. Not given the way she was looking at him right now, with expectation and—heaven help him—longing. He couldn't bring himself to look into her deep green eyes, sparkling like jewelry in the moonlight, and pretend he wasn't interested in spending more time with her. He might very well hate himself for it later, and Saleh was sure to read him the riot act. The other man was already quite cross with him, to begin with, about this whole trip. And especially about attending this ball. But Ray couldn't bring himself to pass on the chance to spend just one more day in Mel's company. Damn the consequences.

"That's the best offer I've had in a long while," he answered after what he knew was too long of a pause. "I'd be honored if you'd show me around your great city."

CHAPTER SEVEN

"I DON'T SEE any frogs."

"You do realize it's mid-December, right?" Mel laughed at Ray's whimsical expression. He was clearly teasing her.

"I don't see any frozen frogs either."

"That's because they aren't here any longer. And if they were, they'd most definitely be frozen." She handed him the rented skates.

"But I thought you said we were going to a pond of frogs. Boston does have a very well-known aquarium."

"I figured you must have already been to the aquarium. And besides, they don't harbor any frogs there."

Okay. She obviously hadn't been very clear about exactly what they'd be doing. Mel had decided an authentic winter experience in Boston wouldn't be complete without a visit to the Frog Pond. It was the perfect afternoon for it: sunny and clear, with the temperature hovering just near freezing. Not a snowflake to be seen. She'd figured they could start their excursion with a fun hour or so of skating, then they would walk around the Common, Boston's large inner-city park, which housed the ice rink in the center.

"I said we'd be going to the Frog Pond."

"So where are the frogs?" he asked, wanting to know.

"They're gone. This used to be a swampy pond years ago. But now it's a famous Boston attraction. During the hot summer months, it's used as a splashing pool. In the winter, it turns into an ice-skating rink. I figured it would be fun to get some air and exercise."

"I see." He took the skates from her hands and followed her to a nearby park bench to put them on. "Well, this ought to be interesting."

An alarming thought occurred to her. "Please tell me you know how to skate."

He sat down and started to unlace his leather boots. "I could tell you that. But I'd be lying to you."

Mel would have kicked herself if she could. Why had she made such an assumption about a businessman from a Mediterranean island? She'd planned the whole day around this first excursion, neglecting to ask the most obvious question.

"Oh, no. I didn't realize. I'm so sor—"

He cut her off with a dismissive wave of her hand. "How difficult could it be? I'm very athletic, having played various sports since I could walk. I almost turned pro, remember?"

There was no hint of bragging or arrogance in his tone; he was simply stating a fact.

He motioned toward the rink with a jut of his chin. "If those tiny tots out there can do it, so can I."

Ray quickly proved he was a man of his word. After a couple of wobbly stumbles, where he managed to straighten himself just in time, he was able to smoothen his stride and even pick up some steam.

"Color me impressed," she told him as they circled around for the third time. That was all it took for Ray to complete a full pass around the rink without so much as a stumble. Just as he said, he'd been able to pick it up and had done so with a proficiency that defied logic. "I don't know if you're quite ready to a triple lutz in the center of the rink, but you seem to have got the hang of it."

He shrugged. "It's not all that different from skiing, really."

"Do you ski often?"

"Once or twice a year. My family owns an estate in the Swiss Alps."

Mel nearly lost her balance and toppled onto her face. An estate. In the Alps.

Not only was Ray a successful businessman in his own right—he would have to be to be working directly for the king of his nation—he came from the kind of family who owned estates. There was no doubt in her mind that there was probably more than just one.

Oh, yeah, she was so far out of her league, she might as well have taken a rocket ship to a different planet.

She was spared the need to respond when a group of school-age children carelessly barreled into her from the side. The impact sent her flying and threw her off balance. Unable to regain her footing, she braced herself for the impact of the hard ice. But it never came. Suddenly, a set of strong, hard arms reached around her middle to hold her steady.

"Whoa, there. Careful, love."

Love. Her heart pounded like a jackhammer in her chest, for reasons that had nothing to do with the startle of her near fall.

For countless moments, Mel allowed herself to just stand and indulge herself in the warmth of his arms, willing her pulse to slow. His breath was hot against her cheek. He hadn't bothered to shave or trim down his goatee this morning. The added length of facial hair only served to heighten his devilish handsomeness. She'd never been attracted to a man with a goatee before. On Ray, it was a complete turn-on. He managed to pull it off somehow in a sophisticated, classic sort of way.

"Thanks," she managed, gripping him below the shoulders for support. It was surprising that her tongue even functioned at the moment.

"Sure thing."

"I guess I should have thought this out more." In hindsight, ice-skating wasn't such a good idea, given that Ray hadn't even done it before and how disastrous it would be if she suffered another stumble. "Maybe I should have chosen a different activity."

He glanced down at her lips. "I'm very glad you did choose this. I'm enjoying it more than you can imagine."

She couldn't be misreading his double meaning. They were standing still in the outer ring of the rink, with other skaters whisking by them. The same group of kids skated by again and one of them snickered loudly as they passed. "Jeez, get a room."

Mel startled back to reality and reluctantly removed her hands from Ray's biceps. A quick glance around proved the kids weren't the only ones staring at them. An elderly couple skating together gave them subtle smiles as they went by.

How long had they been standing there that way? Obviously, it had been long enough to draw the attention of the other skaters.

"Just be careful," he said and slowly let go of her, but not before he tucked a stray strand of her hair under her knit cap. "We can't have you falling again. Not when your bruises appear to be healing so nicely."

She wanted to tell him it was too late. She was already off balance and falling in another, much more dangerous way.

* * *

They decided they'd had enough when the rink suddenly became too crowded as the afternoon wore on. Ray took Mel by the elbow and led her off the ice. In moments, they'd removed their skates and had settled on a park bench. Someone nearby had a portable speaker playing soulful R & B. Several middle school–age children ran around the park, pelting each other with snowballs.

All in all, it was one of the most relaxing and pleasurable mornings he'd spent. No one was paying the slightest attention to him, a rare experience where he was concerned. Mel sat next to him, tapping her leather-booted toe in tune with the music.

"Those kids have surprisingly good aim," he commented, watching one of the youngsters land a clumpy snowball directly on his friend's cheek. Mel laughed as the "victim" made an exaggerated show of falling dramatically to the snow-covered ground. After lying there for several seconds, the child spread out his arms and legs, then moved them up and down along the surface of the snow. He then stood and pointed at the snow angel he'd made, admiring his handiwork.

"I haven't made a snow angel in years," Mel stated, still watching the child.

"I haven't made one ever."

She turned to him with surprise clearly written on her expression. "You've never made a snow angel?" She sounded incredulous.

He shrugged. "We don't get that much snow in our part of the world. And when we're in the Alps, we're there to ski."

She stood suddenly, grabbing him by the arm and pulling him up with her. "Then today is the day we rectify that sad state of affairs."

Ray immediately started to protest. Anonymity was one thing, but he couldn't very well be frolicking on the ground, in the snow, like a playful tot. He planted his feet, grinding them both to a halt. "Uh, I don't think so."

Her smile faded. "Why not? You have to do it at least once in your lifetime! What better place than the snow-covered field of Boston Common?"

He gave her a playful tap on the nose. "Making a snow angel is just going to have to be an experience I'll have to forgo."

She rolled her eyes with exaggeration. "Fine, suit yourself."

To his surprise, she strolled farther out into the park and dropped to the ground. She then lay flat on her back. He could only watch as she proceeded to make an impressive snow angel herself.

Ray clapped as she finished and sat on her bottom. "That's how it's done."

He walked over, reached out his hand to help her up.

And realized too late her sneaky intention. With surprising strength, she pulled him down to the ground with her.

"Now that you're down here, you may as well make one, too," she told him with a silly wiggle of her eyebrows.

What the hell? Ray obliged and earned a boisterous laugh for his efforts. By the time they stood, they were both laughing like children.

Suddenly, Mel's smile faltered and her eyes grew serious. She looked directly at him. "You didn't grow up like most boys, did you? Making snow angels and throwing snowballs at friends."

Her question gave him pause. In many ways, he had

been a typical child. But in so many other aspects, he absolutely had not. "Yes. And no."

"What does that mean?"

"It means I had something of a very structured up-bringing."

She studied him through narrowed eyes. "That sounds like you never got in any kind of trouble."

He shook his head. "On the contrary. I most definitely did."

"Tell me."

Ray brushed some of the snow off his coat as he gathered the memories. "Well, there was the time during my fifth birthday party when an animal act was brought in as the entertainment."

"What happened?"

"I insisted on handling the animals." Of course, he was allowed to. People didn't often turn down the request of the crown prince, even as a child.

"That doesn't sound so bad."

He bit back a smile at the memory. "There's more. See, I didn't like how the poor creatures were confined, so I set them free. Just let them loose in the garden. Several reptiles and some type of rodent."

Mel clapped a hand to her mouth and giggled at his words. Ray couldn't bring himself to laugh, for he vividly recalled what had happened in the immediate aftermath.

His father had pulled him into his office that evening as soon as he'd arrived home from a UN summit. Ray distinctly remembered that event as his first lesson on what it meant to be a prince. He was expected to be different from all the other children, to never make any mistakes. To never break the rules. He would always be held to a higher standard, as the world would always be watching him. It was a lesson that had stayed with him throughout the years. On the rare occasions he'd forgotten, the repercussions had been swift and great.

"What about as a teen?" Mel asked, breaking into his thoughts.

The memory that question brought forth was much less laughable. "I got into a rather nasty fistfight on the field, during one particularly heated ball game. Walked away with a shiner that could compete with the one you've recently been sporting."

Mel bit her lip with concern.

"But you should have seen the other guy," he added with a wink.

Again, he wouldn't tell her the details—that the mishap had led to a near-international incident, where diplomats were called in to discuss at great length what had essentially been a typical teen tantrum over a bad play. As expected, the press had gone into a frenzy, with countless speculative articles about the king's lack of control over his only son and whether said son even had what it would take to be a competent king when the time came. His father had been less than happy with him. Worse, he'd been sorely disappointed. Yet another memorable lesson that had stayed with Ray over the years. Suddenly, the mood in the air had turned heavy and solemn.

"Come," Mel said after a silent pause, offering him her hand. "I think we could both use some hot cocoa."

He took her hand and followed where she led.

He hadn't been quite sure what to expect out of today. But Ray could readily admit it had been one of the most enjoyable days he'd ever spent. Now he stood next to Mel on the second level of Faneuil Hall, one of the city's better-known attractions.

"So this is Faneuil, then," he asked. He'd heard about

the area several times during his research on Boston and on previous visits to Massachusetts. But he'd never actually had the chance to visit for himself. Until now.

"The one and only," Mel answered with a proud smile.

Ray let his gaze wander. He'd be hard-pressed to describe the place. It was an outdoor plaza of sorts, with countless shops, restaurants and pubs, all in one center area. But it was so much more. Several acts of entertainment performed throughout the square while adoring crowds clapped and cheered. Music sounded from every corner, some of it coming from live bands and some from state-of-the-art sound systems in the various establishments. Holiday decorations adorned the various shop fronts and streetlights. The place was full of activity and energy.

He and Mel had the perfect view of it all from above, where they stood.

"You're in for a real treat soon," Mel announced. "And we're in the perfect spot to see it." Even as she spoke, several people began to climb up the concrete steps to join them. Before long, a notable crowd had gathered.

"What kind of treat?"

She motioned with her chin toward the massive, tall fir tree standing on the first level. Even at this height, they had to look up to see the top of it. "They're about to light it in a few minutes. As soon as it gets dark."

They waited with patient silence as the night grew darker. Suddenly, the tree lit up. It had to have been decorated with a million lights and shiny ornaments.

Several observers cheered and clapped. Mel placed her fingers in her mouth and let out an impressive whistle.

"So what do you think?" she asked him after they'd simply stared and admired the sight for several moments.

"I know Faneuil can be a bit overwhelming for some people."

Quite the opposite—he'd found it exciting and invigorating. "Believe it or not, it reminds me of Verdovia," he told her.

She glanced at him sideways, not tearing her gaze from the majestic sight of the tree as lights blinked and pulsed on its branches. "Yeah? How so?"

"In many ways, actually. We're a small country but a very diverse people. Given where we're located in the Mediterranean, throughout the years, settlers from many different cultures have relocated to call it home. From Central Europe to Eastern Europe to the Middle East. And many more." He motioned toward the lower level. "Similarly, there appears to be all sorts of different cultures represented here. I hear foreign music in addition to the English Christmas carols and American pop music. And it's obvious there are visitors here from all over the world."

Her eyes narrowed on the scene below in consideration of what he'd just told her. "I never thought of it that way. But you're right. I guess I just sort of took it all for granted. I've been coming here since I was a little girl."

"From now on, when you come, you can think about how it's a mini version of my home country."

Her smile faltered, her expression growing wistful. "Maybe I'll be able to see it someday."

Taking her hands, he turned her toward him. "I'd like that very much. To be able to show you all the beauty and wonder of my nation. The same way you've so graciously shown me around Boston."

"That'd be lovely, Ray. Really."

A wayward snowflake appeared out of nowhere and

landed softly on her nose. Several more quickly followed, and before long, a steady flurry of snow filled the air.

Thick white flakes landed in Mel's hair, covering her dark curls. Ray inadvertently reached for her hair and brushed the snow off with his leathered fingers. He heard her sharp intake of breath at the contact.

Then she leaned in and surprised him with a kiss.

Stunned, he only hesitated for a moment. He wasn't made of stone, after all. Moving his hands to the small of her waist, he pulled her in closer, tight up against his length. She tasted like strawberries and the sweetest nectar.

He let her set the pace—she'd initiated the kiss, after all—letting her explore with her lips and tongue. And when she deepened the kiss and leaned in even tighter against him, he couldn't help but groan out loud. The touch and feel of her was wreaking havoc on his senses.

This was no way to behave. They were in public, for heaven's sake. What was it about this particular woman that had him behaving so irrationally? This was the second time in one day he'd wanted to ravage her in the plain view of countless strangers.

Grasping a strand of sanity, he forced himself to break the kiss and let her go. Like earlier at the ice-skating rink, they'd managed to attract the attention of observers.

"Mel."

She squeezed her eyes shut and gave a shake of her head. "I know. I'm sorry, I shouldn't have kissed you in public like that. Again. I can't seem to help myself."

"I believe the first kiss was my doing. But I had a mistletoe excuse."

She rubbed her mouth with the back of her hand and it took all his will not to take those lips with his own again. He really had to get a grip.

"Why don't we grab a bite?" he suggested, to somehow change the momentum and where this whole scenario might very well be headed: with him taking Mel behind one of the buildings and plundering her mouth with his. "The least I can do after you've entertained me all day is buy you dinner."

"I know just the place."

Within moments, they were down the stairs and seated at an outdoor eatery with numerous heat lamps to ward off the chill. Mel had chosen an authentic New England–style pub with raw shellfish and steaming bowls of clam chowder for them to start with.

Ray took one spoonful of the rich, creamy concoction and sighed with pleasure. He'd had seafood chowder before, but this was a whole new taste experience.

"This chowder is delicious," he told her.

"It's pronounced *chowdah* around here," she corrected him with a small laugh.

"Then this *chowdah* is delicious." Only, with his accent, he couldn't quite achieve the intended effect. The word came out sounding exactly as it was spelled.

Mel laughed at his attempt and then nodded in agreement. "It's very good. But I have to tell you, it doesn't compare to the chowder they serve in the town where I grew up. They somehow make it taste just a bit more home-style there. Must be the small-town charm that adds some extra flavor."

"You didn't grow up in the city?"

She shook her head. "No. About forty minutes away, in a coastal town called Newford. I moved to Boston for school and just ended up staying. Things didn't exactly turn out the way I'd intended after graduation, though."

The spectacle of her failed marriage hung unspoken in the air.

"Tell me more about your hometown," Ray prompted, in an attempt to steer the conversation from that very loaded topic.

A pleasant smile spread across her lips. "It was a wonderful place to grow up. Overlooking the ocean. Some of the small islands off the coast are so close, you can swim to them right from the town harbor. Full of artists and writers and creative free spirits."

"It sounds utterly charming."

She nodded with a look of pride. "It is. And we can boast that we have more art studios per block than most New England towns. One of which I could call a second home during my teen years, given all the hours I spent there."

That took him back a bit. "Really? At an art studio?" There was so much about her he didn't know.

"We had a neighbor who was a world-renowned sculptor. A master at creating magical pieces, using everything from clay to blown glass. He took me under his wing for a while to teach me. Said I had a real talent."

"Why haven't you pursued it? Aside from studying art history in college, that is."

She shrugged, her eyes softening. "I thought about maybe creating some pieces, to show in one of the galleries back home, if any of the owners liked them. But life got in the way."

Ray fought the urge to pull her chair closer to him and drape his arm around her. Her dreams had been crushed through no fault of her own. "Do you still see this sculptor who mentored you? Maybe he can offer some advice on how to take it up again."

Mel set her spoon down into her bowl. "Unfortunately, he passed away. These days, if I go back, it's only to visit an old friend of my mom's. She runs the only bed-and-breakfast in town. They also serve a chowder that would knock your socks off."

"I've never actually stayed at one of those. I hear they're quite charming."

"I'm not surprised you haven't frequented one. They're a much smaller version of the grand hotels your king probably likes to invest in. Tourists like them for the rustic feel while they're in town. It's meant to feel more like you're staying with family."

He was definitely intrigued by the prospect. A hotel stay that felt more like a family home. He would have to find time to stay in one on his next visit to New England. A pang of sorrow shot through his chest at that thought. He might very well be a married man at that time, unless he could convince the king otherwise. The idea made him lean closer to Mel over the table. He gripped his spoon tighter in order to keep from reaching for her.

Mel continued, "In fact, I should probably check in on her. The owner, I mean. Myrna has been struggling to make ends meet recently. She's on the market for a buyer or investor who'll take it off her hands and just let her run the place."

Ray's interest suddenly grew. The whole concept definitely called to him. But it wasn't the type of property the royal family of Verdovia would typically even take the time to look at. They'd never invested in anything smaller than an internationally known hotel in a high-end district of a major metropolitan city.

Still, he couldn't help but feel an odd curiosity about the possibilities. And wasn't he officially part of the royal family, who made such decisions?

CHAPTER EIGHT

"WHATEVER YOU'VE BEEN up to these past couple of days, I hope you've got it out of your system."

"And a good morning to you, as well." Ray flashed Saleh a wide smile as the two men sat down for coffee the next morning in the main restaurant of their hotel. Not even his friend's sullen attitude could dampen his bright mood this morning. Between the way he'd enjoyed himself yesterday with Mel and the decision he'd made upon awakening this morning, he was simply too content.

"Must I remind you that we're only here for a few more days and we haven't even inspected any of the hotels we've come out all this way to visit?" Saleh asked, pouring way too much cream into his mug. He chased it with three heaping spoonfuls of sugar, then stirred. How the man stayed so slim was a mystery.

"You're right, of course," Ray agreed. "At this point, we should probably split up the tasks at hand. Why don't you go visit two of the hotels on the list? I believe a couple of them are within a city block of each other."

"And what will you be doing, Rayhan? If you don't mind my asking," he added the last part in a tone dripping with sarcasm.

"I'll be visiting a prospect myself, in fact, if all goes as planned."

Saleh released a sigh of relief. "Better late than never, I guess, that you've finally come to your senses. Which one of those on the list would you prefer to check out?"

"It isn't on our list."

Saleh lifted an eyebrow in question. "Oh? Did you hear of yet another Boston hotel which may be looking for a buyout?"

"Not exactly. Though the place I have in mind is indeed interested in locating a buyer. Or so I'm told." He couldn't wait to run the idea by Mel, curious as to what her exact reaction might be. He hoped she'd feel as enthusiastic about the prospect as he did.

Saleh studied his face, as if missing a clue that might be found in Ray's facial features. "I don't understand."

Ray took a bite of his toast before answering, though he wasn't terribly hungry after the large dinner he and Mel had shared the evening before. He'd definitely overindulged. The woman certainly knew what he might like to eat. In fact, after just a few short conversations, she already knew more about him than most people he'd call friends or family. He'd never quite divulged so much of himself to anyone before. Mel had a way of making him feel comfortable enough to talk about himself—his hopes, the dreams he'd once had. Around her, he felt more man and less prince. Definitely a new experience. He knew better than to try to explain any of it to the man sitting across the table. Best friend or not, he wouldn't understand. Ray couldn't quite entirely grasp what was happening himself.

"I'm considering, perhaps, looking at smaller options," he answered Saleh. "Something different than the grand international hotel chains."

"Smaller? How much smaller?"

"So small that the guests feel like they're actually staying with family."

Back to reality. Mel smoothed down the skirt of her waitress uniform and tried to force thoughts of Ray and the time they'd spent together yesterday out of her mind. Her shift would be starting in a few minutes and she had to try to focus. Customers really didn't like it when their orders were delayed, or if they mistakenly got the wrong dish.

It was time to pull her head out of the clouds. She'd done enough pretending these past few days.

"You look different," Greta declared, studying her up and down.

"Probably because my face is almost completely healed."

Frannie jumped in as she approached them from behind the counter. "No, that's not it. Greta's right. You look more—I don't know—sparkly."

Mel had to laugh. What in the world did she mean by that? "Sparkly?"

Both the older ladies nodded in unison. "Yeah, like there's more brightness in your eyes. Your skin is all aglow. You even had a spring in your step when you walked in. Can't say I've seen you do that before."

Frannie suddenly gasped and slapped her hand across her mouth. "Dear sweetmeat! You said you were spending the day with that businessman. Please tell me you spent the night with him, too!"

Mel looked around her in horror. Frannie's statement had not been made in a low voice. Neither woman seemed to possess one.

"Of course not! We simply did some skating, walked

for a bit around the Common and then had a meal together." Try as she might, Mel knew she couldn't quite keep the dreaminess out of her voice. For the whole day had been just that…something out of a dream. "He dropped me off at my apartment at the end of the evening like a true gentleman."

Greta humphed in disappointment. "Damn. That's too bad."

"You two know me better than that."

"We know you're due for some fun and excitement. You deserve it."

"And that you're not an old maid," the other sister interjected. "Not that there's anything wrong with being one."

"I think you should have seduced him!" Again, the outrageous statement was made in a booming, loud voice. Mel felt a blush creep into her cheeks. Though she couldn't be sure if it was from embarrassment or the notion of seducing Ray. A stream of images popped into her head that spread heat deep within her core, intensifying into a hot fire as she recalled how brazenly she'd kissed him on the walkway overlooking the tree above Faneuil.

"He's leaving in a few days, Greta."

Greta waved a hand in dismissal. "Lots of people have long-distance relationships. Think of how much you'll miss each other till you can see one another again."

"Thousands of miles away, along the Mediterranean coast, is quite a long distance," she countered, fighting back a sudden unexpected and unwelcome sting of tears. Just like her to be foolish enough to go and fall so hard for a man who didn't even live on the same continent.

Not that it really mattered. Where they each lived was beyond the concept of a moot point. The fantasy of

Ray was all well and good. But they weren't the type of people who would ever end up together in the long term.

Her family had never owned a European estate. What a laugh. She could barely afford the rent in her small studio apartment on the south side. She could only imagine how elegant and sophisticated Ray's parents and sisters had to be. Mel didn't even want to speculate about what they might think of someone like her. Look at the way her own father had been treated by his wife's family.

"So have some fun in the meantime," Greta argued. "He's still got a few more days in the States, you said."

"And I repeat, you know me better than that. I'm not exactly the type who can indulge in a torrid and quick affair." Though if any man could tempt her into doing so, it would most certainly be the charming man with the brooding Mediterranean looks who'd haunted her dreams all last night.

"Then maybe he should be the one who tries to seduce you," Frannie declared, as if she'd come up with the entire solution to the whole issue. Mel could only sigh. They clearly had no intention of letting the matter drop. She really did have to keep repeating herself when it came to the Perlman sisters.

"I already mentioned he was a gentleman."

The pocket of her uniform suddenly lit up as her phone vibrated with an incoming call.

Her heart jumped to her throat when she saw whose number popped up on the screen. It was as if her thoughts had conjured him. With shaky fingers, she slid the icon to answer.

The nerves along her skin prickled with excitement when she heard his deep, silky voice. Oh, yeah, she had it pretty bad.

And had no idea what to do about it.

"I wanted to thank you again for taking me to so many wonderful spots yesterday." Ray's voice sounded smooth and rich over the tiny speaker.

Mel had to suppress the shudder of giddiness that washed over her. She realized just how anxious she'd been that he might not reach out to her again, despite his assurances last night that he'd be in touch before leaving the United States. "I had a lot of fun, too," she said quietly into the phone. Greta and Frannie were unabashedly leaning over the counter to get close enough to hear her end of the conversation.

"Believe it or not, I'm calling to ask you for yet another favor," Ray said, surprising her. "One only you would be able to help me with."

"Of course," she answered immediately, and then realized that she should at least inquire what he was asking of her. "Um. What kind of favor?"

"You gave me an idea last night. One I'd like to pursue further to see if it might be worthwhile."

For the life of her, she couldn't imagine what he might be referring to. Was she forgetting a crucial part of the evening? Highly unlikely, considering she'd run every moment spent with him over and over in her mind since he'd left her. Every moment they'd spent together had replayed in her mind like mini movies during her sleepless night. She'd felt light-headed and euphoric, and she hadn't even had anything to drink last night.

"I did?"

"Yes. Are you free later today?"

For him? Most certainly. And it wasn't like she had an active social life to begin with. She could hardly wait to hear what he had in mind. "My shift ends at three today, after the lunch crowd. Will that work?" It was impossible to keep the joy and excitement out of her voice. Something about this man wreaked havoc on her emotions.

"It does. Perfectly."

Mel's heart pounded like a jackhammer in her chest. She'd be spending the afternoon with him. The next few hours couldn't go by fast enough.

"I'm glad. But I have to ask. What is this idea I gave you?"

She could hardly believe her ears as he explained. Her off-the-cuff remark about the bed-and-breakfast in Newford had apparently had more of an impact on him than she would have guessed. She'd actually forgotten all about it. Ray's proposal sent a thrill down her spine. By the time she slid her phone back into her pocket, her excitement was downright tangible.

"Well, what was that all about?" Frannie demanded to know. "From the dreamy look on your face, I'd say that was him calling. Tell us what he said."

"Yeah. Must have been something good," Greta added. "You look like you're about ready to jump out of your skin."

All in all, it was a pretty apt description.

"Why, Melinda Lucille Osmon, let me take a look at you! How long has it been, sweetie?"

Ray watched with amusement as a plump, short older woman with snow-white hair in a bun on top her head came around the check-in counter and took Mel's face into her palms. "Hi, Myrna. It's been way too long, I'd say."

"Now, why have you been such a stranger, young lady?"

"I have no excuses. I can only apologize."

"Well, all that matters is that you're here now. Will you be staying a few days?"

It was endearing how many little old ladies Mel had in her life who seemed to absolutely adore her. She might not have any more living blood relatives, but she seemed to have true family in the form of close friends. Ray wondered if she saw it that way.

Right now, this particular friend was making a heroic effort to avoid glancing in his direction. No doubt waiting for Mel to introduce him and divulge what they were doing there together on the spur of the moment.

Not too hard to guess what conclusion the woman had jumped to about the two of them arriving at the bed-and-breakfast together. The situation was bound to be tricky. Both he and Mel had agreed on the ride over that they wouldn't mention Ray's intentions about a potential purchase. Mel didn't want to get the other woman's hopes up in case none of it came to fruition.

Mel hesitantly cleared her throat and motioned to him with her hand. "This is a friend of mine, Myrna. His name is Ray Alsab. He's traveling from overseas on business. He wanted to see an authentic bed-and-breakfast before leaving the States."

"Why, I'm honored that mine is the one he'll be seeing," the other woman said with a polite smile.

Ray reached over and took her hand and then planted a small kiss on the back, as was customary in his country when meeting older women. "The honor is all mine, ma'am."

Myrna actually fanned herself. "Well, you two happen to have great timing. It's the night of the annual town Christmas jamboree. To be held right here in our main room."

Ray gave Mel a questioning look. "It's a yearly get-together for the whole town," Mel began to explain. "With plenty of food, drink and dancing."

"Another ball, then?"

Myrna giggled next to him. "Oh, no. It's most definitely not a ball. Nothing like it. Much less fancy. Just some good old-fashioned food and fun among neighbors." She turned to Mel, her expression quite serious. "I hope you two can stay."

This time it was Mel's turn to give him a questioning look. She wasn't going to answer without making sure it was all right with him. *Why not*, Ray thought. After all, the whole reason he was here was to observe the workings and attraction of a small-town lodge. To see if it might make for a worthwhile investment.

Yeah, right. And it had absolutely nothing to do with how it gave him another excuse to spend some more time with Mel. He gave her a slight nod of agreement.

"We'd love to stay and attend, Myrna. Thank you."

Myrna clasped her hands in front of her chest. "Excellent. Festivities start at seven o'clock sharp."

"We'll be there."

"I'm so happy you're here. Now, let's get you two something to eat." She laid a hand on Mel's shoulder and started leading her down the hall. "Ruby's thrown together a mouthwatering beef stew, perfect for the cold evening." She turned to Ray. "Ruby's our head cook. She does a fine job."

Ray politely nodded, but his mind was far from any thoughts of food. No, there was only one thought that popped into his head as he followed the two women into a dining area. That somehow he was lucky enough to get another chance to dance with Mel.

* * *

"So, what do you think of the place?" Mel asked him as he entered the main dining room of the Newford Inn with her at precisely 7:00 p.m.

"It's quite charming," Ray answered truthfully. The establishment was a far cry from the five-star city hotels that made up most of his family's resort holdings. But if he was to deviate from that model, the Newford Inn would be a fine choice to start with. It held a New England appeal, complete with naval decor and solid hardwood floors. And the chef had done an amazing job with the stew and fixings. He still couldn't believe just how much of it he'd had at dinner. But Myrna had put bowl after bowl in front of him and it had been too good to resist.

"I'm so glad to hear it." She gave him a genuine smile that pleased him much more than it should have.

"Mel? What are you doing here?"

They'd been approached by a tall, lanky man who appeared to be in his thirties. He had a fair complexion and was slightly balding at the top of his head. The smile he greeted Mel with held more question than friendliness.

"Carl," Mel answered with a nod of her head. Her smile from a moment ago had faded completely.

"Wow, I wasn't expecting to see you here tonight."

"It was something of an unplanned last-minute decision."

The other man looked at Ray expectedly, then thrust his hand in his direction when Mel made no effort to introduce them. "I'm Carl Devlin. Mel and I knew each other growing up."

"Ray. Nice to meet you."

Carl studied him up and down. "Huh. Eric mentioned

you were seeing someone," he said, clearly oblivious to just how rude he was being.

Mel stiffened next to him. "You and Eric still talk about me?"

Carl shrugged. "We talk about a lot of things. We're still fantasy-ball buddies."

Yet another American term Ray had never really understood the meaning of. It definitely didn't mean what it sounded like. As if American sports fans sat around together fantasizing about various sports events. Though, in a sense, he figured that was how the gambling game could be described.

Mel gave him a sugary smile that didn't seem quite genuine for her part either. "I'm so terribly happy that the two of you have remained friends since I introduced you two at the wedding. After all this time."

"Yeah. I'm really sorry things didn't work out between you two."

Ray felt the ire growing like a brewing storm within his chest. The blatant reminder that Mel had once belonged to a man who so completely hadn't deserved her was making him feel a strange emotion he didn't want to examine.

Luckily, Mel cut the exchange short at that point. She gently took Ray's arm and began to turn away. "Well, if you'll excuse us then, I wanted to introduce Ray to some friends."

Ray gave the other man a small nod as they walked away.

"I'm sorry if that was unpleasant," she said as she led him toward the other corner of the room. "I should have remembered that he and Eric still keep in touch."

"No need to apologize," he said and put his arm around her waist. "Though it occurs to me that we have the same predicament as we had the other evening at the holiday ball."

Her eyebrows lifted in question. "How so?"

"Looks like we'll have to put on a good show for your old friend Carl." He turned to face her. "Shall we get started?"

She responded by stepping into his embrace and giving him just the barest brush of a kiss on the lips.

CHAPTER NINE

"THIS MIGHT VERY well be the silliest dance I've ever done."

Mel couldn't contain her laughter as Ray tried to keep up with the line dance currently in play in the main room. Had she finally found the one thing Ray might not be good at? He was barely keeping up with the steps and had nearly tripped her up more than once when he'd danced right into her.

She had to appreciate the lengths he was going to simply to indulge her.

"You'll get the hang of it," she reassured him. "You're used to dancing at high-end balls and society events. Here at the Newford Inn, we're much more accustomed to doing the Electric Slide."

"It appears to be more complicated than any waltz," he said with so much grim seriousness that she almost felt sorry for him.

The song finally came to an end before Ray had even come close to mastering the steps. The next song that started up was a much slower love ballad. The dancers on the floor either took their leave and walked away, or immediately started to pair up. Ray reached for her hand. "May I?"

A shiver meandered down her spine. With no small amount of hesitation, she slowly stepped into his arms.

She wasn't sure if her heart could handle it. The lines between pretending to be a couple for Carl's benefit and the reality of her attraction to him were becoming increasingly blurry.

She had no doubt she was beginning to feel true and strong emotions for the man. But for his part, Ray's feelings were far from clear. Yes, he seemed to be doing everything to charm her socks off. But how much of that was just simply who he was? His charm and appeal seemed to be a natural extension of him. Was she reading too much into it all?

And that kiss they'd shared the night before while they'd watched the tree lighting. She'd felt that kiss over every inch of her body. She wanted to believe with all her heart that it had meant something to him as well, that it had affected him even half as much as it had affected her. The way he'd responded to her had definitely seemed real. There had been true passion and longing behind that kiss—she firmly believed that. But she couldn't ignore the fact that she'd initiated it. How many men wouldn't have responded? She didn't exactly have the best track record in general as far as men were concerned. Look at how badly she'd read Eric and his true intentions. In her desire to belong to some semblance of a family again, she'd gone ahead and made the error of a lifetime.

She couldn't afford to make any more such mistakes.

At the heart of it, there was only one thing that mattered. Ray would be gone for good in a few short days. She had to accept that. Only, there was no denying that he'd be taking a big part of her heart with him.

How foolish of her to let that happen.

Even as she thought so, she snuggled her cheek tighter

against his chest, taking in the now-familiar, masculine scent of him. It felt right to be here, swaying in his arms to the romantic music.

Any hope she had that he might feel a genuine spark of affection died when he spoke his next words. "We definitely seem to have your friend Carl's attention. He seems convinced I can't keep my hands off you. If Eric asks, I'm sure he'll get the answer that we're very much enamored with each other."

Something seemed to snap in the vicinity of her chest. She yanked out of his arms, suddenly not caring how it would look. To Carl or anyone else.

"I don't care."

He blinked at her. "Beg your pardon?"

"I don't care what Eric thinks anymore. It was childish and silly to go through so much trouble just to prove a point to a selfish shell of a man." She swallowed past the lump that had suddenly formed in her throat. "A man I should have never fallen for, let alone married."

There was a sudden shift behind his eyes. He reached for her again and took her gently by the upper arms. "Come here."

Mel couldn't allow herself to cry. Since they'd walked into the room, all eyes had been focused on them. There was zero doubt they were being watched still. It would be disastrous to cause a scene right here and now. The last thing she wanted was gossip to follow her on this visit.

She couldn't even explain why she was suddenly so emotional. Only that her heart was slowly shattering piece by piece every time she thought of how temporary this all was. A month from now, it would be nothing more than a memory. One she would cherish and revisit daily for as long as she lived. More than likely, the same could not be said for how Ray would remember her.

Or if he even would.

The thought made her want to sob, which would definitely cause a scene.

"Please, excuse me," she pleaded, then turned on her heel to flee the room. She ran into the outer hallway, making her way past the desk and toward the small sitting area by the fireplace. Ray's footsteps sounded behind her within moments. He reached her side as she stood staring at the crackling flames. She wasn't quite ready to turn and face him just yet.

"What's the matter, Mel?" he asked softly, his voice sounded like smooth silk against the backdrop of the howling gusts of wind outside.

She took too long to answer. Ray placed a gentle hand on her shoulder and turned her around. The concern in his eyes touched her to her core.

"Nothing. Let's just get back and enjoy the dancing." She tried to step to the side. "I guess I'm just being silly."

He wasn't buying it. He stopped her retreat by placing both hands on either side of her against the mantel. Soft shadows fell across his face from the light of the fire and the dim lighting in the room. With the heat of the flames at her back and that of his body so close to hers, she felt cocooned in warmth. Ray's warmth. Her stomach did a little quiver as he leaned closer.

"*Silly* is the last word I would use to describe you."

She wanted to ask him how he would describe her. What were his true, genuine thoughts as far as she was concerned?

The sudden flickering of the lights, followed by a complete blackout, served to yank her out of her daze. Now that the music from the other room had stopped, the harsh sound of the howling wind sang loudly in the air.

She'd been a New Englander her whole life and could

guess what had just happened. The nor'easter storm forecast for much later tonight must have shifted and gained speed. The roads were probably closed or too treacherous to risk. Attempting the forty-minute ride back into Boston would be the equivalent of a death wish.

They were almost certainly snowbound for the night.

"I'm sorry, dear. Unfortunately, the one room is all I have. Between the holidays, the storm warnings and this annual holiday jamboree, we've been booked solid for days now. I only have the one small single due to a last-minute weather-related cancelation."

Mel had been afraid of that. She stood, speaking with Myrna in the middle of the Newford Inn's candlelit lobby. Most of the partygoers had slowly dispersed and headed back to their rooms or to their houses in town. Ray stood off to the side, staring in awe at the powerful storm blowing outside the big bay window. The power wasn't expected to come back on in the foreseeable future and Myrna's backup generators were barely keeping the heat flowing. "I understand. I'm not trying to be difficult. I hope you know that."

Myrna patted her hand gently. "Of course, dear." She then leaned over to her and spoke softly into her ear so that only Mel could hear her. "Are you scared in any way, dear? To be alone in a room with him? If you are, even a little bit, I'll figure something out."

Mel felt touched at her friend's concern. But fear was far from being the issue. She didn't know if she had the emotional stamina to spend a night alone in a small room with Ray.

She shook her head with a small smile. "No, Myrna.

I'm not even remotely in fear of him. It's just that we haven't known each other that long."

"I'm so sorry, Mel," Myrna repeated. "Why don't you sleep with me in my room, then? It will be tight, but we can make do."

That offer was beyond generous. Mel knew Myrna occupied a space barely larger than a closet. Not to mention she looked beyond exhausted. Mel knew she must have been running around all day to prep for the jamboree. Then she'd had to deal with the sudden power outage and getting the heat restored before it got too cold. All on top of the fact that Mel and Ray hadn't been expected. She felt beyond guilty for causing the other woman any inconvenience.

Ray suddenly appeared at her side and gently pulled her to the corner of the room. "Mel, I must apologize. I feel responsible that you're stranded here. With me."

The number of people suddenly apologizing to her was beginning to get comical. All due to a storm no one could control or could have predicted.

Ray continued, "Please accept whatever room the inn has available for yourself. I'll be perfectly fine."

"But where will you sleep?"

He gave her hand a reassuring squeeze. "You don't need to concern yourself with that."

"I can't help it," she argued. "I am concerned." The only other option he had was the SUV. "You're not suggesting you sleep in your car, are you?"

"It won't be so bad."

"Of course it will. You'd have to keep it running all night to avoid freezing. You probably don't even have enough gas to do that after our drive here."

"I can handle the cold," he told her. "I have roughed it in the past."

She quirked an eyebrow at him.

Ray crossed his hands in front of his chest. "I'll have you know that military service is a requirement in my country. I spent many months as a soldier training and surviving in worse conditions than the inside of an SUV during a storm. I can survive a few hours trying to sleep in one for one night."

He'd been a soldier? How much more was there about this man that she had no clue about?

Nevertheless, they had more pressing matters at the moment.

Mel shook her head vehemently. She couldn't allow him to sleep outside in a car during a nor'easter. Especially not in a coastal town. Plus, she felt more than a little responsible for their predicament. She was the native New Englander. If anything, she should have been prepared for the storm and the chance that it might hit sooner than forecast.

"Ray, setting aside your survival skills learned as a soldier, making you sleep outdoors is silly. We can share a room for one night."

He studied her face and then tipped his head slightly in acceptance. "If you insist."

She turned back to Myrna, glad to be done with the argument. What kind of person would she be if she allowed herself to sleep in a nice, comfortable bed while he was outside, bent at odd angles, trying to sleep all night in a vehicle? Military service or not.

"We'll take the room, Myrna. Thank you for your hospitality."

The other woman handed her an old-fashioned steel key. "Room 217. I hope you two stay warm."

"Thank you," she said with a forced smile, trying to convey a level of calm she most certainly didn't feel.

"Have a pleasant sleep," her friend added, handing her two toothbrushes and a minuscule tube of toothpaste.

That was doubtful, Mel thought as she motioned for Ray to follow her. It was highly unlikely she'd get much sleep at all. Not in such close quarters with a man she was attracted to like no one else she'd ever met.

Not even the man she had once been married to.

Ray placed his hand on Mel's as she inserted the key to open the door to what would be their room for the night. "My offer still stands," he told her, giving her yet another chance to be certain. "I can go sleep outside in the vehicle. You don't need to do anything you're not completely comfortable with."

He'd never forgive himself for the predicament he'd just put Mel in. Who knew the weather along the northeastern coast could be so darn unpredictable? He wasn't used to accommodating unexpected whims of the forecast where he was from.

"I appreciate that, Ray. I do." She sighed and turned the key, pushing open the wooden door. "But we're both mature adults. I've spent enough time with you to know you're not a man to take advantage. Let's just get some sleep."

"You're sure?"

She nodded. "Yes. Completely."

Grateful for her answer—he really hadn't been looking forward to being sprawled out in the back seat of an SUV for hours in the middle of a storm—he followed her in. The room they entered wasn't even half the size of one of his closets back home in his personal wing of the castle. But the real problem was the bed. It was barely the size of a cot.

Mel must have been thinking along the same lines.

Her eyes grew wide as they landed on it. He could have sworn he heard her swear under her breath.

"I'll sleep on the floor," he told her.

She immediately shook her head. "There's only the one comforter. That wouldn't be much better than sleeping in the car."

He took her by the shoulders and turned her to face him. "Again. I'm sorry for all of this. I can assure you that you can rest easy and fall asleep. I won't do anything to make you uncomfortable. You don't have to worry about that."

She gave him a tight nod before turning away. Again, she muttered something under her breath he couldn't quite make out.

Despite his unyielding attraction to her, he'd sooner cut off his arm than do anything to hurt her. It was hard to believe how much he'd come to care about her in just the short time since they'd met. She had to know that.

They both got ready for bed in awkward silence. Mel climbed in first and scooted so close to the wall she was practically smashed up against it. Ray got into bed and lay on his side, making sure to face the other way.

"Good night, Mel."

"Good night."

Wide-awake, he watched as the bedside clock slowly ticked away. The wind howled like a wild animal outside, occasionally rattling the singular window. Had Mel fallen asleep yet? The answer came when she spoke a few minutes later.

"This is silly," she said in a soft voice, almost near to whispering. "I'm close to positive you aren't asleep either. Are you?"

Just to be funny, he didn't answer her right away. Several beats passed in awkward silence. Finally, he heard Mel utter a chagrined "Oh, dear."

He allowed himself a small chuckle, then flipped over onto his other side to face her. "Sorry, couldn't resist. You're right. I'm awake, too."

"Ha ha. Very funny." She gave him a useless shove on the shoulder. The playful motion sent her body closer against him for the briefest of seconds, and he had to catch his breath before he could speak again.

"I've never experienced a New England snowstorm before," he told her.

"It's called a nor'easter. We get one or two every winter, if we're lucky. If not, we get three, maybe even four."

"They're pretty. And pretty loud."

He felt her nodding agreement in the dark. "It can be hard to fall asleep, even if you're used to them."

"Since neither of us is sleeping," he began. "I was wondering about something."

"About what?"

"Something you said tonight."

"Yes?"

"When you told me you no longer cared about what Eric thought. Did you mean it?"

The sensation of her body so near to his, the scent of her filling his nostrils compelled him to ask the question. He realized he'd been wanting to all night, since she'd spoken the words as they'd danced together earlier.

He felt the mattress shift as she moved. "Yes. I did mean it. And I realize I haven't cared about his opinion for quite a while."

He wanted to ask her more, was beyond curious about what had led to their union. She seemed far too good for the man Eric appeared to be—she was too pure, too selfless. But this was her tale to tell. So he resisted the urge to push. Instead, he waited patiently, hoping she would continue if she so chose.

She eventually did. "I honestly don't know exactly what drew me to Eric. I can only say I'd suffered a terrible loss after my parents' passing. It's no excuse, I know."

"A person doesn't need an excuse for how they respond to grief," he told her.

"You speak as if you're someone who would know." She took a shaky breath. "Have you lost someone close to you?"

That wasn't it. He wouldn't be able to explain it to her. As the heir to the crown, he'd been to more ceremonial funerals than he cared to remember. Words had always failed him during those events, when confronted with the utter pain of loss that loved ones experienced.

"I haven't," he admitted. "I've been quite fortunate. I never knew my grandparents. Both sets passed away before I or my sisters were born."

She stayed silent for a while. "I lost the two most important people in the world to me within a span of a few months," she said, reminding him of their conversation from the other day. "I guess I longed for another bond, some type of tie with another person. So when Eric proposed…"

"You accepted." But she'd gone above and beyond the commitment of her marital vows. "You also put him through school."

"I never wanted finances to be an issue in my marriage. Money was the reason I had no one else after my parents died."

"And you never fought to get any of it back? To get your life back on track or even to pursue your own dreams?"

He felt her tense up against him. Maybe he was getting too personal. Maybe it was the effect of the dark and quiet they found themselves in. Not to mention the tight and close quarters. But he found he really wanted to understand her reasoning. To understand *her*.

"It's hard to explain, really. I didn't have the stomach to fight for something I readily and voluntarily handed over."

"Is that the only reason?"

"What else?"

"Perhaps you're punishing yourself. Or maybe trying to prove that you can be independent and rebound. All on your own."

He felt her warm breath on his chest as she sighed long and deep. "I thought I was in love. To me, that meant a complete commitment. Materially and emotionally." The statement didn't really answer his question. But he wasn't going to push.

She didn't need to explain anything to him. And he suddenly felt like a heel for making her relive her grief and her mistakes. Gently, softly, he rubbed his knuckles down her cheek. She turned her face into his touch and he had to force himself not to wrap his arms around her and pull her closer, tight up against him. As difficult as it was to do so, he held firm and steady without moving so much as a muscle. For he knew that if he so much as reached for her, it would be a mistake that could only lead to further temptation.

Temptation he wasn't sure he'd be able to control under the current circumstances.

Mel couldn't believe how much she was confiding about herself and her marriage. To Ray of all people—a man she'd just recently met and barely knew. But somehow she felt more comfortable talking to him than anyone else she could name.

She was curious about things in his past, also.

"What about you?" she asked, not entirely sure she really wanted to know the answer to what she was about to ask him. "There must have been at least one significant relationship in your past. Given all you have going for you."

"Not really. I have had my share of relationships. But none of them amounted to anything in the long run. Just some dear friendships I'm grateful for."

"I find that hard to believe."

He chuckled softly. The vibration of his voice sent little bolts of fire along her skin. "You can believe it."

"Not even at university? You must have dated while you were a student."

"Sure. But nothing that grew serious in any way."

She had no doubt the women he was referring to would have much rather preferred a completely different outcome. Ray seemed to have no idea the trail of broken hearts he must have left in his wake. Her eyes stung. She'd soon be added to that number.

After pausing for several moments, he finally continued, "I never really had much of a chance to invest any kind of time to cultivate the kind of relationship that leads to a significant commitment. As the oldest of the siblings, familial responsibilities far too often fell solely on my shoulders. Even while I was hundreds of miles away, studying in Geneva."

Ray sounded like he bore the weight of an entire nation on those shoulders. "Your family must be very important in Verdovia."

That comment, for some reason, had Ray cursing under his breath. "I'm sorry, Mel," he bit out. "For all of it."

He had to be referring to all the pain and anguish of

her past that she'd just shared. Mel couldn't help but feel touched at his outrage on her behalf. The knowledge that he cared so deeply lulled her into a comfortable state of silence. Several moments went by as neither one spoke.

She wasn't sure how she was supposed to sleep when all she could think about was having Ray's lips on hers.

So it surprised her when she opened her eyes and looked at the clock, only to see that it read 7:30 a.m. A peaceful stillness greeted her as she glanced outside the window at the rising sun of early morning. The only sound in the room was the steady, rhythmic sound of Ray breathing softly next to her.

At some point, the winds had died down and both she and Ray had fallen asleep.

The air against her face felt frigid. Her breath formed a slight fog as she breathed out. The generators must not have been able to quite keep up with the weather, as the temperature in the room had gone down significantly. She came fully awake with a start as she realized exactly how she'd fallen asleep: tight against Ray's chest, snuggled securely in his arms. She hadn't even been aware of the cold.

CHAPTER TEN

THE AWKWARDNESS OF their position was going to be unbearable once Ray woke up. Mel racked her mind for a
possible solution. She didn't even know what she would
say to him if he woke to find her nestled up against his
chest this way.

There was no doubt she'd been the one to do the nes-
tling either. Ray remained in exactly the same spot he'd
been when they'd got into the bed. She, on the other hand,
was a good foot away from the wall.

She did the only thing she could think of. She pretended to snore. Loudly.

At first he only stirred. So she had to do it again.

This time, he jolted a bit and she immediately shut her
eyes before he could open his. Several beats passed when
she could hear him breathing under her ear. His body's
reaction was nearly instantaneous. Heaven help her, so
was her response. A wave of curling heat started in her
belly and moved lower. Her fingers itched to reach for
him, to pull him on top of her. Electricity shot through
her veins at the images flooding her mind. She didn't
dare move so much as an inch.

Mel heard him utter a soft curse under his breath.
Then he slowly, gently untangled himself and sat up on
the edge of the mattress. She felt his loss immediately.

The warmth of his skin, the security of his embrace—if she were a braver, more reckless woman, she would have thrown all caution to the wind and reached for his shoulder. She would have pulled him back toward her and asked him for what she was yearning for so badly.

But Mel had never been that woman. Especially not since her divorce and the betrayal that had followed. If anything, the fiasco had made her grow even more guarded.

Ray sat still for several more moments. Finally, she felt his weight leave the mattress.

She wasn't proud of her mini deception, but what a relief that it had worked. The sound of the shower being turned on sounded from behind the bathroom door. There was probably no hot water. But Ray probably didn't need it.

She rubbed a shaky hand down her face. Hopefully he would take his time in there. It would take a while for her heart to steady, judging by the way it was pounding wildly in her chest.

Before long, the shower cut off and she heard him pull the curtain back.

Mel made sure to look away when Ray walked out of the bathroom, wearing nothing but a thick terry towel around his midsection. But it was no use, she'd seen just enough to have her imagination take over from there. A strong chiseled chest with just enough dark hair to make her fingers itch to run through it. He hadn't dried off completely, leaving small droplets of water glistening along his tanned skin. She had to get out of this room. The tight quarters with him so close by were wreaking havoc on her psyche. Not to mention her hormones. She sat upright along the edge of the mattress.

"You're awake," he announced.

She merely nodded.

"I…uh… I'll just get dressed."

"Okay." She couldn't quite meet him in the eye.

He began to turn back toward the bathroom.

"Do you want to take a walk with me?" she blurted out.

"A walk?"

"Yes. The wind and snow has stopped. We won't be able to start driving anywhere for a while yet. The salt trucks and plows are probably just now making a final run to clear the roads."

"I see. And all that gives you a desire to walk?" he asked with a small smirk of a smile gracing his lips.

"The aftermath of a snowstorm in this town can be visually stunning," she informed him. "I think you'd enjoy the sight of it."

He gave her an indulgent smile. "That sounds like a great idea, then."

She gave him a pleasant smile. "Great, you get dressed. I'll try to scrounge us up some coffee from the kitchen and meet you up front."

"I'll be there within ten minutes," he said with a dip of his head.

It was all the cue Mel needed to grab her coat and scarf, and then bolt out of the room.

As soon as she shut the door behind her, she leaned back against it and took several deep breaths. A walk was definitely an inspired idea. The air would do her good. And she knew just where to take him. Newford was home to yet another talented sculptor who put on a stunning display of three or four elaborate ice statues every year, right off the town square. At the very least, it would give them something to talk about, aside from the strange night they'd just spent in each other's arms.

But first, caffeine. She needed all the fortitude she could get her hands on.

Ray made sure to be true to his word and took the center staircase two steps at a time to find Mel waiting for him by the front doors. They appeared to be the only two people up and about—in this part of the hotel anyway.

"Ready?" she asked and handed him a travel mug of steaming hot liquid. The aroma of the rich coffee had his mouth watering in an instant.

He took the cup from her with a grateful nod and then motioned with his free hand to the doors. "Lead the way."

He saw what she'd meant earlier as soon as they stepped outside. Every building, every structure, every tree and bush was completely covered in a thick blanket of white. He'd never seen so much snow in a city setting before, just on high, majestic mountains. This sight was one to behold.

"It looks like some sort of painting," he told her as they started walking. The sidewalks still remained thick with snow cover, but the main road had been plowed. He was thankful for the lined leather boots he was wearing. Mel was definitely more accustomed to this weather than he was. She maintained a steady gait and didn't even seem to notice the cold and brisk morning air. He studied her from the corner of his eye.

Her cheeks were flushed from the cold, her lips red and ripened from the hot brew she was drinking.

His mind inadvertently flashed back to the scene this morning. He'd awoken to find her snuggled tight in his embrace. Heaven help him, it had taken all the will he possessed to disentangle her soft, supple body away from his and leave the bed.

In another universe, upon waking up with her that way, he would have been the one to put that blush on her cheeks, to cause the swelling in those delicious ruby red lips.

He blinked away the thoughts and continued to follow her as she made her way to what appeared to be the center of town.

"Do we have a destination?" he asked, trying to focus on the activity at hand and not on the memory of how she'd felt nestled against him earlier.

"As a matter of fact, we do," she replied. "You'll see soon enough."

As he'd thought, they reached the center of town and what seemed to be some sort of town square. The sound of the ocean in the near distance grew louder the farther they walked. There was nothing to see in the square but more snow. How in the world would all this get cleaned up? It seemed an exorbitant amount. Where did it all go once it melted?

Verdovia's biggest snowstorm in the past decade or so had resulted in a mere light covering that had melted away within days.

"This way," Mel said.

Within moments, she'd led them to a small alleyway between two long brick buildings, a sort of square off to the side of the main square. In the center sat a now quiet water fountain of cherubic angels holding buckets.

But the true sight to behold was the handful of statues that surrounded the cherubs. Four large ice sculptures, each an impressive display of craftsmanship.

"Aren't they magnificent?" Mel asked him with a wide smile.

"Works of art," Ray said as they walked near to the closest one. A stallion on its hind legs, appearing to bray at the sky.

"They certainly are," Mel agreed. "This spot is block-aded enough by the buildings that the sculptures are mostly protected from the harsh wind or snow, even during nasty storms like the one last night," she explained.

True enough, all four of them looked none the worse for wear. He couldn't detect so much as a crack in some of the most delicate features, such as the horse's thick tail.

After admiring the statue for several moments, they moved on to the next piece. A mermaid lounging on a rock. The detail and attention on the piece was astounding. It looked like it could come to life at any moment.

"One person did all these?"

Mel nodded. "With some minor help from assistants. She does it every year. Arranges for large blocks of ice to be shipped in, then spends hours upon hours chiseling and shaping. From dusk till dawn. Regardless of how cold it gets."

He smiled at her. "You New Englanders are a hearty lot."

"She does it just for the enjoyment of the town."

"Remarkable," he said. Mel took him by the arm and led him a few feet to the next one.

"Take a look at this piece. This one's a repeat she does every time," she told him. "It's usually my favorite." She ducked her head slightly.

It was a couple dancing. That artist's talent was truly notable, she had managed to capture the elegance of a ballroom dance, even depicting an expression of sheer longing on the faces of the two entwined statues. With remarkable detail, the man's fingers were splayed on the small of the woman's back. She was arched on his other arm, head back atop a delicately sculpted throat. Icy tendrils of hair appeared to be blowing in the wind.

"She's really outdone herself with this one this year," Mel said, somewhat breathless as she studied the frozen couple.

Ray was beyond impressed himself. And he knew what Mel had to be thinking.

They'd danced that way together more than once now. He couldn't help but feel touched at the thought of it.

Mel echoed his thoughts. "It sort of reminds me of the holiday ball. I think you may have dipped me just like that once or twice."

Mel hadn't exaggerated when speaking of the artistic talent of her small town. These pieces were exquisitely done, even to his layman's eye. He'd never seen such artwork outside of a museum. Yet another memory he would never have gained had he never met the woman by his side.

He turned to her then. "I don't know how to thank you, Mel. This has truly been the most remarkable holiday season I've spent."

She blinked up at him, thrill and pleasure sparkling behind her bright green eyes, their hue somehow even more striking against the background of so much white. "Really? Do you mean that?"

"More so than you will ever know."

"Not even as a child?"

"Particularly not as a child."

She gripped his forearm with genuine concern. "I'm really sorry to hear that, Ray."

He took a deep breath. How would he explain it to her? That Christmas for him usually consisted of endless events and duties that left no time for any kind of appreciation for the holiday. By the time it was over, he was ready to send the yuletide off for good.

In just the span of a few short days, she'd managed to show him the excitement and appeal that most normal people felt during the season.

He was trying to find a way to tell her all of that when she surprised him by speaking again. She took a deep breath first, as if trying to work up the courage.

"If you end up buying the Newford Inn," she began, "do you think you'll come back at all? You know, to check on your investment?"

The tone of her question sounded so full of hope. A hope he would have no choice but to shatter. He'd allowed this to happen. Mel was conjuring up scenarios in her head where the two of them would be able to meet up somehow going forward. Scenarios that couldn't have any basis in reality. And it was all his fault.

What had he done?

Ray might not have spoken the words, but his stunned silence at her question was all the answer Mel needed.

He had no intention of coming back here, regardless of whether he purchased the property or not. Not to check on an investment. And certainly not to see her. His expression made it very clear. Another thing made very clear was that he was uncomfortable and uneasy that she'd even brought up the possibility.

She'd done it again.

How much battering could a girl's pride take in one lifetime? If there was any way to suck back the words she'd just uttered, she would have gladly done so.

Foolish, foolish, foolish.

So it was all nothing but playacting on his part. She no longer had any doubt of that. Both at the ball and last night at the party. He'd never told her otherwise. She'd gone and made silly, girlish speculations that had no basis in reality.

"Mel," Ray uttered, taking a small step closer to her.

She held a hand up to stop him and backed away. "Please. Don't."

"Mel, if I could just try to ex—"

Cutting him off again, she said, "Just stop, Ray. It's really not necessary. You don't have to explain anything. Or even say anything. It was just a simple question. I'm sorry if it sounded loaded in any way with an ulterior motive. Or as if I was expecting anything of you with your answer."

Something hardened behind his eyes, and then a flash of anger. But she had to be imagining it. Because anger on his part would make no sense. He was the one rejecting her, after all.

"I didn't mean to imply," he simply stated.

"And neither did I."

She lifted her coffee cup and took a shaky swig, only to realize that the beverage had gone cold. The way her heart just had. Turning it over, she dumped the remaining contents onto the white snow at her feet. It made a nasty-looking puddle on the otherwise unblemished surface. Matched her mood perfectly.

"I appear to be out of coffee. I'd like to head back and get some more, please."

He bowed his head. "Certainly."

Suddenly they were being so formal with each other. As if they hadn't woken up in each other's embrace earlier this morning.

"And we should probably make our way back into Boston soon after. With our luck, another storm might hit." She tried to end the sentence with a chuckle, but the sound that erupted from her throat sounded anything but amused.

For his part, Ray looked uncomfortable and stiff. She had only herself to blame. The forty-minute ride back into the city was sure to be mired in awkward silence. So different from the easy camaraderie they'd enjoyed on the ride up. How drastically a few simple words could change reality overall. Words she had no business uttering.

The walk back to the hotel took much less time than the one to get to the statues, most of it spent in silence. In her haste, she almost slipped on a hidden patch of ice in the snow and Ray deftly reached out to catch her before she could fall. Tears stung her eyes in response to his touch, which she could feel even through her thick woolen coat. It was hard not to think of the way he'd spent the night touching her, holding her.

"Thanks," she uttered simply.

"You're welcome."

That was the bulk of their conversation until they reached the front doors of the bed-and-breakfast. Ray didn't go in; instead, he pulled the car keys out of his pocket. "I'll just go start the car and get it warmed up. Please, go get your coffee."

"You've seen all you need to see of the hotel, then?"

He nodded slowly. "I believe I have. Please thank Myrna for me if you see her. For all her hospitality and graciousness."

"I'll do that. It might take me a few minutes."

"Take your time. Just come down when you're ready."

Mel didn't bother to reply, just turned on her heel to open the door and step into the lobby. So it was that obvious that she needed some time to compose herself.

Clearly, she wasn't as talented at acting as Ray appeared to be.

CHAPTER ELEVEN

RAY REALLY NEEDED a few moments alone to compose himself.

He knew she was angry and hurt. And he knew he should let it go. But something within his soul just couldn't let the issue drop. He hadn't misread her intention when she'd asked about him returning to the United States sometime in the future. He couldn't have been that mistaken.

Regardless, one way or another, they had to clear the air.

Ray gripped the steering wheel tight as Mel entered the passenger seat and shut her door. Then he backed out of the parking spot and pulled onto the main road. It was going to be a very long ride if the silent awkwardness between them continued throughout the whole drive back.

She didn't so much as look in his direction.

They'd traveled several miles when he finally decided he'd had enough. Enough of the silence, enough of the tension, enough of all the unspoken thoughts between them.

He pulled off the expressway at the next exit.

"Where are we going?"

"I'd like a minute, if you don't mind."

She turned to him, eyes wide with concern. "Is everything all right? I can take over the driving if you'd like to rest your legs. I know you're not used to driving in such weather." Even in her ire, she was worried about his state. That fact only made him feel worse.

"It's not my legs," he said, then turned into an empty strip mall. The lone shop open was a vintage-looking coffee stop. "Did you mean what you said back in Newford? That you really don't expect anything of me?"

Mel stared at him for several beats before running her fingers along her forehead.

"Yes, Ray. I did. You really don't need to concern yourself." She let out a soft chuckle. "It really was a very innocuous question I asked back by the ice statues."

He studied her face. "Was it?"

"Absolutely."

He could prove her wrong so easily, he thought. If he leaned over to her right now, took her chin in his hand and pulled her face to his. Then if he plunged into her mouth with his tongue, tasted her the way he'd so badly wanted to this morning, it would take no time at all before she responded, moaning into his mouth as he thrust his fingers into her hair and deepened the kiss.

But that would make him a complete bastard.

She deserved better than the likes of him. The last thing he wanted was for her to feel hurt. Worse, to be the cause of her pain.

Instead, he sighed and turned back to look out the front windshield. "Well, good," he said. "That's good."

A small hatchback that had seen better days pulled up two spots over. The occupants looked at him and Mel curiously as they exited their car. It occurred to Ray just how out of place the sleek, foreign SUV must look in such a setting. Especially with two people just sitting inside as it idled in a mostly empty parking lot.

"Fine," Mel bit out.

She certainly didn't sound as if she thought things were fine. He inhaled deeply. "I'd like to clear the air, Mel, if I could. Starting with the bed-and-breakfast."

"What about it?"

"I should have been clearer about Verdovia's potential investment in such a property. Please understand. A small-town bed-and-breakfast would not be a typical venture for us. In fact, it would be a whole different addition to the overall portfolio of holdings. I would have to do extensive research into the pros and cons. And then, if the purchase is even feasible or even worth the time and effort, I'd have to do some real convincing. I haven't even run the idea by my fa—" He caught himself just in time. "I haven't run it by any of the decision makers on such matters. Most notably, the king and queen."

"I understand. That sounds like a lot of work."

"Please also understand one more thing—I have certain responsibilities. And many people to answer to." An entire island nation, in fact. "A certain level of behavior is expected of me. With a country so small, even the slightest deviation from the norms can do serious damage to the nation's sovereignty and socioeconomic health."

He refrained from biting out a curse. Now he sounded like a lecturing professor. To her credit, Mel seemed to be listening intently, without any speculation.

He watched as she clenched her hands in her lap. "You can stop trying to explain, Ray. See, I do understand. In fact, I understand completely," she told him through gritted teeth. "You mean to say that I shouldn't get my hopes up. About the Newford Inn, I mean." Her double meaning was clear by the intense expression in her blazing green eyes and the hardened tone of her voice. "I also understand that Verdovia is much more accustomed to making bigger investments, and that nothing gets decided without the approval of the royal couple. Who have very high expectations of the man who obtains property and real estate on their behalf. Does that about sum it all up?"

Ray had to admire her thought process. It was as clear as day. She had just given him a perfect out, a perfect way to summarize exactly what he needed to say without any further awkwardness for either of them. He couldn't decide if he was relieved, annoyed or impressed. The woman was unlike anyone he'd ever met.

"I'm sorry." He simply apologized. And he truly was. She had no idea. The fate and well-being of an entire nation rested on his shoulders. To do what was best for Verdovia had been ingrained in him for as long as he could remember. He couldn't turn his back on that any more than he could turn his back on his very own flesh and blood. Verdovia needed a princess, someone who had been groomed and primed for such a position.

Even if he could change any of that, even if he turned to Mel and told her the complete truth about who he was at this very moment, then called his father and asked him to scrap the whole marriage idea, what good would any of it do?

Mel wasn't up to withstanding the type of scrutiny that any association with the Verdovian crown prince would bring into her life. Not many people could. If the international press even sniffed at a romantic involvement between Rayhan al Saibbi and an unknown Boston waitress, it would trigger a worldwide media frenzy. Mel's life would never be the same. He couldn't do that to her. Not after all that she'd been through.

He resisted the urge to slam his fist against the steering wheel and curse out loud in at least three different languages. The real frustration was that he couldn't explain any of that to her. All he had left were inadequate and empty apologies.

Mel finally spoke after several tense beats. "Thank you, but there's no need to say sorry. I'll get over it."

She turned to look out her side window. "And Myrna will be fine, too. The Newford Inn will find a way to continue and thrive. You said it yourself this morning. We New Englanders are a hearty lot."

Again, her double meaning was clear as the pure white snow piled up outside. With no small degree of reluctance, he pressed the button to start the ignition once more.

"I should get you home."

He had no idea what he would say to her or do once he got her there.

Mel plopped down on her bed and just stared at the swirl design on the ceiling. She felt as if she'd lived an entire year or two in the last twenty-four hours. Ray had just dropped her off and driven away. But not before he'd looked at her with some degree of expectation. She suspected he was waiting for her to invite him up so they could continue the conversation that had started when he'd pulled over to the side of the road.

She couldn't bring herself to do it. What more was there to discuss?

Not a thing. Once Ray left, she would simply return to her boring routine life and try to figure out what was next in store for her.

Easier said than done.

It occurred to her that she hadn't bothered to look at her cell phone all day. Not that she expected anything urgent that might need her immediate attention. Frannie and Greta weren't expecting her at the diner and no one else typically tried to contact her usually.

But this time, when she finally powered it on, the screen lit up with numerous text messages and voice mail notices. All of them from one person.

Eric.

Now what?

Against her better judgment, she read the latest text.

Call me, Mel. I'd really like to talk. I talked to Carl last night.

That figured. She should have seen this coming.

She had to admit to being somewhat surprised at his level of interest. He'd wasted no time after speaking with Carl to try to get more information out of her about the new man he thought she was seeing. What a blind fool she'd been where Eric was concerned. The man clearly had the maturity level of a grade-schooler.

No wonder she'd fallen for Ray after only having just met him.

But that was in itself just as foolish. More so. Because Ray wasn't the type of man a lady got over. Mel bit back a sob as she threw her arm over her face. Ray had certainly put her in her place during the car ride. He'd made it very clear that she should harbor no illusions about seeing him again.

She'd managed to hold it together and say all the right things, but inside she felt like a hole had opened up where her heart used to be.

She might have been able to convincingly act un-affected in front of Ray, but she certainly wasn't able to kid herself. She fallen head over heels for him, when he had no interest nor desire in seeing her again once his business wrapped up in the States.

She couldn't wallow in self-pity. She had to move on. Find something, anything that would take her mind off the magical days she'd spent with the most enigmatic and attractive man she was likely to ever meet.

She hadn't done anything creative or artistic in nearly two years. This might be an ideal time to ease herself back into using her natural talent for sculpting and creating something out of a shapeless slab of raw material. The idea of getting back into it sent a surge of nervous anticipation through the pit of her stomach.

She called up the keypad and dialed the number of the glass studio in Boston's Back Bay. A recorded voice prompted her to leave a message. She did so, requesting a date and time for use of the studio and materials. Then she made her way to the bathroom and hopped in the shower.

Studio time wasn't much in the way of adventurous, but at least it gave her some small thing to look forward to.

Her cell rang ten minutes later as she toweled off. Mel grabbed the phone, answering it without bothering to look at the screen. The studio had to be returning her call.

Mel realized her mistake as soon as she said hello. The caller wasn't the studio at all. It was her ex-husband.

"Mel? I've been calling you all day."

"What can I do for you, Eric?"

She had an urge to simply disconnect and hang up on him. She really was in no mood for this at the moment. But he'd simply keep calling and hassling her. Better to just have it out and get this over with.

"Carl called me last night. He mentioned you were visiting Newford. And that you weren't alone."

Well, he'd certainly gone and cut to the chase. Mel released a weary sigh. "That's right. I don't see how it's any of your business. Or Carl's, for that matter."

"I told you, Mel. I still care about you. We were man and wife once. That has to mean something."

"As much as it did the day you took off with your dental assistant, Eric?"

He let out an audible, weary sigh. "That's kind of why I'm calling. I've been giving this a lot of thought. I messed up, Mel. I shouldn't have walked away from our marriage."

What?

She nearly lost her grip on the phone. She had no idea where all this was coming from. But she had to nip it in the bud without delay. The whole idea of faking a pretend boyfriend in front of her ex-husband had backfired bigtime. She'd simply meant to prove she'd moved on, and that she could attend a yearly event, even though he'd left her. The disaster happening right now hadn't even occurred to her as a remote possibility. Her ex-husband had made it more than clear two years ago that he had moved on and would be spending his life with another woman.

Or so Mel had thought.

She gripped the phone tight and spoke clearly. "Eric, you don't know what you're saying. I'm guessing you and Talley had a fight. And now you're simply overreacting."

He chuckled softly. "You're right about one thing."

"What's that?"

"We had a fight, all right. She became upset because I couldn't stop talking about you. And why you were with that businessman."

Mel had been ready to tell him the complete truth about Ray—she really had. If only just to end this nightmare of a phone call and return Eric's wayward thoughts back to where they belonged, to his wife-to-be.

But the way he said it, with such an insulting and derisive tone, made her change her mind. She didn't owe this man anything, not an explanation, not any comfort. Nothing. Eric wasn't even worth her anger. He simply wasn't worth her time. No, she didn't owe him anything. But the truth was, he did owe *her*.

"Please, Mel. Can we just get together and talk?"

Ray's words from last night echoed in her mind. "Actually, maybe there is something we can talk about."

"Anything."

Mel figured he wouldn't be so enthusiastic once she brought up the subject matter. But Ray was right. She needed to stand up for herself and ask for what was rightfully hers. "I think we need to discuss some ways for you to pay me back, Eric. At least partially."

A notable silence ensued over the speaker. She'd shocked him.

She continued before he could say anything, "Other than that, you really need to stop concerning yourself with me and go resolve things with your fiancée. Now, if you'll excuse me, I'm waiting for an important phone call."

She didn't give him a chance to respond before continuing. "I wish you well, Eric," she said and meant it.

Then she disconnected the call.

CHAPTER TWELVE

MEL HUNG UP her apron and reached for her handbag atop the freestanding cabinet in the back kitchen. It had seemed a particularly long shift. Probably because she hadn't been able to focus on a thing to do with her job. Her mind kept replaying scenes from the past week over and over. Scenes which starred a handsome, dark-haired businessman who sported a shadow of a goatee on his chin and a smile that could charm a demon.

Hard to believe three days had gone by since Newford and the nor'easter that had stranded them overnight. It didn't help matters that she relived the entire experience every night in her dreams, as well as several times during the day in her imagination.

Suddenly Greta's scratchy voice sounded from the dining area. "Well, lookie who's here."

Mel's mouth went dry and her blood pounded in her veins. She wasn't sure how, but she knew who her friend was referring to. *Ray.* He was here.

The suspicion was confirmed a moment later when Greta yelled yet again. "Mel, you should come out here. Someone to see you."

Mel threw her head back and closed her eyes. Taking a steadying breath, she grasped for some composure. She could do this. Even if the chances were high that he was simply here to tell her goodbye. For good.

Masking her emotions as best she could, she pushed open the swinging door and went out of the kitchen. Her breath stopped in her throat when she saw him. Again, he hadn't bothered with a coat. A crisp white shirt brought out the tanned color of his skin and emphasized his jet-black hair. His well-tailored dark gray pants fitted him like a glove.

She smoothed down the hem of her unflattering waitress uniform and went to approach him, her bag still clutched in her hands and a forced smile plastered on her face.

"Ray, I didn't expect to see you."

He jammed his hands in his pockets before speaking. "I took a chance you may be at work. I was going to try your apartment if you weren't here."

"I see. Did you want to sit down?" As luck would have it, the only clean booth was the one they'd sat at together for breakfast that morning not so long ago—though now it seemed like another lifetime.

She'd been well on her way then, but hadn't yet quite fallen in love with him. Because that was exactly what had happened. She could no longer deny it. She'd fallen helplessly, hopelessly in love with Ray Alsab.

"I came to tell you that I've come to a decision. And it looks like we'll be moving forward."

She had to rack her brain to figure out exactly what he was talking about. Then it occurred to her. The bed-and-breakfast.

"You'll move forward with buying the Newford Inn, then?"

He nodded with a smile. "I wanted to tell you myself. We haven't even contacted Myrna yet."

Her heart fluttered in her chest, though whether it was the result of hearing the good news or seeing Ray's dashing smile again, she couldn't be sure.

"I've been speaking to all the appropriate people for the past three days," he added. "We've all decided to move ahead. The attorneys are drawing up the paperwork as we speak."

She was happy to hear it, she really was. Particularly for Myrna, who would have so much of the burden of owning the inn taken off her shoulders. But she couldn't just ignore the fact that all she wanted to do right now was to fling herself into his arms and ask him to take her lips with his own. Did he feel even a fraction the same?

It didn't appear so. Because here he was, and all he could talk about was the business deal he'd come to Boston for in the first place.

"It wouldn't have happened without you, Mel. I mean that. And this is just the start."

"The start?"

"That's the best part of it all. I told you the inn was much too small compared to Verdovia's hotel holdings. So we've decided to make it part of something bigger. We'll be investing in several more. A chain of resorts and inns throughout New England, all bearing the royal name. And you were the catalyst for it all."

She didn't know what to say. As much as she appreciated the credit he was giving her, all she could think about was how much she'd missed him these past few days, how she hadn't been able to get him out of her mind. There was no way she was going to tell him that, of course. But, dear heavens, she had to say something.

The words wouldn't form on her tongue, so she just sat there and continued to smile at him stupidly.

"Well, what do you think?" he finally prompted.

If he only knew.

"I think it's wonderful news, Ray. Really. I'm so glad it will work out. Sounds like your business trip will be a success. I'm happy for you."

His eyes suddenly grew serious. He reached across the table and took her hand in his. "There's something else I need to talk to you about."

Mel's pulse quickened and her vision suddenly grew narrow, her only focus at the moment being Ray's handsome face.

"I need to return home to get some things settled once and for all."

Mel felt the telltale stinging behind her eyes and willed the tears not to fall. She was right. This was simply a final goodbye. But his next words had her heart soaring with renewed hope.

"But then I'm going to call you, Mel. Once the dust is settled after I take care of a few things."

That was it, she couldn't hold back the tears, after all. He wasn't giving her the complete story, clearly, but neither was he shutting the door on the two of them. She would take it. With pleasure. She swiped at her eyes with the back of her arm, embarrassed at the loss of control.

He let out a soft chuckle and gripped her hand tighter. "Why are you crying, sweet Mel?"

She didn't get a chance to answer. Ray's phone lit up and vibrated in his front shirt pocket. With a sigh of resignation, he lifted it out. "I have to take this. I'm sorry, but it's about the inn and we're right in the middle of setting up the deal."

She nodded as he stood.

"I'll be right back."

Something nagged at the back of her mind as she watched Ray step outside to take the phone call. She'd got a brief look at the screen of his phone just now as his call had come through. The contact had clearly appeared on the screen as a call from someone he'd labeled as *Father*.

But he'd just told her the call was about the offer he was making to buy Myrna's bed-and-breakfast.

Why would his father be involved in a deal he was doing for the king?

Ray had never mentioned his father being in the same line of work. It didn't make any sense.

She gave her head a shake. Surely she was overthinking things. Still, the nagging voice continued in the back of her mind. The fact was, she'd had the same curious sense before. There seemed to be too many holes in the things Ray had told her about himself. Too many random pieces that didn't quite fit the overall puzzle.

She'd resisted looking at the questions too closely. Until now.

With trembling fingers, she reached into her handbag for the mini electronic tablet she always carried with her to work and logged on to the diner Wi-Fi. Ray was still outside, speaking on the phone.

Mel clicked on the icon for the search engine.

Ray rushed back to the booth where Mel still sat waiting for him, anxious to get back to their conversation.

Something wasn't right. Mel's fists were both clenched tight on the table in front of her. Her lips were tight, and tension radiated off her whole body. One look at the screen on the tablet in front of her told him exactly why.

"Mel."

She didn't even bother to look up at him, keeping her eyes fixed firmly on what she was reading. Ray had never considered himself to be a violent man, save for that one youthful indiscretion on the ball field. But right now, he had a near-overwhelming desire to put his fist through a wall. The gossip rags never failed to amaze him with the unscrupulous ways they so often covered his life.

Mel had gone pale. She used her finger to flip to another page on the screen. Ray didn't need to read the specific words to know what she was seeing. The international tabloid Mel currently stared at was a well-known one. One that featured him just often enough. Ray didn't bother lowering his voice as he bit out a vicious curse.

"Mel. Hear me out."

She still refused to look at him, just continued to read and then clasped a shaky hand to her mouth. Her gasp of horror sliced through his heart.

"Oh, my God," she said in a shaky whisper. "You don't just work for the royal family. You *are* the royal family."

"Mel." He could only repeat her name.

"You're the prince!" This time she raised her voice. So loud that the people around them turned to stare.

"It's what I was trying to explain." Even as he spoke, Ray knew it was no use. Too much damage had just been done. She was going to need time to process.

"When?" She pushed the tablet toward him with such an angry shove, it nearly skidded off the table before he caught it. "When exactly were you going to explain any of this?"

One particular bold headline declared that the Verdovian prince had finally chosen a bride and would be married within months. Somehow they'd snapped a picture of him with a young lady Ray didn't even recognize.

Damn.

"What's there to explain anyway?" she bit out through gritted teeth. "You lied to me. For days."

She was right. He'd been fooling himself, telling himself that not telling Mel the complete truth was somehow different from lying to her.

That itself was a lie.

He had no one to blame but himself. He rammed his hand through his hair and let out a grunt of frustration.

"Is it true?" she demanded to know. "That you're due to be engaged soon?"

He refused to lie yet again. "Yes."

"I need to get out of here," Mel cried out and stood. Turning on her heel with a sob that tore at his soul, she fled away from the table and toward the door.

Ray didn't try to chase after her. He didn't have the right.

And what would he tell her if he did catch up to her? That what she'd seen was inaccurate? The fact was he *was* the crown prince of Verdovia. And he had deceived her about it.

Greta and Frannie stood staring at him from across the room with their mouths agape. For that matter, the whole diner was staring.

"You'll make sure she's not alone tonight?" he asked neither sister in particular. They were both giving him comparably icy glares.

"You bet your royal patootie."

"Don't you worry about it," Frannie added. At least he thought it was Frannie. Not that it really mattered. All that mattered was that Mel was looked after tonight. Because of what he'd done to her.

As he left, Ray heard one of the diner patrons behind him.

"Told you this place was good," the man told his dining companion. "We got dinner and a show."

Ray was the prince. The actual heir to the crown. An heir who was due to marry a suitable, noble young woman to help him rule as king when the time came for him to take over the throne. Mel felt yet another shiver of shock and sorrow wash over her. Greta rubbed her shoulder from her position next to her on the couch. Frannie was fixing her a cup of tea in the kitchen. She didn't know what she'd do without these women.

"How could I have been so clueless, Greta?" she asked for what had to be the hundredth time. "How did I not even guess who he might have been?"

"How would you have guessed that, dearie? It's not every day a prince runs you over in the middle of a busy city street, then insists on buying you a dress to make up for it."

Mel almost laughed at her friend's summary. In truth, that accident had simply been the catalyst that had set all sorts of events in motion. Events she wasn't sure she would ever be able to recover from.

Her doorbell rang just as Frannie set a tray of cookies and steaming tea on the coffee table in front of them.

All three of them looked up in surprise. "Who could that be?"

Greta went over to look through the peephole. She turned back to them, eyes wide. "It's that fella that was with your prince. The one who was at the hospital that day."

Her prince. Only, he wasn't. And he never would be.

Mel's heart pounded at the announcement. "What could he possibly want?"

"Only one way to find out," Greta declared and then pulled open the door without so much as checking with Mel.

The gentleman stepped in and nodded to each of them in turn. He pulled an envelope out of his breast pocket. "Sal?"

He gave her a slight bow. "My full name is Saleh. Saleh Tamsen."

Okay. "Well, what can I do for you, Mr. Saleh Tamsen?"

"It's more what I'm here to do for you," he informed her. What in the world was he talking about?

"The kingdom of Verdovia is indebted to you for your recent service in pursuing a business contract. This belongs to you," he declared and then stretched his hand out in her direction.

Mel forced her mouth to close, then stood up from the couch and stepped over to him. He handed her the envelope. "What is it?"

"Please open it. I'm here to make sure you're satisfied and don't require a negotiation."

Negotiation? Curiosity piqued, Mel opened the envelope and then had to brace herself against Greta once she saw what it contained.

"Yowza!" Greta exclaimed beside her.

She held a check in her hand for an exorbitant sum. More money than she'd make waitressing for the next decade.

"I don't understand."

"A finder's fee. For bringing the prince to the Newford Inn, which he is in the process of acquiring on behalf of the king and the nation of Verdovia."

"A finder's fee? I hardly found it. I grew up near it." None of this made any kind of sense. Was this some type of inspired attempt on Ray's part to somehow make things up to her? That thought only served to spike her anger. If he was trying to buy her off, it was only adding salt to her wounds.

"Nevertheless, the check is yours."

Mel didn't need to hesitate. She stuck the check back in the envelope and handed it back to Saleh. "No, thank you."

He blinked and took a small step back. "No? I assure

you it's standard. We employ people who do the very thing you accomplished. I can also assure you it's no more or less than they receive. Take it. You've earned the fee."

She shook her head and held the envelope out until he reluctantly took it. "Nevertheless, I can't accept this. Thank you, but no."

Saleh eyed her up and down, a quizzical gleam in his eye. "Fascinating. You won't accept the money, even though you've earned it."

"No, I won't. And please tell His Royal Highness I said it's not necessary."

Saleh rubbed his chin. "You know what? Why don't you just tell him yourself? He's waiting downstairs for me to return."

CHAPTER THIRTEEN

To HIS CREDIT, Ray looked pretty miserable when he walked through her door. Though she doubted his misery could even compare to the way she was feeling inside—as if her heart had been pulled out of her chest, torn to shreds and then placed back inside.

Greta and Frannie had gone into the other room in order to give them some privacy. No doubt they had their ears tight against the wall, though, trying to hear every word.

Ray cleared his throat, standing statue still. "Mel. I didn't think you'd want to see me."

She didn't. And she did.

She gave him a small shrug. "It just didn't feel right. You know, leaving a prince waiting alone in a car. The last time I did that, at the inn, I didn't actually realize you were a prince. So you'll have to forgive me," she added in a voice dripping with sarcasm.

"You have every right to be upset."

If that wasn't the understatement of the century. "How could you, Ray?" She hated how shaky her voice sounded. "How could you have not even mentioned any of it? After all this time?"

He rubbed his forehead in a gesture so weary that it nearly had her reaching for him. She wouldn't, of course. Not now. Not ever again.

"It wasn't so straightforward. You have to understand. Things seldom are for someone in my position."

"Not even your name? You're Rayhan al Saibbi. Not Ray Alsab."

"But I am. It's an anglicized version of my name. I use it on business matters in North America quite often." He took a hesitant step toward her. "Mel, I never purposely lied to you."

"Those are merely semantics and you know it, Ray." She wanted to sob as she said the last word. She wasn't even sure what to call him now, despite what he was telling her about anglicized business aliases.

"It would have served no purpose to tell you, love. My confiding it all would have changed nothing. I'm still heir to the Verdovian throne. I still have the same duties that came with my name. None of my responsibilities would have changed. Nor would the expectations on me."

Mel had to gulp in a breath. Every word he uttered simply served to hammer another nail into her wound. She felt the telltale quiver in her chin, but forced the words. "The purpose it would have served is that I would have preferred to know all that before I went and fell in love with you!" Mel clasped a hand to her mouth as soon as she spoke the words. How could she have not contained herself? How could she have just blurted it out that way? Well, there was no taking it back now. And what did it matter anyway? What did any of it matter at this point?

Ray took a deep breath, looked down at his feet. When he tilted his head back up to gaze at her, a melancholy solace had settled in the depths of his eyes. "Then allow me to tell you the honest truth right now. All of it."

Mel wanted to run out of the room. She wasn't sure if she could handle anything he was about to tell her. Nothing would ever be the same again for her. No matter what he said right now. Her broken heart would never heal.

Ray continued, "The truth is that I completely enjoyed every moment you and I spent together. In fact, it might very well be the first time I actually spent a Christmas season having any fun whatsoever. In a different universe, a different reality, things would be very different between you and me. You are a bright light who also lights up everyone you're near. You certainly lit a light inside me. You should never forget that, Mel." He stepped over to her and rubbed the tip of his finger down her cheek in a gentle caress. "I assure you that I never will."

She couldn't hold on to her composure much longer. Mel knew she would break down right there in front of him if he said so much as one more word.

"I think you should leave now," she whispered harshly, resisting the urge to turn her cheek into his hand.

He gave her a slight tilt of his head. "As you desire."

She held back her tears right up until the door closed behind him. Then she sank to the floor and simply let them fall.

"Well, that went about as well as could be expected."

Ray slid into the passenger side of the car and waited as Saleh pulled away and into traffic.

"Your lady is definitely not a pushover, as the Americans say."

Ray didn't bother to correct his friend. Mel certainly couldn't be referred to as his lady in any way. But he so badly wished for the description to be accurate.

"Did you even convince her to take the fee?" Saleh asked.

"No. I know there's no use. If she refused it from you, she will most definitely refuse it from me."

Saleh clicked his tongue. "Such a shame. The young lady is being stubborn at her own expense and detriment."

Ray nodded absentmindedly. He couldn't fully focus on Saleh's words right now. Not when he couldn't get Mel's face out of his mind's eye. The way she'd looked when she'd told him she'd fallen in love with him. What he wouldn't give to have the luxury of saying those words back to her.

But his friend kept right on talking. "Sometimes one should simply accept what he or she is owed. Or at least be adamant about asking for what they're owed, I would think. Don't you agree?"

Ray shifted to look at the other man's profile. "Is there a point you're trying to make?"

Saleh shrugged. "I simply mean to remind you that you are a prince, Rayhan. And that your father is the current ruling king."

"I think you should have taken the money!" Greta declared and popped one of the now-cold cookies into her mouth. The whole cookie. She started chewing around it and could hardly keep her mouth closed.

Frannie turned to her sister. "Why don't you go make us tea, Greta? It's your turn."

Greta gave a grunt of protest but stood and walked to the kitchen.

"You doin' all right, kid?" Frannie asked, taking Greta's place on the couch.

Mel leaned her head against the back of the couch and released a long sigh. "I don't know, honestly. It feels like there's a constant stabbing pain around the area of my heart and that it will never feel better." She sniffled like a child who'd just fallen and skinned her knee.

"It will. Just gonna take some time, that's all." Frannie patted Mel's arm affectionately. "Tell me something?"

"Sure."

"What's makin' you hurt more? That he didn't tell you who he was? Or that you can't have him?"

Mel blinked at the question. A friend like Frannie deserved complete honesty. Even if the question was just now forcing her to be honest with herself.

"I think you know the answer to that," she replied in a low, wobbly voice. Now that she was actually giving it some thought, she realized a crucial point: it was one thing when there had still been a chance for her and Ray, regardless of how miniscule. When she thought he was a businessman who might change his mind and return to the States because he couldn't bear to live without her. But he was a prince. Who had to marry someone worthy of one. Someone who was the polar opposite of a divorced, broke waitress who now lived in South Boston. It was almost exactly how her parents' relationship had started out. Only without the happy ending and loving marriage they'd shared.

"You didn't tell him that," Frannie declared. "You didn't even ask him how he felt. Don't you think you deserved to know? From his own mouth and in his own words, I mean?"

Mel closed her eyes. This conversation was making her think too hard about things she just wanted to forget. In fact, thinking at all simply made the hurt worse. "Well, as he pointed out himself, Frannie, none of it would have made any sort of difference." She knew her voice had taken on a snarky tone, but she couldn't summon the will to care. Hopefully the older woman would just drop the subject.

No such luck. Frannie let out a loud sigh. "Not so sure about that. Now, I may be old but I can count to two."

Mel gave her friend a confused look. "Is that some sort of South Boston anecdote?"

"All I'm saying is there appears to be at least two instances in your adult life where you didn't come out and ask for what was rightfully yours. Damn the consequences."

Mel couldn't be hearing this right. "You can't be including my ex-husband."

"Oh, but I am."

"Are you suggesting that I shouldn't have walked away from Eric? That I should have fought for him, despite his betrayal?" The question was a ridiculous one. She'd sooner have walked through the tundra in bare feet than give that man a second chance. Especially now, after these past few days with Ray.

Frannie waved her hand dismissively. "Oh, great heavens, no. Getting away from that scoundrel was the best thing that could have happened to you."

"Then what?"

Frannie studied her face. "He took your money, dear. Just took it and walked away with another woman."

"I gave him that money, Frannie. It was my foolish mistake."

"Your biggest mistake was trusting that he would honor his vows and his commitment. He didn't."

Of course, the older woman had a valid point. But this train of conversation was doing nothing for her. She loved both Frannie and Greta, and she was beyond grateful for all the support and affection they'd consistently shown her. But Frannie had no idea what it was like to come home one day and find that your husband wouldn't be returning. That he'd found someone else, another woman he preferred over you. Frannie was a widow, whose husband had adored her right up until he'd taken his last breath. They'd had an idyllic marriage, much like her own parents'. The type of union that was sure to elude Mel, given her track record with men so far.

"Well, it just so happens I did ask Eric for the money back. At least some of it." Though she wasn't going to admit to her friend that it had been a half-hearted effort that was meant more to just get Eric off the phone the other night. And to make sure he didn't start harboring any illusions about the two of them reuniting in any way.

But Frannie had her figured out pretty well. Her next words confirmed it. "But you're not really going to fight for it, are you?"

Mel didn't bother to answer. She couldn't even think about Eric or what he owed her right now. Her thoughts were fully centered on Ray and the hurt of his betrayal.

"It's a cliché, but it's true," Frannie went on. "Some things are worth fighting for."

Mel clenched her hands. "And some fights are hardly worth it. They leave you bloodied and bruised with nothing to show for it."

"You might be right," Frannie admitted. "Matters of love can be impossible to predict, regardless of the circumstances. I'm just saying you should at least fight for what belongs to you." She nodded toward the door, as if Ray had just this instant walked out, rather than over two hours ago.

"And that man's heart belongs to you."

CHAPTER FOURTEEN

RAY COULDN'T REMEMBER the last time he'd tried to sleep in. He wasn't terribly good at it. But he felt zero incentive to get out of bed this morning. For the past few days, he'd awoken each morning with the prospect of seeing or at least speaking with Mel.

That wasn't the case today. And wouldn't be the case from now on. Hard to believe just how much he would miss something he'd only experienced for a short while.

His cell phone rang and his father's number flashed on the screen. He had half a mind to ignore it but couldn't quite bring himself to do so. In all fairness, he was way past the point where he owed the king a status report.

He picked up the phone. "Hello, Father."

"Good morning, son."

"Morning."

"Is there anything you'd like to tell me?"

So it was clear his father had heard something. Ray rolled onto his back with the phone at his ear. "Which tabloid should I be looking at?"

"Take your pick," his father answered. "There's some American man who claims to have been at something known as a 'jamboree,' where you were in attendance. Apparently, he took plenty of photos and is now selling them to whoever will pay."

Ray pinched the bridge of his nose. "I apologize, Your Majesty. I was conducting myself with the utmost discretion. But I failed to anticipate an unexpected variable."

"I see. I hope you've resolved the matter with the young lady in question."

"I'm working on it, sir."

His father paused for several beats before continuing, "You do realize the depth of your responsibilities to Verdovia, don't you, Rayhan? Don't lose sight of who you are. Loose ends will not be tolerated, son."

Ray felt a bolt of anger settle in his core. The way his father referred to Mel as a loose end had him clenching the phone tight in his hand.

He hadn't wanted to do this over the phone, but he'd come to a few decisions over the past few days. Decisions he wasn't ready to back away from.

"With all the respect you're due, Your Majesty, I feel compelled to argue that the lady in question is far from a loose end."

The king's sharp intake of breath was audible across the line. Ray could clearly picture him frowning into the phone with disappointment. So be it.

"I'm not sure what that means, son. Nor, frankly, do I care. I simply ask that you remain mindful of who you are and of your duties."

Ray took a deep, steadying breath. He'd been hoping to wrap things up here and have this conversation with his father in person. But fate appeared to be forcing his hand.

"Since we're discussing this now, Father, I wondered if we might have something of a conversation regarding duty and responsibility to the sovereign."

Silence once again. Ray couldn't remember a time

he had tested the king's patience in such a manner. Nor his authority.

"What kind of conversation? What exactly is it you would like to communicate with me about responsibility and your honor-bound duties as prince?"

His father was throwing his words out as a challenge. Normally Ray would have been the dutiful, obedient son and simply acquiesced. But not this time. This time he felt the stakes too deeply.

"Thank you for asking, sir," Ray replied in his sincerest voice. "I'm glad to have an opportunity to explain."

His father sighed loudly once again. "If you must."

"I've been going over some numbers, sir."

"Numbers? What kind of numbers exactly?"

"I've been looking at our nation's holdings and overall wealth and how it impacts our citizens. Particularly since the time you yourself took over the throne. Followed by the growth experienced once I graduated university and began working for the royal house as a capitalist."

"And?" his father prompted. He sounded much less annoyed, less irritated. The discussion about figures and wealth had certainly gained his attention, just as Ray had known it would.

"And a simple analysis easily shows that the country has prospered very nicely since you started your reign, sir. And it continued that growth once I started acquiring investments on behalf of Verdovia. As a result, we've seen increased exports, higher wages overall for our citizens and extensions of most social benefits."

His father grunted, a sure sign that he was impressed. "Go on. Is there a point to all of this, son?"

"A simple point, sir. Maybe our duty shouldn't need to go any further than such considerations—to further the quality of life for our citizens and nationals. And that maybe we even owe a duty to ourselves as well, to ensure our own fulfillment and happiness. Despite being members of the royal house of al Saibbi."

Ray wouldn't blame her if she didn't open the door. He'd texted her last night to say he wanted to stop by this morning. She hadn't replied. Well, he was here anyway. On the off chance that she would give him one more opportunity and agree to see him.

The possibility of that seemed to lower with each passing second as he braced himself against the blowing wind, while standing on the concrete stoop outside her door.

He was just about to give up and turn around when he heard shuffling footsteps from the other side of the wood. Slowly, the lock unlatched and Mel opened the door.

She stepped aside to let him in.

"Thank you for seeing me, Mel. I know it's short notice."

She motioned toward the sofa in the center of the room. "I just brewed a pot of coffee. Can I get you some?"

"No. Thank you. I won't take up much of your time."

She walked over to the love seat across the sofa and sat as well, pulling her feet underneath her. Ray took a moment to study her. She looked weary, subdued. He saw no hint of the exuberant, playful woman he'd got a chance to know over the past week. He had no one but himself to blame for that.

"So you said you wanted to talk about a business matter? Do you have questions about the Newford Inn? If so, you could have called Myrna directly."

He shook his head. "This business matter involves you directly."

Her eyes scanned his face. "I hope you're not back to

offer me another check. I told your associate I'm not interested in taking your money. Not when I didn't really do anything to earn it."

Ray leaned forward, braced his arms on his knees. "Well, we'll have to agree to disagree about whether you earned that money or not. But that's not why I'm here."

"Then why?"

"To put it simply—I'd like to offer you a position."

Mel's eyes narrowed on him, her gaze moving over his face. "Come again? Aren't you a royal prince, who'll eventually become king? What kind of position would someone like that offer a waitress?"

It was a valid question. "I am. The royal house is the largest employer in Verdovia. And a good chunk of the surrounding nations, in fact."

"Okay. What's that got to do with me? I'm a waitress in a diner."

At that comment, he wanted to take her by the shoulders and give her a mild shake. She was so much more than that.

"I mentioned to you earlier, that day at the diner, that we were looking to purchase several New England inns and B and Bs. I'd like to charge you with that. Your official title would be project manager."

Mel inhaled deeply and looked off to the side. "You're offering me a job? Is that it?"

He nodded. "Yes, I think you'd be perfect for it. You know the way these establishments operate and you know New England. The first part will be to get the Newford Inn purchased and renovated. That will give you a chance to slowly get your feet wet. What better way to ease into the job?"

When she returned her gaze to his face, a hardened

glint appeared in her eyes. "It sounds ideal on the surface."

"But?"

"But I'm not sure what to tell you, Ray. What if you'd never accidentally met me that day? Would I be the person you would think of to fill such a position?"

Ray gave her a small shrug. "It's a moot point, isn't it? The fact that we met is the only reason these deals are happening."

"I guess there's a certain logic in that," she agreed.

He pressed his case further. "Why worry about what-ifs? I need someone to assist with these acquisitions, and I think you'd do well."

She chewed the inside of her lip, clearly turning the matter over in her mind.

"Please, just think about it, Mel."

"Sure," she said and stood. "I'll think about it."

Something in her tone and facial expression told him she was simply humoring him. But he'd done what he could.

She walked him to the door.

He turned to her before she could open it. "Mel, please understand. Cultural changes don't happen quickly. Especially in a country so small and so set in its ways."

"You don't have to explain, Ray. I understand the reality of it all. You're here to offer me the only thing you feel you can. A job in your employ."

Damn it, when she put it that way...

"Thank you for stopping by. I promise to give your proposal a lot of consideration." She cracked an ironic smile that didn't quite reach her eyes. "After all, it's not like I'm all that great a waitress."

Mel watched through the small slit in her curtains as Ray walked down her front steps to the vehicle waiting for him outside. He hesitated before pulling the car door open and turned to stare at her building. It would be so easy to lift the window and yell at him to wait. She wanted to run out to him before he could drive away, to accept his offer, to tell him she'd take anything he was willing to give her.

But the self-preserving part of her prevailed and she forced herself to stay still where she was. Eventually, Ray got in and his car pulled away and drove off. She didn't even have any tears left; she was all cried out. In hindsight, she had to admit to herself that none of this was Ray's doing. She was responsible for every last bit of it.

Melinda Osmon alone was responsible for not guarding her heart, for somehow managing to fall for a man so far out of her league, she wasn't even in the same stratosphere. To think, she'd believed him to be out of reach when she knew him as a businessman. Turned out he was a real live prince.

He'd had a point when he'd told her that he'd never lied to her outright. He'd never led her on, never behaved inappropriately in any way.

And he'd just shown up at her apartment with the offer of a job opportunity because he knew she was disappointed and defeated.

Mel leaned back against the window, then sank to her knees.

No. She had no one to blame but herself for all of it.

So now there was only one question that needed to be answered. What was she going to do about it? A part of her wanted so badly to take what she could get. To do anything she could to at least inhabit a spot in his orbit, however insignificant.

But that would destroy her. She wasn't wired that way. To have to watch him from a distance as he performed the duties of the throne, as he went about the business of being king one day.

As he committed himself to another woman.

And what of much later? Eventually, he would start a family with the lucky lady who ended up snaring him. Mel could never watch him become a father to someone else's children without shattering inside. Bad enough she would have to see it all from a distance.

Even the mere thought of it sent a stab of pain through her heart. She wouldn't survive having to watch it all from a front-row seat.

She knew Ray thought he'd found a workable solution. He'd offered her the only thing he could.

It just simply wasn't enough.

Ray sat staring at the same column of numbers he'd been staring at for the past twenty minutes before pushing the laptop away with frustration. He'd never had so much trouble focusing.

But right now, all he could think about was if he'd done the right thing by offering Mel a job. He might very well have crossed a line. But the alternative had been to do nothing, to walk out of her life completely. At least as an employee of Verdovia's royal house, he could be confident that she was being taken care of, that she had the backing of his family name and that of his nation. It was the best he could do until he figured out what to do about everything else.

One thing was certain. He wasn't going to go along with any kind of sham engagement. If there was anything he'd learned during these past few days in the States, it was that he was unquestionably not ready. If that meant upsetting the council, the king and even the constituency, then so be it.

The sharp ring of the hotel phone pulled him out of his reverie. The front desk was calling to inform him there was some sort of package for him that they would bring up if it was a convenient time. Within moments of him accepting, a knock sounded on the door.

The bellhop handed him a small cardboard box. Probably some type of promotional material from the various endeavors he was currently involved in. He was ready to toss it aside when the return address caught his eye.

Mel had sent him something.

With shaky fingers, he pulled the cardboard apart. He couldn't even begin to guess what the item might be. She still hadn't given him any kind of answer about the job.

The box contained a lush velvet satchel. He reached inside the bag and pulled out some type of glass figurine. A note was tied to it with a red satin ribbon, almost the identical color of the dress she'd worn the night of the mayor's charity ball. He carefully unwrapped the bow to remove the item.

And his breath caught in his throat.

A blown-glass sculpture of a couple dancing. It wasn't quite a replica of the one made of ice they'd seen in the town square after the storm. She'd put her own creative spin on it. This couple was wrapped in a tighter embrace, heads closer together.

Her talent blew him away. She'd somehow captured a singular moment in time when they were on the dance floor together, a treasured moment he remembered vividly.

He gently fingered the smooth surface with his thumb before straightening out her note to read it.

Ray,
Though I can't bring myself to accept your offer,
I hope that you'll accept this small gift from me.
I didn't realize while creating it that it was meant

for you, but there is no doubt in my mind now that you were the intended recipient all along.

I hope it serves as a cherished souvenir to help you to remember.

As I will never forget.

M

Ray gently set the figurine and the note on the desk and then walked over to the corner standing bar to pour himself a stiff drink. After swallowing it in one swig, he viciously launched the tumbler against the wall with all the anger and frustration pulsing through his whole being.

It did nothing to ease his fury.

CHAPTER FIFTEEN

RAY STILL HADN'T cleaned up the broken glass by the time room service showed up the next morning with his coffee tray. The server took a lingering look at the mess but wisely asked no questions.

"I'll get Housekeeping to clean that up for you, sir," the man informed him as Ray signed off on a tip.

"There's no rush. It can wait until their regular rounds."

"Yes, sir."

So he was surprised when there came another knock on the door in less than twenty minutes.

Ray walked to the door and yanked it open. "I said there was no hur—"

But it wasn't a hotel employee standing on the other side. Far from it.

"Mother? Father? What are you two doing here?"

His mother lifted an elegant eyebrow. "Aren't you going to invite us in, darling?"

Ray blinked the shock out of his eyes and stepped aside. "I apologize. Please, come in."

The queen gave him an affectionate peck on the cheek as she entered, while the king acknowledged him with a nod.

He spoke after entering the room. "Your mother grew

quite restless with the girls away on their performance tour of Europe and you here in the States. She wanted to surprise you. So, surprise."

That it certainly was.

"How are you, dear?" his mother wanted to know. "You look a little ragged. Have you been getting enough sleep?"

Ray couldn't help but smile. Shelba al Saibbi might be a queen, but first and foremost she was a mother.

"I'm fine, Mother."

She didn't look convinced. "Really?"

"Really. But I can't help but think there must be more to this visit than your boredom or a simple desire to spring a surprise on your son." He looked from one to the other, waiting for a response.

"Very well," his mother began. "Your father has something he needs to discuss with you. After giving the matter much thought."

The king motioned to the one of the leather chairs around the working desk. Ray waited until his father sat down before taking a seat himself. The queen stood behind her husband, placing both hands on his shoulders.

"What's this about, Your Majesty?"

"Saleh called me a couple of days ago," his father began. "He wanted to make sure I was aware of certain happenings since you've arrived in the US."

Ray felt a throb in his temple. Why, the little snitching...

His mother guessed where his thoughts were headed. "He did it for your own good, dear. He's very concerned about you, it seems."

"He needn't have been."

"Nevertheless, he called and we're here."

"Does this have anything to do with your impending engagement?" his father asked.

Ray bolted out of the chair, his patience stretched taut beyond its limits. Perhaps Saleh was right to be concerned about him. He'd never so much as raised his voice around his parents. "How can there be an engagement when I don't even really know the women I'm supposed to choose from? How can I simply tie myself to someone and simply hope that I grow fond of them later? What if it doesn't work out that way?" He took a deep breath before looking his father straight in the eye and continuing, "I can't do it. I'm sorry. I can't go forward with it. Even if means Councilman Riza continues to rabble-rouse, or that Verdovia no longer has the specter of a royal engagement to distract itself with."

"And what of your mother?" the king asked quietly, in a low, menacing voice.

Ray tried not to wince at the pang of guilt that shot through his chest. "Mother, I'm sorry. Maybe we can hire some more assistants to help you with your official duties. I can even take over some of the international visits myself. But I'm simply not ready to declare anyone a princess. I'm just now starting to figure out what type of relationship I might enjoy, the kind of woman I might want to spend my days with. It's not anyone back in Verdovia, I'm afraid."

His father stared at him in stunned silence. But to his utter shock, his mother's response was a wide, knowing grin.

"Well, goodness. You should have just told us that you've met someone."

Ray blinked at her. How could she possibly know that? Saleh might have called his parents out of concern, but Ray knew the other man would have never betrayed that much of a confidence.

"Is that so?" his father demanded to know. "Is all this

turmoil because of that woman you were photographed dancing with?"

Ray forced himself to contain his ire. Not only were these people his parents, they were also his king and queen. "That woman's name is Melinda Osmon. And she happens to be the most dynamic, the most intriguing young lady I've ever met."

"I see." His father ran a hand down his face. "Is that your final say, then?"

Ray nodded. "I'm afraid so."

"You do realize that this will throw the whole country into a tailspin. Entire industries have been initiated based on speculation of an upcoming royal engagement and eventual wedding. Also, Councilman Riza will pounce on this as a clear and damning example of the royal family disappointing the people of Verdovia. A royal family he believes serves no real purpose and which is part of a system he believes should be abolished."

Ray swallowed and nodded. "I accept the consequences fully."

His mother stepped around the table to face her husband. "Farood, dear. You must think this through. We cannot have our only son bear the full brunt of this simply because he has no desire to be engaged. And we certainly can't have him miserable upon his return home."

She turned back to her son. "Do not worry about me, I can handle my duties just fine. Frankly, I'm getting a bit tired of all the fuss over my health. I'm not a fragile little doll that needs anyone's constant concern," she bit out, followed by a glare in her husband's direction.

Ray couldn't hide his smile. "I believe I've come across stone blocks more fragile than you are, Mother."

The queen reached over and gave her son an affectionate pat. "I believe there's someone you need to go see, no?" She indicated her husband with a tilt of her head. "Do not worry about what this one will have to say about it."

For several moments, none of them spoke. A thick tension filled the air. Ray clenched his hands at his sides. The king had never been challenged quite so completely before. But he refused to back down.

It was what the Americans liked to call a "game of chicken." Finally, his father threw his hands up in exasperation. "I don't know what the two of you expect me to do about any of this."

The queen lifted her chin. "May I remind you, dear, that you are in fact the king?"

The statement echoed what Saleh had said to him all those nights ago.

His mother then added in a clipped tone, "I'm sure you'll think of something."

Mel tried not to turn her nose at the morning's breakfast special as she carried it out to the latest customer to order it. Lobster-and-cheese omelet. It appeared to be a big hit among the regulars, but for the life of her, she couldn't fathom why.

The holiday shoppers supplied a steady flow of patrons into the diner, despite the wintry cold. The forecasters were predicting one of the whitest Christmases on record. Though she'd be remembering this year's holiday herself for entirely different reasons. How would she ever cope with the Christmas season ever again when everything about it would forever remind her of her prince?

The door opened as several more customers entered, bringing with them a brisk gust of December wind and a good amount of snow on their covered boots and coats.

She nearly dropped the plates she was carrying as she

realized one of those customers happened to be a handsome, snow-covered royal.

Mel couldn't help her first reaction upon seeing him. Though she hadn't forgotten the hurt and anguish of those few days, she'd realized she missed him. Deeply. She set her load down quickly in front of the diners before making a complete mess. Then she blinked to make sure she wasn't simply seeing what her heart so desperately wanted to see. But it really was him. He really was here.

Ray walked up to her with a smile. "Hey."

"Hey, yourself."

He peeled his leather gloves off as he spoke. "So I was hoping you could help me order an authentic New England breakfast. Any recommendations?"

She laughed, though she could barely hear him over the pounding in her ears. "Definitely not the day's special."

He tapped her playfully on the nose. "Should you be discouraging people from ordering that? You're right, you're not that great a waitress."

"What are you doing here, Ray? I thought you'd be heading back home. Myrna mentioned that the deal has already been settled and signed."

"I came to offer you a proposition."

Mel's heart sank. The happiness she'd felt just a few short moments ago fled like an elusive doe. He was simply here to make her some other kind of job offer.

"I'm afraid I'm still not interested," she told him in a shaky voice. "I should get back to work."

He took her by the arm before she could turn away. The touch of his hand on her skin set her soul on fire. She'd give anything to go back to the morning when she'd woken up in his arms at the inn. And to somehow suspend that moment forever in time.

She tried to quell the shaking in the pit of her stomach. Seeing him again was wreaking havoc on her equilibrium. But she refused to accept his crumbs. She'd made that mistake once already to avoid being alone, and she wouldn't do it again. Not even for this man.

"I can't do it, Ray. Please don't ask me to work for you again. I don't want your job opportunity."

He steadfastly held on to her arm. "Don't you want to hear what it is first?" he asked with a tease in his voice.

Something about the lightness in his tone and the twinkle in his dark eyes gave her pause. Ray was up to something.

"All right."

He tapped the finger of his free hand against his temple. "I've come up with it completely myself. A brand-new position, which involves a lot of travel. You'll be accompanying a certain royal member of Verdovia to various functions and events throughout the world. Maybe even a holiday ball or two."

He couldn't mean… She wouldn't allow herself to hope. Could she? "Is that so?"

He nodded with a grin. "Definitely."

Oh, yeah, he was definitely up to something. "What else?" she prompted, now unable to keep the excitement out of her voice. Was he really here to say he wanted to spend time with her? That he wanted to be with her? Or was it possible that she had not actually woken up yet this morning and was still in the midst of the most wonderful dream.

Ray rubbed his chin. "I almost forgot. There'll be a lot of this—" Before she could guess what he meant, he pulled her to him and took her lips with his own. The world stood still. Her hands moved up to his shoulders as she savored the taste of him. It had been so long.

She couldn't tear herself away, though a diner full of people had to be watching them. This was all she'd been able to think about since the moment she'd first laid eyes on him on that Boston street.

Someone behind them whistled as another started a steady clap. Mel knew Greta and Frannie had to be the initiators of the cheers, but pretty soon the whole diner had joined in.

In response, Ray finally pulled away with a small chuckle and then twirled her around in a mini waltz around one of the empty tables in the center of the room.

"I miss dancing with you," he whispered against her ear and sent her heart near to bursting with joy.

The applause grew even louder. Catcalls and whistles loudly filled the air. But she could hardly hear any of it over the joyous pounding of her heart.

Ray dipped Mel in his arms in an elaborate ending to their mini waltz and gave her another quick kiss on the lips.

He turned to where Frannie and Greta stood over by the counter, grinning from ear to ear. He gave them both a small nod, which they each returned with an exaggerated curtsy that almost had Greta toppling over.

"If it's not all that busy, would you mind if my lady here takes the rest of the day off?"

Their answer was a loud, resounding "Yes," which was said in unison.

Mel laughed in his arms as he straightened, bringing her back up with him.

"Get your coat and come with me before I have to carry you out of here."

Behind them, Ray heard a voice that sounded vaguely

familiar. "I'm telling you, these guys should sell tickets. It's better than going to the movies."

The man was right. This was so much better than any movie. And Ray knew without a doubt there'd be a happy ending.

EPILOGUE

"THOSE TWO MAKE for the most unconventional brides-maids in the history of weddings," Ray said, laughing, motioning across the room to where Greta and Frannie sat with his two sisters at the bridesmaids' table.

Mel returned his chuckle as she took in the sight of the four of them.

"One would think those four have known each other for years."

"They certainly don't seem to mind the vast age difference," Mel added with a laugh of her own.

Ray took her hand in his on top of the table and rubbed his thumb along the inside of her palm. A ripple of arousal ran over her skin and she had to suck in a breath at her instant reaction. The merest touch still set her on fire, even after all these months together.

"They're pretty unconventional in lots of ways," she said with a smile, still trying to ignore the fluttering in her chest that was only getting stronger as Ray continued his soft caress of her hand.

Verdovia's version of a rehearsal dinner was certainly a grand affair, a sight straight out of a fairy tale—with a string quartet, tables loaded with extravagant foods and desserts, and even a champagne fountain. In fact, Mel felt like her whole life had turned into one big fantasy. She was actually sitting at a table with her fiancé, the crown prince, as his parents, the king and queen, sat beaming on either side of them.

Mel cast a glance at her future mother-in-law, who returned her smile with a wide one of her own. She looked the perfect picture of health and vibrancy. The king was equally fit and formidable. It didn't look like she and Ray would be ascending any throne anytime soon. A fact she was very grateful for. No one would ever be able to replace her real parents, Mel knew. But her future in-laws had so far shown her nothing but true affection and kindness. In fact, the whole country had received her with enthusiasm and acceptance—a true testament to the regard they felt for their prince and the royal family as a whole. And all despite Mel's utter unpreparedness for the rather bright proverbial spotlight she'd suddenly found herself in once her and Ray's engagement had been announced to the world.

Her fiancé pulled her out of her thoughts by placing a small kiss on the inside of her wrist. A sensation of pure longing gripped her core.

"I can't wait to be alone with you," he told her.

"Is that so?" she asked with a teasing grin. "What did you have in mind?"

He winked at her. "To dance with you, of course."

Mel gave in to the urge to rest her head against his strong shoulder. "There's no one else I'd rather dance with," she said, her joy almost too much to contain.

"And there's no one else I'd rather call my wife."

His words reminded her that the true fantasy had nothing to do with the myriad of parties being held for them over the next several weeks or even the extravagant wedding ceremony currently being planned. All that mattered was the complete and unfettered love she felt for this man.

Her husband-to-be was a prince in many more ways than one.

* * * * *

A ROYAL CHRISTMAS PROPOSAL

LEANNE BANKS

This book is dedicated to all the parents
who have gone the extra mile, two miles or
one hundred miles for your child's well-being.
Thank you for your love and devotion.
You've made the world a better place.

Chapter One

Princess Fredericka hoped her brother wasn't going to be impossible.

She knew she had made more than her share of mistakes. She'd been a wild child when she'd been a teenager and terrified her family with her antics. Everyone had breathed a sigh of relief when she'd gotten married, because she'd appeared to calm down. In many ways she had, but she'd learned things didn't always turn out the way one expected. She'd managed to make the best of what life had dealt her. Ericka knew her brother Stefan, the ruling prince of Chantaine, however, would have a hard time seeing her as a competent single mother to her adorable son, Leo.

She resisted the urge to fidget as she waited to be invited into her brother's office. She nodded at staff members as they hung holiday greenery and put candles in the window. Ericka suspected the Christmas decorations had been ordered by Eve, her brother's wife. Ericka barely remembered seeing Christmas decorations when she had been growing up in the palace. With the exception of the huge Christmas tree in one of the formal rooms, one might not have known the holiday existed. Of course, the deep chill between her mother and father hadn't helped matters.

Her father, Prince Edward, had been a philanderer and an absentee father and husband. Her mother had felt trapped and bitter. Ericka remembered wishing only that she could run away. She'd done exactly that in more than one way, which was why she suspected this was going to be a messy discussion. Stefan was extremely protective.

The door to Stefan's office finally opened. "Your Highness, Princess Fredericka, please come in," Stefan's assistant said.

She nodded. "Thank you very much," she said, then entered her brother's office while the assistant left the room. "Stefan," she greeted, walking toward her brother. She noticed a wisp of a couple gray streaks on the sides of his dark hair. The burden of his position was obviously weighing on him.

She kissed his cheek and he kissed hers. "How are you?" she asked.

"I'm well," he said. "I'm more concerned about you and Leonardo."

Ericka smiled. "Leo and I are great. I'm happy to be back in Chantaine after spending the last year with Tina in Texas."

"You could have spent the last year here in Chantaine," he said, and rounded his desk to sit in his chair.

Ericka sat in the chair across from her brother, watching him as he tented his fingers and studied her. "I think it was good to be with Tina in Texas during my pregnancy and delivery. She and her husband were supportive, and it was fun having their daughter, Katarina, around. She's quite the spitfire. Little ones put everything in perspective."

"True," Stefan said, giving a serious nod. "I think it would be best for you and Leo to live at the palace."

Ericka's stomach twisted and she bit the inside of her lip. She hated to go up against Stefan but knew it was necessary. "I think not," she said. "I've found a lovely gated cottage and a nanny. I think this will be best for Leo and me."

Stefan frowned. "But what about security? You and Leo need to be protected. That would be much easier within the palace walls."

Ericka shook her head. "The palace isn't the place for me. If you think about it, it's not the place for most of us. None of your siblings live here. I apologize for how this may sound, but the palace feels claustrophobic. I don't want that for Leo."

"He's a baby," Stefan said. "How will he know?"

"Babies sense more than you think. He would sense my tension. Leo and I need our own place. As I said, I have found a wonderful nanny and I've arranged for therapy for his hearing disability."

Stefan pressed his lips together. "Is there any chance you're wrong about his hearing? He's so young."

"No," she said, remembering the grief she'd suffered when she'd learned her perfect Leo couldn't hear. The doctors had tested Leo before she'd left the hospital with him, and many more tests had followed. "He has a hearing disability and I'm determined to make sure he gets the best treatment available."

"I can't believe you don't think living in the palace would make your life easier," Stefan said. "And your son's life safer."

Ericka shook her head. "Don't try to guilt me into doing things your way, Stefan. I have to follow my best inner guidance. I have to be my own expert. I'm counting on you to be supportive."

Stefan sighed. "This situation is going to put a lot of pressure on you. I hesitate to bring up the past, but—"

"You're talking about the time I spent in rehab in my teens," she said. Ericka couldn't blame any of her family for being concerned, but if she'd successfully survived her most recent humiliation, she could handle anything. "I'm lucky I learned to avoid chemicals early on. I haven't had a drink in nearly a decade. I learned to wake up every morning and make the decision that I'm not going to drink or use drugs that day."

Stefan nodded. "It's obvious you've come a long way, but I still don't want you to be overwhelmed."

"I'm going to be overwhelmed at times," she assured him. "I have a baby. Being a mother is new. But I'm a Devereaux and I'm not the weak link you may have once thought I was."

"I never said you were the weak link," he said with a dark frown.

"Well, maybe you just thought it," she said gently with a smile and lifted her hand when she could see he was going to protest. "It doesn't matter. You'll soon see there's more to me than you thought. I'll be very happy in my cozy cottage."

"Okay," he said reluctantly. "As you wish. However, I insist on providing you with security. You'll have a guard within the next couple of days."

Ericka made a face. "If you insist," she said. "Just make sure whoever you choose is low-profile or they'll get on my nerves. No one too pushy."

"I do insist, and I'll make sure you have the best security possible. You're working for the palace, so protection is more than appropriate. The new rules specify that if any of the Devereaux family is working for Chantaine, they shall be given security. You're taking over the coordination for the conference for The Royal Society for A Better World, although I don't know how you expect to do it with a baby and no husband," he said.

"Single mothers have been accomplishing great things for ages," she said. "I'll have a nanny and two sisters willing to help."

"Along with Eve," Stefan said of his wife. "She would kill me if I didn't offer her assistance."

Ericka smiled still amazed at the change Eve had wrought in her brother. The two were soul mates. Her happiness faded a little when she thought of her own future romantic prognosis. She wasn't sure her soul mate existed. Brushing the thought aside, she knew it was silly for her to waste one moment on any ideas about romance. She had no time or energy for a man in her life right now.

"You're always welcome at the palace if you should change your mind."

"Thank you, but I won't," she said. "Now shall we cover a few issues about the upcoming conference?"

Stefan shot her a smile that held a hint of approval. "Down to business already?"

"I've been ready," she said, and powered up her tablet.

Two days later, Stefan sent Ericka a text message informing her that one of his assistants would be bringing her security detail to her for introduction. Ericka frowned at her phone in response. This wasn't the best time. She was tired and hadn't even taken a shower yet. Leo hadn't slept well and had been fussy throughout the night. Even though Nanny Marley was more than able to care for Leo, Ericka had wanted to soothe him. Ericka was finding it more difficult than she'd planned to turn Leo's care over to someone else.

Silly. Ericka had never considered herself overly nurturing, but Leo had provoked powerful changes within her. Of course now that sunlight streamed through the windows of the cottage, Leo slept peacefully.

Yawning, she pulled her hair into a topknot and quickly changed clothes. She dashed to the bathroom to splash water on her face and brush her teeth. The introduction with her security detail shouldn't take any longer than five minutes. After that, she planned to sneak in a little nap before working. Before Leo, Ericka would never have considered meeting someone without being turned out to as close to perfection as possible. Having a baby had changed her priorities.

A knock sounded at the door and she rushed to answer it. Leo was already being treated for his hearing disability with infant hearing aids, and Ericka never knew what sounds might awaken him.

Spotting her brother's assistant through the glass

window beside the door, she opened it. She imme-diately caught sight of a man standing just behind her brother's assistant. He stood at least as tall as her brother-in-law from Texas. Over six feet tall. How was this subtle? she wondered. He would stick out like a sore thumb in Chantaine. What had her brother been thinking?

"Hello, Your Highness. Rolf here," her brother's assistant said as he made a quick bow. "I'm here to introduce you to your primary security detail. Mr. Montreat Walker."

Ericka nodded toward Rolf then turned to Mr. Walker out of politeness. "Mr. Walker."

He gave a half-hearted dip of his head. "You can call me Treat," he said in a Texas twang.

"Oh, really," she said, thinking he was not a treat. With his stubborn chin and too-broad shoulders, he looked as if he would be a pain in her derriere. "Mr. Walker," she said then turned to Rolf, who appeared to be cowering from both her and Mr. *Treat* Walker. "Thank you so much for stopping by. I'll be in touch with Stefan."

"I'd like to check your home security system first," Mr. Walker said.

"Excuse me," she replied, unable to hide her dis-approval.

"Yes," the overly tall, overly muscular, overly American man, said. "I've been hired to protect you. I need to make sure your home is adequately secure."

"I have a security system," she told him.

"Then you won't mind me checking it," he said.

Actually, she would, but she couldn't say that. She shrugged and opened her door widely. "Don't wake my baby."

He lifted his eyebrows for a half-beat then stepped forward. "I'll do the best I can, but I will need to test your alarm system."

Ericka stared at Rolf. "Please tell my brother I'll be in touch," she said.

"Yes, Your Highness," he said before he dipped his head and walked away.

"I'm a done deal," Mr. Walker said to her. "Your brother has made his decision."

Ericka tried to look down her nose at him, but he was too darn tall. "Nothing is a done deal."

Mr. Walker shrugged. "Good luck. I'll check your system."

Ericka frowned at him as he swaggered through the hallway. "I told you not to wake my baby."

Mr. Walker paused and turned to look at her. "How strong is his hearing disorder?"

Ericka could have cried at his question. If only she knew how extensive his hearing loss was. Even the doctors had told her the measurement for his hearing disorder could change. "Profound. He's been awake most of the night."

Mr. Walker nodded. "I'll check the house. I'll have

to test the alarm system some time. You let me know when I can do that without startling him."

If only he *could* startle Leo, Ericka thought. If only she could make a sound that would startle him. Ericka stared after Mr. Walker, hating him and liking him at the same time. What could he possibly know about having a child with special needs? Nothing, she suspected. His life had probably been perfect. No troubles. No trials.

Leo's future was full of trials. She stiffened her back. She needed to cushion her child in his infancy and make him strong for his future years. Her job was to provide the perfect amount of support and hope. Whatever that was.

A flash of fur passed between them.

Mr. Walker frowned. "Was that a cat?"

"Yes. The doctor said Leo would benefit from a pet."

He frowned in confusion. "A cat? Don't they sleep twenty-three out of twenty-four hours a day?"

"Sam is awake much more than that, plus he watches after Leo."

"You mean, he stalks your baby," Mr. Walker said.

She blinked. "He does no such thing. Sam protects Leo. He's probably studying you right now to make sure you won't hurt the baby."

Mr. Walker lifted a dark eyebrow. "This is one more challenge for implementing a sound security system."

She lifted her head. "Sam stays. We brought him back from Texas. My brother insisted he was neutered before we arrived. Stefan doesn't want any more potent cats on the island. He's afraid Chantaine will end up with too many cats."

"Understandable," Mr. Walker said. "Practical."

"Mr. Walker, you need to understand that you're dealing with a very human element. My son. I know that the people of Chantaine don't hold a grudge against me. They're delighted I have returned."

"But there could be one person who's not delighted," he said. "And I'm here to protect you from that person."

Ericka stared into his dark eyes and knew he would protect her from anything. She held his gaze for a long moment and saw a flash of tenderness. It surprised her. How could a man who appeared so hard be kind?

If he couldn't be kind to her son, she had no use for him. If he couldn't tolerate her cat, he would be dismissed.

Treat Walker looked into Princess Fredericka's disapproving blue eyes. He'd read her file. She'd been known as the teenage wild-child beauty. She'd even made a few trips to rehab before she'd gotten herself straightened out and married a French film director.

Although the princess had returned to Chantaine frequently for public and family events, she'd seemed to prefer life out of the limelight. With the exception of red carpet appearances with her husband, Fredericka had focused more of her time on studies in fine arts.

When her husband fell for a younger actress, Fredericka's life began to fall apart. The combination of the scandal and her pregnancy had been overwhelming, so she'd disappeared to live in Texas with her older sister during her pregnancy.

At first glance, she looked a little too perfect. With her aristocratic bone structure, she could have modeled for a Renaissance sculptor. Although she was trying to hold him in cool contempt, he glimpsed humanity and a little bit of fear in her eyes, a hint of purple shadows that showed she wasn't sleeping well.

Taking care of an infant with serious hearing loss could be hard on anyone, especially since she appeared to be trying to do most of it on her own. "Your son," he said. "He's lucky you have the resources to give him the best help he needs. Not everyone can get their child the right kind of help."

Her eyebrows knitted slightly. "Money can't solve everything. The choices may be difficult," she said before she turned away from him.

Ericka spent the day juggling caring for Leo and planning her work schedule. Since the nanny had gone to market, Ericka carried Leo in a cloth baby carrier against her chest as she talked on the phone.

Leo quickly drifted off to sleep and Ericka answered a few calls. When he began to drool against her collar, she suspected he was ready for genuine nap in his crib. Just as she pulled him from the cloth carrier and set him in his crib, he let out a squeak of protest.

Wincing, Ericka immediately placed her hand over his tummy. Her sister had taught her this trick. Leo didn't like the abruptness of being detached after being held. A little more of a human connection seemed to soothe him and he gave a little snorty baby sigh. Ericka held her hand on him for several more moments, staring at his rosy, plump cheeks and dark eyelashes against his perfect skin. Pride and love welled up inside her. He was the most beautiful thing she'd ever seen in her life.

Carefully backing away, Ericka turned around and pulled the door partway closed behind her. Then she walked straight into a wall. Or, it felt like a wall until it swore under its breath. Her heart hammering in panic, she opened her mouth to scream at the same time she looked up into the hard face of Mr. Walker.

She slumped in relief and he immediately clasped her arms as if he thought she were going to faint. The notion annoyed her, "Remove your hands from me," she said in the icy tone she'd learned from one of her governesses.

He immediately released her and she stumbled backward, glaring at me. "I thought you had left to get an alarm system. What are you doing here now? And why didn't you knock?"

"First, since I'm your security detail, I'm like a member of the family. I don't have to knock," he said.

"Oh, yes, you do," she said. "You're not family. You're staff. All staff knocks before entering."

"Plus I didn't want to wake your baby if he was sleeping," he continued.

She opened her mouth then closed it, feeling as if someone had let the air out of her balloon. "Well," she said, desperate to establish some boundaries with this man who seemed to take up entirely too much space. "You shouldn't come up behind me like that and startle me. There's no excuse for that."

"I was examining the hallway for the best alarm system."

He was so implacable, she thought, her irritation growing. "I'm not sure this is going to work," she said, and walked past him. "My nanny and I are working perfectly well together. Your presence is disruptive."

"Give me a couple days," he said. "You'll barely notice I'm around."

That did it, she thought. Mr. Walker was going back to the States. She would talk with Stefan that afternoon.

Except Stefan wasn't picking up his private cell phone, and his assistant said he was indisposed. Stalling tactics. Ericka recognized them because he'd used them before on rare occasions when he wanted things his way. She considered calling Stefan's wife, Eve, but with two young children and another on the way, Eve had her hands full. Besides, this was between her and Stefan.

Ericka made another call. "Bernard, this is Ericka again. How are you?"

"Quite well, Your Highness."

"I realize Stefan is quite busy today," she said.

"Yes, yes, he is," Bernard said.

"Lots of activity in his palace office," she said.

"It's often busy in the Prince's office. As you know, he works hard for the people of Chantaine."

"Of course he does. Since he is at the Palace office today, I'll just scoot over for a quick visit. I promise it won't take more than a moment or two. Ciao," she said.

"But, but, but—"

Ericka disconnected the call and smiled grimly to herself. Two could play this little game. Stefan would be hard-pressed to avoid her if she was standing outside his office.

Ericka found Nanny Marley taking a well-earned break reading in the sunroom. "Marley, I need to make a quick trip to the palace. I won't be gone long."

"Yes, Your Highness. I'll keep an ear out for him."

Ericka shook her finger at the sweet middle-aged woman. "We've already discussed this. You're not supposed to address me as 'Your Highness.' Please call me Ericka."

"I keep forgetting," the woman said. "It just doesn't feel respectful."

"It's my wish," Ericka said. "So that makes it respectful. Please?"

"Yes, Miss Ericka," Nanny Marley said.

Ericka smiled. "That's a little closer. I'll be back soon."

"No hurries on my account, ma'am," the nanny said.

Ericka drove her tiny smart car through the winding streets of Chantaine. Her route to the palace took her past the view of the azure ocean trickling against a white sandy beach. She'd never realized how much she'd missed her homeland until she'd returned. In fact, she'd fought the idea of ever returning. She'd had too many memories of feeling confined and suffocated in Chantaine. Leaving had felt so freeing.

Even now, she felt twinges from her memories, but she was determined to keep her feelings and future in perspective. One of her most important decisions had been not to live at the palace. Another important decision had been to hire Nanny Marley. The next decision would be to get rid of her assigned security man, Mr. Walker.

As she pulled up to the palace, the gates were opened and she was waved through. Parking her car at the side of the main building, she touched her finger to the sensor that would allow her inside the door. Her shoes echoed on the marble floor of the hallways as she made her way to her brother's office. The same office had once belonged to her father, although her father had spent far less time performing royal duties and much more time on his yacht with his mistress du jour. She'd always found it amazing that her father had managed to sire six legitimate children despite his numerous affairs. Now that Ericka was grown, she could look back and see that her mother had continued to have children in hopes of truly winning her father's heart. Unfortunately, her mother's wish had never come true.

Ericka's stomach knotted as she remembered feeling that same sense of desperation at losing her husband. She'd been all too aware of the deterioration of his feelings for her. In fact, she'd made love with him in a final effort to win him back. When she thought of how weak she'd been, she could hardly bear it. It had taken her over a year to find herself again and get centered. She never wanted to be that weak woman, dependent on a man again. Never.

Reaching her brother's office, she knocked on the door and waited. Impatience nicked at her and she knocked again.

The door swung open and one of her brother's assistants dipped his head. "Your Highness," he said.

"I need to see my brother," she said.

"But he's—"

"It won't take long. I promise. Stefan," she called. "I know you're in there. Do you really want me yelling outside your office?"

Her brother's assistant groaned and seconds later, he backed away, allowing her entrance. Stefan frowned at her. "I just got off a conference call with two dukes from Spain and Italy."

"Great timing," she said, and shot him a broad smile. "I thought you might be signing off around this time."

"I actually had some other items on my list," he said, his irritation clear.

"I imagine they could wait until tomorrow. Eve and your little ones would probably love to see you tonight."

His hard gaze softened. "You're probably right. Eve is worn out by the end of the day with this pregnancy, although she would deny it."

"You married a strong woman," she said.

"So I did," Stefan said. "I suspect you're here to complain about your new security man."

"Your suspicion is correct. I specifically requested someone low key, who won't interrupt my routine or bring undue attention."

"Mr. Jackson will work out with no problem. He comes highly recommended. I wanted the best for you and Leo."

"You gave me the Texas version of the Jolly Green

Giant. He's been an interruption since he walked through the door. He doesn't like the cat—"

"Can't blame him there," Stefan muttered.

"Leo likes the cat," she said.

"Leo doesn't know any better," Stefan retorted. "Listen, you haven't even given Mr. Walker a chance. He hasn't been there a whole day. The least you can do is give him a trial period."

"One more day," she said.

Stefan shook his head. "At least a week. He left an assignment in the States at my request."

"I don't need this kind of invasion into my privacy. I can't believe you think Leo or I are at risk here in Chantaine."

"You forget Eve's encounter with that crowd before we were married," he said.

"That's different. I won't be doing nearly as many appearances since I'm focusing on the conference. Any time I'm making an appearance, you can assign someone from your security detail for me."

Stefan sighed. "I don't like to frighten you, but I don't trust your ex-husband. How do you know he won't try to use Leo to get some sort of settlement?"

Ericka's blood ran cold at the thought. She swallowed over a lump of fear and shook it off. "My ex-husband couldn't be less interested in Leo. He knew I was pregnant when I left."

"He could change his mind. If he does, I want to be ready for him."

Chapter Two

Treat heard two voices coming from the den of the house as he walked down the hall. He stopped outside the den and watched as the princess used sign language while she gazed at her computer tablet. The baby sat next to her with his eyes closed, apparently asleep.

"So, how did you like that, Leo?" she asked and turned to look at her child. She gave a soft laugh. "Bored you to sleep, right?"

She sighed. "Well, maybe we can get you to extend your little nap in your crib," she said as she gently picked up the baby and stood. She turned and met his gaze.

Treat saw the way her body stiffened slightly.

"Anything I can do for you? I've decided to focus security around the perimeter of the property and give you and your nanny a panic button."

"Fine," she said with a total lack of interest. "I'm going to try to put Leo down now. He has a hard time sleeping unless he can see me or I'm holding him."

"Maybe it has something to do with his other senses being heightened. Do you leave a light on in the bedroom?" he asked.

"No. I hadn't thought of that," she said. "I use room darkening shades for him during the day."

Treat shrugged. "Just something to think about. He's probably a very visual guy."

She studied him for a moment. "I'll do some research."

He nodded. "Looked like you were doing well with the sign language," he said.

"You know sign language?" she asked.

"A little. Not enough to get any—" he said, and wiggled his hands for the sign for applause.

Her lips twitched in an almost smile. "I've got a long way to go. Right now, though, I'm putting my big guy to bed. I'm glad you won't be concentrating as much on alarming the house. Leo may not be able to hear the alarms, but it would be startling for Nanny and me."

"I hear you," he said. "Listen, do you mind if I take a swim in the pool at night? It's one of the ways I like to stay in shape."

He felt her gaze dip to his shoulders then she blinked and cleared her throat. "Of course not," she said. "Excuse me while I put Leo to bed."

Treat felt something wrap around his ankles and watched Sam wind around him. He frowned.

"Looks like Sam likes you," Princess Fredericka said.

Treat watched her as she retreated down the hallway. He shifted from one foot to the other and narrowed his eyes. Sam looked up at him and gave a meow. He glared down at the cat, but the cat continued to mark him. Glancing toward the hallway, he thought about the woman who'd just left the room. He'd expected a snooty princess. At first glance, maybe she was. But in less than twenty-four hours, he'd glimpsed something else. A princess trying to teach herself and her baby son sign language? She wasn't what he'd expected.

Treat felt a strange gnawing sensation in his gut. He hadn't felt anything like it in a long time. In fact, he hadn't felt much of anything for a long time. He'd made sure not to invest in anything too emotional. His life hadn't allowed for it once he'd suffered that last professional football injury. Treat hadn't gotten truly involved with a woman in several years. He'd been too busy trying to make a living. Once he'd switched to security, he'd decided to make his fortune with it. The past few years he'd worked nonstop with his partner to build their security business.

Now, he was making the step to take the business international.

He needed cooperation from Princess Fredericka and he also needed not to get emotionally involved. No problem, he told himself.

Another near-sleepless night, Ericka thought as she rubbed her face when the sun shone through the crack of her window coverings. She wasn't sure when Leo had fallen asleep for more than an hour, but she planned to check out night lights and anything else that might help him. She'd finally turned on a lamp in the hallway. She wondered if that had helped.

Nanny was more than ready to step up, but Ericka had a hard time handing over Leo's care when he seemed so distressed. Now, however, she had calls and plans to make and she wouldn't feel quite so guilty handing Leo over to his nanny. Ericka was so exhausted that she knew she needed help.

Lying on her back in her bed, she took several deep breaths and stared up at the ceiling. She needed to open the blinds, she told herself. She'd recently read that exposure to light during the first thirty minutes of her day would make her feel more awake.

"Wake up, Ericka," she urged herself and dragged herself from her bed. She thrust herself under a shower, brushed her teeth then stumbled toward the kitchen where Nanny sat at the table.

"You should have woken me. That's why I'm here," she said, offering Ericka a cup of coffee.

"He was just on the edge," Ericka said, accepting the coffee and taking a long draw. "He kept going to sleep and waking up. Then going to sleep and waking up."

"You should have awakened me after the first time," Nanny said.

"I think it became a challenge," Ericka said.

"Oh," Nanny said in a dark voice. "That's bad. No one should ever challenge a Devereaux."

Ericka laughed and took another long drink from her coffee. "You're so right." She paused a half beat. "The security man suggested I do something with light to help Leo. Something about his sight being a strong sense. So I'm going to do some research."

"This from the American?"

Ericka nodded. "Who knew?"

Nanny shook her head. "I would not have expected that."

"Neither would I have," Ericka said.

Nanny lifted her hands in the sign language for applause. "Good for you. Good for Leo."

Ericka smiled and echoed the sign language. "We're working on it," she said. "In the meantime, it's time for me to go to work."

"Drink another cup of coffee," Nanny said.

Ericka extended her mug up toward the woman, who refilled her cup. "I'm so glad I don't have to meet face-to-face with anyone today. Thank goodness this is a phone day."

"Take a nap midday then have juice and a cookie," Nanny said. "It will be good for you."

Ericka chuckled, but she couldn't help thinking Nanny had a good point. Maybe, if everyone took a nap after lunch followed by a snack of juice and a cookie, then the world would be a better place. She would be less cranky. That was for sure.

She made several calls throughout the day. Coffee kept her going. Just before dinner, she signed off and typed some final notes on her laptop. The conference planning was coming along. She was pleased with her progress.

Ericka stood and shook her body to release her stiffness and tension. A short dip in the pool would do her good, she thought, and she went to her bedroom to change into a bathing suit. It was dinner time, but she was more interested in the sensation of sinking into water than eating. Thank goodness the pool was heated.

Ericka stepped down the stairs into the pool, pausing before the last step. The water was cooler than she'd expected. She finally took that last step and let out a little squeal. Sinking down to her neck, she shivered, but quickly adjusted.

She took a deep breath then plunged her face in the water and began to swim. She made it to the far wall and turned then swam back. Out of breath, she paused and chastised herself. "Go," she muttered to herself and swam another lap. She returned and grasped the side of the pool, gasping for air.

A warm hand covered hers on the side of the pool. "Are you okay?"

Surprised, she inhaled water and coughed. And coughed. And coughed. She felt a splash beside her and a thump on her back. She hacked a couple more times then took a low, careful breath through her nostrils.

"Did you have to startle me?" she finally managed, looking up at Mr. Walker who was fully dressed in jeans and a polo shirt. Drenched, he stared down at her, his shirt clinging to his perfectly muscled body.

"I thought you were drowning," he said. "You kept gasping for air but ducking your head under the water."

"I was pushing myself to go a little farther. I realize it may look pathetic in your eyes, but I haven't had a lot of physical exercise during the last few months."

"Oh," he said, watching her as she continued to catch her breath.

"Have you ever had a baby?" she asked.

His mouth twitched in a cockeyed smile. "Not that I can remember."

Ericka took a deep breath and headed toward the

steps. She felt his hands on her waist guiding her. "That's not—"

"No problem," he said, continuing to help her up the steps.

Her heart raced at his touch and she didn't like the sensation. "Let go of me. I'm fine."

He didn't release her until she was steady. She resented the fact that she wasn't steady one minute earlier. She resented him, too.

"I was just taking a swim," she said.

He stepped up beside her in his wet street cloths and looked down at her. "Maybe you shouldn't do as many laps next time."

"I didn't do that many," she retorted.

"Cut yourself some slack. Isn't your baby still waking up every night?" he asked.

"Yes," she said.

"And you don't let the nanny take over nearly often enough, then," he said.

Ericka took another deep breath, hating that he was speaking the truth. She so wanted him to be wrong. "I can handle it."

"I'm your security detail," he said, and extended his hand. "I can't let you drown yourself."

She ignored his hand and walked away, her limbs heavy from her exertion. "You ruined my swim."

"I saved you from drowning," he corrected.

She turned around and stared at him. "You are a total pain and you will be gone in six days."

He gave a crooked smile again. "Your brother insisted that you give me a trial period."

Ericka scowled. *I hate you*, she wanted to say. "Good night. You'll be gone soon enough," she said, and then turned to walk away.

"You know Beethoven wrote some of his most famous work when he was deaf," he said.

She stopped and her heart stopped, too. Ericka took a deep breath, more moved by his words than she would ever want to admit. "Good night," she repeated, although even she would admit she sounded less hostile.

Although she turned on a light in Leo's room, he still awakened in the middle of the night and screamed bloody murder. Nanny was there to help, but Ericka felt responsible. She was his mother. She was the one who should soothe him back to sleep. As soon as she drew him into her arms, he quieted.

As she rocked him in the middle of the night, she wondered if she would ever be the mother he needed. He was such a precious soul. How could she be all he needed?

She dozed a bit with him in her lap then rose and carefully placed him in the crib, keeping her hand on him for several moments. She felt him drift to sleep and carefully walked away.

An hour later, he awakened again. This time, she let Nanny take him. At the same time, she felt like a failure. Why couldn't she help her son so that he would sleep through the night?

Exhausted, she awakened later than usual and forced herself to climb out of bed. Stumbling toward the bath, she splashed her face with water and brushed her teeth then headed for the kitchen for coffee. She wanted to mainline it through her veins.

Nanny offered her a cup. "Would you like cream and sugar, ma'am?"

"That sounds wonderful," Ericka said. "Have you gotten any sleep since four am?"

"Yes, ma'am, I have," Nanny said. "His royal self gave it up after half a bottle. Men," she said, shaking her head. "It's all about food."

Ericka chuckled and took a sip of her coffee. "So true. And this morning?"

"He's still asleep," Nanny said.

"That can be good," Ericka said. "And bad."

Nanny nodded. "I'll take a nap in just a few moments," she said.

"I'm thinking of hiring back-up assistance for cooking and cleaning," Ericka said.

"It shouldn't be necessary," Nanny said. "I know our arrangement is for me to return to my apartment a few days every month. Is that a problem?" the woman asked with a worried expression.

"Not at all. Trust me, you are irreplaceable. I think a little additional back-up may help. For both of us,"

Ericka said. "Leo has us coming and going. There's too much of cooking and cleaning left to do."

"Well, it's not as if you're a woman of leisure," Nanny said. "You work very hard."

Ericka felt a sliver of relief. "Thank you for saying that. I somehow feel as if I should manage all of this on my own."

Nanny shook her head. "Never. It's not as if you have a husband," she said, and then covered her mouth as if she were shocked by her frank words.

Ericka shook her head. "Don't worry. What you say is true. I'm just trying to figure it all out."

"And you're doing a wonderful job," Nanny said. "Don't be so hard on yourself. It won't help you get any job done, motherhood or your other duties."

Ericka made more phone calls to continue to secure the arrangements for the upcoming conference. Her sister Bridget called in between calls. "Hello, Bridget, how are you?"

"Pregnant and busy with the twins and all the animals my husband insists on having at our so-called ranch. When I agreed to marry a Texan doctor, I didn't realize he was serious about recreating home on the range here in Chantaine," Bridget said in a mock huffy voice.

Ericka smiled at her sister's tone. Although Bridget had been known as the socialite in her family, she'd been tamed when she'd fallen in love with her doctor husband and the two nephews he'd adopted. "More animals? Horses, cattle, goats. You're turning into a zoo,"

"Oh, darling, we became a zoo a long time ago," she said. "Now, I know you're busy, but Pippa, Eve and I want to have a get-together for lunch before I get much closer to my due date. Before you know it, it will be Christmas. Or I'll be in labor. One of the two."

"I'd love to," Ericka said, "but I'm feeling strapped for time. Between caring for Leo and planning the conference…"

"I feel terrible that you've had to take over the conference, but when the doctor put me on limited activity, it squashed my schedule even more. You have a nanny and back-up, don't you?"

"I have a wonderful nanny, but I think I'm going to have to get someone part-time for shopping and errands," Ericka said.

Bridget made a tsk-ing sound. "You should have done that right away. Trying to do too much. You're starting to act like overachiever Valentina before her husband took her away from us."

Ericka smiled at the description. Bridget had nailed Tina's personality perfectly. "I'm not sure I'll ever measure up to those standards," Ericka said.

"Well, you have too much right now, so I think you should ask for a loaner or referral from the palace. Anyone they recommend will have been properly vetted. You can ask for a few choices," Bridget said.

"I've been trying to avoid placing any extra burdens on the palace," she confessed.

"Oh, yes. I know all about it. Stefan is huffing and puffing because you won't stay at the palace where he can make sure you're safe and secure. Can't blame you for wanting to escape, though. Even though I live in a circus with these five-year old twins and all these animals, I much prefer living outside the walls. But I insist you let the palace help you out. I also insist you join us for lunch day after tomorrow. No arguments," Bridget said in her best no-nonsense voice.

"All right," Ericka said. "When did you become so bossy?"

"You get a family of instant twin baby boys and you'll be amazed how bossy you become. Ciao, darling. Go eat some chocolate and have some wine. Drink an extra glass for me."

Although reluctant, Ericka put in a call to palace personnel. Two applicants would apply tomorrow. She fed the baby and carried him around for a while. Suddenly it was eight o'clock and she was tired and cranky. Thank goodness for Nanny. She thought about how Bridget had suggested wine and chocolate, but she was in the mood for something different. Something she'd had when she was pregnant and living in Texas.

A peanut butter and bacon sandwich.

* * *

Treat followed the scent of bacon inside the house. He'd missed that smell. "Bacon?" he said.

Ericka whirled around to look at him. "Technically pancetta."

"Smells like bacon," he said.

"It's not quite the same thing," she said. "But I'll make do. If I burn it enough and put it on top of peanut butter, it won't matter that much."

"Peanut butter?" he echoed, impressed by her determination.

She nodded and turned back to her frying pan. "My brother-in-law from Texas turned me onto this when I was pregnant. It has turned into one of my favorite stress foods."

She flipped the pancetta onto a paper towel while she slathered a slice of bread with a peanut butter.

"Hey," Treat said. "Do you have any extra bacon?"

"Pancetta," she corrected.

"It smells great," he said.

She chuckled. "Here you go."

"I think I want to try it with peanut butter," he said.

She slid him a sideways glance. "I don't have a lot of extra peanut butter," she said. "My sister from Texas sends it to me."

"Okay," Treat said. "I'll just take the bacon."

She gave a heavy sigh and pulled out two more slices of bread. Slapping some peanut butter on a slice, she followed with a helping of crispy pancetta and squished the sandwich together. She handed it to him on a plate. "Eat at your own risk."

"I'll brave it," he said, then took a big bite and savored the flavors. He took another bite to assess. "It's delicious. The pancetta's a little strong, but it's still delicious."

"Agreed," Ericka said. "I'm trying to figure out how to get American bacon, although I know I've just offended every Italian I've ever met."

"The pancetta's not bad," he said, taking another big bite of the sandwich.

"No, but I want cheap bacon," she said, and took a bite of her own sandwich.

"If anyone should be able to get it, you should," he said. "You're a princess."

"We have importation rules," she said, and continued to eat her sandwich. "I wonder if I talked to Stefan. Or if I kept my mouth shut and asked Tina to send me American bacon…"

"What a scandal that could be," he said. "Princess Fredericka imports forbidden bacon."

She slid a quelling glance at him, then chuckled. "I suppose you're right. I could be importing so much worse."

He swallowed the rest of his sandwich and nodded. He brushed off his hands. "So right. Time for bed?"

She met his gaze and choked on her sandwich.

Treat smacked her on her back. He wondered if he should perform the Heimlich.

Ericka coughed then stepped away from him. "I'm fine," she insisted, coughing.

"You sure?" he asked.

"Yes," she said, still coughing.

He poured a glass of water and offered it to her.

Ericka sipped it then took a shallow breath. "I think you're right. It's time to go to bed."

Treat nodded. "Let me know if you need me for anything."

"I'm fine, Mr. Walker," she said.

"Call me Treat," he said.

"Treat?" she echoed and shook her head. "What an interesting name."

"Montreat," he said. "The name was shortened."

"Oh," she said, and then nodded.

"Kinda like Fredericka was shortened to Ericka."

"Interesting," she said. "Mr. Walker. Good night."

"Good night, Princess Fredericka," he said.

"I need to clean up," she said.

"I can do that," he said. "Go on up to bed. You need your sleep."

She paused a moment. "If you insist, Mr. Walker."

"Treat," he corrected.

She paused a long moment. "Treat," she finally said in a soft voice. The sound of his name from her lips did something to him. He would have to figure that out later.

"Night," he said as he watched her leave the room. Treat cleaned the pan and dishes then prowled the kitchen. Fifteen minutes later, he heard the sound of Leo crying. He knew Ericka would get up and cradle her baby. He also knew she needed rest.

Treat climbed the stairs. He nearly bumped into Ericka.

"What are you doing here?" she whispered.

"I'm checking on your baby," he said.

"I can take care of that," she told him.

"But maybe you shouldn't," he said. "Even Saint Ericka needs a rest."

She scowled at him. "I've never said I'm a saint."

"Then stop trying to look like one," he said. "Go back to bed."

"Who will hold Leo?" she asked.

"I will," he said.

"You?" she asked. "You look like you would be better with a football."

"Football, baby, they're close to the same."

"A baby is close to a football?" she said, clearly alarmed.

"I'm joking," he said. "I've rocked a baby before. Trust me."

"Why should I?" she asked.

"Your brother did," he said. "He vetted me six times from Sunday."

Ericka sighed, clearly so weary she could hardly stand. "Just for a few minutes," she said. "Just a few minutes. Then wake me up. I can handle this." She turned toward her room and Treat felt a crazy quiet sense of victory as he entered the nursery and picked up the baby.

Chapter Three

Ericka awakened in the night and listened for sounds from the baby monitor. Nothing. She stared up at the ceiling then closed her eyes and told herself she should go back to sleep. Leo wasn't crying. All was well.

Except the football player was looking after her baby. Rising and pushing her covers aside, she shook her head at herself. She must have been out of her mind to put Leo in his care. Rushing to the nursery, she carefully pushed the door open and saw Treat moving the beam of a flashlight against the ceiling. He saw her and lifted his fingers to his lips to urge her to remain quiet.

Ericka looked at Leo whose sleepy gaze followed

the light. His eyelids drooped then opened then finally closed. She tilted her head and looked at Treat in silence. He placed the flashlight on the small dresser then stood and ushered her out of the room, gently closing the door behind them.

"What was that about?" she asked.

"I told you he might like more light," he said.

"That's why I put a nightlight in there," she said.

"I think he likes something more active. It's a challenge to track a moving light. He's a smart little guy," he said.

Ericka took in Treat's last words and it was all she could do not to burst into tears. Although she believed Leo was smart, she hadn't heard anyone else say those exact words. He'd been called beautiful and alert, but no one had called him smart. Ericka bit her lip, determined to pull her emotions in check. "Yes, he is smart," she said as she crossed her arms over her chest. "Thank you for looking after him. It's not really your job."

"I don't require a lot of sleep," he said.

"I envy you that," she muttered. Suddenly she realized how close he stood to her. She could smell the faint scent of soap and shampoo. He was so tall, she thought, and told herself she found that fact offputting. She looked into his eyes and her stomach took a strange dip. *What was that?* She took a quick short breath and looked away. "You can go to bed.

Nanny and I should be able to handle it now. Thank you again."

"No problem," he said, and walked past her down the hallway to the front door. He slept in the small guest suite. Attached to the cottage, the suite had its own door. For a moment, she wondered what he did all day in that suite when he wasn't figuring out new ways to protect her and Leo. It occurred to her that all that solitary confinement would make her batty. Sure, she enjoyed quiet moments enjoying art. She especially missed those moments lately, but Ericka needed human connection. She wondered if Treat did.

Suddenly realizing she'd been thinking about him for at least three full moments, she shook her head and reminded herself that she didn't care if Treat needed human connection or not. She just wanted him to stay out of the way so she could do what she needed to do.

Treat returned to the guest suite but felt like a caged animal. He felt he shouldn't leave the property to go for a run, so he decided to take a swim. Maybe that would relax him. He slid into the pool and the water felt warm against his skin, probably because the night air was cool. Automatically swimming several laps, he waited for the exercise and the monotony of motion to ease his mind.

Being around the princess's baby brought back

memories of his disabled brother, Jerry. Jerry had been born with multiple deformities, both mental and physical, but he'd had a good soul. Treat had seen it in his young brother's eyes and smile.

Treat had noticed that Leo didn't smile as frequently. Leo looked as if he were trying to figure everything out. The baby appeared to want every bit of information he could get and he wanted it immediately. A demanding baby, he thought, and not just because of his hearing loss.

His brother, Jerry, had been demanding due to his health issues which had been enormous. After Treat's father died when he was a teenager, Treat had watched his mother struggle to pay medical bills. He had cared for Jerry whenever he could, but his mother had pushed him to take a football scholarship. It had always been Treat's dream to make a lot of money so that he could take care of both his mother and Jerry.

But Jerry had died during Treat's junior year in college and he'd lost his mother just one year later. She hadn't even seen Treat graduate. Treat had felt like a rudderless boat after that.

Even though he knew the princess's situation was far different than his mother's, he caught glimpses of the same emotions he'd seen in his mother's eyes. Fear, worry, weariness. He also saw a helluva lot of determination. Ericka would make sure Leo received every bit of education and attention he needed. She could have taken an easier way out, but he could tell she would be actively involved in every decision in that baby's life. Leo was damn lucky, not just because his mother was a princess, but because she was so devoted.

Treat swam a few more laps. The vision of the princess and Leo stomped through his mind. Swimming hadn't extricated them from his consciousness, but maybe the exercise would help him sleep. Her Highness was making a bigger impact on him than he'd expected.

Ericka rose early and conducted two tele-conferences. She much preferred regular phone calls because for those, she didn't need to apply make-up or fix her hair. During another call later in the morning, she received the disturbing news that young royals from Sergenia were in danger and needed to leave their small country due to unrest.

Ericka turned off her phone and did a session with Leo. She showed him several works of art and signed the best she could. "Here is da Vinci's Mona Lisa," she said, lifting her computer tablet. "He was a brilliant artist. As was Raphael." She pulled up a photo of one of Raphael's paintings. "I can't wait to show you Michelangelo's sculpture of David," she told her son. "It's beyond amazing. There's nothing like it," she said, and waved the hand toward her face making the sign for amazing.

"I must have been way behind," Treat said from the doorway. "I didn't know anything about da Vinci until I was in my teens. Unless you count the Teenage Mutant Ninja Turtles."

"Who are they?" she asked, feeling a strange rush of pleasure when she saw him.

"Cartoon turtle characters named after some of the great artists of the Renaissance," he said. "Michelangelo, Raphael, Donatello and Leonardo."

"How clever," she said.

He chuckled. "You learned about the real artists. I learned about the cartoon characters."

Ericka frowned in sympathy. "How unfortunate," she said.

He chuckled again. "No worries. I received a little more education later on and saw pictures of the Renaissance artists. I'm okay. Just not as cultured as you are."

Ericka met his gaze and felt her stomach jump. "You can learn."

"I do my best. Are you ready to go out for your luncheon with your sisters?"

"Yes" she said, standing as she remembered. "Nanny will take care of Leo."

"I'm sure he's exhausted from his morning lecture," he said.

She narrowed her eyes at him. "Are you saying I'm boring him?"

Treat lifted his hands. "Not me."

"I need to freshen up," she said. "I'll be back in a moment. Nanny Marley," she called and walked down the hall.

Treat walked over to look at Leo. "How ya doing big guy? Wanna talk football?"

Leo kicked and stared at him, making grunting sounds.

"Just so you know, Bonnie Sloan was one of the first deaf NFL football players. You can do anything you want," Treat said. "When you get a little older, maybe we can toss the pigskin."

A half-beat later, Nanny Marley entered the room. "How's he doing?"

"He's just received a very cultural tutoring session," Treat said.

Nanny nodded and smiled. "Her Highness is highly motivated to expose Leo to art, culture and science."

"What about sports?" he asked.

"That may be someone else's job," Nanny said.

Princess Fredericka strode into the hallway. "Ready," she said, and quickly ran to Leo to give him a kiss on his chubby cheek.

"Yes, Your Highness," Treat said, and walked with her out of the house.

"You don't have to call me 'Your Highness,'" she said.

"Oh, really," he said. "Then what do I call you?"

"For the remainder of your service, you may call

me Ericka in private," she said as she walked to the car.

"And what do I call you in public?" he asked.

"Miss," she said. "Just call me Miss."

"Done and done, Ericka," he said as he helped her into the car.

Just a few moments later, Treat drove to the café where Ericka planned to meet her sisters and sister-in-law. Although she was more than willing to hop out as he approached the curb, he refused to let her out. "I'll escort you into the café," he said.

"Well, don't expect to stay," she told him as he parked the car. "There will already be security for the rest of the crowd. You'll be superfluous."

"Superfluous," he echoed as he walked her into the café.

She gave a heavy sigh. "It's not an attack against your masculinity. When it comes to security, my brother Stefan provides overkill."

"I'm glad he's protective. You are all valuable to him and many others," Treat said. "There's your table. I'll be outside. Call me if you need me."

Ericka was still contemplating his statement about how valuable she and her sisters were, but Bridget stood, in her immense pregnancy, and extended her arms.

"Ericka, come here and give me a big hug. I need it. Maybe you can squeeze away some of my swelling," Bridget said.

Ericka smiled and rushed toward her sister and gave Bridget a hug as big as her pregnancy. "So good to see you. You look great."

"I'll look so much better in a few weeks. Look at Eve. She's doing fabulously. Six months pregnant and she looks like she could deliver after a full day of plowing fields."

"I hope not," Eve said, kissing Ericka on the cheek. "How's our little boy Leo?"

"Wonderful when he sleeps," Ericka said. "Which doesn't seem to happen at night."

"Oh, no," Pippa, Ericka's other sister said. "Hopefully, he'll sleep soon."

Ericka felt Pippa search her face and wished she could hide her emotions.

"You should call me for help," Pippa said.

"You're busy with your own baby," Ericka said.

"Not too busy for family. Any news on treatment?" Pippa asked.

"We're still working with hearing aids, but we haven't seen any improvement. Surgery may be in his future, but I want to make sure he's ready for it. Even with surgery, I'll teach him sign language. Of course, I'm learning it, too."

"You know the rest of us will be right there with you," she said. "We're happy to learn sign language. It would be good for the children. It would be good for all of us."

Ericka's heart swelled and she felt her eyes fill

with tears. "You're so sweet," she said, embracing Pippa. "So very sweet."

"Oh, stop," Pippa said. "Let's have a nice holiday lunch."

Ericka sat down with her sisters and sister-in-law and enjoyed a non-alcoholic cranberry spritzer along with a salad then a chicken crepe. Afterward, the women enjoyed chocolate mousse pie.

"Delicious," Bridget said.

"I agree," Ericka said.

"Stefan says you're doing a great job with the royal society conference," Bridget said.

Eve nodded. "He said the same to me."

"And me," Pippa added.

Ericka felt her cheeks heat with self-consciousness. "Thanks. Our colleagues have been very responsive."

"Good to hear," Eve said.

"I did receive an unsettling call this morning. You know that Sergenia is experiencing some unrest and the princesses and prince need a place to go. I think Chantaine would be perfect."

"But we're such a small country. How could they possibly hide here?" Pippa asked.

"Different identities and jobs." Ericka said. "They're amenable to such a plan."

"But would Stefan agree?" Bridget asked. "He has always wanted to remain neutral."

"Perhaps with the proper pressure," Ericka said, then glanced at Eve. "I hate to ask you."

"Give me more details later and I'll see what I can do. He's a stubborn, but wonderful, man," Eve said. "That's why we all love him."

"True," Pippa murmured then lifted her glass of soda. "To good health, happiness and the future of the Devereaux family."

"Here, here," Eve said. Bridget echoed the cheer as did Ericka.

"And next week, we meet publicly for the lighting of the royal Christmas tree," Eve said. "Bridget excused."

"If I can be there, I will," Bridget said, and then took another sip of her cranberry beverage. "In the meantime, we've just added a couple new goats to our zoo. Too many in my opinion. Do any of you want a goat?"

Silence followed. No takers. Ericka nearly choked over her spritzer, but she swallowed hard to quell the urge so that Bridget wouldn't mistake any sound she made as interest in taking on one of her goats.

After hugs all around, the women headed out the door. Ericka waited for her sisters and sister-in-law to leave then strode outside. A crowd awaited her, taking her by surprise.

"Hello," she managed and Treat appeared by her side.

Several people rushed toward her and Treat stepped in front of her. "Go to the car," he instructed her. "It's behind you."

Ericka rushed into the vehicle and Treat followed, driving her away from the crowd. "Next time, you won't leave last," he said sternly. "The crowd caught on after your sisters left."

"I was merely being polite," she protested.

"Next time you'll leave at the same time they leave or before," he said. "Think about it. If I hadn't been there, you could have been crushed."

She wanted to argue, but she knew he was right. She had underestimated how much the people wanted to connect with the royals. Now that she was a mother, she had to think more carefully about her safety. Thank goodness Treat had been there to protect her.

As he drove into her gated cottage, she felt a sense of safety settle over her. He helped her out of the car. "Thank you," she said quietly. "I was so busy fighting for my independence that I didn't realize I was sacrificing security." She looked into his gaze and noticed a scrape and a trickle of blood on his forehead. "You were hurt."

He shook his head. "Someone just got a little pushy."

Horrified, she lifted her hand. "I'm so sorry. We need to bandage it," she said.

"It's no big deal," he said. "Trust me. I've suffered much worse. Are you okay?"

"Me?" she echoed. "I'm fine. You took care of me."

"Good," he said. "Go inside. Take a break or a

nap. I'll be in the guest room unless you want to go anywhere."

"Of course," she said, standing on the porch as he walked away, wanting to put a bandage on his wound.

She felt a bit stupid after fighting her brother and Treat. As much as she wanted to think she could walk around like anyone else, she just couldn't. And she needed to face that fact for both herself and Leo.

The next day, the artificial pre-lit Christmas arrived outside her well-secured gate. Treat brought it inside. "Good news. There are only three pieces."

She looked at the mark on his forehead and pressed her lips together in concern.

"Stop staring at my little mark," he said, waving his hand in her face. "We need to get this tree put up for Leo. Where is the little sleep-stealer, anyway?"

"I hate to wake him," she said.

Treat dropped his chin and shook his head. "Well, he sure doesn't mind waking you. Besides, this will be a great visual experience for him."

"You're right," she said, clapping her hands as she strode toward the nursery and went against every motherly instinct by waking him. His sweet little eyebrows frowned as she lifted him from his crib.

"Trust me," she said. "You're gonna love this." Ericka was determined to continue talking to Leo even though he couldn't hear a word she was saying. In a few months, if he got the surgery, he would be able to hear her, so she needed to keep talking to him. Shifting him slightly, she grabbed his infant seat and walked to the den. "We're ready," she said as she set Leo into his seat.

"All right, all right," Treat said. "Let's rock and roll."

In a stunningly short amount of time, he put the tree up. Leo squirmed and sucked on his pacifier, but didn't cry.

Treat plugged in the lights and Leo stopped squirming and sucking, gaping at the lights.

"He loves it," Ericka said, delighted. "He loves the lights."

Treat smiled and nodded. "Bet he'll love it even more after we put on the ornaments."

"Oh," she said. "In the top of my closet in my bedroom. My sister gave them to me. I'll get them."

"No," he said. "You stay here. I'll get them."

Ericka turned to Leo and cooed. "You like the lights, don't you? Christmas is a wonderful time of love and hope, Leo," she said to her sweet infant son. "Never ever forget that."

Treat returned with the two boxes of ornaments and garland. "I hope you have some ornament hangers."

'I'm sure Valentina included them. We just need to find them," she said, and opened the boxes. It took only a few seconds to locate the hangers. "Here they are."

"Let's get moving, then. Garland first," he said as he began to spread the garland around the tree.

Ericka helped adjust the greenery. A half beat later, he grabbed a handful of hangers. Before she knew it, he hung five ornaments.

"Wait a minute," she muttered and began to hang silver and red balls. "You seem quite experienced at this."

"I was usually assigned the job of setting of the Christmas tree and decorating it," he said.

"Did you set a speed record?" she asked, hanging more ornaments.

"I wanted the tree decorated and then I wanted out of the house," he said, adding five more ornaments in no time at all.

"Why?" she asked, searching his gaze. "Why did you want out of your house?"

He shrugged as he hung the ornaments. "It wasn't all silver bells and gingerbread at my house," he said. "But that tree was good for everyone and I liked seeing it every time I came into the house. It was sad when we took it down on New Year's Day."

Ericka nodded. "I don't remember putting up the tree or taking it down. The rest of the palace felt cold. I remember wishing I could sleep under the tree, but, of course that wasn't possible. Last year, I spent Christmas with my sister in Texas. It was a totally different experience. I want to give that to Leo."

"You are," Treat said, and hung several more ornaments.

Within five minutes, they had mostly finished decorating.

Treat stepped away and gazed at the tree in approval. "Looks good."

Leo gave a high-pitched squeal of delight.

Ericka looked at her son then at Treat. "That's a first," she said.

"Well, it's his first Christmas. I'm gonna take that as a thumbs up. If he was looking at a Picasso, I might interpret it differently."

Ericka shook her head and laughed. His comment gave her a wonderful, surprising sense of lightness that she'd rarely experienced since she'd given birth to Leo. Everything felt so serious, so important. So dire.

She looked at Leo and he smiled and laughed. Joy filled her, starting in her belly and shooting up to her chest, throat and cheeks. She laughed again, staring at Leo and savoring his joy.

The moment was delightful and sacred. She couldn't have explained it in any language, but she was so glad she'd brought Leo to Chantaine and decided to have Christmas in this cottage. Her heart was so full that her eyes burned with tears.

"Thank you," she said, then began to repeat it in

every language she knew. *"Grazie, Merci, Gracias, Danke..."*

He put his finger over her mouth. "I get it," he said. "You're welcome." He looked at Leo and grinned. "You're very welcome."

Ericka sucked in a teeny tiny breath into her tight chest and nodded.

"I need to check the perimeter," he said, and met her gaze. "You've done well."

"Me?" she squeaked. "You're the one who put this together in no time."

"Don't underestimate yourself. Or Leo," he said, and walked away.

She watched him leave, then she burst into tears and stroked Leo's face as he stared at the Christmas tree in wonder.

That night, Treat did his job and he made sure the house was secure. He made sure the princess and Leo were secure. He stayed away from his precious charges but watched over them.

Grabbing a sandwich, he ate it then took a swim. He swam several laps and the water felt good over his body. Finally, he stopped and hung over the edge of the pool. He took several deep breaths to clear his head.

Images of Leo swam through his brain. The princess permeated his mind. Treat shook his head and swam several more laps. He was caught between driving himself to the point where he was forced to sleep and the point where he had to stay awake to take care of the princess and Leo.

Chapter Four

The cat greeted Treat as he entered the den the next morning, and he immediately realized that he needed to secure the tree. He raced to his room to retrieve twine then returned to the den.

"What are you doing? Why are you running around?" Princess Fredericka asked, appearing in the doorway, her hair mussed from sleep as she pulled a light robe around her.

"Because I need to secure this tree," he said. "I should have done it yesterday."

"Why?" she asked, clearly bemused.

"Because you have a cat," he said. "And cats love to tear up Christmas trees."

"Oh," she said, her sexy, sweet lips forming a perfect O.

Treat scanned the floor to make sure Sam hadn't already grabbed a few ornaments. Then he wrapped twine around the tree and tied it around a vent plug. He wrapped more twine around the tree and a chair leg. He wasn't all that happy with that choice, but he figured it was better than nothing.

Treat decided to place a nail in the wall and wrap yet another bit of twine around it.

"You think that's enough?" she asked.

"I hope so," he said. "But cats are clever and destructive."

"Sam won't be destructive. He's very sweet."

"How long have you had a cat?" he asked.

"Three months here. Longer in Texas," she said.

"How much longer in Texas?" he asked.

She shrugged. "Four months. Why?"

"Has Sam ever seen a Christmas tree?"

"No," she said then winced. "Problem?"

"Not now," he said, making a final tie from the tree.

The tuxedo cat looked at Treat innocently and began to wrap around his ankles. "Oh, look," she said. "He likes you."

"No, he's trying to rub his scent on me probably because he doesn't like my human smell."

Fredericka sniffed. "I don't smell anything."

Sam gave a meow.

"Time for breakfast," she said

Treat watched as the cat proudly strode to the kitchen with its tail upright. "What are Sam's habits?"

Fredericka shrugged. "He sleeps a lot during the day. He jumps on the shelf above Leo's crib and watches over him at night. He meows if we don't respond quickly enough to Leo's cries."

"Hmm," he said as he walked around the kitchen. He glanced on the top of the refrigerator and saw several plush toys. Pulling them down, he glanced at Fredericka. "Did you put these up here?"

She glanced at the toys and frowned in confusion. "No. Two of those are Leo's toys. One is a Christmas tree ornament."

Treat nodded. "Cats are sneaky," he said.

Fredericka frowned. "Maybe so, but Sam watches over Leo, so it's okay if he takes a few toys. It's not as if Leo will notice. He has tons of toys. Christmas is coming."

"You're defending your cat against your son?"

"Sam watches over Leo. Soon enough, Leo will hold onto his toys and Sam won't get any of them." She shot him a sideways glance. "Why don't you like Sam?"

Discomfort flooded through him. "It's not Sam."

"Then what is it?"

"I brought home a kitten one time. My dad made me give it away," he confessed.

"Oh," Fredericka said, her voice full of sympathy.

"Don't feel sorry for me," he said.

"Oh, I don't," she said. "I wanted a puppy when I lived at the palace and that was a big no-go." She glanced downward. "Sam is hugging your ankles again."

Treat looked down at the cat as he wound around his feet and shook his head. "I'm telling you he doesn't like my scent, so he's trying to replace the way I smell with the way he smells."

"Is that why he's purring?" she asked, crossing her arms over her chest.

Treat heard the sound and stared at the cat. He felt a softening toward the feline. Then he shook it off. "I have no idea why he's purring."

"I do," she said. "He's purring because he likes you. He's purring because you're a guy and he's glad to have another guy in the house."

You're nuts, he wanted to say, but he didn't. "I need to get some work done. Call me if you need me." He felt the gazes of both Fredericka and Puss in Boots on him as he strode back to the guest suite. This gig was getting weird.

After making a few calls, Ericka diapered and dressed Leo for a trip to the hospital to test his hearing. Before she left, Treat stepped in front of her car and waved his hands.

"Where are you going?" he called.

She pressed down the button to push down her window. "I'm taking Leo to get his hearing checked," she said.

"Why didn't you tell me?" he asked, stepping next to her window. "It's not on the schedule you gave me."

"I didn't put all the appointments on there. The doctor told me I could wait a week or two later for testing, but I don't want to wait," she said, and shook her head. "It may sound crazy, but I need to prepare myself if he's going to have surgery. It's serious surgery," she said. "It won't be performed until after Christmas, but I don't want to wait a long time for it. This surgery could help him speak and perform just like other kids by the time he hits five or six years old. At the same time, we'll continue sign language and other therapy. It's complicated. I don't expect you to understand."

Treat shoved his hands into the pockets of his jeans. "I understand more than you think," he said.

Ericka felt a crazy connection and bit her lip. "I need to go," she said.

"Well, get into the passenger seat because I'm going with you," he said as he opened her car door.

"This is not necessary," she told him. "I can handle this on my own."

"Not this time, Princess," he said with the smile of a shark.

"Don't call me princess," she said while she rounded the car to take the passenger seat.

"Okay," he said, sliding into the driver's seat. "If I don't call you princess, what do I call you?"

"Ericka," she said through her teeth.

He drove to the hospital and she wasn't sure if she was glad for his presence or not. She squirmed in her seat and glanced back at Leo as he dozed in his infant safety seat.

"You okay?" he asked.

"I'm fine, thank you," she said.

"You don't sound fine," he said.

She took a deep breath, but didn't reply.

"What's the worst thing that could happen during this examination?" he asked.

She frowned at his question. "I hadn't thought of that."

"Well, do," he said as he drove toward the hospital. "Are you afraid he has a tumor?"

"Oh, heavens, no," she said. "No tumors. I was just hoping his hearing would improve."

"And if it doesn't?" he prompted.

"Then we'll learn sign language and he'll get surgery. The prospect of surgery terrifies me," she said, her stomach knotting.

"Will he have the surgery tomorrow?" he asked.

"No," she said, staring at him. "It will be months."

"So you'll have time to prepare," he said.

She took a deep breath. "Yes, I will."

"Take more deep breaths," he said. "You're a strong woman. You can handle this. You'll get Leo through this."

Ericka knitted her eyebrows. "How do you know that?"

"I'm an excellent judge of character," he said. "Before I met you, I thought you were a prissy princess. You've already proved you're more than that."

Nonplussed, Ericka didn't know how to respond. She wasn't sure if she should be insulted or complimented. "Why did you think I was prissy?" she asked.

"Press," he said. "Press was all wrong."

She felt a soft warmth infuse her. She sank back into her seat and smiled. "I didn't like you when I first met you."

"I know," he said.

She glanced over at him. "You're too tall, too big."

"Someone may have felt more secure because of that," he muttered.

"I found you intrusive," she said, and slit her eyes at him. "Sam didn't, though."

"Sam wants another man around the house. He likes Leo, even though he steals his toys."

"I had no idea Sam was stealing toys and ornaments," she said.

"Cats are crafty," he said.

"You like Sam," she said. "Admit it."

"I don't trust him," he said. "But he seems like a good cat."

"You don't trust easily," she said.

"I don't," he admitted.

"Neither do I," she told him and looked out the window as he pulled into the hospital parking lot.

"Want me to wait or come in?" he asked as he pulled to the outpatient entrance.

"Wait please," she said as she got out of the passenger seat. She released Leo from his infant seat and held him against her. "We'll be back in about an hour."

Treat guided the car into a parking space and sat for five minutes that felt like forever. He got out of the car and paced the parking lot for thirty minutes. He checked his watch and did a few push-ups followed by planks. Glancing at his watch, he took several breaths and paced five more times around the parking lot.

Standing next to the car, he jogged in place and looked at the door to the hospital. Finally Ericka appeared with Leo in her arms. She didn't look happy as she walked toward the car.

"Hey," he said.

"Don't ask," she said with tears in her eyes. She began to put Leo in his infant safety seat. Treat helped her. She opened the door to the passenger side of the car and stepped inside.

Treat slide inside the vehicle and started the engine. Despite the sound of the engine, the silence between Ericka and him was deafening. She must have been terribly disappointed by the test results.

He backed out of the parking space and began the drive home. After five minutes of complete silence, he spoke. "Do you know who Thomas Edison is?"

"Of course, but I don't know much about him," she said.

"He was an American inventor," he said. "He invented the light bulb and is credited as the father of electricity. He was deaf."

She took a quick sharp breath. "I didn't know that."

"Leo is going to be an amazing man. He has an amazing mother."

Ericka looked away from him, outside the window and squished her eyes together. She didn't want to cry. She really, really didn't want to cry, but tears streams out the sides of her eyes. *Oh, heaven help her.* She sniffed and prayed that Treat wouldn't hear her.

She couldn't manage a word during the rest of the trip home and she breathed a sigh of relief as Treat pulled into the driveway. "Thanks for driving us," she said.

"No problem. I'm supposed to keep you safe," he said. "Another thought. Francisco Goya was a successful deaf artist."

She met his gaze and smiled at him. "Thank you for the encouragement."

"Even bad news isn't bad news," he said. "With any kind of news, you can make a plan."

She felt the click of certainty inside her. "Thank you," she said. "Really."

He shrugged. "Anytime. Let me help you with Leo."

"I can handle it," she said.

"Of course you can," he said. "But you don't always have to."

Treat picked up the baby from his infant seat and carried him inside the front door.

"Oh, brilliant," she said, seeing a package. "It's a rotating solar toy that promises to gently light up the nursery ceiling. I ordered it a few days ago."

"It could work," he said.

"You don't believe in it," she said.

He lifted one of his hands because he was carrying Leo in the other. "It's got to be better than waving a flashlight around in the middle of the night."

She pressed her lips together. "True."

Treat took Leo to the nursery. He set the baby down in his crib. "I'll set it up for you while you change his diaper."

"Are you afraid of dirty diapers?" she asked with a sly smile.

"I wouldn't use the term *afraid*," he said, then

returned to the front door to get the package while Nanny Marley appeared in the doorway.

"Oh, you're back," she said. "I was doing a bit of laundry so I didn't hear you come in at first. Any news on little Leo's hearing?" she asked as she headed for the nursery.

"I don't think the test showed any improvement," Treat said, carrying the package.

"Oh, dear," Nanny said, and sighed. "We have so many reasons to remain positive. He is a beautiful, healthy baby."

"That, he is," Treat agreed as he allowed Nanny to precede him into the nursery.

"Why, thank you," she said. "What a lovely gentleman."

Ericka looked up at him and twitched her lips in humor. "Gentleman?"

"Hey, I know a few things about manners. I wasn't raised in a barn. Let me open this box and see what tools I'll need," he said.

"And I'll take the baby. Perhaps he could use a bit of tummy time after riding in the car," Nanny said.

"Perfect," Ericka said, lifting the baby from the crib and kissing him on both chubby cheeks. "You can do some push-ups and planks and rolling over followed by a bottle. Then you'll have the best nap ever."

Leo smiled his toothless grin in response and Ericka gave him another squeeze. Then she handed him over to Nanny.

"You're a good mother," he said, and then turned back to the project.

"Thank you," she said, then gave a soft deprecating chuckle. "I'm muddling through. Are you sure I can't help you put the solar system together?" she asked.

"I've got it," he replied. "Don't you usually have some calls to return?"

"Always," Ericka said. "I'll check in later."

Treat watched Ericka walking away, enjoying the sway of her hips. Her blond hair skimmed her shoulders and her shapely pale calves peeked beneath the dress she wore. Treat couldn't help imagining what she would look like if that dress fell from her delicate shoulders down her back, over that ripe rear end to the floor.

Then he realized he was imagining the woman he was supposed to protect naked. Treat swore under his breath and gritted his teeth. He needed to keep his distance. He needed to keep a clear head. This job would make a huge difference in his future. Treat could *not* be attracted to the princess. For too many reasons to count.

Ericka frowned as she talked to the man speaking on behalf of the country of Sergenia's royal family. "I'm sorry, but I don't understand what you're asking," she said to a man named William Monroe.

"As you know, Sergenia has two princesses and a prince to represent their kingdom, but there is so much unrest. The royal family is in danger."

"And how can I help you with that?" she asked, drumming her fingers on an end table as she pumped her crossed leg.

"The royal family of Sergenia would like to seek asylum in your country," Mr. Monroe said.

"Asylum," she echoed, automatically stiffening. She knew Stefan would never agree to such an arrangement. "Public asylum? Do you really think that's wise? If there are people who have ill will for the Sergenia family, shouldn't they be secretly sheltered?"

"Possibly, but—"

"Mr. Monroe, I know my brother will not be willing to make a public issue. If you are looking for a place for the royal family to hide, then that may be a different situation," she said.

Silence followed. "The royal family would be grateful for the opportunity to reside in your country until the unrest in Sergenia has subsided," he finally said.

Ericka bit her lip. Heaven help her, this was not her area of expertise. "I'll research the matter and get back to you."

"Please don't wait long," Mr. Monroe said, then disconnected the call.

Ericka rubbed her forehead and stood. She felt as if she'd been given a huge responsibility. If she didn't respond appropriately, then the lives of the Sergenia royal family could be at stake. She said a silent prayer as she paced the den. She knitted her hands together. She would have to convince Stefan that hiding the Sergenia royals in Chantaine was the right thing to do.

Heaven help her.

Taking a deep breath, she headed for the kitchen and fixed herself a cup of tea. Sipping it, she sank into a seat. All was quiet in the house. Surprisingly enough, Leo was still napping after his active morning and early afternoon. She half wondered if she should awaken him. She didn't want him napping so long that he wouldn't sleep tonight.

Wandering down the hall, she spotted Nanny Marley reading in the sitting room.

"He's still asleep?" Ericka asked.

Nanny looked up from her book and nodded. "Yes, ma'am. I can wake him if you like," she said.

"I hesitate to do that," she said. "Sleeping babies and all that."

"True," Nanny said. She nodded toward the video screen. "He must've worn himself out this morning."

"Maybe we should do that more often," Ericka said, then laughed.

"Perhaps," Nanny said. "We must be careful not to coddle him due to his—"

"Hearing issues," Ericka finished for the woman and nodded. "He's a strong, smart baby. He needs exercise and stimulation. Treat mentioned that he especially needs visual stimulation due to his deafness."

"That sounds right to me," Nanny said. "Although heaven knows you've exposed him to sign language. You've been as perfect a mother as could be."

Ericka sighed. "I'm not sure about that, but I'm working on it. We're so lucky to have you."

Nanny smiled. "You're a lovely girl. Leo will turn out fine. Trust my word," she said.

Ericka could only hope Nanny's words would be true. Soon enough, Leo awakened. Ericka fed him and conducted the sign language lesson even though Leo seemed a bit bored. She lifted his hands so that he could physically experience the meaning of the signs. He seemed to enjoy the physical engagement.

Deciding to take him outside for a bit, she put a tiny hat over her ears and put him into his stroller. The second she opened the gate, however, Treat appeared.

"An evening walk?" he asked, meeting her gaze.

"I thought he might enjoy it," she said. "I don't get him out often enough."

"Aside from his busy day today," he said, walking beside her.

She noticed again his height and his wide shoulders. "Do you exercise every day?"

"Five out of seven days," he said. "Why do you ask?"

"I just wondered. You seem very athletic," she said.

"I always have been," he said. "I went to college on a football scholarship. I thought my future was in football."

"But not," she said.

"An injury can change your life in an instant," he said.

"But you don't appear injured," she said.

"I exercise to compensate," he said. "I was told that another football injury could cripple me."

"Yet, you're a security man," she said. "You don't worry."

He laughed. "Security is much more mental than football. If someone tackles me, they probably won't weigh over two hundred pounds. If they do, I'll mess up my knee for a better reason than chasing pigskin."

Her respect for him went up another notch. "I'm starting to understand why Stefan chose you," she said. "Not that I like it any better."

Treat chuckled again. "I told you I would disappear into your household."

"Not yet," she said. "I didn't get a chance to look at the solar system ceiling light. What do you think?"

"Really?" he asked.

"Really," she said as she studied him.

"I want one of my own."

Ericka couldn't contain a laugh. "Why?"

"This thing is slick. Glow-in-the-dark planets with a remote control battery-operated light. I don't sleep that well, but I think this thing might lull me to sleep," he said.

"It sounds even better than I thought it would be," she said.

"If you ever decide to get rid of it…"

She smiled at him, liking his combination of toughness and masculinity. How could she explain that she liked the fact that he coveted her son's new solar system night light? How utterly strange.

Chapter Five

Despite Leo's new toy, he still didn't sleep through the night. Ericka discovered, however, that after a change and some cuddles, she could set him down in the crib and put on the solar system light and he would fall asleep. Although she was weary, her mind was busy with concerns about the Sergenian royals, not to mention the public service announcement she, a British Duke and an Italian royal would make to support clean water for everyone that was scheduled for the next day. Her sister Pippa was in town and had agreed to entertain the visitors with sightseeing and dinner after the commercial was filmed. She tossed and turned until Leo's cries awakened her early the next morning.

After feeding him, she handed him over to Nanny while she showered and got ready for the shooting of the commercial. As she fixed her hair and applied cosmetics, she realized she'd forgotten how long it took to transform herself to the polished state that was de rigueur when she lived in France with her ex-husband. Now that she was a mom, she couldn't imagine investing so much time in a daily routine.

She brushed a kiss on Leo's forehead, leaving a lipstick print. "Oops. I didn't mean to mark you," she said, and dabbed at it with her fingers.

"Oh, don't worry about it," Nanny said. "I'll take care of it. Besides, it just shows how much he's loved."

"If you say so," Ericka said skeptically. "Something tells me he won't like a lipstick print from me once he hits his teen years. Oh, heavens, I can't believe that thought crossed my mind. I'm so focused on getting him to his one-year birthday."

"And that's the way it should be," Nanny said. "I've had two teenaged children. No need to go there before necessary. I hope your photo shoot goes well."

"Thanks, Nanny," she said as she walked out the front door to where Treat stood by the car. Dressed in a jacket, white shirt and dark slacks, he looked dark and powerful. With his sunglasses hiding his eyes, he had an air of mystery.

She felt a twist of awareness at his extreme masculinity. He did nothing to tone it down, although she wasn't sure if that was even possible.

"Good morning," she said. "How are you?"

"Good," he said as he opened the passenger door then rounded the car to get inside. "And you?" He started the car and used the remote to open the gate.

"Well, thank you. You'll be happy to know the new solar system seemed to help Leo with his sleep. He woke up in the middle of the night, but then fell right back to sleep after I turned on the timed light. I wish I could say the same about my own sleep. Too much on my mind," she said. "Did you sleep well?"

"I got about four hours," he said.

She cringed. "That's not enough for me."

"I don't require much. You know how it goes. Everything gets quiet and your mind wakes up. I took a swim and that helped."

"In the middle of the night? I didn't hear you," she said, wondering what thoughts kept him awake at night.

"I hope not," he said with a chuckle.

"Maybe I should try that next time I have a hard time sleeping," she said. "Go for a swim."

"Let me know if you decide to do that," he said as he continued to drive toward the beach selected for the shooting of the public service announcement. "I don't want you drowning."

"I'll have you know I'm an excellent swimmer. I was raised on an island and my father made sure all of could swim. He didn't pay much attention to us other than that, but he was adamant that we all learn to swim well."

"He didn't pay much attention to you?" he echoed. "Don't you have several siblings? Why have children if you don't want to pay any attention to them?"

"Yes, there are six of us. He had children for the sake of progeny. Plus, if there were more of us, he could send us off to make appearances and he could go yachting. He loved his yacht. More than anything," she murmured, remembering how often he'd been absent due to his love of the sea and perhaps several women.

"Interesting," Treat said. "That wasn't in the report Stefan gave me."

"Oh, it wouldn't be. Stefan rarely says anything disparaging privately about my father and he would never put such a thing in writing. What was in that report, anyway?"

"Just every fact about you since your birth," he said.

"Oh, Lord," she said, feeling a rush of embarrassment. "I'm sure he made sure to note the face that I was the bad princess during my teenage years."

"It wasn't worded exactly that way, but…"

"I've changed," she said firmly.

"I can tell," he said. "He also gave a few details about your ex-husband."

"Stefan doesn't trust my ex-husband," she said.

"Should he?"

"I suppose not," Ericka said as she looked out the window. "I prefer not to think about him. I don't see him or have to deal with him, so to me, he doesn't exist."

"What about the fact that he is Leo's father?" he asked.

"He knew I was pregnant when I left him and he's made no effort to contact me since. Leo's birth made the news, but I've stayed out of the spotlight and I won't discuss him during interviews except to say that Leo is beautiful and growing by leaps and bounds."

"Works for me," he said, and pulled alongside the beach where several others were already setting up the commercial.

Fighting a sudden attack of nerves, she took a deep breath. "I hope this goes quickly," she muttered as he helped her out of the car.

"Why? Many women would envy your beauty," he said.

"I've never enjoyed being in front of the camera," she told him.

"But you married a filmmaker," he said.

"I wasn't in the films," she told him. "The reason I married my husband was because he took me away from Chantaine. My life wasn't studied under a microscope in France. At that time, I just wanted to escape scrutiny. The only time I had to put on a show was for a premiere or awards show."

"If you hate it so much, why did you agree to do it?"

"It's for an excellent cause. It's a very small sacrifice on my part to raise awareness. If my tiny contribution can wield influence, than I should use it." She gave a silly half smile, half moue. "Time to be a grown-up."

Treat walked behind her as she headed for the small group on the beach. She wore a simple blue dress that skimmed her curves without being too tight. Classy, feminine and, in his mind, sexy. Walking in the sand exaggerated the sway of her hips. She probably cursed the way her hair fluttered in the wind. To others, she may have appeared a smiling, friendly, blue-eyed blonde, but he knew there was a lot going on under that pale, creamy skin and "Her Highness" label.

Ericka was complicated with a heart like a mama bear for her baby and devotion to her country and sisters and brothers. She was so busy with the demands of her life that Treat wondered if she had any idea how beautiful she was. He was finding himself thinking about her far more than he should. She was a job, a means to an end. He'd protected other beautiful women. Why was she different?

He watched as she patiently did her part during

each take, and there were several. Finally, two hours later, the director appeared satisfied and Ericka took several moments to speak to each person at the shoot. She also gave Pippa a hug and thanked the Duke and Italian royal for their participation.

Treat escorted her to the car and she sank into her seat. "Thank goodness that's over," she said. "Everyone was wonderful, but we all seemed to mess up on different takes."

"Where to now?" he asked, sensing she'd felt a little trapped by the experience. It wasn't quite midday.

She glanced at him in surprise. "Home, I guess."

Treat nodded. "Home, it is."

She let out a sigh. "Well, maybe we could make one stop along the way."

Treat nodded again. "Where?"

"Gelato. There's a place in town that makes fabulous gelato, almost as good as Italian. I already know I want dark chocolate," she said. "You'll have to get some, too, but you're not allowed to choose vanilla."

Treat smiled, but mentally planned the visit in his head in order to protect Ericka from unpleasant surprises. "What if I like vanilla?"

"Then you'll have to choose that a different time," she said.

"As you wish, Your Highness," he said.

"Don't start with that now," she warned him, but laughed.

Treat hadn't seen her this playful even when she

was playing with her son. It was as if every exchange with Leo had a serious undertone. Following her directions to the gelato shop, he secured a parking spot down the block and escorted her to the shop.

"You're going to love this," she told him as he constantly watched their surroundings both inside and outside.

Two servers, one male and one female, dressed in uniforms stared at Ericka in surprise.

"Your Highness?" the young woman finally managed.

"You weren't supposed to notice," Ericka whispered and smiled. "You have the best gelato in Chantaine and I want a scoop of dark chocolate."

"Yes, of course, ma'am," the woman said as she prepared Ericka's gelato.

"What kind do you want?" Ericka asked Treat with a curious expression on her face.

"You choose," he said, his attention focused on their surroundings.

"That's no fun," she said, her face falling. "Do you prefer fruit or chocolate?"

"Fruit," he said. "I'll take the berry gelato."

Treat took a bite of his and was surprised by the vivid flavor.

"Excellent, isn't it?" she asked, savoring a bite of her own.

He watched her lick her lips and felt his gut tighten in awareness.

Suddenly the waitress came up to their table again. "Your Highness, would you possibly allow us to take a photo with you?"

Ericka wrinkled her nose. "Then everyone will think I'm playing hooky," she said.

"Oh, no," the female server said. "We can say your visit was official business."

Ericka laughed. "Okay, but I'm not sure how you can sell that. Treat, would you mind taking a photo with this lovely woman's smart phone?"

Treat nodded and took the photos. "Just give us ten minutes before you post it for the world to see," he told her. "Finish in the car?" he asked Ericka. At her nod, he escorted her to the car. He inhaled his small portion of the dessert and started the car.

"Already finished?" she asked, still taking slow bites of her own.

"I wanted to get on the road before there's a crowd," he said.

"Oh, I was so busy enjoying the outing that I forgot you're working," she said.

"Your brother wouldn't forgive me if I forgot to protect you," he said. "That's always number one."

She sighed and took her last bite of gelato. "Well, it was nice while it lasted. Hope it wasn't too much of a trial," she said, and shot him a glance from beneath her eyelashes that almost looked flirtatious.

Treat felt that pull in his gut again. He would have to put a stop to it. He'd figure out how soon enough, he promised himself. In the meantime, he shook his head. "I can't think of any man who would consider that a trial," he told her in a dry tone. At the same time, she seemed to be playing havoc with a place inside him he'd considered sewn up tight and under wraps.

"Thanks for the field trip." She sighed and leaned her head back against the headrest in the car. "Maybe my sister Bridget is right. She keeps saying I need to get out more, but I don't like leaving Leo."

"You could take him out every now and then. Has he been to the beach?"

"Not since he was an infant. I'm afraid the paparazzi will catch a photo of him wearing his hearing aids. I want to protect him as long as I can," she said.

Treat shrugged. "You could always go early in the morning and put a hat on him," he said. "For that matter, you could put him in the pool, too."

"I'll see," she said. "Like you said, my number one job is to protect him."

"Are you afraid of the questions?" he asked.

She looked away for a moment as if she didn't appreciate his query. "Perhaps. I don't have all the answers. I may never. I don't want anyone to make fun of him. That would break my heart."

"Oh, I don't know about that. You've got a strong mama-bear thing going on. If anyone caused harm to your baby in any way, I wouldn't be surprised if you broke some bones."

"That may be a slight exaggeration. I'm not normally a violent person."

"But if someone threatened Leo?"

"I like to think it would never get that far," she said.

Treat gave a short, emphatic nod and pulled the car past the gate to the front door. Cutting the engine, he rounded the car and helped her out of the vehicle.

"Thank you," she said. "My new part-time genie planned to prepare an afternoon meal today. Would you like to join us?"

"Thanks," he said, knowing such a move would be dangerous. "But I have computer work."

Her eyes darkened with a twinge of disappointment. "Of course. Ciao, then," she said as she walked into the cottage.

Treat stood there, looking after her, for a full moment after she closed the door behind her. His attraction to her was ridiculous. She was the princess of a Mediterranean island for Pete's sake. He was a wrong-side-of-the tracks kid from Texas. He knew he wasn't the kind of man who would normally catch her eye. He had to be careful. He knew enough about security to know that these situations could be emotionally intense for some people although he'd never had a problem before. He sure as shooting didn't need a problem now, especially since this job could help him expand his company internationally. He'd worked hard the past several years. He didn't want to lose all his hard-won progress just because he was developing a stupid crush on a princess.

Raking his hand through his hair, he returned to the guest suite and turned on his laptop then grabbed one of the jars of peanut butter he'd brought with him from the States and slapped a peanut butter sandwich together before he returned to his desk. The welcome screen rose to greet him. There was always work to do, he told himself. Work that would help him forget everything he had lost so quickly in his college year. Work was a panacea. Always.

Treat checked the perimeter several times then knocked on the door to the house that evening. Nanny answered. "How are you tonight, Mr. Walker?"

"I'm fine. How are you, the princess and the baby?" he asked.

"All well. The baby appears quite charmed with his new ceiling mobile of the solar system. Her Highness has either been working all afternoon or playing sign language games with Leo. I swear that woman hardly ever stops. I would just like to see her get a full night's rest."

Treat smiled and nodded. He could always count on Nanny giving him a mouthful of information. "I'm glad to hear everything is going well. I hope everyone has a good evening. I'm only a few steps away. Call me if you need me."

"Yes, sir," she said.

Treat returned to his suite and made a few calls.

His agreement with Stefan allowed him to continue to make future business plans and contacts. So far, it was quiet job, but he never let down his guard. Not even when he slept. He'd set multiple alarms and had a backup with the palace.

Hours later, he looked at the clock and realized he needed to hit the sack. He did a weight workout in the suite, but still felt restless, so he put on a swimsuit and went to the pool. Lap after lap, he took then felt a slight disturbance in the water. Rising, he looked around and saw Ericka hanging on to the side of the wall.

He took several breaths. "What are you doing here?" he asked.

"You said you swim when you can't sleep. Why can't I do the same?" she asked.

He studied her for a long, hard moment and saw that she wasn't being coquettish. She, like him, just wanted a decent night of sleep. "Have you tried meditation?" he asked.

She sighed. "The trouble with meditation is that I keep interrupting the oms with what I worry about."

He chuckled, easily identifying with her quandary, although he struggled with more regrets than worries. "Okay, start your laps. I'll sit on the side to make sure you're okay."

"I'll do fine," she told him with a prim frown and began swimming.

He couldn't fault her form and he liked that she

didn't move too quickly. A nice, steady pace. She did a flip turn against the wall and he was impressed yet again. On her back, she kicked like a pro. After the next turn, she did a great breaststroke, tagged the wall and did another length of breaststroke.

She smiled as she approached him, taking several heaving breaths. "I was never good at butterfly."

"Looks like you're good at everything else," he said.

She gulped in several more breaths. "Again, my father encouraged competitive swimming."

"That can be good and bad," he said.

"It was probably one of the few good things he did," she said. "I need a few more laps."

She did a few more and he couldn't help admiring her body. He liked her combination of athleticism and feminine softness. She relied on the breaststroke for a couple more laps then turned on her back and did the backstroke for two more laps.

She grabbed the side of the pool and gasped for breath. "I think that's enough for now," she said.

"Should you have stopped sooner?" he asked.

"No. You always have to push yourself when you're swimming," she said, still taking deep breaths. "Even if you feel like you're dying."

"And this is why I want you to let me know if you decide to do night swimming," he said.

"Spoilsport," she said as she rested her head on

the side of the pool. "The water feels nice at night, doesn't it?"

He nodded. "Do you worry about Leo at night?"

"Yes," she said. "I worry about what I may have done during my pregnancy that caused his deafness."

"Isn't this a genetic issue?"

"Most likely," she said. "But I still wonder. I wonder if I could have prevented it."

"You couldn't have," he said.

"How can you be so confident? How can you know that I did everything possible to protect Leo during my pregnancy?"

"Because I know you did. I know you couldn't prevent his deafness," he said. "And you can't make his world perfect now. It's okay that you can't. You just need to be his mom and love him no matter what. You can't fix everything. You don't have to."

Ericka sighed. "I wish I had superpowers and could fix everything."

"Stop wishing," he said. "Just do what you can every day. You get to the end of the day, say a prayer and enjoy a full night of rest every night."

She chuckled. "A full night of rest every night?" she echoed. "That's a fantasy world for me."

"Do another four laps," he said.

"I'm tired," she protested.

"Not tired enough," he told her. "You're still arguing."

She groaned, but did the laps, albeit slowly. After

the fourth, she dragged herself out of the pool. "You're not as bad as my father, but you're close. I'm way tired."

"Good. Maybe you'll sleep now," he said. "Let Nanny do her job if Leo awakens during the night."

"It makes me feel like a slacker when I don't get up with him at night," she said.

"Take a break. It's not as if you have a husband to take a turn," he said.

Ericka bit her lip. "And that's another subject. No father figure for him."

"He's got plenty of father figures. More than most," Treat said. "Your brothers. Your brothers-in-law. I hear there's more one road to Mecca. You're taking it."

"If you say so," she said, wrapping a towel around her.

"I do. Now you're growing very sleepy. Very sleepy. Your eyes are closing," he said.

"You're a good guy, Treat, but you're no hypnotist."

"Bet you fall asleep within five minutes," he said.

"But will I stay asleep?" she asked.

"Yes," he said, then waited until she left to swim ten more laps. He wanted Ericka more than ever.

Chapter Six

The next night, Ericka sent Treat a text informing him that she planned to take Leo for an early morning trip to the ocean. Ericka had strange feelings about Treat. He showed her a lot of heart then totally backed away as if he wanted to remain as professional as possible.

That's what he should do, she told herself as she crawled into bed and pulled the sheets up to her chin. That's what she and Stefan wanted. A true professional. It was his good heart that was wearing her down. It was his good heart that made her feel both weak and strong. And she totally needed to get over those feelings.

She took a deep breath and tried the meditation

exercise she'd learned earlier in the day, and surprisingly enough, she drifted off to sleep.

Reality smudged with dreams. *Treat took her into his arms and his body felt so strong and muscular. His heartbeat drummed against her chest.*

"I want you," he confessed. "I want you, but I shouldn't."

She felt herself melt in his arms. "I want you, too. I was afraid I was the only one."

"No," he said, and lowered his mouth to hers. He slid his tongue between her lips and she drank in the taste of him. She couldn't prevent herself from rubbing her chest against his.

He groaned in response. "You feel so good," he said. "I want more of you," he told her. "I want you naked."

Her heart beat so quickly she wondered if she would faint. She slid her fingers through his short hair and opened her mouth for a soulful kiss.

Moments later, as if through magic, her clothes floated away, as did his. Her nipples meshed against his hard chest. She felt him naked against her from head to toe. He took her mouth and the kiss seemed to go on forever and ever.

"I can't get enough of you," he muttered against her lips as he slid his hand between them and rubbed her where she was swollen and needy. "Can't get enough."

"I want you," she said. "I need you..."

Groaning, he pushed her legs apart and...

Ericka reached for him, arching her body.
"Treat..."

A sound permeated her dream. A baby crying. Ericka sat up in bed, fully aroused and full of want and need. She gasped for breath and shook her head, chasing consciousness. "Oh, my—"

She shook her head again and realized she was hearing Leo's cry. Rubbing her forehead, she climbed from her bed and went to the nursery. She clicked on the light for the solar system and waited a few seconds. She could hear Leo squirming in his crib then he quieted. She felt him slurp his thumb into his mouth as he studied the lights on the ceiling.

He was comforting himself, she realized. He needed a little extra help, but he was working at it, sucking his thumb and staring at the solar system. Her chest tightened and she felt a tear run down her cheek at the realization. Her baby boy was doing the best he could. She would do the best she could for him even if the best she could do frightened her nearly to death.

Ericka returned to bed and waited for sounds from Leo, but he remained quiet, hopefully sleeping. She tried meditation, but she fell asleep during the middle of it. Proof she was exhausted, but also felt safe. She would have to think about that safe feeling tomorrow. Or the next day.

* * *

The next morning, Ericka arose to the sound of her alarm and dragged herself out of bed. Despite her drowsiness, excitement raced through her. She was taking Leo to the beach!

She stripped then pulled on her bathing suit followed by a pair of shorts and a t-shirt. She went to her bathroom, splashed her face with water and brushed her teeth.

"Your Highness?" Nanny said, wearing her night robe, as Ericka entered the hallway. "I believe the baby is asleep."

"For how long?" Ericka asked.

"Most of the night," the older woman said. "I only heard him once and he quickly went back to sleep or I would have gotten up with him."

"It's the solar system," Ericka whispered. "I pray it continues to work. In the meantime, I'm taking him to the beach."

Nanny's eyes widened. "The beach? Are you sure that's wise? Won't the water be too cool for him?"

"If it is, he can enjoy the sand. This baby lives on an island and he's only been to the beach once. I want him to experience the ocean, if only for a few minutes."

Nanny gave a thoughtful nod. "I think it's a good idea. The boy loves new experiences."

Ericka smiled, glad Nanny approved of her idea. Even though Ericka knew it was the right thing to do,

Nanny's affirmation added to her confidence. "See you later," she said. "Go back to bed."

"As you wish, ma'am," Nanny said, tightening the belt of her robe and returning to her room.

Ericka rushed to the nursery and broke one of her cardinal rules. She awakened Leo. He blinked his sleepy eyes and rubbed them then met her gaze as she changed his diaper.

"Good morning," she whispered, even though she knew he couldn't hear him. She signed the words and repeated them then smiled.

He smiled his toothless grin in return.

"Aren't you handsome," she said to him and stroked his forehead. She grabbed a few more articles of clothing and a bottle. He was hungry and quickly downed the formula. Ericka lifted him against her shoulder and a burp escaped. "Aren't you the efficient one this morning?" she asked, then grabbed her diaper bag and raced out the door.

Treat was waiting next to the car. Her heart leaped at the sight of him. She told herself to ignore her wayward reaction to him.

"You think he's ready for the ocean?" he asked.

"We'll start with the sand and end with the ocean. I don't want him to get too cold," she said, and placed Leo in the infant safety seat. "I think he's ready for an adventure."

"He's always ready for an adventure," Treat said.

She glanced at him. "And how do you know that?"

Treat shrugged. "He's just that kind of guy."

Ericka stuck a pacifier in Leo's mouth and he suckled it for all he was worth, as if he knew this would be one of his first great adventures.

Sliding into the passenger seat, Ericka gave Treat direction to the privately owned beach of the Devereaux family. Although the beach was private, it was no match for the long lenses of cameras from the paparazzi. Since it was December and early morning, however, they had a great shot at avoiding the photographers.

Treat pulled down a sandy road and stopped when the beach was in sight. "I think we're here."

"I think we are," she said, excitement thrumming through her. Pulling on a baseball cap, she got out of the car before Treat could assist her and started to release Leo from his safety seat. She began to pick him up.

"Hat," Treat reminded her, and she paused.

"Right. Thanks," she said as she put a ball cap on the baby's head.

Leo stared at her, still sucking on his pacifier. His expression seemed to say, *Are you sure you know what you're doing? I don't know if I like this thing on my head.*

"You're gonna love the cap," she told him and pulled him against herself.

The trio walked toward the gentle lap of the waves on the beach. Not too far from the surf, she sank onto the sand and put Leo between her legs. "How do you like this?" she asked, and stroked his head while keeping his cap in face.

Leo continued to suck on his pacifier as he stared at the surf.

Ericka lifted a handful of sand and spilled it over his tiny palm. He glanced down at his hand and she repeated the motion. His sucking slowed as he studied the sand in his hand. A few seconds later, he dipped his hand into the sand and squeezed his fingers through it.

"Good for you," she said, patting his arm. "You're a smart one."

Leo played in the sand for the next several moments and Ericka loved watching him explore.

"Are you sure you want to try the ocean? It may be a bit cold," Treat said.

"I agree," she said. "Maybe we could just dip his feet in it."

Treat grabbed Leo against him and pulled Ericka rise to her feet. They took a few steps into the ocean.

"A little chilly," she said.

"We can let him have his own opinion," Treat said and, still holding Leo against him, he dipped the baby's feet in the ocean.

Leo paused again in suckling his pacifier.

"How was that for you, big guy?" he asked, and then dipped his tiny feet into the surf again.

Leo kicked his feet and legs.

Ericka laughed. "I don't know if that's a yes or no."

"He's not screaming, so let's call it a yes," Treat said as he dipped the baby's feet in a wave once more. Leo opened his mouth and cackled, dropping his pacifier. Treat caught the paci before it fell into the ocean.

Ericka stretched out her hands for Leo, and Treat passed the baby to her. "You may be an ocean baby, after all," she said. "We'll have to bring you again."

"Are you going to take a dip?" Treat asked.

"Not this time," she said. "It's a little cool for me."

He nodded, staring out at the ocean. "I only went to the ocean twice when I was growing up. Loved it both times. Once, we went in winter and I swam even though it was freezing cold," he said, then chuckled.

"You should go now," she urged.

He shook his head. "I can't be protecting you if I'm swimming in the ocean."

She sighed. "Well, darn."

"I'll come back another time on my day off," he said.

"What day off?" she asked as they walked out of the water. "You haven't taken a day off since you started."

"I will sometime," he said.

"But then I won't get to see you swim in the ocean," she said.

"I'm sure I wouldn't win any prizes for form," he told her. "You won't be missing much."

"I bet you dive into the waves," she said.

He looked at her and his lips lifted in a half-grin. "Who are you? The psychic princess?"

She walked on the sand toward the car. "That's what I want to see. You diving into the waves."

"Why?" he asked.

"I'd like to see what you were like as a kid," she said.

He shook his head. "The kid in me doesn't come out very often. The kid had a complicated childhood."

"How complicated?"

"I told you more than enough. You're a client," he reminded her.

His statement felt like a smack in her face. She took a quick breath. "You were just part of an amazing, private experience. How many times have you taken a baby with his mom for a dip in the ocean?"

"Never," he admitted.

"Leo and I are not just clients," she told him tersely, and put Leo into his car seat. "Do you have his pacifier?"

"Here," he said, and pressed the pacifier into her hand.

He opened the passenger door and she slid into her seat without looking at him. She heard and felt Treat get into the car and start the ignition. She kept her gaze trained forward. She was so incredibly insulted and not sure why. Why should she care what staff thought of her?

"Sorry," he said as he pulled past the gate to the front door and stopped. "That was out of line. I've dealt with kids before, but not infants. And not you. I just need to keep my head on straight."

Her heart turned over at the intent expression on his face. His gaze forced her to think more about how she was feeling at this moment. This *was* a job for him, one that would end. He was a human being with feelings. Deeper feelings than she'd expected. He was the first man who'd inspired crazy emotions inside her. Emotions she hadn't felt in a long time. The situation was very complicated, but that didn't change the fact that she wanted him.

"I understand," she said. "I'll get Leo inside for his bottle and a nap."

"And your morning full of work," he said, stepping out of the car. He unhooked Leo from his car seat. "You did good, big guy," he murmured to the baby. "Want me to bring him inside?"

"I can do it," she said, taking Leo into her arms. She inhaled his baby scent and gave him a kiss on his chubby cheek. "Thank you," she said, and walked into the cottage. Feeling Treat's gaze on her as she walked, Ericka felt a tiny sliver of comfort. He was as affected by her as she was by him. She wasn't completely alone. Small comfort, she told herself. Neither could do anything about their feelings.

Ericka looked down at Leo as he stared up at

her. Maybe doing nothing was for the best. She had enough on her hands and in her arms.

That afternoon Ericka decided to pay a visit to the palace. She needed to talk to Stefan personally. Despite the fact that her biggest concern was Leo, thoughts of the Sergenian royals plagued her. She needed to get Stefan on her side.

Treat insisted on driving her and she did all she could not to think about the dream she'd had the other night and how much he affected her and how hard it was to be this close to him. When they arrived at the palace, she nearly leaped out of the car. "I'll be back soon."

She'd called ahead and Stefan had agreed to meet with her provided she wasn't complaining about security. Truth was, her security could complain about her, but that was another story.

His assistant opened his office door at her second knock. "Your Highness," the assistant said.

"Good afternoon," she said as she walked toward Stefan.

He stepped from behind his desk and kissed her on the cheek. "You sounded upset," he said.

She kissed him on the cheek in return. "I'm concerned. I received a call about the royal family of Sergenia."

"The country has experienced a lot of unrest," he said.

She nodded. "The royal family is in danger. They need a place to go."

He gave her a thoughtful look. "You know we don't get involved in the politics of other countries."

"This isn't about politics," she said. "It's about people. What if one of us had needed a place to go because Chantaine had become more violent?"

"We take care of our people," he said. "We put our people first. That's why Chantaine is peaceful."

"But this isn't asking a lot. They just need a place to disappear," she said.

Stefan shook his head. "I appreciate your good heart, but I have to think about the greater good. I don't want violent people from Sergenia taking revenge on our citizens."

"But if we kept it secret—"

"Fredericka," he said. "The answer is no."

She understood her brother's point, but her heart still tugged at the thought of the young Sergenian royals in danger. She'd done research on them. They were good people.

She bit her lip. "You know I could have done this behind your back."

He narrowed his eyes in a way that would have intimidated her five years ago. Not so much today. "I hope your honor as a Devereaux means more to you than that."

"I hope you'll think about the Devereaux honor and how we're trying to make a new name for ourselves. Please reconsider." She lifted her hand when he opened his mouth. "Don't say anything, just please reconsider. Have a good evening in your very safe palace, in your very safe country. Not all are quite so fortunate," she said as she walked out of his office.

Striding out of the palace, she found Treat waiting for her just outside the door. He quickly exited the car and assisted her inside. Ericka jerked her seatbelt into place.

"That was fast," he said, sliding back into his seat and pulling out of the parking area.

"Fast, but not successful. Being honest and honorable can be a total pain," she muttered.

Ericka felt Treat's gaze on her as he stopped at a stop sign. "Honor? Honest? You want to explain?"

"Not really," she said, feeling extremely frustrated. "Everyone thinks I have this superficial job where all I do is plan meetings with other members of royalty, but other things can happen. I can get calls that are more than fluff. What am I supposed to do about those calls?"

"What are you talking about?" he asked.

Ericka took a deep breath and crossed her arms over her chest. "Nothing."

"Doesn't sound like nothing to me, but as long as it doesn't affect your security," he said.

"Of course it doesn't affect my security," she said, and sighed. "It affects the security of the royals in Sergenia, but if you repeat that, I truly will kill you."

He gave a whistle. "Sergenia. Oh, that place is a mess."

"Yes, it is, and the royals need a place to go," she said.

"Here? Chantaine? Why here?" he asked. "Why not a larger country?"

"You must agree we're a bit more isolated. We're not a target," she said.

"True, I guess. I take it Stefan didn't agree."

"He didn't, but I'm not giving up," she said. "I put in the initial guilt screws. I'll try again in a few days."

He glanced at her and chuckled. "You're a little scary when you get determined."

She smiled back at him. "I'll take that as a compliment."

Shortly later, they arrived back at the cottage and Ericka thanked Treat as she entered the house. Nanny greeted her, holding Leo in her arms.

"He's been a bit fussy this afternoon. The hearing doctor called the house phone. I couldn't get to it in time. I think he left a message."

Ericka glanced at her cell phone and spotted a missed call from Leo's doctor. She listened to the message and her stomach fell. The doctor confirmed what she had already sensed. Leo was profoundly deaf. But he could have life changing surgery in January or February.

The news left her in a quandary because the surgery presented a fair amount of risk. The possibility of endangering Leo crippled her. In normal circumstances, she would want to put it off. The flip side was that if Leo's surgery was successful, he would be able to speak normally and hear more than he ever could with hearing aids.

Ericka went to Nanny and extended her arms. "I'd like to hold him for a while," she said.

"Of course," Nanny said. "Simon left groceries and dinner. Would you like some soup?"

"That sounds perfect," Ericka said as she carried Leo to the den. He stared up at her with his wide blue eyes. "How are you doing, little man? I thought you would be all tuckered out from your adventure in the ocean this morning."

Leo squirmed in her arms and Ericka realized her darling baby had gas. "Maybe I can help," she said, sitting down and putting his tummy over her knees. He gave several burps and let air out his backside then seemed to relax.

She pulled him onto her lap. "Better now?"

He made a moue, but didn't cry. "Bet you're hungry now," she said. "Let's get a bottle." She went to the kitchen and pulled a bottle from the refrigerator as Nanny heated soup on the stove.

"Gas," Ericka said.

"That explains the crankiness. I hope he'll sleep well tonight," Nanny said.

"Me, too," Ericka said as she gave Leo his bottle.

He sucked it down in no time. She burped him repeatedly then put him to bed. He was so drowsy he looked as if he were craving rest.

Crossing her fingers, Ericka returned to the kitchen and accepted the bowl of soup Nanny had heated for her. "Thank you so much," she said. "It's been quite a day."

"I'll say," Nanny said. "You've been up since nearly the crack of dawn. I bet you're ready for some sleep yourself."

"I am, but I hate for you to take the tortured night shift," Ericka said as she sipped her soup.

"Remember, I can sleep when he does. You have work to do. Don't you worry about me," Nanny replied, and patted Ericka's back.

But Ericka couldn't help feeling *she* should be the one getting up with Leo.

Chapter Seven

Despite her qualms, Ericka gave into her longing for a full night's rest and allowed Nanny to take the night shift. She heard a couple of peeps from the baby monitor, but no prolonged crying. When she rose, she felt rested and refreshed, a condition she rarely experienced these days.

Making her way into the kitchen, she found Nanny sneezing into a tissue. "Bless you and good morning," Ericka said. "I hope Leo didn't keep you up too much last night."

"Not at all, ma'am, but I fear I'm getting a cold. I've been washing my hands, but I feel as if I need to spray myself with anti-germ cleaner so I won't pass this on to you or the baby," Nanny said then sneezed again.

"You look miserable," Ericka said. "Perhaps you should take a day or two to recuperate."

"I hate to leave you without help," Nanny said.

"I have Simon for food and errands. You've just given me the gift of a full night of sleep. I think I can manage for a couple days."

"Are you sure?"

Ericka nodded. "You'll get better sooner if you rest. And take some of Simon's soup with you. He made quite a bit of it," she said, going to the refrigerator and pulling out the crock of soup. She poured some into a storage container and gave it to Nanny.

"You're too good to me," Nanny said.

"Not at all," Ericka said. "I hope you feel better soon."

Nanny left for her small apartment in town and Ericka quickly took a shower then started working on a spreadsheet of workshops for the upcoming conference. In the middle of a telephone call with one of the prospective speakers, she heard Leo cry out. Quickly ending the call, she went to the nursery, changed his diaper and brought him into the den with her. She gave him his bottle, made the sign for milk and moved his hand to make the same sign.

Leo clapped his hand against hers and cackled.

Ericka couldn't resist smiling. "We'll keep working on it," she said, while he sucked down his formula. As soon as he finished, she burped him several times. A gassy baby was not a happy baby.

"Time for sign language class," she said, then clicked on the pre-recorded video on her laptop. Sitting on the floor, she propped Leo on her lap and repeated the words from the tutor and performed the signs then helped move his hands into the signs.

A knock sounded at the front door and she glanced toward it. Who—

Treat poked his head inside and she felt an unwelcome surge of pleasure at just the sight of him. *Oh, please. Get a grip*, she told herself.

"Just checking on you. I noticed Nanny left earlier."

"We're fine. Nanny was fighting a cold and losing, so I thought it would be best for everyone for her to take a couple days off."

"Good call," he said. "How's he doing with sign language?"

She chuckled and shook her head. "I think he's more interested in giving me a high five and having fun, but I've been told most babies don't start signing until six months."

"Nothing wrong with both of you having fun," he said. "He's a fun kid."

She felt a slight easing inside her and let out a breath. "I'm trying so hard to do everything correctly that I sometimes forget about having fun."

"Think about when you were a kid. Didn't you learn better when you were having fun?" he asked.

She thought back to her childhood and remembered strict nannies and teachers. There had been one or two that had relaxed the rules at times. "I guess you're right."

Sam strolled into the room and began to rub his face on Treat's jeans. He looked down at the cat in confusion. "He does this nearly every time I come into the house. Doesn't he know that I'm not really a cat person?"

Amused, she tried to keep a serious face. "It's obvious that he's determined to make you love him," she said.

Treat rolled his eyes, but bent down to rub the cat behind his ears. Sam closed his eyes in contentment.

Leo squirmed and let out a little shriek, waving his hands toward Sam. Hearing the baby, Sam obligingly strolled next to Ericka and Leo. Leo patted the cat. He hadn't quite learned the technique of stroking. Sam tolerated the petting then slinked toward the kitchen.

"Does the cat always let Leo pet him?" Treat asked.

"More times than not," she said, rising from the floor. "I think Sam believes his job is to watch Leo."

"A watch cat instead of a watch dog," he said. "Looks like it's working. I'll let you get back to whatever you're doing."

"I'm getting ready to eat lunch. Simon brought soup and a pasta meal that could feed a dozen. Would you like to join us?" she asked.

She saw a flicker of hesitation, as if he wanted to stay. He shook his head and she hated the knot of disappointment she felt in the pit of her stomach.

"Thanks, but I'll have to pass," he said.

Why? she wanted to ask, but swallowed the question. She wasn't asking for a lifetime commitment. She just wanted a little company, and the more time she spent with him, the more curious she became about him. But he was clearly determined to keep his distance. She should accept that and be done with her thoughts about him.

Deliberately forcing herself to stop thinking about Treat, she made sure Leo got in some tummy time, watching him grunt and groan as he did baby push-ups. She placed one of his favorite toys in his peripheral vision to see if she could tempt him to roll over. He worked hard but wasn't quite ready. When he started to cry, she scooped him and gave him the toy, praising him even though she knew he couldn't hear him. She wanted to stay in the habit of praising him for the day when he could hear her, possibly after his surgery in January.

He was drooling like a fountain and rubbing his eyes, so she put him down for his afternoon nap and returned to her work. Less than an hour later, she heard him crying. Surprised, she turned on his solar system toy. That only worked for a few more minutes. She brought him with her into the den and put him in his infant seat with toys hanging in front of him, but he continued to fuss.

She spent most of the rest of the afternoon walking the floor with him in his arms. Fearing he might be catching Nanny's cold, she touched his face and body, but he didn't appear to have a fever. He did, however, seem to be chewing on his pacifier more than sucking on it.

"You're teething," she said, feeling like a dumb bunny. "Maybe some ice?"

The night turned into an endless search of relief for Leo's sore gums. She felt as if she tried everything, but nothing worked for more than fifteen minutes.

Changing into her pajamas, Ericka rocked Leo in the rocking chair beside his bed. He calmed and she put him in his crib then headed for her own bed. Not long later, he cried again and Ericka tried the solar system, but it was clear that Leo was hurting. She rocked him again, put him down and headed again for her bed. Just as she fell asleep, Leo cried out again.

For the five hundredth time during the past four months, Ericka encountered the truth again: *this is single motherhood.* Sometimes it was one day at a time. Other times it was five minutes at a time. Tonight was the latter. She rocked then turned on the solar system light until it all became a blur. Sometime after midnight, she wondered if this night would ever end.

Treat took a swim and looked at the lights in the cottage. He noticed that some form of light kept illuminating the nursery. The room went dark and he swam a few more laps then paused. The light from the nursery flickered on again.

Deciding to give it a few more minutes, he returned to the guest suite, took a shower and pulled on sweat pants and a tank. Restless, he walked outside and looked at the nursery window. The light was on. Well, darn. He was going to have to do something.

Treat waited a few more moments and the room went dark. Edgy, he decided to check on the princess and her baby. He unlocked the door, approving of the fact that Ericka had indeed locked it, and walked down the hall to the nursery. The door was ajar, so he walked inside to silence. Ericka was crumpled into a rocking chair, clearly asleep. Treat walked closer to the crib and saw that Leo was sprawled on his back, also asleep.

Putting his hands on his hips, Treat assessed the situation. He definitely didn't want to wake the baby, but Ericka needed to be in bed. As soon as possible. Taking a silent deep breath, he approached her and touched her arm. She didn't awaken. It must have been a rough evening, he thought. Sliding his hands underneath her, he picked her up and carried her to her room.

He gently put her on her bed and her eyelids flickered. She looked up at him and batted her eyes again, as if to clear them. "Treat?"

"Yeah," he said, his face inches from her.

Her eyebrow wrinkled. "What—"

"You fell asleep in the nursery and looked uncomfortable, so I brought you back to your bed," he said.

"Leo?" she asked and his heart softened because she automatically asked about her son even though she wasn't totally conscious.

"He's sleeping. Looks like a deep sleep," he said.

"Oh, thank goodness. Poor thing. He's teething," she said.

"Ah," he said, unable to pull away from her.

For a fraction of a second, she lowered her eyelids then looked him straight in the eye. "Thank you," she whispered and wrapped her hand around his neck and kissed him.

Her mouth was so soft and sweet he immediately wanted more. He wanted to taste her. And heaven forbid, take her. He slid his tongue past her lips and tasted a delicious combination of citrus and mint. He felt her lift her fingers through his hair and a rush of arousal raced through him.

Her combination of sweet and spicy undid him. Treat couldn't stop himself from devouring her mouth. She opened easily to him, making him want more and more. She pulled him down against her. He gave into her urging and relished the sensation of her warm, feminine body beneath his. It would be all too easy to kiss away her nightclothes then kiss her all over her body. All too easy to touch her in all her secret places and make her ready and wanting for him. All too easy to thrust inside…

Treat was suddenly so hard with need he trembled from it. She kissed him again, thrusting her sweet tongue in his mouth. He swallowed a thousand curses at how she made him feel. Strong, tender, fierce. Out of control.

He couldn't get out of control. He could not.

Even as she wriggled beneath him and took him with her mouth, he knew he needed to draw back. For her sake and his.

It was tough, but he did it. He pulled back, gasping for air. "Whoa," he muttered.

"Wow," she said, her eyelids half-shuttering her eyes in a sexy glance. She slid her hands down his shoulders to his arms.

She made him feel strong, sexy and all too aware of the fact that he hadn't been with a woman in a long time. But she was different. She wasn't just any woman.

"I didn't mean for that to happen," he said.

"But it was a good thing to happen," she said. The expression in her eyes was so inviting he had to look away.

"Can't deny that," he admitted, and kissed her on her cheek. Her lips were far too dangerous. "You need sleep," he said. "Get it while you can."

"I won't forget that kiss," she whispered.

"Neither will I," he said, and forced himself to rise from the bed. Then he forced himself to walk out of her bedroom and out of the cottage. His body was hot, his heart was hammering in his chest and he was hard with want and need. Returning to the guest suite, he headed straight for the bathroom. He stripped off his clothes and stepped into a cold shower. Standing under the cold spray, he waited for relief from his need for Ericka. He waited for fifteen minutes, but relief never arrived.

Leaving the shower, he dried himself off and pulled on a pair of underwear. He went to his self-made gym and began to work out. An hour later, his muscles were tired, but his brain still drifted toward the sensation of Ericka's body and mouth beneath his. He wondered if he would ever be able to rid himself of the memory.

Ericka slept like the dead until Leo's cry awakened her from the baby monitor. Stumbling from her bed, she walked to the bedroom and spotted Sam mewing on the shelf above Leo. "Okay, okay," she said. "I'm here."

She looked down at Leo and put her hand on his tummy. "How are you feeling today, sweetie?"

Leo squirmed and wiggled then smiled at her. Ericka's heart squeezed tight. "Good for you, sweetheart," she cooed as she changed his diaper. "How are your gums? Are they a little better?" she asked.

Leo giggled and her heart caught again.

"You are clearly a morning guy," she said while she lifted him into her arms. Carrying him to the kitchen, she pulled a bottle from the fridge and sat in the den and fed him. Burping was compulsory and she squeezed several gas bubbles from him.

"So let's do little sign language while you're fresh," she said, turning on a video lesson.

She lifted his hands to follow the signs during the lessons, but again, Leo seemed to prefer playing patty-cake. She laughed. "Come on. Give me a try for cat. You can do that," she said, pointing at Sam who stared at them as if they crazy. She gave the sign of stroking a cat's whiskers and helped Leo do the same. "Cat," she repeated.

Sensing he was being discussed, Sam came closer and allowed Leo to pet him. He gave a meow then walked away. Leo grunted and waved toward Sam.

"Leo loves Sam, doesn't he?" she said then gave her baby a squeeze.

Leo wasn't drooling quite as much today, so she hoped he would rest more comfortably during his naps. She put him down for his morning nap and was surprised that he slept soundly, but Ericka was no fool. She used the time to make several phone calls and get work done. When he awakened over an hour later, Ericka fed him and kept him awake until he grew cranky. Then she put him to bed.

After that, Ericka couldn't stop thinking about Treat and how his body had felt against hers, how his mouth had felt against hers. She couldn't remember when she had felt more like a woman, more wanted in a man's arms. She could still taste him on her lips.

Her heart hammered in her chest at the thought of him. She wanted to be with him, to feel his mouth on hers, to feel him on her…inside her.

Ericka bit her lip, thinking and plotting and planning. The last time she'd attempted to seduce a man, it had been her ex-husband. This, her second time, she planned to seduce her bodyguard and the thought of it made her so nervous she could hardly stand it.

Leo was cooperative. He awakened early evening and she fed and played with him. Apparently his gums weren't hurting tonight. Great for her and him.

She rocked him to sleep and he easily settled into sleep. It seemed like a miracle to her. Or, perhaps, destiny, she thought, and dressed in a skimpy black tank dress. She fluffed her hair and said a crazy prayer then pressed the intercom button for Treat. "Do you mind coming over to the cottage?"

"No problem. I'll be right over," Treat said.

Ericka sat on the sofa. Then she stood. Then she sat down again.

Treat walked through the front door. "Problem?" he asked.

"Yes," she said, her heart thumping in her chest. "My problem is that I want you very, very much."

Treat took a deep breath. "Ericka," he said.

"I've put my feelings on a plate. Can you do the same?" she asked.

Treat closed his eyes and looked away. "You know this is wrong," he finally said.

"Wrong?" she echoed, rising from the sofa. "But we're adults. We can determine what's best for us."

Treat shook his head. "I can't do this," he said. "If I'm with you, I don't know how I can be rational and protect you the way I need to," he said. "It's not that I don't want you," he said.

Ericka struggled with his rejection. "Right," she said, trying to figure out her next step since her first step had clearly failed.

"No, really—"

"Oh, stop," she said. "You clearly have no problem resisting my attempt at seduction. Enough humiliation. Let's just go to our separate beds."

"You're wrong," he said, moving toward her. "I do want—"

"Stop," she said, lifting her hand. "I made a mistake and now we're both uncomfortable. Let's just try to forget it all."

"I can't do that," he said.

"You may have an easier time than I will," she

said. "Good night, or as my sister-in-law Eve would say, sweet dreams."

Ericka walked to her bedroom and stripped off her dress. She suddenly felt a century old and as sexy as a stone. Humiliated, she put on her comfy jammies and climbed into her bed. Treat was not in her future and she needed to forget that mind-blowing kiss they'd shared. It had been an illusion. He might say that he wanted her, but he clearly didn't want her as much as she wanted him.

She needed to shut those desires and needs down. Now and forever.

The following afternoon, Nanny returned appearing less congested and more rested.

Ericka decided she needed a little outing, so she told Treat she wanted to visit her sister but also told him she wanted to drive herself. He could follow in his own vehicle. After her failed attempt at seduction last night, she couldn't bear the prospect of him in such close quarters with her.

Driving her small car onto Bridget's ranch, she pulled to a stop and skipped to the front door. She knocked.

Seconds later, Bridget, immensely pregnant, opened the door and squealed. "You're here. Where's the baby?"

"Resting," Ericka said. "I just needed a sister visit."

"Well, you've got one. Come on inside," Bridget said, and led her inside to a comfortable sunroom. "You picked a good day. The twins are in a quiet mood. Playing Lego. Under all that quietness, I'm convinced they're trying to take over the world. My husband says swelling from my pregnancy is making me crazy, but I know better."

Ericka gave a circular nod. "If you say so."

"I'm just kidding," Bridget said. "How's sweetie-pie Leo?"

"Perfect," she said, sinking into a comfortable couch. "But I think I may need to get out a little more often."

"Getting a little crazy?" Bridget asked.

"I wouldn't have put it that way," Ericka said, but knew Bridget had nailed it.

"Well, why not kill two birds with one stone?" Bridget asked, clapping her hands together. "As you know, the royal family is hosting a holiday art event. I know a hot, young Italian guy who could cheer you up," she said.

"Italians flatter too much," Ericka said.

"There are times when we could all use a little flattery. I'm not asking you to marry him. Just enjoy him for the evening. You don't even have to take him to bed," Bridget said.

Ericka stared at her sister in shock. "Bridget, shame on you. I'm not that desperate."

"Of course you aren't," she said. "But you could

use a little fun. I'm looking out for your mental health," she said.

Ericka couldn't help chuckling. "I'm not sure this is a good idea. I was thinking a luncheon or a visit to our museum."

"This is similar to a visit to a museum. You'll just dress up a little more and enjoy the company of an attractive man. Like I said, it's not forever. You could use a little fun. You're looking a little unnecessarily serious and cranky," Bridget said.

Ericka blinked. "That's sounds a bit insulting."

"Just tell me you'll go on the date," Bridget said.

Ericka took a deep breath. She clearly needed to get out. She was getting way too hung up over a bodyguard who didn't want to be with her. "I'll do it."

Bridget clapped her hands together. "Great. I can't wait to talk to Antonio."

Ericka visited with the twin boys and a few of the animals. She promised to bring Leo soon. As she got into her small car, she spotted Treat waiting. She waved at him because it seemed like the right thing to do. Then she drove home. Along the way, she wondered if she should have agreed to the blind date via Bridget, but she hoped it would be a very welcome distraction.

She needed to stop thinking about Treat. Maybe Antonio would help. Arriving at the cottage, she stepped out of the car and waved toward Treat as he pulled in behind her. "I'm going to a formal event tomorrow night. Representing the Devereaux family. The palace will provide a car."

He met her gaze. "This is new."

She shrugged. "Good to know we're keeping the job interesting. Ciao," she said as she walked into the cottage.

Chapter Eight

The next day, Ericka awakened early to the sound of Leo's lusty cry. She waved Nanny back to her bed as she made her way to her son's room. Today, she was determined to brighten her outlook. Perhaps Bridget was right. She'd become too serious for anyone's good. She had plenty going for her. She had a healthy, happy baby. Her child's nanny adored him. She had a supportive family and she lived in a lovely cottage on a beautiful neighborhood.

Ericka looked down at Leo as he whined. "Good morning, beautiful boy," she said, putting her hand on his chest to comfort him then stroking his face. She smiled and he quit crying. After changing his diaper, she put in his hearing aids even though she now knew they helped his hearing very little, if at all.

"I bet you would like a bottle," she said, and carried him to the kitchen where she grabbed a bottle from the refrigerator. He slurped down his nourishment and she helped him burp. If she were following her normal schedule, she would share a little sign language session with him then move on to tummy time, but the sun was shining brightly and she'd heard the weather should be reasonably warm.

She decided to take Leo for a stroll. With a cap over his head covering his hearing aids, even if the paparazzi took a picture, they wouldn't spot anything unusual. She changed into jeans and a light jacket and put a jacket on Leo, grabbed the stroller and headed out the door. The sun was so bright Leo squinted his eyes.

"Sorry about that, sweetie," she said as she pulled the top of the stroller forward to offer him a little shade. She walked to the gate and pushed the button for it to open. Just as she walked through it, she heard footsteps behind her. Glancing behind her, she saw Treat and felt a strange combination of excitement and annoyance.

"What are you doing?" he asked, catching up to her.

"I'm taking Leo for a stroll," she said.

"You're supposed to tell me," he said.

"Nothing personal, but I didn't want to invite

you." She shrugged. "Well, maybe it is personal," she said. "I'm not going far."

"It doesn't matter. I need to have eyes on you if you leave the gate. Anything could happen," he said.

"But it probably won't at seven a.m.," she pointed out. "Most of the citizens of Chantaine don't rise much before nine." She frowned. "This is Leo's first stroll in a week. Don't ruin it."

He blinked and lifted his hand. "Okay. Just pretend I'm not here."

"Not likely," she muttered under her breath but gave it a good effort. She looked at the trees and her neighbor's well-tended garden. She tried to take a deep breath and fill her mind with so many good thoughts that they would crowd out her awareness of Treat. After a few moments of walking, she stopped to check on Leo. The little sneak appeared to be sleeping.

"You little rascal," she said, adjusting his jacket.

She felt Treat look over her shoulder. "Sleeping on the job?"

"I was hoping this would be stimulating for him, offering him a new experience." She chuckled.

"You really can't blame him. He's nicely bundled and shaded. The temperature is perfect with a little breeze. The movement of the stroller probably lulled him to sleep. Perfect nap situation," he said.

She looked up at him and began pushing the stroller again. "Are you a nap person?"

"I can be, but I'll only go fifteen minutes tops."

"When I sleep, I like it to last for hours and hours without interruption," she said.

"Says the single mother of a baby," he said with a nod of understanding. "There's a reason sleep deprivation is used as a form of torture."

"It's really much better than those first couple of months. It helps if I look back at how things were when I first came home from the hospital with him. I have Nanny and she's an enormous help."

"And the solar system on the ceiling," he added with a half grin.

That half grin made her stomach take a dip. She looked away. "Yes, the solar system." She turned silent and fretted over her feelings.

"You don't need to be uncomfortable with me because of what happened the other night," he said.

Upset by his ridiculous comment, she rounded on him. "Of course I'm uncomfortable with you. I tried to seduce you and you didn't want me in return. The situation is beyond awkward and—"

"I didn't say I didn't want you," he said. "I just know I can't have you. It's for the best."

Her heart skipped a beat when he confessed in a double negative sort of way that some part of him perhaps did want her. Her heart seemed to want to ignore the latter part of what he'd just said. Her heart was being very foolish, she told herself and she closed her eyes, shaking her head. "I'm not sure talking about this is going to help," she said, and opened her eyes. "But I'm doing some things to help alleviate my…" She took another breath. "Complete humiliation."

"Ericka…" he said.

She lifted her hand to cut him off. "Please. If we must talk, choose another subject." She turned the stroller around and headed for the cottage at a brisk pace.

Treat stayed right by her side. "How do you like those Broncos?"

She glanced at him in confusion. "Broncos? What on earth—"

"You said change the subject. I said the first thing that came to mind. Denver Broncos," he said. "Football."

"Oh, American football," she said. "I remember that Valentina's husband is a big fan, but he favors another team. Rangers?" she guessed.

"That's baseball. Sounds like he could be a Texas fan," he said.

"Texans. That's what it is," she said. "And Ackies?"

"Aggies. That's college football. They're from Texas, too," he said.

"Where are these Broncos from?" she asked. "Didn't you grow up in Texas?"

"Yes, but I had to expand my loyalties when I played pro for Kansas City," he said.

"I didn't realize you played professionally. Was Kansas City a good team?" she asked.

"They were pretty good when I was with them, but I was on the injured list way too often," he said.

"Does it ever hurt?" she asked. "Wherever you were injured," she said.

He chuckled. "I got injured all over my body at one time or another, so I'd be in bad shape if I hurt all over. But my left knee took the worst of it. I work out every day, but I can tell you when it's going to rain because my knee lets me know."

"How upset were you when you had to quit playing?" she asked.

"I was pretty disappointed, but I didn't have time to mope. With no family left, I didn't have a place to land. I had to switch gears as quickly as possible. Luckily I had a buddy who wanted a partner for a security business. I lived on SpaghettiOs for a while, but I'm eating better now."

"SpaghettiOs?" she echoed.

"Spaghetti and meatballs in a can," he said.

"Oh, that sounds disgusting," she said. "Your palate must be destroyed from that. No wonder you turn down Simon's food."

"I'm sure Simon's food is delicious. I just don't want you to think you've got to feed me. I can handle that."

She nodded. "I'm curious. How do you handle that? What do you eat?"

He rubbed his jaw as if her question made him uncomfortable. "Nothing you would want," he said.

"Okay," she said. "But answer my question."

He sighed. "I didn't want you to know that I eat a lot of peanut butter and canned soup."

She wrinkled her nose. "That's ridiculous. You're so determined to stay away from me in the cottage that you give up gourmet food for peanut butter. Unless you're eating peanut butter and bacon. Otherwise you deserve your bad food," she told him.

He stared at her in surprise.

"I feel better now. And look, we're at the gate so you can go back to your man cave and eat some peanut butter. Ciao," she said as she pushed the stroller to the front door. Pulling Leo up into her arms, she hugged him close. "When you grow up to be a man, try not to drive women crazy," she told him.

Leo looked up at her with wide, innocent eyes and smiled. Her heart swelled with love. "Oh, darn. You're already too gorgeous. The female race is doomed," she said, then kissed his chubby cheek.

Ericka divided the rest of her day between caring for Leo and doing work for the palace. She would likely be out late tonight due to the Christmas Art Show, and she tried to balance the demands of childcare with Nanny so that Nanny wouldn't become overwhelmed. Ericka treasured Nanny's presence and was actually a bit terrified of losing her. She couldn't imagine replacing the sweet woman.

As she showered and fixed her hair and make-up, she felt a mixture of emotions. Part of her regretted her decision. What had she been thinking? She wasn't ready to start dating and she truly didn't have time for it. At the same time, a shot of excitement raced through her when she picked out an emerald-green dress she'd worn pre-pregnancy from her closet, *and it fit.*

It hit her that she had totally lost confidence in herself. Before her marriage, she'd had plenty of male admirers. Since her divorce and pregnancy, when she looked in the mirror she saw a tired woman, dumped by her husband, with zero sex appeal. Because she'd been so busy trying to take care of Leo and make a life for her baby and herself, she hadn't realized how much her husband's betrayal had affected her self-esteem as a woman.

Ericka closed her eyes for a moment then looked in the mirror. Maybe it was time to push the reset button. She was no longer the young naive woman who'd married her husband and agreed to follow wherever he led. True, she was often tired and felt more vulnerable than she liked. But she was stronger now.

Treat wasn't all that comfortable with the event tonight. He was accustomed to Ericka staying in the cottage with the baby. Although he knew he shouldn't care, he did. He worked out, took care of online reports, showered and shaved, but he still didn't feel great about tonight. He needed to keep his feelings hidden, however. He dressed in slacks, dress shirt, tie and sport jacket. That should do the trick. At least for tonight.

He went outside and waited for the car from the palace. He understood that he would be riding in the front with the driver while some Italian businessman rode in the back with Ericka. The thought of it made him lose his taste for everything, but he needed to conceal his feelings.

The expansive limousine arrived and Treat waved them into a spot in front. He held up the universal sign for stop then went into the cottage. Nanny was holding Leo. "Is she ready?" he asked.

"I think so," Nanny said as she walked down the hallway. "I think your vehicle has arrived, miss," she called to a closed door.

The door flung open and Nanny gasped. "You're so beautiful."

Ericka rounded the corner in the hall and smiled. "You're so sweet," Ericka said, and then walked down the hall in a formal emerald-green dress and a cream-colored stole.

Treat succeeded in staring at her without dropping his jaw, but it was tough. She looked more beautiful than a beauty queen. She looked like a princess.

She glanced at him and nodded. "Good evening," she said. "I may need a little extra help getting in and out of the palace vehicle. I haven't been wearing heels much lately."

"I can do that," he said.

"Thank you," she said, walking toward Nanny and Leo. She pressed a kiss against the baby's cheek, leaving a lipstick stain that many men would welcome, including himself.

Treat escorted her to the vehicle and Mr. Italian stepped outside. He was a not-too-young man with model looks and a muscular frame. Treat had wondered if Antonio was just a pretty face, but apparently the man operated several companies.

Antonio bowed slightly then took Ericka's hand and lifted it to his lips.

At that moment, Treat hated Antonio.

"You look very beautiful, Your Highness. Please allow me to assist you into the limousine."

She met his gaze and smiled. "Thank you so very much, Antonio. I appreciate your help."

And Treat hated the man even more.

The couple neglected to close the window between the driver and backseat, so Treat was able to hear nearly every word Antonio and Ericka exchanged. Antonio flirted. Ericka responded lightly. Antonia flirted more. Ericka smiled and sat closer to him.

He couldn't stand it when she smiled at Antonio. It made him want to break every window in the car, but he held it all in. He had a job to do.

Treat escorted the couple into the event for the

Christmas Art Exhibit. As Ericka allowed Antonio to hold her hand, he clenched his fists together. The two of them wandered through the exhibit, studying and discussing the works of art.

After a time, Antonio grabbed two glasses of champagne and offered one to Ericka. She accepted, smiled and clicked her glass against his.

Antonio pressed a kiss against her wrist and it lasted a few seconds too long for Treat. Frowning, he wondered if Ericka was asking for more than she wanted to deliver.

Should he question her?

At the same time, Treat was concerned that Antonio might be expecting more from the end of the night than he might get. He forced himself to block out his jealous feelings and focused on his job as protector.

Another hour passed and he watched as Antonio kissed her hands and drew her against him. Ericka laughed and appeared to flirt with him. Treat could tell that Antonio was becoming more intent and drawn in by Ericka.

Antonio finally took a break and dismissed himself, most likely to the restroom. Treat approached Ericka. "May I have a word with you?" he asked.

"Of course," she said, and allowed him to guide her to the lobby of the art center. "Is there a problem?"

"There could be," he said. "I'm concerned that

Antonio may want more from you than you want to give."

She lifted her chin. "Maybe I can deliver what he wants. At least he finds me attractive and he's not afraid to admit it."

Treat ground his teeth. "I'm not afraid to admit my attraction for you," he told her. "I'm just trying to draw a line of professionalism."

"Enjoy that line," she told him and turned away.

"Ericka," he said, tugging her arm.

The princess glanced down at his hand on her arm. "Yes?"

He pulled her closer and pressed his mouth against hers, sliding his tongue inside, tasting and taking her. She was deliciously sweet in a forbidden way. She tasted like sin and heaven at the same time.

He forced himself to draw back and looked deep in her eyes.

"You are such a pain in the butt," she said breathlessly, and stalked away from him.

Treat stared after her, completely aroused. This *cake* assignment was turning into his worst nightmare.

Ericka tried her very best to pay attention to Antonio, but he mind was stuck on the kiss she'd shared with Treat. Her lips burned, her heart hammered and all her womanly places swelled and moistened. Staring into Antonio's lustful eyes, she couldn't summon the least bit of interest.

"Antonio," she said. "I'm so sorry, but I think I should leave. I'm not feeling well."

"You are ill?" he asked, his brown eyes tilting in concern.

"The nanny for my son has been sick. I hope I haven't caught her cold." That much was true, although Ericka was suffering from a different kind of illness. Complete lust for her bodyguard.

"I'm so sorry, but I think I should go home," she said.

Disappointment crossed Antonio's handsome face. "Of course," he said. "Let's leave right away."

Antonio escorted Ericka to the palace limo with such a gentlemanly attitude that she felt guilty. At the same time, she knew she shouldn't lead him on. They rode quietly through the streets of Chantaine toward her cottage. Finally, they passed through the gates and the doors of the limo opened.

Antonio attempted a passionate kiss, but Ericka couldn't find it in herself to pretend. She pulled back and smiled. "Thank you. I really should go."

"Call me if you change your mind," he said.

"Good night," she said as she stepped out of the car.

Treat took her hand and helped her stand.

As the limo rode away, Treat turned away. "Regrets? You wish you had stayed with him?"

"You made that plenty difficult when you kissed me," she said.

"Maybe I shouldn't have," he said.

"Don't start with that now," she said. "My American brother-in-law once gave me a great quote. *Go big or go home.* What are you going to do?"

"If I followed my professional guidance, I would walk you to the cottage door and go back to my room," he said.

She crossed her arms over her chest. *If he rejected her again…*

"If I follow every other urge and need, I would take you back to my room and make love to you."

She bit the inside of her lip. "What are you going to do?"

"Are you sure you want this?" he asked her. "Because once I take you into that room, I'm not going to want to stop."

Ericka bit her lip. She couldn't remember a time that she'd wanted a man more than at this moment. "Take me with you," she whispered.

Sweeping her into his arms, he took her to his room and bed, releasing her onto his mattress. "You're so beautiful. You have no idea," he said, pulling off his tie, jacket, shirt and slacks.

Ericka's heart slammed so hard against her chest she couldn't find any words to respond to him. She opened her mouth, but no words came out.

"Just tell me what you want," he told her. "Because I want to give it to you."

How could she say that all she wanted was him? She took several deep breaths and swallowed hard. "You," she finally managed. "All I want is you."

She slid her hands over his muscular chest and arms and lower.

"Oh, Ericka, you're too much, but you make me want more," he said.

He kissed her and caressed her body with his hands and mouth. Every breath, every heartbeat made him want more of her. Her lips tasted like cherries and felt like sex.

"You're just too good," he said.

"I want you," she said, sliding hers hands down between his legs.

Treat nearly burst out of control, but he reined himself in. "I'm trying to pace myself," he told her, covering her hands with his.

"Don't do that," she said, meeting his gaze. "Give me all of you."

Her expression nearly sent him over the edge, but he hung on long enough to put on protection. Then he pushed her sweet white thighs apart and plunged inside.

She gasped.

He stopped. "Okay?"

She closed her eyes, then wriggled against him.

He swallowed a groan. "What are you doing?" he muttered.

"You. I'm doing you," she said. She wriggled again as she lifted her mouth to his.

That's when Treat lost control. He just wanted her way too much. Thrusting inside her, he watched her as her eyes darkened in arousal.

She felt so good and tasted so sweet, he thought as he clutched Ericka's derriere, then flew into the most intimate moment he'd ever experienced. He flew high in the sky and wanted more than anything to take Ericka with him.

"Come with me," he urged, sliding his hands over her sweet body.

When he felt that she hadn't gone over the top, he slid his hand between their bodies. She wiggled against him. Again and again.

"Give me you," he said. "Give me you." He continued to rub her sweet spot and she clung to him.

Finally she clenched and rippled against him, her climax producing a ricochet through her to him. "Oh," she whispered. "Wow."

He couldn't help smiling at her response at he pulled her against him. "Yeah. Oh. Wow."

Chapter Nine

"You know this wasn't the wisest thing for us to do," he said. "I don't want anything to damage your reputation. I'm not concerned about my own situation—"

"Oh, stop being a saint and stop trying to play my big brother when you're my lover," she said.

"I'm not trying to play your big brother," he told her. "But it's my job to protect you."

Sighing, she pushed her hair behind her ear. "It's lovely of you to protect me, but I'd rather you make love to me."

"But you need to make a decision. Do you want to keep this between you and me? Or do you want it public?"

Frowning, she sighed again. "I actually don't want anyone in my business. I don't want anyone studying Leo. I don't want anyone analyzing you and me under a microscope. It's strange, but I feel protective of my relationship of you and me. Do we need a contract for this?" she asked.

He gave a rough chuckle and pulled her against him. "No." He slid his fingers through her hair and rubbed his mouth against hers. "No contract. This is just between you and me," he said, then he made love to her again.

At 2:00 a.m., she awakened to silence and listened for the sound of Leo. It took a few moments for her to realize that she was in Treat's bed and man cave. She sat up. "I need to go," she whispered.

Treat slid his hand over her arms. "What's wrong?"

"I need to check on Leo. I can't hear if he's crying. I can't hear if he's okay," she said. "I'm sorry."

"No. It's okay," he said, rising. "Let me walk you to the cottage."

Both of them dressed. It felt odd to Ericka to put on her now crumpled formal gown. She ran her fingers through her hair. "Hopefully Nanny won't be up for my walk of shame, although I'm actually quite proud. How am I going to hide my feelings from Nanny?" Ericka asked him. "She's so intuitive."

"It'll be okay. Just don't discuss it," he told her

as he escorted her from his suite. "She's too discreet to ask."

"That's true," she said. "Otherwise I would blab on and on about my feelings.

"Brush your teeth," he suggested.

"What?" she asked then covered her mouth. "Is my breath bad?"

"No," he said. "Just tell her you need to brush your teeth because there was too much garlic in the appetizers. She'll run. Who wants to smell too much garlic?"

She narrowed her eyes at him. "Are you sure I don't smell like garlic?"

He lowered his mouth and gave her a soulful, thorough kiss then pulled back. "What do you think?"

"Guess not," she said, and flung her arms around his neck. "Oh, I want to stay with you, but I need to check on Leo."

He returned her embrace. "I'm here. Not going anywhere."

Ericka slumped against him for one luxurious moment, and then pulled back. "Good night," she said as she walked into the cottage.

Closing the door quietly behind her, she stood in the foyer and listened. Was Leo awake?

Silence pervaded the cottage. Who would have thought? she thought and walked on tiptoe to her bedroom, listening for any sound, especially any sound from Leo. But there was nothing. She quickly changed into bedclothes and sat on her bed waiting for sounds from Leo on the baby monitor. Nothing.

Unable to still her concern, she broke her second cardinal rule of the evening and peeked into the nursery. She walked next to the crib and saw that Leo was breathing. No need to put a mirror under his nose and mouth. He was sleeping.

Go, go, she told herself and headed for her bedroom. She brushed her teeth then dashed into bed, wishing Treat were with her. His body had warmed and comforted her. Her feelings for him were far more than sexual, and that was dangerous. But withering from fear and need…wasn't that more dangerous?

Stumbling into bed, she fell into a deep, deep sleep.

What felt like fifteen minutes later, Leo's cry broke into her slumber. She checked her alarm clock. It had been five hours not fifteen minutes, actually.

Dashing out of bed, she raced to the nursery and changed his diaper. "Need a bottle?" she asked, giving the sign language for bottle.

Leo's gaze was fixed on her face.

She slowed down and smiled at him.

After a few seconds he smiled and kicked in return.

"Aren't you the best baby in the world," she cooed as she lifted him in her arms. She carried him to the kitchen and brought his bottle out of the refrigerator. He immediately began sucking it down. She was thankful for his appetite. To her, it was a sign of a healthy baby. In that case, he was extremely healthy.

She burped him several times then carried him into the den and put him on her shoulder. He wiggled and rooted then settled down and took a little nap.

"Thank you," she whispered, and leaned her head against the back of the sofa. She drifted off to sleep.

A half hour later, Leo awakened and gave a cry. Ericka shrugged off her slumber and took a sniff. Definitely time for a diaper change. She encountered a very messy diaper and decided to give him a quick bath. Leo had a love-hate relationship with baths, so Ericka always made sure his water temperature was very warm, but not quite hot.

Talking to him the entire time despite the fact that he couldn't hear a word, she bathed him in the kitchen sink. Quickly washing him, she rinsed him then pulled him out of the sink and wrapped him in a towel.

"How's that?" she asked. "Pretty darn good, don't you think?"

Leo nuzzled against her and for several moments, he remained still, safe and warm in the towel. She pressed a thousand kisses on his sweet forehead.

Leo began to squirm. Ericka gently rubbed him with a towel then diapered and dressed him. Putting him in his crib she rested her hand on his chest.

He kicked and played and fussed a little then fell asleep again

When he fell asleep, she was certain she had the best baby in the world.

Treat paced the man cave. He was clearly an animal. How could he have given into his feelings for Ericka? He was supposed to protect her, not ravish her.

Continuing to pace, he thought about the night they'd shared. He couldn't remember feeling such desire for a woman. He'd barely kept his head on straight until that Italian guy had begun to vie for her affection. It was crazy, but after that he couldn't deny his feelings. He had wanted her so much. He still wanted her.

He realized he may as well kiss his plans for business expansion via Prince Stefan good-bye. But he couldn't quit on Ericka and Leo. He didn't know how he could ever quit on them. They'd wrapped their tentacles around his heart. The only way he could turn away from her now was if she officially told him she didn't want him. Treat knew deep inside that the time would come when she didn't want him in her life. How could a life between a princess and a boy born on the wrong side of the tracks in Texas ever work out?

Still glowing from the night she'd shared with Treat, Ericka had to force herself to concentrate on her work for the palace. Toward the end of her designated work time, she received a sobering call with another urgent request for the Sergenian royal family to stay in Chantaine. She had to figure out how to persuade Stefan to give his permission. Feeling her frustration build, she decided to step outside for some fresh air and bumped into Treat.

Her heart jumped in her chest. "Hi," she said, feeling suddenly shy.

"Hi to you," he said, his gaze seeming to envelope her from head to toe. "Everything okay? I thought I would check in." He paused a half-beat. "Are you okay?" he asked and his second query somehow felt more personal.

"We're fine. I'm mostly fine," she said as she walked to take a seat by the pool. Treat sat across from her. "I just received another more urgent request for the Sergenian royal family to come to Chantaine. Stefan has already said no. I wish I could find a way to change his mind."

Treat nodded thoughtfully and leaned forward. "There are a few things you can try. Start out the conversation with something you've accomplished. Is there something you've done lately that would impress him?"

"I think he'll be impressed with two of the speakers who have given me last-minute acceptances for the conference. They're both internationally renowned in their fields and one is a winner of a Nobel prize in medicine."

"Sounds good. The next step is to talk to him at the right time of day. When is quitting time for him?" he asked.

"Usually between four and five. Why does that matter?"

"It means he won't have anything else he's trying to get off his plate," Treat said. "Finally, give him reasons that this decision is in his best interest."

"That's going to be difficult," she said glumly.

"It doesn't have to benefit him immediately. The potential benefit could come down the road."

She nodded. "I'll ask Stefan's assistant to look at his schedule for tomorrow and plan to go then. In the meantime, Simon has brought over an immense pan of lasagna. There's no way Nanny and I can eat it. And I won't even force you to dine with me in the cottage," she said, unable to keep herself from making the cheeky comment.

Treat leaned forward and lightly touched her knee. "Ah, but dining with you would make it taste so much better."

In a flash, he'd gone from consultant to seducer and she felt the difference throughout her body. "I've been thinking about you and me all day," she said. "I realized it's not going to be all that easy for us to—" She cleared her throat. "Be together." She frowned, feeling both anxious and extremely uncomfortable.

"I want to have time with you without prying eyes, but Nanny is here five days a week or more. I want you, but I want our privacy. Nanny is off two days from now."

"It's okay," he said, squeezing her leg. "It will be okay. I won't sneak into your bedroom unless you invite me."

The sensual expression on his face made her so weak in the knees that she was grateful she was sitting down. "It's not that I don't want to invite you," she whispered.

"We'll work it out," he said, and rose to his feet.

Ericka stiffened her own knees and walked toward the door to the cottage. "Why does it seem so much easier for you than me?" Ericka asked. "You appear to be in perfect control, when I'm not." Unable to resist the urge, she stood on tiptoe and brushed her lips against his. He swept her away from the cottage door and windows and took her mouth in a sensual, all-encompassing kiss.

He drew back and his eyes looked like black fire. "Does that look like complete control?" he asked.

Ericka tried to catch her breath and mind so she could form words. "I don't know if it's perfect control or not," she said, and then took another breath. "But I like it."

Treat chuckled. "I do, too," he said. "I'll check in on you later."

Ericka returned to the cottage and immediately

fixed a glass of ice water for herself. Like many Europeans, she'd never been big on ice, but after that blazing kiss from Treat, she wondered if an ice bath would be appropriate.

Treat popped in for a few moments later that evening and accepted a large helping of lasagna. Ericka was relieved Nanny wasn't in the room because the electricity between Treat and herself was so strong she was surprised her hair didn't stand on end.

Ericka spent the rest of her evening trying not to think about Treat and preparing for her meeting with her brother. While Nanny took care of Leo, Ericka wrote out every word she wanted to say and when she reread it, she could see that Stefan would fall asleep if she talked this long without taking a breath, so she edited it twice.

By that time, she was putting herself to sleep. Crawling into bed, she couldn't help remembering how wonderful it had felt to have Treat's arms around her. A little damning voice inside her reminded her she had no time for his warm arms and lovemaking, but she pushed it aside. For now.

The following afternoon, Treat drove her to the palace. Ericka was too nervous to chat. When he pulled outside the side entrance, she grabbed for the door. He stopped her with his hand. "Take a deep breath," he said. "Or two. Remember, you're very persuasive."

She took a deep breath and winced. "It's just Stefan is so accustomed to saying no. Sometimes I wonder if it's his favorite word."

"You don't have to take no for an answer," he told her. "You didn't take it last time. Your will is just as strong as his, maybe more if it's something you care about passionately."

She gave a quick nod. "Thanks for the support." She went into the palace. She gave a tight smile of welcome to the staff she encountered then paused long enough to take another deep breath before she knocked on Stefan's office door. His assistant immediately allowed her inside and Stefan stood as she entered.

"You're looking well," he said, and stepped from behind his desk and kissed her on the forehead. "Is Leo letting you have a little more sleep?"

"When he's not teething, he is. I bought a new gadget that hangs from the ceiling and lights up. I think it gives him a temporary distraction," she said.

"You'll have to tell Eve about it. She's got several months before her due date, but it never hurts to be well-prepared when you have an infant," he said as he motioned to one of the two chairs beside his desk.

Ericka sat down and he followed. "You had something you wanted to discuss with me,"

"Yes, first I wanted to tell you about the two speakers who've recently accepted invites to the conference. Hector Suavez, a foremost expert in making sanitary water available in developing countries, has agreed to speak. Along with Dr. Albert Shoen, winner of the Nobel Prize in physiology."

Stefan gave a nod of approval. "Well done. I can see that you were the right person to take on the task of this conference. I'm very pleased."

"I am, too. It also appears that several of the attendees want to put together a roundtable so they can discuss how to make trips to various countries in need of assistance."

"Again, well done," Stefan said.

"Now onto a concern that I have," she began.

"This isn't about your bodyguard, is it? I know his probationary time period has passed," he said.

"No. He's fine. Not too intrusive and he's surprisingly good with Leo," she said.

"Good to hear," he said, leaning back in his seat.

"I've heard from a representative for the Sergenian royals again," she began.

"I've already discussed this. I said no and I meant it," he said.

"What if the royals temporarily gave up their identities and took jobs?" she asked. "We don't have to announce that they're living here, and the whole situation is temporary. They're not asking to become citizens and stay here forever."

"But why here?" he asked. "Why not a large city where they could easily get lost?"

"You're forgetting that their country doesn't have

many large cities. Part of the reason they want to stay in Chantaine is because it's not as well-known as other places."

"That's still no reason for us to get embroiled in this kind of controversy," he said.

Ericka ground her teeth in frustration. "You've always said you want to be a better ruler than our father. Here is a chance for you to show it. He avoided controversy like the plague. You are stronger than that," she said. "This is the right thing to do."

When Stefan stared at her in silence, she lifted her chin. "What if these were your children? Wouldn't you want someone to show some compassion toward them?"

His expression changed minutely. His eyes softened and he rubbed his finger between his eyebrows. "I'll think about it," he said.

"No," she said. "The royals need to come to Chantaine now. You must say yes."

"I must?" he echoed.

"Yes, you must," she said without flinching.

Stefan sighed. "You're going to nag me to death until I agree to this, aren't you?"

"Yes, I am," she said.

"Okay, but there will be strict rules. They can't be seen in public with each other. They'll have to temporarily give up their identities and they will have to work," he said.

"Done," she said, then stood. "Thank you. I knew I could count on you."

He rose to his feet. "I'm still not sure this is going to work," he said.

"I'll make it work," she said, and kissed her brother on his cheek.

"You've turned into quite the soldier, Ericka," he said. "I'm proud of you."

Her eyes filled with a surprising burst of moisture. "High praise from you."

Calmly walking from the palace, she stepped toward the car. Treat helped her inside and shot her a look of inquiry.

"He's going to let them come to Chantaine. I'm so happy I could dance on the roof," she said.

"I wish I could take you to one," he said, grinning at her obvious joy.

It was all she could do not to throw herself into his arms in celebration. "On second thought, I'm not sure dancing on a rooftop is a good idea, but I do know a wonderful little bar on the ocean. I could have a martini and you could have a beer," she suggested, delighted with the prospect.

"Are you sure this is a good idea? You, me in public like that?" he said.

"As long as we don't kiss each other, it should be okay. It's just a drink on a Monday night. They can't be busy," she said.

"If you're sure," he said, looking decidedly un-excited.

"If you can't be a little more cheerful then just let me go into the bar by myself so I can enjoy my martini in peace," she said.

"As if I would ever allow that," he said.

"Allow?" she echoed in irritation. "Just because you're my security detail doesn't mean you have to watch me every minute."

"You say that like it's a trial," he said, tossing her a glance full of heat.

His expression took the punch out of her defiance. She closed her eyes and smiled. "I'm just going to enjoy this moment," she said.

Moments later as they arrived at the bar, Treat watched Ericka pulled her hair into a ponytail and perch her sunglasses on her nose. "Ready," she said.

"It's dark outside. Don't you think you'll look a little odd wearing your sunglasses?" he asked.

"It will make me less recognizable," she said, and stumbled on the walkway.

He quickly righted her. "And if you fall because you can't see?"

"Then you'll catch me," she said with a smile full of charm.

Treat wasn't sure what to expect next from her. From the beginning, he'd known she was a strong-willed woman and she could be heartbreakingly fervent about people she was determined to protect. But that wasn't all. He'd held her in his arms and she'd kissed him with a passion that that made his head spin. She'd apparently just taken Stefan to task, yet now she was determined to savor the moment.

As Ericka had predicted, only a few patrons occupied the bar when they entered.

"Let's take a table by the ocean," she urged, leading the way and stumbling again.

Treat grabbed her around her waist and guided her to a table. "If you keep falling, they're not going to want to serve you any more alcohol," he said.

"Oh, posh," she said dismissively and waggled her fingers toward a server who immediately responded.

"Good evening. How can I help you?"

"Years ago, you made this lovely martini during the holidays. I can't remember the name," she said.

He nodded. "We called it Hollytini," he said, and then listed the ingredients. "We renamed it the Holiday Princess because rumor has it that it was one of Princess Fredericka's favorite drinks."

Ericka cleared her throat. "Is that so? Isn't that something?" she said to Treat.

"Isn't it?" he said. "I'll take a glass of beer."

"Yes, sir. And you'd like the Holiday Princess," he confirmed.

"Yes, please, but can you leave out the alcohol?"

He paused then nodded. "Of course," he said as he walked away.

"I thought you wanted to celebrate with a drink," Treat said.

"I don't drink anymore," she said nonchalantly. "What I really wanted was to look at the ocean while I sit in this romantic bar with my lover."

Her words delivered a one-two punch. In another circumstance he would be all over her, but this time he couldn't. He had to show restraint.

The server delivered the drinks and she lifted hers. "Cheers," she said.

He took a drink of beer. "To Chantaine's Holiday Princess."

They lingered a few moments and Ericka told him about one of the many times she'd sneaked away from the palace to hit the clubs with friends.

"You must have been a terror," he said. "No wonder your brother hired me. You should know that you wouldn't have succeeded in any of that if I'd been your security detail."

"I would have detested you for being a fussbudget," she said.

He shook his head. "Wouldn't have changed a thing."

She smiled and took another sip of drink. "I'm way past high school."

"I'll say," he agreed and paid the bill before they left. As soon as they got into the car, she threw herself in his arms.

"I want to be with you. How can I possibly wait

for Nanny's day off?" she whispered and pressed her mouth against his.

Treat kissed her in return then pulled back. "We need to go back to the cottage. Now fasten your seatbelt and stay in your seat," he instructed firmly.

As soon as he pulled into the driveway, she began kissing him again. After just a few minutes, the windows steamed up and Treat felt like a horny teenager. Taking a deep breath, he set her away from him. "We're adults. We can handle this."

She frowned at him. "There you go being all responsible. You make it look so easy."

"I told you it's not easy," he said, his lower body hard with need. "I'll show you at the right time. Unless you want Nanny to know about us, now is the not the right time."

She sighed. "You're right. I apologize. You probably think I'm some desperately needy woman."

He put his hand on hers. "I don't. I think you're an amazing and passionate woman. I need to protect you, and not just because it's my job."

Chapter Ten

The next morning, Treat received a call from the palace. "Mr. Walker, this is Glendall Winningham from the Palace Public Relations Department. We understand a story with photos about Princess Fredericka has hit an online paparazzi site. The palace prefers to be informed ahead of time of any possibilities of these kinds of stories. We will make a statement if necessary, but I had to tell you because interest in the princess may be elevated due to this story. I'm emailing the link to the story right away. Good day."

Treat blinked as the call was disconnected. He hadn't said a word, but he'd sure gotten an earful from the palace. Dread rumbled in his stomach. A story about Ericka? With photographers?

He pulled up his email and immediately read the story. Who Is Princess Fredericka's New Mystery Man? A dark photo of her wearing her sunglasses sitting at bar with Treat supplemented the story.

He swore under his breath. This was what he'd wanted to avoid. If the paparazzi decided Ericka was interesting, she and Leo would be hard-pressed to find a moment of peace outside the gated cottage. He'd glimpsed the few steps she'd taken to enjoy a few outings. Now that would be nixed unless she was willing to risk more invasions of her privacy.

Rubbing his face, he considered doubling the warning system all the way to the curb. It would result in extra false alarms, but if it kept a telescopic lens from capturing little Leo wearing hearing aids, it would be worth it. Ericka was finding her way of dealing with the delights and challenges of meeting Leo's special needs. She didn't need any extra pressure from the press about it.

After he'd examined ways to extend the boundary around the fence, he walked next door to the cottage and knocked on the door before entering. Ericka, wearing pink pajamas with her hair piled on top of her head and sleepy-looking eyes, looked up from feeding Leo a bottle and smiled.

Treat felt his heart turn over at the sight of her. He'd seen her all glammed up, but something about the way she looked at this moment got to him. "Noisy night?" he asked.

"He had a rough time starting around four a.m. I think I'm going to throw a party when this tooth makes it through his gums," she said. "How about you?"

"I got my four hours, so I'm good. I got a call from the palace this morning," he said.

"I think I may have heard my phone vibrate, but I had to change a diaper and get his bottle, so I decided I'd check after he's feeling more human," she said. "Who was it?"

"Glendall Winningham," he said.

"Oh, my. Mr. Stuffy PR. Bet that was a fun call. Why in the world did he call you?" she asked.

Treat glanced down the hallway. "Before I finish, where is Nanny?"

"Asleep. She'll get up in an hour and leave this afternoon for her night off," she said. "What is this about?"

"Apparently an online paparazzi newspaper has published a photo of you. And me," he said.

Her eyes widened. "Where?"

"At the bar last night. The title of the article is Who Is Princess Fredericka's New Mystery Man?"

Ericka stared at him for a moment then burst out laughing, accidentally pulling the bottle from Leo's mouth. The baby glanced up at her, his little mouth forming a pout, clearly gearing up for a good wail.

"Oh, no, no. You're fine," she said to her baby, rubbing the nipple of the bottle against his lips. He let out a half cry then happily found the nipple and began feeding again.

"Why are you laughing about this?" Treat asked.

"Because it's Stefan's fault," she said, and giggled again, this time with more restraint so she wouldn't upset Leo. "I told him to get a low-profile security man or even a woman, but no, he chose you. No one will possibly believe that you're a nanny for Leo or my assistant. You're just too—" She sighed. "Male."

"So you're not at all worried about this?" he asked. "Because the PR guy warned you could receive additional unwanted attention because of this."

She made a face. "That's true, but I can't tell you how many times they've made up stories about me or my sisters or brothers. Hopefully it will pass soon enough." She paused. "There was only one photograph? If they'd taken one of me kissing you in the car…"

"Only one," he said. "But this means we have to be more careful."

"I think you mean I have to be more careful. I'll try to control myself in public," she said.

"I'm not sure it's a good idea for you and I to—"

"You're bailing on me after a dark photo. The palace will make a statement that there's no mystery man and that you are merely security." She closed her eyes. "I don't want to feel as if I'm begging you."

"You're not begging," he said, feeling torn between doing what he thought was best for her and what he wanted. "I just—"

"I don't want to talk anymore. I've had more than my share of wishy-washy men," she said, rising to her feet.

He blinked at her. "Wishy-washy?"

"Thank you very much for the information. I have other things to do. Good day," she said as she walked away from him.

Treat nearly got frostbite from her abrupt, icy and very royal dismissal. Whoa. He wondered if she'd learned that in princess school. Lord help him if he had to deal with that on a regular basis.

Treat returned to the man cave and focused on his work. He noticed Nanny's car departing the driveway and Simon arriving with food and fresh laundry delivery. The more the thought about Ericka, the more he realized that the woman had a point. Her husband had bailed on her and Treat had given her a ton of mixed messages.

He walked to the cottage and knocked on the door then stepped inside. Ericka was trying to lure Leo into turning over by moving one of his toys next to his side. "Come on," she said. "You can do it."

Sam scampered next to the toy, his head moving every time Ericka moved the toy.

Leo let out a loud guttural yell.

Accurately reading her baby's sound of frustration, she gave the toy to Leo and he clutched it as he continued his push-ups. Sam looked disappointed and wandered to Treat to wind around his ankles and stamp out his human smell.

"Close. Very close," she said, but didn't meet Treat's gaze. "If you're checking on us, as you can see we're fine."

"I came to apologize," he said.

Her head jerked upward and she gaped at him. "Excuse me?"

"I've been thinking about it and I have been sending you mixed signals. One minute, I'm pushing you away because I'm trying to be professional. The next I'm all over you and can't get enough of you."

She stood and crossed her arms over her chest. "Which is the real Treat Walker?"

"You already know the answer to that. Both. I could quit and we could see how things go," he said.

"I don't want you to quit. I want you to stay." She shook her head in frustration. "Can't we just take this one day at a time right now? Can you just let it be okay that you like me?"

His feelings for her ran much deeper than like, but he didn't want to muddy the waters any more than he already had. "Yeah. I'll give it a try."

"Good," she said. "Simon brought Chinese food tonight. Would you like to take it back to the man cave with you? Or would you like to join me?"

"I'd like to join you," he said. And it occurred to

him that she deserved a man who would court her. He suspected there had been plenty of men who had tried to win her over, but somehow he'd had the dumb luck of getting her attention. He wouldn't take the gift of her interest and passion lightly, but he still didn't know how this could turn out without a world of hurt for one or both of them.

Treat and Ericka shared the delicious meal and Ericka charmed him with more stories from her childhood years in the palace. It turned out her sister Bridget had instigated quite a bit of mischief, and the sisters had often plotted how to loosen up their stuffy older brother.

"Bridget was always a fashionista. She was very adept at getting out of palace duties until Valentina and I married our husbands. Then she fell for an American doctor who had become a father to his brother's baby's twins. At first, no one believed it. She's the kind to wear heels on the beach," she said, rolling her eyes.

"It sounds like you managed to enjoy at least part of your childhood," he said.

"I did. We all did. I think Stefan and Valentina took the brunt of the work. It was drilled into Stefan from the time he was born that he was the heir, so he needed to always excel. My mother died when my sister Valentina was in college," she said. "That was hard on all of us."

"You miss her," he said.

"I miss what I wished I'd had with her. I'm determined to make sure Leo has a totally different experience with his mother," she said.

Treat nodded. "Good for you."

"And what about you? What about your parents?" she asked.

He wanted to turn away, but her eyes were warm with compassionate interest. "My dad died young and my mother was overworked. She tried, but I can hardly remember time when she wasn't tired. Between taking care of my brother and trying to make a living, she could hardly catch a break."

"Your brother," she said. "You have a brother. Is he like you?"

He shook his head. "He had some health problems."

"Oh. I'm sorry," she said.

He shrugged. His inability to make life better for his mother and brother was his life's greatest failings. Now that they were gone, he would never have that opportunity again. They were gone forever.

Leo interrupted his sad memories with a plaintive sound.

Ericka immediately turned to him in his baby seat. "Are you feeling a bit ignored?" she asked her baby and rubbed his chin. He kicked and stared up into her face intently.

"How does it feel to have a little person adore you so completely?" he asked

She smiled softly. "It's the most wonderful thing I've experienced. Of course, he doesn't adore me every minute. If he's hungry or uncomfortable or teething, that whole adoration thing goes right out the window. Diaper change, bath and bottle now," she said, and then shot him a sly look. "Wanna help?"

"I think I'll leave that to the expert," he said, and rose. "I'll check the perimeter and confirm that the alarm system is in place." He paused. "I could come back if you like."

She nodded. "I'll see you in about an hour."

Anticipation thrummed through Treat as he conducted his evening duties. As much as he fought it, he wanted to hold Ericka against him and taste her lips again. He'd tried his best to stop thinking about the night they'd shared together, but her memory was blazed on his mind and body. And the more he learned about her, the more he wanted her.

Returning to the cottage, he gave a soft knock then entered and found her sitting on the sofa reading from her computer tablet. She looked up and rose from the sofa. "I just put the kettle on. Would you like a cup of tea?" she asked.

He wrinkled his nose. "The only kind of tea I drink is sweet iced tea. I'll fix myself a glass of water."

"As you know, I spent most of my pregnancy in Texas with my sister Valentina. Her husband is a big fan of your iced tea." She made a face. "I much prefer mine hot with a little milk." She poured her own cup and led the way back to the den. "I was just reading about the surgery Leo will be receiving as early as January or February. I'm terrified that they will have to perform general anesthesia. When I think about it, I'm not sure I can go through with it. But I must if I want to give him the best possible future. It will not magically heal him, but he will be able to hear when he's wearing the external device."

"Will it affect his speech?" he asked.

"It should. Even with the surgery, there are many adjustments that will need to be made and lots of training. We're fortunate because Stefan has connections in Italy where there are several highly trained surgeons who've performed the surgery many times. It's likely that Leo and I will travel there for the actual surgery. Every time I think about it, my hands shake from nervousness," she said, and set her tea on the small table next to the sofa.

Treat felt an odd twisting sensation in his chest. He hated seeing her so distressed. Put down his glass of water, he covered her trembling hands. "You don't need to let this upset you. My mom always said we've got plenty to worry about today. We don't need to borrow trouble from tomorrow."

"She sounds like a wise woman," she said.

"She was," he said.

"I'll bet she was very proud of you," she said.

"Hope so," he said. He hoped he'd been some comfort to her during her hard, hard life.

"Distract me," she whispered, leaning closer to him. "Distract me from worrying about the future."

She was so sweet and genuine he couldn't possibly refuse her. He lowered his head and gently took her mouth. Her lips were sweet and plump, her response both giving and wanting. The combination made him hungry, but he was determined to take his time. As much as he wanted to run his hands all over her and sink inside her, he wanted to savor the taste of her, rub his fingers over the bones of her cheeks and stroke her silky hair.

He kissed her for what could have been seconds or hours, but he knew when she wanted more. She squeezed his shoulders and rubbed her breasts against his chest. Arousal thrummed through his body like a drum. Knowing the tempo and his need would only increase, he continued to make love to her mouth.

Her arms stretched around his neck, pushing her into him. He lowered his hand to cup her breasts and she gave a soft moan. The sound tripped his trigger and he was filled with a ferocious need to show her with his body how beautiful she was.

He unbuttoned her blouse and bra then touched her breasts, lingering over her swollen nipples. Her felt her breath hitch in her throat when he lowered his head to taste her.

"Oh, Treat,' she whispered.

Urgency pounded through him. He pulled off his shirt and felt her naked breasts against him. "So good," he told. "You feel so good."

He felt her lower her hand to where he was hard and aching for her. She stroked him through his jeans, and the fabric of her jeans and his became the worst tease. He reached for the top of hers.

Leo's cry broke through the smoke of his arousal. He heard the cry again as Ericka pulled back. They stared into each other's eyes for several seconds. Sam entered the room and mewed in complaint.

Ericka took a deep, deep breath and reached for her bra. "I have to get him," she said as she fumbled with the fastening of her bra. She tried to put her blouse on backward, but Treat helped her with it. His own hands were unsteady from the force of his arousal.

"Sorry," she managed and went to the nursery.

"I'll be here when you get back," he said, and paced the den to bring his body back to earth.

Ericka checked Leo's diaper, but he was as dry as a bone. She knew he couldn't be hungry. Picking him up, she saw him gnaw on his pacifier and she immediately identified the problem. "Your gums are sore. Let me get a cold rag for you."

She went to the kitchen and wet the rag, then lifted

it to Leo's mouth for his to gum it. Treat walked into the kitchen and gave a questioning look.

"Teething," she said. "You don't have to hang around. I'm going to rock him for a while."

"I can catch up on one of my football games if I get my laptop," he said.

"That's nice of you, but he can get pretty noisy," she said.

Treat shrugged. "I can handle it," he said.

"Okay," she said. "I'll be back when he falls asleep."

Unfortunately Leo awakened every time she put him in his crib. Not even the solar system helped. Hearing the faint sound of a ballgame coming from the den, she was surprised that Treat had stayed so long. Any other man would have given up hours ago.

She paced the bedroom until she grew tired then rocked, rapidly. If she didn't move quickly enough, he cried again. She guessed the movement distracted him from his discomfort.

She didn't know how long had passed when Treat appeared in the doorway, his broad shoulders blocking the soft light from the hallway. A twist of irony tightened inside her. The evening had held such promise. Being held by Treat had made her feel so wonderful she couldn't even describe it to herself let alone anyone else. Now, though, she had to focus on Leo. She had no regrets, but couldn't help feeling a little wistful. She couldn't blame Treat for wanting to return to his suite.

"You wanna let me take a turn?" he asked.

Ericka stared at him in disbelief. She couldn't have heard him correctly. "Pardon me?"

"I said, do you want to let me take a turn with him? If you're not afraid I'll do something wrong," he added.

Her heart swelled in her chest and she felt her eyes burn with unshed tears. Blinking furiously, she shook her head then nodded. "Are you sure you want to do this? He's very cranky. You'll either have to pace or rock."

"I can do that," he said, and extended his arms.

Ericka carefully placed her baby into his arms. "Cradle him a little," she instructed, moving his hands into position.

Leo pouted and wiggled. Treat began to walk and the baby calmed.

"Are you sure—"

"I'm sure," he said. "Remember, I can get by on four hours of sleep. Less if necessary. Go take a nap," he told her.

Ericka took in the sight of her big strong bodyguard pacing the room with her helpless baby and took a mental picture she resolved to store forever. No matter what happened in the future, she wanted to always remember this moment.

Giving into her weariness, she went to her bedroom, changed into her pajamas and fell into bed. She slept so hard she didn't even dream. Some part of her must have sensed a ray of sunshine sliding past through her curtains, but she had a hard time rousing herself. Finally, she forced her eyes open and automatically listened for Leo, but she didn't hear anything.

Frowning, she rose, looked at the baby monitor and listened again. Uneasiness grabbed at her. Rushing from bed, she raced to the nursery. His crib was empty. Alarm swept through her and she ran to the den.

"Looking for us?" Treat asked as he sat on the sofa feeding a bottle to Leo. "I can't promise I did a great job with the diaper. He can be a squirmy little thing when you try to change him, can't he?"

"I—" She stared a him in surprise. "Did you stay the rest of the night?"

"Yep," he said. "He settled down for an hour twice, so I just dozed in the rocking chair."

Guilt nicked at her. "Why didn't you wake me?" she demanded. "I didn't expect you to stay the whole night."

"Why not?" he asked.

"Well, because," she said. "He's not your responsibility."

Treat glanced down the baby. "He is in a way," he said. "He's part of you."

She hadn't thought he could take her breath away

again, but he did. She sank onto the sofa. "I'm sorry the evening didn't turn out. I loved the idea of you staying the night, but I had really wanted to be conscious for it."

Treat met her gaze. "Next time," he said, his dark eyes holding the promise of pleasure.

Watching him feed Leo, she couldn't help taking another mental photograph. Some part of her sensed Treat wouldn't be around forever. Their relationship was a fleeting moment in time, but with each new day, being with him made her feel a little stronger. He reminded her that she was human and there was nothing wrong with that. He reminded her that she was a desirable woman. She couldn't imagine him wanting to deal with a single mother princess forever, but she would cherish these moments because it restored her faith in possibilities.

Chapter Eleven

Nanny never arrived at the cottage. By late afternoon, Ericka grew worried and called Nanny's house. An hour later, she received a call from Nanny herself. Nanny had been in an automobile accident and had been taken to the clinic for examination.

Horrified, Ericka gasped. "How horrible. Are you okay?"

"I'm so sorry, ma'am," Nanny said. "I'm sure it's just a scrape from the windshield splattering, but they want to make sure I'm not carrying around any extra glass. I'm so sorry."

"Please stop apologizing," Ericka said, worried for Nanny's safety. "I just want you to be okay. Take whatever time you need and get back to me with your progress."

Ericka hung up the phone and struggled with how to modify her arrangements for Leo for the evening. As she fretted over her options, she heard a knock on the door just before it opened.

Treat poked his head inside. "Checking in," he said.

"Thanks. I just received sad news," she told him. "Nanny has been in an automobile accident. She sounded shaken up, but she says she's okay."

"That's rough. Is she being checked out by a doctor?" he asked.

"Yes, of course, but I don't expect her in tonight or tomorrow, and I'm required to attend the palace outdoor Christmas tree festival tonight. Tomorrow the Sergenian royals are scheduled to arrive and I'm to represent my family."

He shrugged. "Do you want me to take care of him?"

"I hate to ask you, but I don't want him anywhere near cameras tonight. With his teething, I can just see him pulling off a hat to reveal his hearing aids. I just don't want to have to answer any questions right now. If my entire family wasn't supposed to be attending, I could ask one of my sisters, but they need to be there, too."

"What about your security?" he asked.

"The palace will send a car with your relief detail,

which you haven't used since you started. Even God rested on the seventh day," she said.

Treat grinned. "God doesn't sleep," he said. "I do."

"You could have fooled me," she said. "Are you sure you don't mind? This is a highly unusual situation."

"I'm okay with it," he insisted. "We'll watch football. He's gonna love it."

So grateful that she could count on him, she reached toward him and hugged him. "You really have no idea how much I appreciate this," she said, her voice breaking.

"Hey, hey," he said, stroking her hair. "What's this? You're not crying are you?"

"No, of course not," she said, blinking back tears.

"You don't have to worry. I'll take care of him. Your boy is safe with me," he assured, hugging her.

She took a deep breath and put a check on her emotions. "I know he is safe with you. Now, I'd better get ready for tonight. Simon has delivered another delicious meal. Coq au Vin. Eat as much as you like," she said, and went to her bedroom to get ready for her appearance.

Within an hour, a guard and driver appeared to take her to event. Darkness was beginning to fall over the island and holiday lights twinkled here and there. The palace would be lit from one end to the other. Stefan's wife, Eve, had insisted on creating more holiday traditions. Bit by bit, Eve was remodeling the palace both externally and in personality. The advisors still insisted on a certain level of decorum, but with toddlers roaming the palace halls, it was hard to require so much formality.

Arriving at the palace, she was escorted to one of the more comfortable meeting rooms. Bridget sat in a chair while her husband fussed over her and chased after their young twin boys. Stefan's daughter sat on the floor calmly coloring in her coloring book while his two-year old tried to keep up with the twins. Eve caught him just before he fell and scooped him up in her arms. Pippa carried her toddler daughter on her hip.

Eve spotted Ericka and moved toward her. "It's good to see you," she said, giving Ericka an affectionate squeeze. "I'm so sorry about Leo's nanny. Do you think she'll be okay?"

"I'll hear more tomorrow, but she was complaining about having to see the doctor, so I suppose that's a good sign."

"I'm glad. Who is watching Leo?"

"My security man," she said.

Eve widened her eyes. "Really?"

"Yes. He's been surprisingly good with Leo. He's not an expert with diapers, but—"

"I don't know many men who are," Eve said. "Hopefully we won't need to keep you too long tonight."

The press representative called them to attention

and reviewed the evening schedule. The children would appear briefly while Stefan ordered the lighting of the Christmas tree. Nannies would then take the children either to bed or to a playroom. Due to her advanced pregnancy, Bridget would be excused early. The rest of her siblings and their spouses would be required to stay until the end.

As she and her family walked toward the large imported pine tree, the crowd cheered with delight. Ericka smiled and waved as did her brothers and sisters and a few of the children.

"Good evening, people of Chantaine," Stefan said to the crowd. "Thank you for joining us for the lighting of the palace Christmas tree. This season celebrates hope, love and peace for the entire world. We are especially grateful for the peace our country continued to experience and I want to thank you, the citizens of Chantaine, for your commitment to your country and to your fellow citizens. You serve as an example to the rest of the world."

The crowd applauded.

"As you can see, the royal family is expanding by leaps and bounds with more expansion on the way," he said, glancing at Bridget.

He crowd chuckled.

"We, the royal family of Chantaine, wish you the happiest Christmas, full of love, hope and peace everlasting."

Stefan gave a nod of his head and the huge tree

was lit. More applause followed, the children waved farewell along with Bridget, and the festivities continued with a performance by a children's choir and a reading from a village priest and instrumental holiday music.

The entire time, Ericka wondered how Leo would have responded. The lights would have fascinated him. He wouldn't have been able to hear the children sing, the music or the applause of the crowd. Her heart twisted. She wanted so much for him. Maybe next year? she wondered and said a silent prayer.

Ericka arrived back at the cottage at ten o'clock, feeling worn out. She entered the cottage to find Treat holding Leo on his lap while he watched his laptop screen. He glanced up at her. "How'd it go?"

"It went very well. I feel as if I should be asking you the same question."

"I let him take the car for a spin, then we went for a swim in the ocean and we had a couple of beers before we got back to watch the game," he said.

Ericka rolled her eyes. "You want to tell me the real story now?"

"Gave him a bottle. Did you know that kid can burp like a trucker?" he asked.

Ericka chuckled. "Yes, and it's better for him to burp. He gets very fussy when he isn't well burped."

"I ate some of the coq au vin. It's a lot better than the peanut butter sandwiches I make, but not as good as your peanut butter and bacon sandwich. We both did some more push-ups. I gave him a bath—"

Ericka looked at him in surprise. "By yourself?"

He shot her an insulted glance. "It's not that hard. You just have to make sure the water's warm enough. I probably didn't do a perfect job, but I figure you can get whatever I missed on the next go-round. Since then I've been explaining different formations and plays. He dozed a couple of times, but I think he waited up to see you."

She sat down next to Treat and extended her hands to her baby. Leo fell toward her and she scooped him up against her chest.

"See? I told you he was waiting up for you," Treat said.

She cuddled Leo and kissed his chubby cheeks. "No signs of teething?"

"Not yet, but it's not the witching hour," Treat said.

"Thank you for taking care of my baby," she said.

"It was cake," he said. "Sam supervised me most of the time except when I bathed him. Then Sam suddenly disappeared."

"I'm sure you could tell that Sam doesn't like the water," she said, then sighed. "I have to get up early in the morning to meet the Tarisse sisters and their brother. Stefan has charged me with emphasizing the rules of our agreement. It's only fair since I twisted his arm. I can take Leo with me and one of the nannies for Eve and Stefan's children will watch him."

"Why would you do that when you can leave him here with me?" he asked.

"Because I feel that I've already imposed."

"I told you I don't mind," he said, rising from the sofa. "What time do you need me here?"

"Seven," she said. "I'll call the palace to give me a ride, but I'm told I'll be meeting them at an inn. I could drive myself."

"Not without security," he said. "I'm going to bed. Hate to admit it, but I'm starting to understand why moms of young ones feel tired."

She stood and pressed her mouth against his cheek. "I thought you're the tough guy who thrives on four hours of sleep."

"That's exactly what I'm going to get. My four hours. Your boy should be ready to hit the sack after one more bottle. If he gets fussy, give me a call. Night, princess," he said. Treat knew she didn't like being called "princess," but the way he said it made it sound sexy.

Seemed like lately the way he said anything was sexy to her.

Leo slept through the night. She almost awakened him the next morning, but restrained herself. Quickly dressing, she grabbed a quick bite to eat and sipped a cup of tea as Treat walked through the door. He looked her up and down then studied her face. "You look like you got a decent night's sleep."

"That's because Leo slept," she told Treat, still surprised.

"And that's because I had a little man-to-man talk with him about letting his mama get some sleep."

She chuckled. "And look how well it worked. I should have asked you to talk with him earlier."

He shrugged. "It's a guy thing."

"If you say so," she said, glimpsing the palace car in the driveway. "I should be back by lunchtime. Don't take him skydiving," she told him, and kissed his cheek.

"Hey, how did you know that was on my list?" he joked.

"Ciao," she said. "And thank you again."

Ericka reviewed Stefan's notes on the way to the inn where she would meet the Tarisse siblings. Stefan had initially requested the Sergenian royals to sign a contract, but Ericka had refused. The siblings shouldn't have to sign their lives away for a temporary stay in Chantaine.

Her security escorted her inside a small inn to a suite on the second floor. When she entered, she noticed one of her brother's top security advisors, Paul Hamburg, along with an assistant and the Tarisse sisters. Both princesses were beautiful, but at the moment both looked tired and irritated.

"Your Highness, Princess Fredericka Devereaux,

please allow me to introduce you to Princesses Sasha and Tabitha," Paul said, performing the formal introductions.

"Please call me Ericka," she said, moving toward the two women. "You must be tired. Would you like some tea?" she asked.

"Yes, please," Sasha said.

Ericka nodded toward the assistant. "Please get some tea and pastries."

Sasha, the elder sister, wore her dark hair in a loose chignon at the base of her neck while Tabitha wore her wavy hair loose over her shoulders. "We're grateful you've welcomed us to your family," Sasha said. "You'll forgive us if we're not at our most congenial."

"Because we've been tricked," Tabitha continued. "We made an agreement with our brother, Alex. He told us he would meet us in Chantaine, but he has disappeared."

"Oh, I'm so sorry. Do you have any idea where he could be?" Ericka asked.

Tabitha crossed her arms over her chest, her eyes nearly spitting sparks. "Who knows? He may be roaming the mountains on the border of our country. Or he may be partying in Italy."

"Tabitha," Sasha said in an admonishing voice. "I apologize."

"I can understand some of your frustrations. I've dealt with my share of sibling skirmishes."

The assistant returned with tea and snacks. Ericka made sure everyone had their own cup and a bite to eat before she began. "It's my pleasure to welcome you to Chantaine, but as you know, we have several conditions during your visit here. These are for both your safety and the safety of our citizens. I'm sure you've been told you'll need to assume different identities. You're not to reveal your true identity to anyone. Sasha, I know you're a talented concert pianist, but while you are here, we ask that you not play in public."

Sasha nodded with a sad expression.

"You can, however, play in private. We'll try to make sure you have access to a piano during your stay."

"Thank you," Sasha said. "It would be difficult for me if I couldn't play at all."

"Tabitha, we're working on finding a position for you within the next few days. In the meantime, the two of you can stay here. However, this is hard for me to say. You must not appear in public together."

Tabitha's face fell. "Never?"

"This is not forever," Ericka reminded her. "This is just during your stay while your country resolves its current turmoil. It's for your safety. Think about it. If the two of you are seen together, it's more likely that someone will figure out your true identities. Think of it as divide and conquer."

Sasha slipped her hand through her sister's. "We

will do what we must, but what do we do about our brother, Alex?"

Ericka looked at Paul Hamburg expectantly.

"We'll make inquiries, but we must tread carefully with the princesses visiting Chantaine. We don't want to arouse suspicion," he said.

"But we have contacts who have contacts," Ericka said.

Paul sighed. "Yes, we do."

"I know you don't take orders from me, but I hope you will give this your best discreet effort."

"I will," he said.

"Thank you," she said then turned back to the sisters. "Now let me tell you about Chantaine."

An hour and a half later, Ericka got into the car and returned to the cottage. She hoped she'd soothed some of their nerves, but she suspected that would take time. It broke her heart to see the fear in their eyes. She wasn't sure how she would arrange it, but she was determined to stay in touch with them. She was also going to make sure they had a Christmas celebration of some kind. After all they were going through, it was unacceptable for them to skip Christmas.

She exited the car and thanked her security man then opened the door to the cottage.

"It's not as bad as it looks," Treat called from the hall bathroom.

Alarmed, she raced down the hall to find Treat and Leo covered in red and blue. "What on earth?"

"I told you it's not that bad. We just need to get cleaned up," he said.

"How do you plan to do that?" she asked, wondering if her baby would be stained with red and blue paint for the rest of his life. "What are you doing?"

"You like art." Treat lifted a sheet of paper with Leo's footprints in red and his handprints in blue.

She reached for the precious image of Leo's sweet baby feet and hands and burst into tears.

"That bad?" Treat asked in a gently joking tone.

"Oh, be quiet. You know better." She swiped at her tears. "How can I help clean up?"

"Just go into the den and let us take care of it. This is a job for the men," he said. Leo giggled and planted a blue finger on Treat's cheek.

At that moment, Ericka felt herself fall hopelessly in love with Treat.

She forced herself to remain on the sofa despite the strong maternal urge to help. Pouring herself a cup of tea, she looked at the "painting" and cried again. She'd taken plenty of photos of Leo, but this was an image she knew she would always treasure. She visualized different frames for the art.

Finally after a few wails that caught at her throat, Treat returned with Leo scrubbed shiny clean, wearing only his diaper. Treat was still multi-colored.

"The bathroom is as clean as a whistle," he said. "I'm headed for a shower."

"Are you coming back?"

He met her gaze for a long moment then nodded. "Yeah."

Ericka dressed Leo and gave him a bottle. He nearly fell asleep, which led her to believe he'd had quite the active morning. She set him down in his crib and he nodded off right away.

She felt a rush of nerves as she waited for Treat to return. The events of the past few days had left her feeling more vulnerable than usual. She piddled in the kitchen and called to tell Simon she didn't want a delivery that afternoon.

She heard a knock on the door then it opened and Treat walked in, his hair damp from his shower, his gaze immediately searching hers. "How was this morning?" he asked.

"Challenging. They're afraid. I can't say I blame them," she said. "I'm hoping the peacefulness of Chantaine will be healing for them."

"It's not a bad place if you need to hide out for a while," he said, then took her hands in his. "You made it happen for them."

"I hope it will all work out," she said.

"What's on your mind?" he asked, dipping his head to study her face. "Looks like it's going a hundred miles an hour."

Her heart hammering in her chest, she wondered

why she was suddenly so shy. "I'm trying to think of a clever way of telling you that Leo is asleep and we have the house to ourselves."

Treat pulled her against him and kissed her. "That's the cleverest thing I've heard all day," he said, and scooped her off her feet and down the hall to her bedroom. "I'll try to take my time, but I swear I feel like it's been a decade."

"It hasn't?" she asked, unfastening his shirt while her fingers still worked.

He kissed her slow and deep, lighting the fire inside her. He ran his lips down her cheek and throat. "You skin is so soft," he murmured and unbuttoned her blouse.

He dipped his tongue in the hollow of her throat, taking her off guard. Another moment of caresses and her bra was gone. She loved the sensation of his naked chest against her breasts.

She rubbed her open mouth against his and he sucked in a quick breath, taking her mouth in another deep, hungrier kiss. His hunger made her hyper-aware of all the achy, needy places in her body.

He slid her skirt and panties down over her hips then followed her down on the bed. "I'm naked and you're not."

"I will be soon enough," he said, then kissed his way down her body.

Ericka fell into a delicious cocoon where only she and Treat existed. He pleasured and seduced her until she couldn't bear being separate from him for one more second. Then he finally slid inside her and they were as close as could be. Afterward, he held her tightly against him, as if he never wanted to let her go.

The rest of the day passed in a sweet haze of togetherness. They both played with Leo and ate leftovers. Treat turned on his laptop and attempted to teach her the finer points of football, but she was too busy soaking up every second. She knew this time together would soon pass. Nanny had already called, insisting she was ready to return to work the following afternoon.

The next day, Ericka found herself sighing in contentment. She couldn't remember feeling this happy in her life. Midmorning, she received a call from Treat. Unusual, she thought. He usually just walked over if he wanted to talk to her.

"Hello to you," she said, still feeling a buzz of happiness.

"There's a man at the gate," Treat said. "His name is Jean Claude and he says he wants to see his son."

Shock coursed through Ericka. She was so stunned she nearly dropped her cup of tea. "Is it really Jean Claude?"

"His identification checks out. But I can send him away."

Ericka closed her eyes and shook her head in disbelief. She'd been so sure her ex would never show any interest in Leo. Why now? Why now?

Remembering what Stefan had said, she felt a surge of raw bitterness and narrowed her eyes. "Let him in."

Chapter Twelve

"I'm here to demand shared custody of my son," Jean Claude announced as soon as he entered the cottage.

Ericka couldn't believe his audacity. At this moment, she couldn't believe she'd ever been in love with this man. "Hello, Jean Claude, I hope you're doing well," she said politely, because someone needed to provide some leadership in civility in this situation. Just beyond Jean Claude, Ericka could see Treat glowering with anger.

"I think you may be confused about the divorce agreement you signed concerning Leo. You waived all rights and responsibilities to your son," she said.

"That showed a lack of forethought," he said. "I

was impulsive because I feared you were trying to trap me in our marriage when I needed to be free."

The way he used the word *trap* made her stomach twist. Ericka had made every effort to save her marriage. "And you are now free."

Jean Claude shifted from one foot to the other. "I want to renegotiate."

"I see no reason to renegotiate. You haven't exhibited one drop of interest in your son since he was conceived let alone since he was born."

Jean Claude stretched his chin. "Must we discuss this in front of the staff?"

Ericka blinked. "Yes, we must. He's my security detail."

"Ericka, I know the Devereaux family has some hidden cash. Look how the royal yachts and the grand palace are always being redecorated. You have yourself a nice place here. You don't appear to be hurting for cash," he said.

"And your point is?" she asked.

"I want shared custody and support for when the baby visits me."

"Support," she echoed, her fury growing. "You don't know what the word means."

"We can make this easy, or I can make it very dirty in the press for you and your family," he said.

Ericka watched Treat move toward her ex and she held up a hand. "You do realize that if you have joint custody, you will also need to contribute to Leo's medical bills. Are you prepared to do that?"

"Why wouldn't I be?" he asked, a hint uncertainty flickering in his. "Is something wrong with him?"

"No, he's perfect. He's also profoundly deaf," she said.

Jean Claude stared at her in shock. "Oh, my—" He shook his head. "Now, I understand why you've kept him hidden from the press. How to explain a defective child. I can't say I blame you. I hope you'll keep him hidden. It wouldn't do anything for your image or mine."

Treat lifted Jean Claude from his feet and tossed him out the door. "Get away from her. You don't deserve either of them."

Jean Claude protested. "Don't you insult me. Don't—"

Treat punched him in the face, sending her ex reeling. Seeing Jean Claude for the opportunistic monster he'd become, she tugged at Treat's arm. "Stop. Please stop," she said, fighting back tears. She turned to Jean Claude. "Just leave."

"My attorney will be in touch," Jean Claude said, rubbing his jaw. "You can't hit just anyone with no repercussions," he said as he walked to the gate.

"I have to let him out of the gate," Treat said, his nostrils still flaring in anger. He did the deed then returned. "Are you okay?" he asked.

"I will be," she said, crossing her arms over her

chest protectively. "I still can't believe he just showed up with no notice."

"The palace keeps a watch over him and it appears he and his new companion have been spending more than he makes," he said as he escorted her back to the cottage.

Treat pulled her into his arms and she savored the protective sensation. "I don't think he'll be back," he murmured, rubbing his mouth over her forehead.

She sighed then pulled back slightly. "You were so angry. I could see it in your eyes."

He looked away. "I lost control. I'm going to have to deal with that," he said.

"What do you mean?" she asked.

"I'll figure it out," he said. "I need to file a report. Don't worry about it. You have enough on your mind," he said, then gave her a quick kiss. "We'll talk later. Put this in your rear view mirror. Your day is gonna get better, okay?"

She nodded, but something about his manner made her feel uncertain.

Treat rehashed the incident with Ericka's ex both verbally and in writing. Nobody was happy that he'd used physical force with Jean Claude, but nobody really blamed him, either. Still, the palace preferred to deal with all matters in a low-profile manner if at all possible. Treat supposed he could have restrained himself if he didn't have such strong feelings of protectiveness for Ericka and Leo.

Pacing the suite, he berated himself for his actions. He had acted out of his emotions instead of with the professionalism Ericka deserved. His partner deserved better. The palace deserved better. Ericka deserved better.

Treat knew what he had to do and it made him feel as if his heart were being ripped from his chest. He sent an official email to the palace, his partner and Stefan. Now for the hard part. He had to tell Ericka.

Treat tried to time his visit with Ericka for when Leo would be napping. He knocked on the cottage door and opened it, realizing this would be the last time he performed this little routine. He found her in the den. She glanced up from her computer tablet and smiled. "Hey, there. I've missed you," she said, rising from the sofa.

She put her arms around him and he inhaled the sweet fragrance of her hair. He wanted to remember that. He wanted to remember everything. Treat held her an extra few seconds then pulled back and took a deep breath.

"I need to talk to you," he said.

"Oh, sounds serious," she said.

"You could say that," he said, then looked away for a moment, searching for the right words. "What I did this morning was wrong. It was unprofessional and I broke my code of ethics by punching your ex.

I reacted emotionally. To tell the truth, I wanted to throw him out the door every time he opened his mouth. I was over the edge when he insulted you. It took everything I had to rein myself in when you held up your hand. When he said those things about Leo—" Treat broke off.

"I understand your feelings," she said. "The whole thing was so bizarre. I was just trying to stay sane."

"Well, you did a better job than I did." He nodded, feeling grim. "I've resigned from my position."

Ericka gasped, staring at him in shock. "What?" She shook her head. "No. No. You can't. Anyone could have responded to Jean Claude that way. He was so degrading."

"I can't be anyone. I've been given the responsibility of protecting you. My emotions were out of control. I lost control. I can't be your security anymore. I thought I could separate my feelings about you from the job I have to do. You don't need to be worrying about what your security guy is going to do. You've got enough going on with the rest of your life. I'm not good for you right now," he said. "I'm going back to the States."

"No," Ericka said. "Please don't do this."

He shook his head. "Ericka, you're not ready to have me in your life and I refuse to add to your troubles right now. I—" He broke off again. "You and Leo mean too much to me."

"But I don't want you to go," she said, her eyes filling with tears. "I want you to stay. Reconsider."

"I can't," he said. "It's done. Your temporary security guy is on his way now. I'm packed."

Ericka stared after Treat in disbelief. She felt as if she'd been spent her entire day in shock. *No, no, no.* She started to run after him, but Leo's cry broke the silence. Feeling as if her world had just been turned upside after everything had felt so right, she automatically went to the nursery.

"Hi, big boy," she said to Leo through her tears. "Need a diaper change?" She chatted with him until her throat closed tight from a wrenching feeling of loss. Then she picked him up and held his sweet warmth again her. Nothing could stop the love she felt for Leo. Nothing. But she'd finally let down her guard and she felt broken to pieces. Even though she'd instinctively known her relationship with Treat might not end with them together, she'd been unprepared for it to end so swiftly.

She'd just grown accustomed to his sense of humor, to feeling his arms around her and just basking in his presence. Her chest felt as if a heavy weight had descended on it. She could hardly breathe. She closed her eyes and his image stomped through her brain.

It was all she could do to keep from sobbing outright, but she had to hold herself together. Leo was counting on her. Within moments, Nanny appeared at the door with a small adhesive bandage on her forehead and a bruise on her cheek.

"Hello, hello," she called cheerily. "Now don't worry over the bruise," she said. "I may be a little scraped up, but not enough to stop me."

Ericka felt a trickle of relief at the sight of the woman although she wondered if Nanny had rushed returning to work. "Are you sure you're okay?"

"I'm fine, truly fine. Thank you, ma'am," Nanny said, then studied Ericka's face. "But you're looking a bit out of sorts. Are you feeling ill?"

Devastated was more accurate. "I'm not feeling all that well," she admitted, biting the inside of her lip to keep from bursting into tears.

"Well, let me take our sweet boy and you go take a little rest. It'll do you good," she said, opening her arms to hold him. "And don't you worry about a thing. I can take the night shift, too. You don't want to get worn down," she said, then made a clucking sound. "Off to bed with you, ma'am."

Following Nanny's encouragement, she went to her room and closed the door. She looked at the bed and all she could think about was the night she'd just shared with Treat. She wanted to run and hide, but he was everywhere. Ericka sank onto the bed and sobbed into her pillow.

Feeling like the emotionally walking dead, she went through the motions of her life. Leo still made her smile, but otherwise she felt joyless during this most joyful of all seasons. She avoided Nanny's worried glances. She shopped online for gifts for her family and visited a local store for toys for Leo and her nieces and nephews.

Just because she felt hollow didn't mean she was going to wallow in it. She bought a few gifts for the Tarisse sisters. Unfortunately, there'd been no sightings of their brother, Alex.

As Leo did his tummy time, Ericka wrapped packages, tossing the cat a shiny ribbon. Sam had been more affectionate lately, as if he knew she was grieving. She scratched the kitty behind the ears then glanced at Leo. He'd turned over and looked a bit disoriented from the experience.

"Look at you," she said, touching his chest and raving over him. "You rolled over. You're so strong," she told him, smiling down into his precious face.

Leo smiled and giggled in return. Ericka felt tears well in her eyes. She wished Treat could have been her for this. He would have been over the moon.

Ericka shook herself for thinking that way. Treat was gone and he wasn't coming back. She needed to face that fact. Her phone rang and she noticed the call was from her sister Pippa.

"Hello, Pippa. How are you?"

"I'm at the hospital," Pippa said breathlessly. "Bridget is in labor. When can you get here?"

"Oh, my goodness," Ericka said, feeling a rush

of excitement for her sister. "Nanny's taking a break watching a television show. How far along is she?"

"Well, you never know with Bridget. She's such a drama queen, but I will say she came in huffing and puffing and she wasn't wearing a drop of make-up," Pippa said.

"That's serious," Ericka said. Bridget refused to be seen in public without her cosmetics perfectly applied. "I'll be there as soon as possible."

Ericka took Leo to stay with Nanny while she watched her television show then rushed to the hospital with her new dour security detail sitting in the passenger seat. He hated when she drove, but he moved too slowly for her. Especially in this case.

Arriving at the hospital, she joined Pippa and Eve in a private waiting room. "I wonder how long it will take," Eve said. "I always get a little nervous when the Devereaux women go into labor."

Ericka nodded. "Valentina gave us a scare, but thank God everything turned out."

Eve continued to chatter, filling the time with conversation about Christmas. The door to the waiting room opened and Bridget's husband appeared, beaming.

"What a healthy mother and healthy baby girl! The boys have taken their turn to meet the baby. Would you like to visit?"

"Of course," Eve said. The three women were led to the birthing room where Bridget was sitting up in bed, her face make-up free, but her hair brushed into place.

She looked up and smiled. "Look what I have."

Pippa took her turn first and cooed over the baby. She kissed Bridget on the cheek. "You look entirely too composed for a woman who just gave birth," she said.

"I agree," Eve said, moving closer to get a better look at the baby. "Oh, she has a lovely pink complexion and that little spray of hair. A beauty," she said. "You did well."

Ericka peeked at the baby and agreed with Eve's assessment. "She truly is a beautiful newborn," Ericka said. "No lopsided head or scrunchy face." She kissed Bridget on the cheek. "I'm so happy for you."

"Thank you, all of you," Bridget said, growing suddenly teary. "I didn't want to let on how frightened I was when the doctor limited my activities. I'm so relieved she's here, safe and sound."

"That's our brave Bridget," her husband said, tenderly stroking Bridget's cheek.

The love between Bridget and her husband was so big it seemed to fill the room. Ericka was happy for her sister, but at that moment, she couldn't help thinking of Treat. She swallowed her bitter twist of loss and lifted her lips in a determined smile.

"We've gotten our peek. Let's give Mom and baby time to rest up," Eve said, and the three of them left the birthing room. "Beautiful," she said. "And

Bridget didn't look a bit ragged. I could complain, but her pregnancy wasn't the easiest. I'll see you and yours on Christmas Eve," she said, giving a quick hug to Pippa and Ericka. "We have so much to celebrate."

"We do," Pippa said as Eve walked away. She turned to Ericka and took her hand. "We need to talk. You look miserable."

Ericka demurred. "I'm fine. Just busy due to the holiday season."

"That's not what I heard. Let's go back to the private waiting room. There was a teapot. We weren't in there long enough to take any," she said, tugging Ericka to the waiting room where she poured tea for both of them.

"I should get back home," Ericka said. "I left a mess of wrapping paper on the floor. Who knows what the cat will do with it?"

"The mess can wait. I'm told your American security man abruptly resigned," she said. "There are rumors that you were romantically involved with him."

Ericka took a sip of tea, but it stuck in her throat. She coughed and set down the cup and the truth just spilled out. "It was a disaster from the start, but he surprised me. He was so kind to me and to Leo. It caught me off guard. I knew I shouldn't get involved, but I just couldn't resist. He was able to resist in the beginning, but the pull between us was so intense."

"He left because something happened with your ex," she said.

"Treat punched Jean Claude," she said. "Jean Claude visited and demanded I share custody and money. He was so insulting. Honestly, he wasn't like that when we first got married. I don't know when he turned into such a horrid person. Treat was horrified that he had behaved unprofessionally and he left," she said. "End of story."

"Is it?" Pippa asked.

"What do you mean?" Ericka asked.

"I must tell you that I see myself in your eyes right now. The misery and loss," she said.

"But you're not miserable," Ericka said. "You're glowing. You're happily married."

"I am now, but only because I went after the man I loved with all my heart. Did you ever tell Treat that you loved him?"

Ericka bit her lip and shook her head. "It happened so fast. I was afraid I would scare him away."

Pippa took Ericka's hands in hers. "How can you truly know what Treat wants if you don't tell him your feelings? You're not a teenager anymore. You're a woman with a child. You've been banged around a bit in the relationship department, but I think you know what you want. Do you think you'll ever meet another man like him?"

Ericka shook her head, feeling her chest tighten with grief again. "No. But I've lost him."

"You could tell him your feelings," Pippa suggested.

"But he's all the way in Texas," she said. "This isn't the kind of thing one sends in an email."

"We have jets leaving for the United States every day from Chantaine," Pippa said.

Overwhelmed by the prospect, Ericka stood and paced the small area. "I couldn't dare. It's almost Christmas. What would I do with Leo?"

"I would gladly take care of him for you," Pippa said.

Ericka's heart hammered in her throat. "I don't know if I can do this. I don't know if I have the courage. What if he turns me away?"

"There's only one way to find out. Let me know when you want to drop off Leo," she said, rising and giving Ericka a tight hug.

Ericka returned home, trying to digest Pippa's challenge to her. She couldn't believe her shy sister had become such a tiger. Ericka took care of Leo after she arrived home, but thoughts of Treat consumed her. She barely slept all night. The next morning, she awakened and decided to accept Pippa's challenge. She was going to Texas to see Treat and she was taking Leo with her.

Packing took little time and before she knew it, she and Leo were flying across the Atlantic. Her baby did surprising well on the flight, taking lots of naps and doing sign language lessons with her on her tablet. Nearby passengers looked at her curiously.

"You're teaching your baby sign language?" the woman from across the aisle asked. "Isn't he a bit young?"

"He is, but he's profoundly deaf, so there's no such thing as starting too soon," she said.

"I'm so sorry," the woman said.

"Oh, don't be. He's the joy of my life," Ericka said, and felt another weight lifted from her chest. One less secret to keep.

Treat sat behind the desk in his cluttered office space and stared at his laptop. Now that he'd messed up the job for the Devereaux family, he was chasing new leads for his business. It was a wonder his partner hadn't ditched him, but Andrew had seemed to sense his misery and chosen not to add to it.

Determined to make up for his failing, he was spending twelve hours a day at the office then falling into bed at night, but rarely sleeping. Visions of Ericka and Leo danced in his head. He didn't know which was worse—thinking about her when he was awake or dreaming about her during his rare moments of sleep.

He slurped down a cup of coffee that resembled tar and added another lead to his list. Unfortunately, with the exception of retail stores, most people didn't have security on the brain. He really should straighten up this office, he thought, looking around at the boxes of files.

A knock sounded at the door and then it flew open. Ericka and Leo swept inside the room. Treat stared at her in shock and shook his head. *Oh, no, he had gone over the edge.* He was seeing things. That was it. Time to check himself into the loony bin.

"Sorry. This isn't how I wanted to start our conversation, but we have a bad diaper situation," she said, and dug a blanket out of the gigantic bag slung across her shoulder. Struggling to hold squirmy Leo in place, she cleaned him, changed his diaper and put him on the blanket.

Leo immediately rolled over.

"He's rolling," he said.

"Yes," she said, smiling and sighing at the same time. "Now that he knows how to do it, he doesn't want to stop."

"Are you really here? Or am I just imagining this?" Treat asked, his heart starting to stretch and fill up at the sight of her.

"I'm really here," she said as she put her arms around him. "Don't I feel real?"

Treat squeezed her tight. "I don't know how or why, but—"

She backed away slightly. "Well, I'm going to tell you," she said, meeting his gaze. "I love you and I want you in my life. No secrets. I know I'll never meet another man like you."

"But I'm not royalty. I came up dirt poor," he said. "I'll never be as polished as most of the guys who've tried to win you."

"Do you have a prejudice against royalty?" she asked.

"No."

"Because you bring it up a lot. Haven't you figured out that part of the reason I fell in love with you was because I could be myself with you? You even seemed to like it when I was myself. You helped me become stronger and more confident. You took my heart by surprise and I'm just now catching up. Say you'll give us a chance."

Treat closed his eyes, feeling his heart nearly burst with joy. He couldn't turn down her offer. He had fallen for her like a brick and he knew there was no recovering from his feelings for her. "I love you," he told her. "Tell me what you want and I'll do my best to give it to you."

"Come home with me for Christmas," she said.

Five days later, the Deveraux family gathered for Christmas Eve. During Ericka's growing up years, she remembered the gathering as stiff and dignified. With all the babies, toddlers and love abounding, it was rollicking good craziness. Bridget's new baby girl was passed around from one adult to the other. Bridget's twin boys couldn't stop kissing the poor baby's pink cheeks. The rest of the children scampered around the room with parents preventing spills and upsets when possible.

Pippa held Leo on her lap and practiced some sign language she'd learned. The sight of her sister adapting to communicate to her son almost brought Ericka to tears. She couldn't remember feeling such love and support.

"Hey, princess, will you skip out to the garden with me?" Treat asked her.

She shot him a chiding look. "Princess?"

"Your Highness?" he said, teasing her.

Ericka asked Pippa to watch Leo for a few moments and walked into the garden with Treat.

He took her hand and loosened his tie at the same time. "Madness and mayhem in there. You Devereauxs sure know how to party," he said.

She chuckled. "Complete with diapers and sippy cups." She looked into his gaze. "Thank you for coming back to Chantaine with me."

"I wouldn't have it any other way," he said, and led her to a bench among the carefully tended blooms and shrubs. "In fact, I have a question for you…" He knelt down on one knee.

Ericka looked at him in surprise. She was even more surprised when he pulled a jeweler's box from his pocket.

"Fredericka Devereaux, I love you and Leo more than life itself. I never dreamed a woman like you could exist. Your strength, your humor, your passion. Will you marry me?"

Ericka was so overwhelmed she could hardly speak. "Oh, Treat. I—I—"

"Don't leave me hanging here too long," he said

"Yes," she managed breathlessly and urged him up from his knees. "I love you so very much. I don't ever want to live without you. Wherever we may go, I want to be with you. Forever," she said

"Will you wear this ring?" he asked and opened the box to reveal a brilliant ruby surrounded by diamonds.

"It's beautiful," she said. "Of course I will." Her hands trembled as he placed the ring on her finger. "The ring is beautiful," she said. "But the man who gave it to me is my true treasure."

Epilogue

Four months later, so many changes had taken place. The conference had been a smashing success. Ericka and Treat had married. Most harrowing of all, Leo had received his surgery.

Today, Ericka sat with Treat, Leo and the specialty audiologist in a small office in Italy. Both nervous and excited, she bounced Leo on her knee. Today the audiologist would activate the external device. This visit wasn't the pot of gold at the end of the rainbow. It was just the beginning. Leo would need to be trained how to best use the device.

"Okay?" Treat asked, covering her hand with his.

She took a deep breath. "A little nervous."

"It's gonna work out," he said, and offered Leo a ring of plastic donuts.

Leo grabbed the first one then tossed it several feet.

"He throws everything these days. It's all that football you let him watch," she whispered.

"Hey, the kid's got a good arm," he said as he gave Leo another donut.

Leo tossed that one on the floor, too.

The audiologist smiled. "I'm going to activate the volume levels on Leo's device now. I'll do it gradually, but as I told you, he may cry when he first hears noise because it can be confusing for the little ones. Here we go."

Ericka held her breath, carefully watching Leo's face. During the first few tests, he showed no response. Suddenly, though he stopped and his eyes widened.

"We may have something here," the audiologist said. "Say hello to your son," she told Ericka.

"Hi, Leo," she said. "Hello, beautiful boy. I love you so much."

Leo looked up at her and put his fingers against her mouth.

She gasped then laughed. "Can you hear me? You can hear, Leo. You can hear, can't you?"

Leo laughed in return and wiggled his head as if he would need to get used to the new sensation.

"That's what we call a late Christmas gift," the woman said.

Ericka looked into Treat's gaze and her eyes filled with tears. He'd been with her through all the up-heaval and challenges of the past few months, and she knew in her heart that he would be there for her and Leo forever.

* * * * *

A PRINCESS BY
CHRISTMAS

JENNIFER FAYE

CHAPTER ONE

AT LAST HE'D lost them.

Prince Alexandro Castanavo of the Mirraccino Islands stared out the back window of the cab as it snaked in and out of traffic. He'd never driven in New York City but his concern deepened when they swerved to the berm of the road. While all of the other traffic was at a standstill, they kept rolling along.

When the cab suddenly jerked to the left, Alex's shoulder thumped into the door. He reached for the armrest and his fingertips dug into the hard plastic. What had he done to deserve the cabbie who thought he was a grand prix driver?

Alex jerked forward as the car screeched to a halt in front of a traffic light. At least the guy obeyed some traffic rules. Another glance out the rear window revealed a bread delivery truck behind them. He breathed a sigh of relief. No one was following them. But then again, how could they? He doubted many people drove as erratically as this cabbie.

"You can let me out here?"

"No. I get you there quick."

Alex reached for his wallet, but before he could grab it, the car lurched forward. He fell back against the seat. What was up with this guy? Didn't he know that he'd make more money by taking his time?

"You don't have to hurry."

The man grinned at him in the rearview mirror. "Hurry? Sure. I hurry."

Alex inwardly groaned. He was about to correct the man when he realized that every time the man spoke, he took his eyes off the roadway. It was best not to distract him if Alex wanted to reach his destination in one piece.

He silently sat in the backseat while the cabbie jock-eyed through the streets of Manhattan. Alex stared out the side window as a fine snow began to fall. Cars and people abounded in every direction, seemingly undisturbed by the deteriorating weather. Garlands and festive wreaths adorned the fronts of buildings while pine trees and shiny ornaments decorated the shop windows. Christmas was definitely in the air, even though it was still a few weeks away.

City life would definitely take a bit to get used to. Not that he planned to live it up while in town. Unlike his usual need for high visibility on behalf of the kingdom, this trip required stealth maneuvers, especially since he'd gone against protocol and stolen away without his security detail. Although in his defense, it was a necessity. Trying to elude the paparazzi was tricky enough, but doing it with an entourage would be impossible.

Soon the stores faded away, traffic thinned out and rows of houses dotted each side of the street. One last glance out the rear window assured him they hadn't been followed. At last, the tension in his neck eased.

When a loud clicking sound filled the car, he noticed they'd turned onto a cobblestone roadway. It was a narrow residential road with no parking on either side.

Alex sat up a little straighter, taking in the sweeping willow trees on either side of the street. This must be the exclusive neighborhood of Willow Heights, aptly named.

The homes in this area sat back off the road. They were older mansions that were well kept and still stunningly beautiful. Being here was like stepping back in time. A wrought-iron signpost came into view. It stood in front of a stone wall and read: The Willows.

Alex glanced up at the stately home with its old-world charm. He wasn't sure what he was expecting. When the problem at the palace had come to light, there had been no time for detailed planning. He'd moved directly into action. His mission was to draw out this game of cat and mouse with the press—not knowing how much time would be needed to resolve his brother's latest fiasco.

The driver turned in to the gated driveway. "That is some swanky place. You some rich muckety-muck?"

He wasn't sure what a muckety-muck was, but it didn't sound good. "No."

"You stay long?"

He wished he knew. "I'm not sure."

"When you need a ride. You call. Freddy take you."

English might be Alex's second language, but this man made him feel as if it was his first—the broken English combined with a very heavy accent left Alex struggling to understand what the cabbie was trying to say. But one thing he knew was that he wouldn't be summoning Freddy for another ride—anywhere.

The paved driveway led them to a spacious three-story flagstone mansion. By the looks of it, this place dated back a century or two. The owner certainly had done a fine job keeping up the outside. Ivy grew up one wall and its vines were dusted with snow. It didn't even come close to the enormity of his family's palace, but the large, sweeping porch draped with garlands gave the place a warm, homey feel.

The car pulled to a stop and the driver cast him a big, toothy grin. Alex reached for his credit card to pay the fare but paused. On second thought, he grabbed some cash from his wallet. It was best to keep his true identity under wraps for now.

Once he and his luggage were settled on the sidewalk, the cab raced off down the driveway. Alex's shoulders slumped as the adrenaline wore off and fatigue weighed him down. He stifled the urge to yawn. He'd never been so happy to have his feet on solid, unmoving ground; now he just had to find his room and get some shut-eye before he dropped from exhaustion.

"Welcome," chimed a sweet voice.

He turned, finding a young woman coming up along the side of the house, lugging a big cardboard box. Her reddish-brown ponytail swayed as she made her way toward him. Her beauty captivated him, from her pink-stained cheeks to her full rosy lips.

Her breath came out in small white puffs in the frigid air. Her forehead creased with lines of exertion from carrying a box that was far too big for her.

Alex sprang into action. "Let me take that for you."

She looked hesitant but then relented. "It goes on the front porch."

"Your wish is my command."

They strolled side-by-side along the walkway. She cast a curious glance his way. "Are you all right? You looked a little shook up when you got out of the cab."

"You wouldn't believe the cab ride I had here." He stopped at the bottom of the steps. "I think the cabbie drove off the road more than he drove on it."

"I take it you didn't enjoy your adventure?"

"Not at all. I am very grateful to be here in one piece. Remind me to think twice before I call that cab company again."

The young lady smiled and he found himself smiling

back. This was not good. He knew better than to encourage the attention of women. It only complicated things when they wanted more than he could offer.

He forced his lips into a flat line as he moved onto the porch. The box landed with a thunk. He turned around to find the young woman standing just behind him.

As he dusted off his hands, he took in her white winter jacket with the logo for The Willows stitched in blue thread on the chest. His gaze skimmed downward, catching her snug jeans and the wheat-colored work boots that completed her ensemble. He drew his gaze up from her peekaboo curves. At last his gaze made it to her eyes—her big brown eyes. He wondered if she knew how beautiful she was. The guys must go crazy over her.

"Thank you for the help." Her gaze strayed to his luggage and back to him. "Can I help you? Are you part of the wedding party?"

"No, I'm not." His voice came out deeper than normal. "I want to check in."

"Rooms are by reservation only."

This young woman must be mistaken. "I have a reservation. Now, if you could point me in the direction of the person in charge."

The young lady pulled off a glove and held out her hand. "You're speaking to her. I'm Reese Harding. And you would be?"

He stepped closer and wrapped his cold fingers around her warm ones. Her skin was smooth and supple. He resisted the urge to stroke the back of her hand with his thumb. When his gaze caught hers, he noticed the gold flakes in her eyes.

"Allow me to introduce myself. I am P—" He caught himself just in time before blurting out his formal title. It took him a moment to recall the alias he'd used on the registration. He'd borrowed his mother's family name. "Alex DeLuca."

Then, realizing he'd held on to her hand longer than necessary, he released his hold on her. He never let a woman affect him to this extent. Being awake more than twenty-four hours was definitely impacting him. If only he could sleep on planes, it'd help.

"You own this place?" he asked, just to make sure he understood her correctly.

"Yes, I do."

His brows gathered as he studied her. She certainly seemed awfully young to be running her own business. "If you don't mind me asking, how old are you?"

"I can assure you I'm older than I look."

Well, now she had him curious. "And that would be—"

"Twenty-five." Her dimpled chin lifted. "Don't tell me you're going to card me too?"

"Um…no." He glanced away. He was letting himself get off track. It must be jet lag, because he wasn't here to pick up women—even one as captivating as the woman standing before him. "About the room—"

"The place is full up until Monday."

"Monday?" That was impossible. The muscles in his neck and shoulders tightened. "I made the reservation for today."

"If you'd like to make another reservation, I can check our calendar." She turned and stepped inside.

He strode after her, closing the door behind him. "I assure you I have a reservation, if you'd just check."

With an audible huff, she stopped in the foyer and turned. "Listen. I don't have your reservation. In fact, I've never spoken to you in my life. I would have remembered the accent."

He would have remembered her honeyed voice, too.

She was as attractive as she was frustrating. "Someone else must have taken my reservation. Surely you're not the only person who works here." Then again, this place was smaller than he'd been expecting. "Are you?"

Her forehead crinkled. "No, I'm not. But anyone you'd have spoken to would have checked the online system and known we were booked."

Not about to give up, he thought back to the phone call when he'd made the reservation. "It was a woman I spoke to about getting a room. She sounded a bit older than you. She took my information."

She frowned. "Maybe you do have a reservation. It's possible it didn't get entered in our system." She lowered her head and shook it. "But it doesn't change the fact that I don't have anywhere for you to stay. We are hosting a wedding this weekend."

He'd boarded three different flights today just to be sure he'd lost the paparazzi. And he'd suffered through a long layover in the Atlanta airport, cramped in a chair. All he wanted to do now was enjoy a warm meal and a soft bed. He held back a yawn. Rather make that a soft bed and then the warm meal. Anything else was unacceptable.

He straightened to his full six-foot-three-inch height and pressed his hands to his waist. He swallowed his frustration and strove for a professional tone. "What about my deposit?"

Her lush lips gaped and her face paled. "You made a deposit?"

"Yes. Check your computer."

Her eyes widened. "Mr. DeLuca, I'll definitely check into getting you a full refund. I'm truly sorry for the inconvenience."

He glanced around at the historic mansion. His gaze scaled up the rounded staircase, taking in the stained-

glass window on the landing. There had to be room somewhere—even if it took a bit of juggling.

"Since you've already accepted my money and this
place looks spacious enough, I am sure you can set up
accommodations for me until this wedding is over." He
flashed her one of his camera-ready smiles. "After all, I
traveled a long way to get here. Now I expect you to hold
up your end of the arrangement."

Her lush lips pressed into a firm line as though she
were considering her options before speaking. "Why
don't you follow me into the lobby while I clear up this
snafu?"

Without another word the spitfire strode away. Her well-
rounded hips sashayed from side to side like the metro-
nome from the days when he'd been forced to take piano
lessons. Only the swing of her backside mesmerized him
in a way the silly rhythm keeper from his childhood never
did. He stared at her until she disappeared back down the
hallway.

Alex gave himself a mental jerk. He couldn't let himself
get distracted—no matter how beautiful the distraction.
He had a job to do. A mission to complete. His sole duty
was to protect the crown of the Mirraccino Islands from
a messy scandal—one that would most certainly rock not
only the palace walls but also the entire nation.

CHAPTER TWO

REESE HARDING STRODE to the back of the mansion, trying not to let the tall, dark stranger get under her skin. All the while, she ignored the prickling sensation at the back of her neck. Let him stare. She wasn't going to go all soft because he was drop-dead gorgeous and his mere touch made her fingers tingle.

Her gut told her that he was used to getting what he wanted—when he wanted—but it wasn't going to happen today. There honestly was no room. And by the way he could make her heart race with just a look, it was for the best.

Reese marched into the office just off the kitchen. She suspected that her mother had accepted his reservation. If that were the case, Reese might very well have a legitimate problem. And she'd have no one to blame but herself. When her mother had finally come out of the dark place she had disappeared to after Reese's father unexpectedly died, she had been so excited to see her mother's desire to help with the inn that perhaps she'd let her mother have too much freedom.

"Hey, honey." Her mother peered in from the kitchen. "What are you doing? You just tracked a trail of snow over my clean floors."

"Sorry." Reese continued rummaging through the

stacks of bills and correspondence on top of the big oak desk. "I need to find something."

"Can I help?" Her mother's face lit up. "I'm feeling like my old self now and would really like to be more helpful around here. I could organize the office for you."

"Mom, we talked about this. I like it the way it is. I can usually find what I'm looking for." And she would this time, too, if Mr. DeLuca didn't have her all flustered. "Besides, we don't want to rush things. You're doing so well and all, I just don't want—"

"I know, honey." Her mother patted her back. "It's just nice to be needed. So what are you looking for?"

"There's some guy waiting in the foyer claiming to have a reservation for tonight. Do you recall taking a phone call from an Alex something or other?"

Her mother's graying head tilted to the side. "I'm not sure. A lot has been happening around here lately."

Reese stopped shuffling through the papers in the organizer and looked directly at her mother. "This is important. Think real hard. Did you take a reservation from a man with a foreign accent?"

Her mother's forehead crinkled. "When would he have called?"

"Last week." Reese grabbed another stack of papers, looking for anything that would confirm that man's words.

"Seems to me I might recall speaking to someone with a foreign accent. I remember because the connection wasn't very good."

"Really? You remember him?"

"If I took his reservation, the money will be in the computer."

Her mother was right. She was wasting her time searching through all of those papers. She could pop on the computer and confirm Alex's deposit had been made. She pushed a button to start the computer.

"I'll leave you alone to figure things out." Her mother made a beeline for the door.

Reese logged into the resort's financial account. There was indeed a deposit—a huge deposit. Surely she'd misread the amount. Even after she blinked and refocused, the same enormous dollar figure remained. Her heart picked up its pace as excitement coursed through her veins. There was more than enough cash here to rent out the entire mansion for a month.

She then checked the inn's online reservation system. There was no mention of Mr. DeLuca. How was that possible?

After some quick sleuthing, she determined that her mother had bypassed the online reservation system and taken his information over the phone manually. Oh, what a mess! She'd have to sit her mother down and have a firm talk about procedures so they could avoid these issues in the future.

Still, this influx of cash was just what they needed to pay the upcoming tax bill, not to mention the bank loan. *Calm down. You're getting ahead of yourself.*

It wasn't like she could accept his money. She didn't have one single room to offer him. All she could do was offer Mr. Sexy Accent a full refund and hope he'd go away quietly.

But nothing about the man said he'd easily back off from what he wanted. Everything from the man's every-strand-in-its-place dark hair to his tailored white shirt that covered an obviously buff chest and down to his polished dress shoes said he was used to getting what he wanted when he wanted and the way he wanted it.

Nonetheless, she didn't have the ability to accommodate

him, much less the obviously large party that he planned
to host. With a weary sigh, she grabbed the checkbook to
write out the refund. The pen hovered over the check and
her grip tightened as she thought of turning away all of
that money.

She wrote out his name and the amount. Life wasn't fair.
In the past year or so, with the economic downturn, she'd
had a hard time attracting people to The Willows and now
she was having to turn away this obviously affluent guest
because of a clerical error.

She really did feel bad for him. Then a thought occurred
to her. The least she should do was help this man locate
some other reasonable accommodations.

Armed with the check and her address book, she returned to the foyer. Upon finding her mother and Mr.
DeLuca conversing in lowered voices, she paused by the
staircase. Neither of them seemed to notice her presence.
What in the world was her mother saying that was so en-
grossing? The man rocked back on his heels and laughed.
The sound was deep and rich.

When she stepped off the carpeted runner and onto the
dark, polished wood floor, her boots made a sound. Both
her mother and Mr. DeLuca turned her way. Reese's hold
on the sizable check tightened. It was best to get this over
with quickly.

The man caught her gaze with his deep blue eyes. She
was struck by their vibrant color, but beyond that they told
her nothing of the man's thoughts. Talk about a poker face.
What sort of things did this international hunk keep hidden from the rest of the world? And what twist of fate had
brought him to her doorstep?

The rise of his brows had her averting her gaze, but not
before her pulse spiked, causing her heart to flutter. Why
was she so intrigued by this stranger? So what if he came

from another land and had the sexiest way of rolling his *R*s? He was still just a guy and she wouldn't let herself want something that she knew could never be. Her attention needed to remain on the mansion and keeping it afloat.

"Ah, there's my daughter." Her mother leaned toward Mr. DeLuca as though they were old friends. "I'm sure she'll have cleared everything up for you. It was nice to meet you. I hope we can talk again." Her mother's eyes twinkled as a mischievous grin played across her lips.

Once they were alone, Reese pulled her shoulders back. "Mr. DeLuca, I've verified your reservation and I must apologize for the inconvenience this has caused you. My mother made a mistake when she gave you the reservation. She didn't realize that we already had a prior commitment."

The man remained silent, not appearing the least bit interested in helping her out of this awkward situation. She held out the hefty check, but he didn't make any attempt to accept it.

"This is the full amount you paid. I double-checked." When he still didn't move, she added, "The check will cover your full deposit."

"I don't want it."

"What? Of course you do. That's a lot of money."

Tired of playing word games, she stepped up to him and stuffed the check in his hand. For the second time in less than an hour, his touch caused a jolt of awareness to shock her nerve endings.

Her gaze lifted and she noticed his eyes were bloodshot, as though he'd been up all night. Then she noticed the lines bracketing his eyes and the dark shadow of beard trailing down his squared jaw. She was tempted to reach up and run her fingertips over the stubble.

She clamped her hands together. "If you'd like, I have

the phone numbers of other facilities around the city that might be able to accommodate your party—"

"That won't be necessary," he said firmly. "I am staying here as arranged."

"But—"

"There are no more buts. I am staying." He pressed the check back into her hand. "And don't tell me again that there is no room. Your mother informed me otherwise."

"She did what?"

He sent her a knowing smile. "She told me there's a bedroom available. It's in some private apartment until one of the guest rooms opens up."

What in the world had gotten into her mother? Sure, she used to be impulsive back before the disaster with Reese's father, but since then she'd been so reserved, so quiet. Now she was getting active in the inn, which was great, but why in the world was she handing out her daughter's bedroom to this total stranger?

Reese shook her head, trying to dispel the image of this tall, dark, smooth-talking stranger in her bed. "She shouldn't have done that, not without talking to me."

His voice softened. "She seemed certain you wouldn't mind. After all, it's only until the other guests check out."

"But that's days away. They aren't leaving until Monday." And the apartment was so small that they'd be bumping into each other, day and…night. She swallowed hard.

At that moment, approaching footsteps sounded on the stairs. Relieved at the interruption, Reese turned away. Sandy, in her blue-and-white maid's uniform, descended the steps with her dark brown ponytail swinging back and forth. The young woman's eyes lit up when they landed on their latest guest. It would appear that being left in the lurch by the father of her child wasn't enough to make Sandy immune to Mr. DeLuca's charming smile.

"Do you need something, Sandy?" Reese asked, hoping the girl would quit openly ogling the man.

Sandy came to a stop next to them. "I…uh…finished cleaning all of the rooms." She tore her gaze from Mr. DeLuca and turned to Reese. "Do you need anything else today? I don't mind staying longer."

"Thanks. But we're good. Enjoy your evening off."

"Um…sure. Thank you." Sandy almost tripped over her own feet as she kept glancing over her shoulder at Mr. DeLuca.

Reese turned back to him, refusing to let his tanned features, mesmerizing blue gaze and engaging smile turn her into a starstruck teenager. "Where were we?"

"We had just resolved my accommodations until the wedding party checks out. Now, if you'll show me to my room."

She pressed her lips firmly together, holding back her response until she gave it some thought. The truth was most women would probably stumble over themselves to have this hunk of a man sleep in their bed. But she wasn't most women. Men couldn't be trusted—no matter how well you thought you knew them.

But this arrangement was all about business—nothing more. What was a few nights on their old, lumpy couch? As it was, she didn't sleep all that much anymore. The concerns about meeting this month's payroll on top of the loan payment kept her tossing and turning most nights.

"I must warn you that the room is nothing special. In fact, it's rather plain."

"Is it clean?"

She nodded. The linens had just been changed that morning. "But I'm certain it won't be up to the standards you're used to or even the normal standards of The Willows. And…and—"

"And what?"

She shook her head. "Nothing important."

She couldn't bring herself to let on that it bothered her to share her tiny apartment with him. And no matter how much she reminded herself that it was business, it still felt personal having him slide between her sheets and lay his head on her pillow. Her pulse picked up its pace. Her gaze strayed to his bare ring finger before she realized her actions and refocused on a nondescript spot just over his left shoulder.

Maybe if he wasn't drop-dead gorgeous she wouldn't be overreacting. But for the first time since she'd started the inn, her hormones were standing up and taking a definite interest in a man. Not that he'd be interested in a college dropout like herself—even if quitting school hadn't been a choice but rather a necessity.

He looked pointedly at her. "If you have something else on your mind, you might as well get it out in the open now."

Heat crept up her neck as her fingers tightened around the check. No way was she confessing to her nonprofessional thoughts. "I was just concerned about where the rest of your party would be staying."

"There's no one else coming. I am the only guest."

"Just you?" Her gaze moved to the check that was now a bit wrinkled. "But this deposit covers all six rooms."

"I am a man who values his privacy."

That or he was so filthy rich that he didn't have the common sense God gave a flea. But hey, who was she to argue with some sheikh or eccentric recluse?

But the money in her hand came with some sticky strings. She'd have to open her home up to him for five days and four nights. She suddenly regretted not doing more with the upkeep of the apartment. But her limited funds had to go toward the debts her father had left as her inheritance. Soon the creditors would be calling and she wasn't sure what she would tell them.

She glanced up at the staircase and balcony with the large stained-glass window. Her mother's family had owned the mansion for generations. She didn't want to think about the tailspin her mother would go into if they had to turn this place over to the bank—not now that her mother had almost recovered from her father's deception. So if it took bunking with this man to secure the necessary funds, she didn't see where she had much choice in the matter.

"Well, Mr. DeLuca, it looks like you've rented yourself a mansion."

What would it be like having a sexy roommate? Did he sleep in boxers? Or perhaps in the buff? And more importantly, did he walk in his sleep? Heat swirled in her chest and rushed up her neck. After all, a glimpse wouldn't hurt anyone.

The lines on the man's tanned face eased and a hint of a smile played at the corners of his full lips. "Now that we're housemates, you may call me Alex."

She wasn't so sure getting personal with him would help her roving thoughts, but she wasn't about to turn away his kindness. "And you can call me Reese."

CHAPTER THREE

THIS WAS WHERE he was to stay?

Alex followed Reese into the tiny apartment. He wondered who lived here or if it was just kept as a spare unit. Although seeing the older furniture and the coziness of the place, it didn't resemble any of the inn's photos he'd observed online. This place definitely wasn't meant for guests.

Reese swung open the door to a small bedroom. "This is where you can sleep."

He stepped up behind her in the doorway and peered over her shoulder. The decorations consisted of miniature teddy bears of all colors and designs. He'd never seen so many stuffed animals in one room. It was definitely interesting decor.

The most important feature was that it had a place for him to sleep. In the middle of the room stood a double bed sporting a royal-blue duvet with white throw pillows. Definitely nothing fancy, but at this point it didn't matter. He didn't think he could take one more step.

And to be honest, staying in these private quarters, as primitive as they were, would only make him that much harder to find. It'd been way too easy to tease the press with a juicy morsel of information about how he'd lost his heart to an American. But what no one knew was that he wanted no part of the *L* word. He'd witnessed firsthand how devastating it could be when you've lost the one person you loved with all of your heart. He refused to let himself become that vulnerable.

"Dinner is at six." Reese backed out of the doorway. "Do you need anything else?"

He stepped past her and hefted his suitcase onto the bed. "Your mother mentioned the room has a private bath."

Reese's brows rose sharply. "She was mistaken."

"I don't think so. She sounded quite certain."

Reese crossed her arms and tilted her head until their gazes met. "Well, she was mistaken, because she was talking about her room and she's not about to give it up to you or anyone."

"You seem very protective of your mother."

"She's all I've got in this world." And without another word, Reese turned and left.

Alex stood there staring at the now empty doorway, mentally comparing the image of the smiling older woman with the very serious young woman who seemed less than happy to have him here. There was a definite resemblance between the two as far as looks went, but the similarities stopped there. He rubbed the back of his neck before stretching. He was probably making too much of the first meeting. He'd see things clearer in the morning.

At last, he gave in to the urge for a great big yawn. The unpacking could wait. After being in transit for much longer than he cared to remember, it'd feel so good to lie down and rest. Just for a moment. After all, it was almost dinnertime.

He leaned his head back against the pillow. Maybe this trip wasn't going to be as bad as he'd imagined. For the time being, he could be a normal person without people looking at him with preconceived notions of what a royal should say or do. For just a bit, he'd be plain old Alex. A regular citizen. A mere tourist. Something he'd never been in his whole life.

The next morning, Alex awoke with his street clothes still on. He'd only meant to lie down for a moment. His stomach rumbled. He hadn't even made it to dinner. Then the events of the prior evening started to play in his mind.

He groaned as he recalled how in his exhausted state he'd been less than gentlemanly, demanding to have his way. He scratched at his two—or was it now a three?—day-old beard. He definitely owed Reese an apology.

After a hot shower and a much-needed shave, he started to unpack. He moved to the dresser and pulled out a drawer. He froze when he spotted a light pink lacy bra. What in the world?

His gaze moved to the right, finding a matching pair of undies. They weren't much more than a scrap of lace with a couple of pink strings. Immediately the image of Reese came to mind. This must be her bedroom. And these were her things. He slammed the drawer shut, but it was too late. His imagination had kicked into overdrive.

Not only had he been unfriendly last evening, but he'd even stolen her bed right out from under her. He groaned. He wasn't so sure an apology was going to be enough to earn his way into her good graces.

He removed a pair of jeans and a sweater from his suitcase—the clothes he'd borrowed from his brother. They were more casual than his normal wardrobe, but this trip called for a very casual appearance. He and his fraternal twin, the Crown Prince Demetrius Castanavo, still wore the same size. Not that his brother would even notice the missing clothes, much less care about them. He had more important things on his mind at the moment.

Alex's next task was styling his temporarily darkened hair. He didn't want anyone to recognize him too soon. Let the paparazzi continue with their hunt. After all, the fun was in the chase. And it'd take them awhile to find him in this out-of-the-way inn.

As he worked the styling gel into his hair, he mulled over his brother's situation. He sympathized with Demetrius. The thought of being responsible not only for the royal family but also for an entire nation was, to say the least, a bit overwhelming. He just hoped Demetrius would come to terms with his inherited position as crown prince and not cause any further incidents—such as the potential scandal everyone was working so hard to cover up.

Next Alex added some saline drops to his eyes to refresh the colored contacts similar to the ones he'd used while he'd been on vacation a few months back. He blinked a couple of times, then inspected his image in the mirror. A smile pulled at his lips. For today, he was no longer Prince Alexandro. He was just plain, ordinary Alex. But first he had some royal business to attend to.

He stepped into the living room and heard a knock at the door. A man handed him a tray of food and Alex's mouth watered. It'd been a long time since he'd been this hungry. He thanked the man and barely got seated on the couch before he took his first big bite.

After finishing every last drop of the herb soup and devouring the turkey sandwich, he logged on to his computer. He scanned one news site and then another and another. His plan wasn't working. The paparazzi weren't following his jaunt to the U.S. the way he'd hoped they would. In fact, he'd fallen out of the headlines. This was not good. Not good at all.

He'd definitely have to up the stakes if he wanted to gain the press's fleeting attention. Uncomfortable with the idea of throwing out a juicy bit of information, he nonetheless started typing a note from a fictitious palace employee to a popular internet gossip site about his recent "activities." This was the only way to keep them from sniffing out the truth—the scandal that was his brother's life. He just wondered what lengths he'd have to go to in order to keep up this charade.

He was able to keep working into the afternoon and catch up on some important emails related to Mirraccino's shipping commerce. Once he'd pressed the send button on the last email, he made his way downstairs. He'd just found his way to the kitchen when Reese came rushing out of it carrying a stepstool. All bundled up in her coat and fuzzy pink earmuffs, she came to a halt when she noticed him blocking the hallway.

"Good afternoon." Her voice was cool and there was no hint of a smile on her face.

This would be so much easier if he hadn't stumbled upon her skimpy undies. Even now he wondered if she had on a matching blue set. Or perhaps she preferred deep purple. Or maybe they were polka-dotted.

"Could you move aside? I was on my way out the door."

He gave himself a mental jerk. He wasn't ready for her to go—not yet. "I smell something delicious. The aroma wafted the whole way upstairs. What is it?"

She lowered the collapsible stool to the floor and leaned it against her leg. "It's homemade marinara sauce. But it's not ready yet. If you want to make yourself comfortable in the living room just off the foyer, I'll make sure someone lets you know when dinner is served."

"Do you want to join me?"

"I can't. I'm headed outside to do some work." She hefted the silver stool.

"But I wanted to speak with you."

"Can it wait? I have a couple of things I need to do before dinner."

"Of course." He kept what he hoped was an impartial expression on his face. "It's not urgent. May I help you?"

She shook her head. "I've got it."

As she headed for the front door, an uneasy feeling came over him. The ladder looked as though it'd seen far better days. Combine that with the ice and snow and it'd undoubtedly add up to trouble. Perhaps this was a way he could earn himself some points with her. But more than that, something told him Reese could use a helping hand—even if she was too stubborn to admit it.

As it was, he'd never been any good at just sitting around doing nothing. If he'd been at the palace, he'd be busy dealing with one situation or another. His country was quite involved with the exportation of its fine wines and fruit as well as being a shipping mecca. But he had to keep in mind that while he was in New York, he was plain Alex on holiday. Still, that didn't mean he had to sit around doing nothing.

He rushed off to grab his coat from the apartment. On the way back down the stairs, he happened upon a young man rushing up the steps, taking them two at a time. The guy had stress marring his face as a distinct frown pulled at his mouth. The guy grunted a hello as he rushed past. Alex couldn't help but wonder if that was the groom.

Why in the world did people put themselves through such stressful situations? He had no intention of saying *I do* any time soon—if ever. He'd seen firsthand how powerful love could be. And when it was over, it left people utterly devastated.

If he took the plunge it would be for something other than love—something worthwhile. After all, a meaningful union was what was expected of a prince. It was his duty.

Lost in his thoughts, Alex yanked open the front door. His hand grasped the brass handle on the glass storm door and pushed. At that moment, he saw Reese off to the side. The door bumped into the stool with her on it. The contraption teetered to the side. Reese jumped off just in time.

"Are you okay?" Alex rushed to her side.

"I'm fine." But she didn't look happy to see him—not that he could blame her.

"I didn't expect to find someone standing in front of the door."

"It's my fault, I should have moved over to the side a little more, but I was having problems stringing the lights right above the door."

He glanced at them. "They look all right to me."

"Look at them from down here." She led the way into the yard, oblivious of the deepening layer of snow.

Alex followed her. When he turned back, he found she'd transformed the porch into a beautiful winter scene. There was garland lining the front of the porch. Small artificial pine trees strung with white lights stood guard on either side of the front door. And then there were strands of white twinkle lights the whole way around the porch, giving it a soft glow.

As Reese stood there puzzling over how to finish stringing the lights, her full lips pursed together. If he were impulsive—like his twin—he might consider stealing a kiss just to see if her lips were as sweet as they looked.

Alex turned to look out over the quiet street. The thought of kissing her still pulled at his thoughts. Besides probably earning him a slap for his effort, he knew kissing her was the sort of spontaneity that had gotten his brother in a world of trouble. Alex still didn't understand how the crown prince could elope with a woman he had only known for a handful of weeks. Frustration churned in Alex's gut. No one would want an impulsive ruler, including Alex himself. That's why the elopement had to be dealt with immediately and quietly without the encroachment of the press.

Alex glanced in Reese's direction to find her big brown eyes studying him. Her gaze was intense and put him off center because it was as if she could see through him—see that he was a fake. Or maybe it was his guilt from not introducing himself properly as the prince of the Mirraccino Islands that had him uneasy.

But it had to be this way. Keeping his identity hush-hush was of the utmost importance. He didn't know this woman any better than a person on the street. There was no reason to take her into his confidence and expect her to keep it. To her he was nothing more than a paying customer—end of story.

Her brow crinkled. "Is something wrong?"

"Not that I can think of."

"Okay. I just thought with you standing out here in the cold instead of inside in the warmth that you must need something important."

This was his opening. He didn't have a lot of practice at apologies and for some reason he really wanted to get this right.

"There's something I have to say." When he had her full attention, he continued. "I am sorry about our first meeting. I was way out of line."

There was a flicker of something in her eyes, but in a blink, it was gone. "Apology accepted. But it wasn't all your fault. You were expecting a room to be waiting for you. No one could blame you for being upset."

"But then to kick you out of your own bed—"

"Don't worry. I don't sleep much anyway."

Before he could inquire about her last statement, she

headed back to the porch to adjust the strand of lights on the banister.

"What do you think?" Reese returned to his side.

He didn't really notice a difference. "Looks much better."

"I don't know." She crossed her arms and studied the lights strung from one end of the porch to the other. "It's not perfect, but I guess it'll have to do."

"Do you always decorate so elaborately?"

She shrugged. "I wouldn't bother, but each home along Cobblestone Way is expected to light up their homes for the holidays."

Reese climbed on the unstable stepstool. When she swayed slightly, Alex rushed to her side.

"Let me do that for you." He held out his hands for the string of lights.

"Thanks, but I've got it. I know exactly how they go."

Instinctively he placed a hand on her hip to steady her while with his other hand he gripped the stool. The heat of her body seeped through her jeans and into his hand, sending a strange sensation pulsating up his arm.

She glanced down at him and their gazes caught for a second more than was necessary. Then she turned away and attempted to string the lights on three little hooks above the door.

"There. That should do." With his hand aiding her, she climbed down the few steps. "Would you mind plugging them in?" She pointed to the outlet on the other side of the porch.

He was glad to help, even if it was just something small. And the fact that this independent woman let him do anything at all must mean that he was making a little bit of progress with her. He liked that thought—not that he was going to let this budding friendship go too far. But it would be nice to have someone around with whom he could strike up a friendly conversation. He quickly found the end of the extension cord and plugged in the additional string of lights.

He turned around to find that she'd returned to the front lawn to inspect her own handiwork. Deciding that she had the right idea, he did the same. He glanced up at the house, finding it looked just as good as before. "You did a great job."

"It's no big deal. But it's nice to know that someone enjoys my efforts."

"Do you need help with anything else?"

"Actually, I do."

Her answer surprised him. "Tell me what you need."

"After dinner, I need to go get a Christmas tree."

She was going to chop down a tree? She might have the determination, but he wasn't so sure that she had the physical strength. He wondered whom she would turn to if he wasn't here. The thought of her leaning on another man didn't sit well with him.

Ignoring the bothersome thought, he followed her back to the porch and helped collect her supplies. "I must admit this will be a first for me."

"Where exactly are you from?"

He didn't want to lie to her, but he knew that he couldn't be totally honest. With his accent there was no way he could pass for an American. There had to be a way around this tricky topic.

He decided to turn things around. "Where do you think I'm from?"

"I don't know." She tilted her head to the side and eyed him. "Let me think about it."

Spending time with Reese could be trickier than he'd imagined. He didn't want to lie to her, but telling her about his homeland was not an option. Maybe he should have stayed in the apartment and avoided her altogether. He inwardly groaned. As if that would be possible with them being roommates.

Besides, he already had a date with her. Correction. He had plans with her.

Oh, boy, was he in deep trouble, and it was only his second day in New York.

CHAPTER FOUR

THIS WASN'T A good idea after all.

Reese closed the side door to the garage and inhaled a steadying breath. She'd been far too aware of Alex at dinner. The deep rumble of his contagious laughter. The way his eyes crinkled at the corners when he smiled, making him even more handsome—if that was possible. And the way he listened to her as though each word she uttered truly mattered.

This was not good.

What had she been thinking inviting this man to go pick out a Christmas-tree with her? It wasn't as if she needed any help. Since her father's death, she'd been managing everything on her own. Why should that change now?

But she reasoned that Alex was an important guest. His enormous fee would help her meet this month's bills... she hoped. It was definitely a good incentive to make his stay here as pleasant as possible. And perhaps he'd recommend his friends stay at The Willows the next time they visited the city.

And if they were all as easy on the eyes, she wouldn't complain. After all, looking didn't hurt anything. It was getting involved with men that set you up for a world of pain. Just ask her mother. And even Reese had been involved with someone after her father died who'd promptly dumped her when he found out she wasn't a rich debutante. The memory still stung. How could she have been so foolish as to fall for her ex's promises?

In the end, she'd learned an important life lesson—don't trust men with your heart. Eventually they'll hurt you when you least expect it.

As for Alex DeLuca, she was so far out of that man's league that it was laughable. So what was she worrying about? She could relax and enjoy having some company for once.

She pressed the automatic garage door opener and started the truck. It coughed and sputtered and the breath caught in her throat. *Please don't let this be another thing I need money to fix.* As though in response to her silent prayer, when she turned the key again the engine caught. She exhaled a pent-up breath and put the vehicle in drive.

In no time at all, Alex was seated next to her. "Reese, thank you for allowing me to ride along."

The *R*s rolled off his tongue in such a divine way. She stopped herself just short of swooning. He could definitely say her name as often as he wanted. Realizing that she was letting her thoughts wander, she reminded herself that he was her guest—nothing else.

"Um…sure. No problem." In an effort to keep her thoughts from straying, she turned on the radio and switched stations until holiday music filled the air. As an afterthought, she said, "I hope you don't mind some music."

"Not at all. Back home my mother used to always have music filling the…house."

She noticed his use of the past tense and then the awkward pause. She wondered if he too was a member of the lost-a-parent-prematurely club. It was not something she'd wish on anyone—no matter the circumstances. But then again, maybe she was reading too much into his choice of words, as English was obviously his second language.

In an effort to change the topic of conversation to something more casual, she said, "That's right, I was supposed to guess where you're from. I'm not great with placing accents, but I'm thinking somewhere in the Mediterranean. Maybe Italy?"

"Very good guess. Maybe you are better at figuring out accents than you think."

English definitely had a different ring to it when Alex was speaking. It had a sort of soothing melody. She could listen to him talk for hours.

"If you don't mind me asking, what brought you to New York?"

"Business. Or should I say, I am between business negotiations. With people being out of the office for the holidays, I decided to stay in New York and experience a white Christmas."

"You hope."

"What?"

She could feel his gaze on her. "I meant you hope to see a white Christmas. Snow around these parts is hit or miss. The snow we're getting now might be all we get until after the New Year."

Was it possible he had no family to go home to? Why else would he rent out an inn for the holiday? Pity welled up in her. She couldn't blame him for not wanting to spend Christmas alone. She'd had a taste of that when her mother was having problems. It was lonely and sad, filled with nothing but memories.

Which led her to her next question: How did such a handsome, obviously successful man end up alone? Surely he wouldn't have a hard time finding a date or two. Oh, who was she kidding? He could probably have a different date for breakfast, lunch and dinner, seven days a week, and still have plenty leftover. Perhaps if her life were different she might have given him a chance.

Alex cleared his throat. "Are you sure we're going in the right direction? We're heading into the city."

She had been distracted by their conversation, but she couldn't imagine she'd turned the wrong way. Just to be sure, she glanced around at the landmarks. "This is the right way."

"But I thought you said we were going to cut down a Christmas tree."

"I said I was going to get one, but I never said anything about cutting it down." She glanced over at him as he slouched down in the seat and adjusted his ball cap. "I'm sorry to disappoint you. But this is really much faster and easier for me."

"Is it much further?"

"Not far at all. In fact, we're here."

She stared out the window at the familiar city lot that was cordoned off with fencing. Pine trees ranging in size from small chubby little guys to tall slender ones littered the lot. People from old to young meandered around, pointing at this tree and that tree. Smiles covered their faces and the years rolled away as each seemed to step back in time and remember the childhood fascination of choosing their very own tree for Santa to leave presents under. If only that feeling of wonderment stayed with everyone. Instead some learned the hard way that things weren't always as they appeared. Sometimes life was nothing more than an empty illusion.

Reese's jaw tightened at the grim thought. Anxious to get this over, she said, "I'll just go check out what's available that will fit in the foyer. Feel free to look around."

"What about a tree for yourself?" When she cast him a puzzled look, he added, "You know, for the apartment?"

"I don't want one. After what happened...oh, never mind. I just don't have the time to bother."

She threw open the truck door and hopped out. She'd already circled around to the sidewalk when Alex's door opened. She noticed that he had the collar on his jacket pulled up and his hat shielded a good portion of his face. He must be cold. If he was here long enough, he'd get used to the cold weather.

He stepped up to her. "Let me know if you need any help."

"I will. Thank you."

His gaze moved up and down the walk. If she knew him better, she'd say he looked stressed. But that couldn't be the case. Who got stressed going to the Christmas tree lot? Maybe a single mom of six active little kids. Now that could be stressful. But not a single grown man.

So what was the true story? Why was Alex all alone for the holidays?

What had he been thinking to agree to come to this very public place?

Alex glanced around to see if anyone had noticed him. It was far too early in his plan to have his true identity made known. Or worse, for someone to snap a picture of him and publish it on the internet. He pulled his ball cap a little lower. Sure, he had his disguise in place, but he knew that it would not hold up under the close scrutiny of the press's cameras.

He slouched a bit more and avoided making eye contact with anyone. Fortunately no one seemed to pay him the least bit of attention. The people meandering about seemed more interested in finding the perfect Christmas tree than the couple of dozen other shoppers.

Thousands of holiday lights were strung overhead. This town certainly had a thing for lights, from the little twinkle ones to big flashing signs. He gazed at the trees, wondering what it'd be like to be here with his own family choosing the perfect tree—not that he had any immediate plans for a family. He knew a proper marriage was expected of him, but the thought didn't appeal to him. His duty was to look after his father, the king.

After all, if it wasn't for him, his mother, the queen, wouldn't have been shot by a subversive. The poignant memory of his mother taking a bullet in the chest brought Alex up short. Because of one thoughtless act, he'd devastated lives, leaving his father brokenhearted and alone to shoulder the weight of Mirraccino's problems.

That long-ago day was still fresh in Alex's mind. He'd grown up overnight and learned the importance of rules and duty. He didn't have the luxury to wonder what his life might be like if he were an ordinary citizen. He was a prince and with that came duties that could not be shirked—the consequences were too much to bear.

Still, that didn't mean he should forgo his manners. And thanking Reese for her hospitality would be the proper thing to do. He stopped in front of a chubby little tree that would look perfect in the apartment. It'd certainly cheer the place up.

A young man with a Santa hat and red apron approached him. "Can I help you?"

"I'd like to buy the little tree in the corner."

The guy eyed him up as though wondering why he'd want something so tiny. The man rattled off a price and Alex handed over the money.

With the little tree stowed in the back of the pickup, Alex sought out his beautiful hostess, who was pointing out a tall, slender tree to an older man with a white beard.

His cheeks were chubby and when he laughed his round belly shook. Alex wondered how many times children had mistaken him for Santa. Even the man's eyes twinkled when he smiled.

The man glanced at Alex before turning back to Reese. "This must be your other half. You two make a fine-looking couple. Is this your first Christmas together?"

"We're not together." Reese's cheeks filled with color. "I mean, we're not a couple. We're...um—"

"Friends," Alex supplied.

Although on second thought, the man's observation did have some merit. In fact, the more he thought of it, the more he wondered if the man was on to something. Reese would make any man the perfect girlfriend.

She was certainly beautiful enough. When she smiled, she beamed. And in the short time he'd known her, he'd gotten a glimpse of her strength and determination.

She'd make the ideal fake girlfriend.

After all, he was supposed to be in the States because of a love interest. And with the speed with which he'd had to put this plan in motion, he hadn't had a chance to find someone to fill the role. But if the need arose, would Reese be willing to play along?

Something told him that with some gentle persuasion, she could be brought round to his way of thinking. Okay, maybe it was more a hope than a feeling. But for now none of that mattered. Hopefully his brother's rushed marriage would be resolved quickly and quietly so that involving Reese wouldn't be necessary. But it never hurt to be prepared. His father's motto was Hope for the Best, But Be Prepared for the Worst.

Perhaps Alex should do a little research and see what challenges he would be up against with Reese. He'd probe the subject with her when they were alone in the truck.

Alex leaned over to Reese. "You found a tree?"

"Yes, I did. I think it'll be perfect." She pointed to the tree the man inserted into a noisy machine. Alex watched as the tree's limbs were compressed and bound with rope.

"It'll make a great Christmas tree. You have good taste."

Reese turned to him and smiled. Such a simple gesture, and yet his breath hitched and he couldn't glance away. Big, fluffy snowflakes fluttered and fell all around them. And the twinkle lights reflected in her eyes, making them glitter like gemstones.

"As soon as they bundle it up we can go home." She moved as if to retrieve the tree, breaking the spell she'd cast over him.

Alex, at last gathering his wits, stepped forward. "I'll get it."

She frowned as though she were about to argue, but then she surprised him by saying, "Okay."

With the tree secured in the bed of the truck, Alex climbed in the heated cab. He rubbed his hands together. "I remembered everything for this outing except my gloves."

Reese's face creased with worry lines. "You should have said something. Here, let me crank up the heat."

"Not necessary. The sting from the pine needles is worse than the cold."

"Let me know if you need anything when we get back to the house. Antiseptic cream, maybe?"

"I will." This was his chance to broach the subject in the forefront of his mind. "What did you think of Santa back there mistaking us for a happy couple?"

"That he needs a new pair of glasses."

"Surely being my girlfriend wouldn't be so bad, would it?"

Once stopped at a red light, Reese gave him a long look.

He started to feel a bit paranoid, as though he had a piece of lettuce in his teeth or something. "What?"

"I'm just looking for some sign that you hit your head when you were swinging that tree around."

"Very funny." When she smiled, a funny sensation filled his chest. "You still haven't answered my question. Would I make good boyfriend material?"

She jerked her gaze forward just as the light changed. "You can't be serious. We—we don't even know each other. And I'm not looking for a relationship. Not with you. Not with anybody."

"Understood." He was at last breaking through her calm reserve. He couldn't push her too hard too fast. "I was just hoping your rejection of the idea of us being a couple wasn't a personal one. After all, I showered and shaved today. My clothes are clean," he teased. "And I carried that great big tree for you."

"That's the best you can come up with?" She smiled and his breathing did that funny little tickle thing at the back of his throat again.

"Pretty much. So if circumstances were different, would I stand a chance with you?"

"I'll give you this much, you are persistent."

"Or maybe I'm a glutton for punishment." He sent her a pleading look.

"And I'm sure those puppy eyes work on all of the ladies, don't they?"

He sat up a little straighter. "Is it working now?"

The chime of laughter filled the truck. "If you aren't a salesman, you certainly missed your calling."

Did that mean he'd sold her on the idea that he was worthy of a second or third look? He didn't know why her answer had suddenly become so important to him. It wasn't as though this part of his plan had to be implemented—yet.

Still, he found himself enjoying the smile on her face. It lit up the night. She should definitely do it more often.

Reese tramped the brakes a bit hard for a red light, jerking him against the seat belt. "I'm sure you'll make some lucky lady the perfect boyfriend."

It was his turn to smile. "Thanks for the ringing endorsement. What would it take to tempt you to play the part?"

"Of what? Your girlfriend?"

In for a penny, in for a pound. "Yes."

She laughed. "Fine. If you must know, if by chance I was looking—which I'm not, but if I were—you might have a chance. But I seriously don't have the time...if I was interested."

"Ouch."

"Is it your hands?"

"No. It was my ego. It just took a direct hit."

She shook her head and smiled. "I'm sure you'll survive."

He leaned back in the seat as she skillfully guided them homeward. With Reese behind the wheel, Alex relaxed enough to let his thoughts wander.

How was it that someone so beautiful and entertaining could be single? Surely she wouldn't be alone for long. The image of Reese in someone else's arms took shape in his mind and with a mental jerk, he dismissed the unsettling idea. Her future relationships were none of his business. Period.

CHAPTER FIVE

PEACE AND QUIET at last.

Reese smiled to herself. The wedding party was off for the rehearsal and dinner. They wouldn't be home until late. She'd even let the staff go early. After all, it was the holiday season and there was nothing here that she couldn't manage on her own. And her mother was upstairs watching her favorite crime drama.

"Reese?" Alex's deep voice echoed down the hallway.

"In here." She was kneeling on the floor, sorting strands of twinkle lights.

He stepped into the room. "What are you doing?"

"Trying to get these lights to work. I need to replace the lightbulbs—one by one. Someday I'll have to buy new strings, but not this year." They would light up—even if she had to sit here all night exchanging the little bulbs. "What do you need?"

"I finished with my work and wondered if I could lend you a hand."

"You spend a lot of time on your computer, don't you?"

"It's a portable office. It allows me to work from anywhere."

She pulled out another bulb and replaced it with one she was certain worked. Still the strand remained dark. "So this isn't a holiday for you?"

"I would rather keep busy. I am not good at sitting around doing nothing." He knelt down beside her. "Let me have a try."

She glanced at him, surprised anyone would voluntarily offer to fix Christmas lights. Before he had a chance to change his mind, she held out the strand to him. "Good luck."

He moved closer. His warm fingers brushed over hers. His touch lingered, sending an electrical current up her arm. The reaction frazzled her common sense. She stared into his eyes as her heart pounded in her ears. He was the first to turn away. A sense of disappointment plagued her.

Regaining her senses, she jumped to her feet. She took a step back, hoping to keep her wits about her. She'd been avoiding him since that awkward moment with Santa—er, that man at the tree lot. Why the man had assumed they were a couple was beyond her. It wasn't as if she looked at Alex with dreamy eyes. Okay, so maybe she just had. But it was just for a moment. And it wasn't as if she was truly interested in him.

But then Alex had continued the conversation in the truck. What was that all about? She still wasn't certain if he had just been joking around or if he'd been hitting on her. At least she'd set him straight—a relationship wasn't in her plans. She refused to be lied to by another man.

Alex pushed a small lightbulb into the socket. Nothing lit up. "I don't smell any food cooking. That's a first. This place always has the most delicious aromas."

In that moment, she realized in her exuberance to let everyone have the evening off that she hadn't thought about dinner. And she didn't have a good history with the stove. Anything she put near it burned—to a crisp.

"I'm afraid that I let the staff have the evening off. With the wedding party gone for the evening and the holidays approaching, I thought they would enjoy some time off. So I'm not sure what to do for dinner, as I'm an utter disaster in the kitchen."

"It doesn't have to be anything fancy. In fact, simple sounds good."

Against her better judgment, she was starting to like this guy. "How simple were you thinking? I can work the microwave, but that's about it."

His brow arched as amusement danced in his eyes.

"Hey, don't look at me like that. A person can't be good at everything. So how about a frozen dinner?"

His tanned nose curled up. "Or we could order a pizza?" He loosened a bulb from the strand. "They do deliver here, don't they?"

She nodded. "I'll check to see if my mother will join us. I'll be right back with the menus."

She rushed out of the room and up the stairs to the little apartment that she'd been sharing with her mother since her father's death two years ago, when her life had changed from that of a carefree college student with the whole world ahead of her to a college dropout, striving to keep a roof over her brokenhearted mother's head.

Not that she would have ever made any other choice. Her mother had always been there for her—she'd made her smile and wiped her tears. Now it was Reese's turn to pitch in and help. That's what families did—took care of each other.

"Hey, Mom," Reese called out, bursting through the door of their apartment. "How do you feel about—"

The words died in her throat as she noticed her mother sitting before a tiny Christmas tree on the coffee table. It was lit up and had a few ornaments on it. What in the world? Where had it come from?

Her mother was staring at it as if she were lost in her

thoughts. Was she thinking about the past? Was her mother remembering how Reese used to beg her father for her very own Christmas tree?

The memories Reese had been suppressing for so long came rushing back. The image of her father's joyful smile as he held a tiny pine tree in his hand had her chest tightening. Back then he'd call her his little princess, and she'd thought the sun rose and set around him. How very wrong she'd been.

"Mom?" Her voice croaked. She swallowed hard and stepped closer to her mother. "Are you okay?"

Her mother blinked and glanced up at her. "I'm fine. But I'm glad you're here. I just had a phone call and your aunt isn't doing well."

Relieved to find that her mother wasn't sinking back into that miserable black hole where she seemed virtually unreachable, Reese asked, "What's wrong with Aunt Min?"

"She's having a hard time adjusting since Uncle Roger passed on. That was her neighbor and she agreed to come pick me up. I know with the holiday approaching and the wedding this weekend that this is the wrong time to be leaving you alone, but no one knows your aunt as well as me."

Reese wasn't so sure about her mother leaving to comfort someone who was grieving. She knew for a fact it was not an easy position to be in. But her mother appeared to be determined, and she supposed there was nothing she could say to change her mind.

"What can I do for you?" Reese asked, ready to pitch in.

"Absolutely nothing. You already have your hands full here." Her mother gave her a hug. "I've got to pack before my ride gets here."

Her mother was headed for the bedroom when Reese called out, "Mom, where did the tree come from?"

"Alex. He thought you might like it."

Her mother disappeared into her bedroom and Reese turned. The long-forgotten handmade ornaments on the little tree caught her eye.

Well, if he was so interested in having a Christmas tree, he could have it in his room—er, her room. She unplugged the lights, carried the tree to the bedroom and pushed aside her collection of miniature teddy bears—some that were as old as she was and some that were antiques collected from her grandmother and yard sales.

She'd always planned to update the room, but once she'd formally withdrawn from college, she'd packed up her apartment and put everything in storage. There wasn't time to worry about knickknacks when there was an entire inn to run. And now she was just too tired after working and smiling at the guests all day to be worried about redecorating a room where she barely spent any time.

She glanced at the bed with its comforter haphazardly pulled up. She imagined Alex sleeping in it. There was something so intimate about knowing that the Mediterranean hunk was sprawled out in her bed. Just as quickly as the thought came to her, she vanquished it.

He was a man—not to be trusted. And he'd only gone and confirmed her thoughts when he went against her wishes with the little Christmas tree—even if it had been an effort to be considerate. Conflicting emotions churned in her stomach. Why couldn't he leave well enough alone?

Not needing or wanting the aggravation, she pulled the door closed on the room. And that's exactly what she needed to do with Alex—close the door on this thing that was bubbling just beneath the surface.

He'd put this off long enough.

Alex retrieved his phone from his pocket. It was time

to let the king know that he was safe. In return, hopefully he would have good news as well. Perhaps this mess with his brother, the crown prince, had been quietly resolved. Then Alex could pack his bags and catch the first flight home—away from his beautiful hostess, who muddled his thoughts and had him losing focus on his priorities.

He dialed the king's private line. The phone was answered on the first ring, as though his papa had been sitting there waiting for him to call.

"Papa, it's me, Alexandro."

"At last, you remember to call."

"I had to move quickly and quietly in order to elude the paparazzi."

"Tell me where you are so I can dispatch your security detail."

"No." Alex's body tensed as he envisioned the dark expression settling over his papa's distinct features. It wasn't often that someone said no to the king. In fact, this was the first time Alex had done it since he was an unruly child. "I have to do this. It's the only way to protect the family. If your enemies learn of Demetrius's rash actions, they'll make it a public scandal by painting him as unfit to rule. They'll gain more support for their planned takeover."

"That's not for you to worry about. The royal cabinet has that under control."

He wanted to believe his papa's comforting words, but Alex had his own sources and they all told him that these subversives meant business. He knew that no matter how old he got, his papa would still try to shield him from the harsh realities of life. But now wasn't the time for being protective. There'd already been one uprising that year. They couldn't risk another.

"I understand, Papa. But trust me when I say I have to do this. It's for the best. As long as the press is curious of my activities, they'll focus on me instead of sniffing around the palace for a piece of juicy gossip."

The king let out a long, weary sigh. "I'll admit that it has been helpful. So far only the necessary staff know of this debacle. The councillor seems to think we should be able to clear this up soon…if only your brother would come to his senses."

"You're still opposed to this marriage?"

"In these uncertain times, we need a strong liaison with one of our allies." There was a strained pause. "If only this girl had some important connections."

His papa sounded much older than he'd ever heard him before. Alex's gut knotted with frustration. When was his older twin ever going to learn that he had responsibilities to the crown, the kingdom and to their papa, who would never step down from the throne until he was secure in the fact that his successor was up to the challenge of safeguarding the kingdom. His father had never rebounded fully after the queen's death. And now his health was waning.

Alex recalled how he'd made it to her side as she drew in her last breaths. Pain arrowed through his chest. She'd told him to take care of his papa. He'd promised to do it. And that's what he'd been striving to do ever since. Not that anything he did could make up for his part in his mother's death.

"Don't worry, Papa. I know what I'm doing."

Alex's thoughts strayed back to their visit to the Christmas tree lot.

You two make a fine-looking couple.

The more he thought of Santa's words, the more he was certain he was right—Reese had the right beauty and poise to pull off the plan he had in mind. Perhaps it was time he started figuring out ways to fit Reese into his agenda.

"Papa, everything will work out. When the time is right, I'll call for my security detail."

There was another pause. He wondered if the king was debating whether or not to command he change his plans and return home immediately.

"Alex?" The sound of Reese's voice trailed down the hallway.

"Papa, I must go. I'll call again soon." And with that he disconnected the call and switched off his phone. "I'm coming." He reached for the cabinet next to the sink, searching for a glass.

"Oh, here you are. I thought maybe you changed your mind about dinner and decided to cook instead."

"I don't cook, either. I just got thirsty." And he truly was thirsty after tap-dancing around, trying to pacify his papa.

After he downed a glassful of water and set it aside, he turned to her. "What did you need?"

"I ran upstairs to get these." She held up an array of menus.

She'd been in the apartment and that meant she must have noticed the little Christmas tree that he'd decorated to cheer up the place. Her mother had supplied some old ornaments. So why hadn't Reese mentioned it?

"Here." She stepped closer with her hand outstretched. "Pick your favorite."

He waved her away. "You pick. Whatever you choose will be fine."

Her gaze didn't meet his. "Are you sure?"

He nodded. He'd made enough decisions for tonight. He didn't feel like making any more, even if it was something as simple as pizza. In some ways, he used to envy his brother for being the crown prince, with the way people looked up to him. But as Alex got older, he was relieved to have been delivered second. It was very stressful and tiring making decisions day in and day out that impacted so many people.

Sure, to the world being royalty was all glamour and five-star dinners and balls. But behind palace walls in the executive suite there were heated debates, and the newspapers were quite critical of the decisions made by the monarchy. There was no way to please everyone all of the time.

But in this one instance, Alex was needed to keep the Mirraccino Islands together and peaceful. He would do whatever it took to keep the paparazzi from finding out the truth. Because he knew all too well what happened when a royal forgot his allegiance to the kingdom—the price was much too dear.

He cleared the lump in his throat. "While you call in the order, I can set up the tree in the living room."

"Did you get the lights to work?"

"Yes, I did. It was one bulb that was burned out. I replaced it and at last, there was light."

"Thank you." Her tone held no warmth. "Um, about the tree…I usually set it up over there next to the staircase. But I can do that myself—"

"Consider it done."

"I thought maybe you'd be tired of decorating."

So she had noticed the little tree. And it didn't seem as though she was pleased. Sure, she'd told him not to bother, but he'd thought she was too busy to do it herself and would enjoy the surprise. Her cool demeanor told him that her reason for not wanting a tree went much deeper than that.

"Christmas is one of my favorite holidays." He wondered if maybe she'd open up a little.

"That's nice." Her frosty tone chilled him. "I put the boxes of decorations next to it."

"You'll need to show me. I don't know how you want it decorated."

"Oh, that's easy. I always start with the white twinkle lights. Then I add gold ribbon and red glass ornaments."

"Do you trim the tree by yourself?"

"Yes. I find it is easier. I know how it should look, so why bother explaining how I want it when I can just as easily do it myself? In fact, you don't need to bother with it. I'll just place this call and be right back."

Reese strode out of the room like a woman on a mission. He thought it was sad that she insisted on doing so much around this place by herself. It sounded very lonely. Well, this Christmas would be different. He walked over to the tree and moved it to a spot next to the steps.

This Christmas he'd help her find the joy of the holiday.

CHAPTER SIX

Why didn't he listen to her?

Reese frowned when she returned to the foyer. Alex was busy stringing the lights. And he didn't have the tree in the right spot. She usually moved it a little closer to the stairs to keep it out of the way. She knew she was being picky. She'd known for a long time that it was one of her faults. But things must be in their proper place or it drove her to distraction.

Alex turned to her. "I went ahead and started."

She nodded, trying to not let it bother her that the tree was out of place. Or that the lights needed to be redone if they were going to make it the whole way to the top.

"You don't like it?"

She knew that he'd tried his best and she really did appreciate it. She shifted her weight from one foot to the other and continued holding her tongue. Why did it have to bother her so much? She was being silly.

"What is it?" His eyes beseeched her.

She let out a pent-up breath. "The tree needs to be moved back out of the way."

"I know. But it is easier to decorate it here."

"And the lights, they need to be spread out a little more or you'll run out before you get to the top."

He arched an eyebrow. "You can try to get me to quit, but I won't. I'm going to help you decorate this tree."

"You're stubborn."

"And you're picky."

"Something tells me we have that in common." She could give as good as she got.

He smiled. "Maybe I am. But I know what I like."

His gaze was directly on her as he stepped closer. Her heart shot into her throat, cutting off her breath. His gaze dipped to her mouth before returning to meet her curious stare.

"You're very beautiful." The backs of his fingers brushed her cheek.

She should move, but her feet wouldn't cooperate. Shivers of excitement raced down her neck and arms, leaving goose bumps in their wake. She stared into his mesmerizing blue eyes, drowning in their depths. It'd been so long since a man had been interested in her. And she hadn't realized until now how lonely she'd become. After Josh—

The memory of her ex jarred her to her senses. She stepped back. This couldn't happen. She'd promised herself that she'd keep men at a safe distance.

Alex's hand lowered to his side. If she didn't know better, she'd say there was a flicker of remorse in his eyes. What should she say to him? After all, he wasn't Josh. Her ex had been needy and demanding. Alex was thoughtful and understanding. They were opposites in almost everything. So why was she backing away? After all, he'd soon be moving on and returning to his home—far away.

Maybe she shouldn't have backed away. Maybe she should have satisfied her curiosity to see if his kisses were as passionate as she imagined them in her dreams.

But the moment had passed. There was no recapturing

it. She moved to the tree and knelt down to start adjusting the string of lights.

"Could you help me on the other side of the tree?" She tried to act as though the moment hadn't shaken her.

"Just tell me what you need me to do."

To Alex's credit, he let the awkward moment pass without question. By the time they moved the decorated tree into the correct position, Reese had to admit that she'd enjoyed her evening. Alex was actually quite entertaining with his various bits of trivia. Who would have guessed it?

It wasn't until after the wedding guests streamed through the front door that she was able to lock up the house. She climbed the steps to the tiny apartment, anxious to call it a night. She was just about to close the door when she heard footsteps bounding up the stairs. She didn't need two guesses to know that the heavy footsteps didn't belong to the anxious bride across the hall or one of her smiling attendants. No, it was the one man who got under her skin. She thought of rushing off to her mother's bedroom, but she felt the need to thank him for making a chore that normally came with some harsh, painful memories into a pleasant experience.

She turned to him. Her gaze settled on his lips. The memory of their almost kiss sent her stomach spiraling. "I—I'm heading to bed. I just wanted to thank you for the help tonight. If it wasn't for you, I would still be working at it."

"You're welcome. And it turned out well, even if it isn't exactly how you normally do it." His brows drew together as his gaze swept around the room. "What happened to the little Christmas tree?"

"I moved it to your room. I thought you could appreciate it better in there."

"But I did it for you."

"And I told you that I didn't want a tree."

"But the tree downstairs—"

"Is the price of doing business. Guests expect an inn to be decked out for the holidays, and it's my job to fulfill those expectations. But that doesn't mean I have to decorate my personal space."

"I was only trying to help."

"That's not the type of help I need." The words were out before she could stop them. Exhaustion and worry had combined, causing her thoughts to slip past her lips. "I'm sorry. I didn't mean to snap at you."

He shook his head. "You're right. I thought—ah, it doesn't matter what I thought."

The hurt look in his eyes had her scrambling for an explanation. "It's just that Christmas brings back bad memories for me and my mother. And I'm afraid that it'll upset her. I'll do anything to keep her from going back to that lonely dark place where she went after my father died."

He eyed her up as though he were privy to her most private thoughts. "Your mother seems like a strong lady. Perhaps she's stronger than you think."

Reese shook her head, recalling how her mother had crumbled after learning that her father had been on his way to his mistress when he'd died in a car accident on Christmas Eve. Loss and betrayal combined to create the perfect storm to level her mother—a woman she'd always admired for her strength. It had brought her mother to her knees and Reese never wanted to witness anything so traumatic again.

Reese pressed her hands to her hips. "You don't know her like I do."

"That's true. But sometimes an outsider can see things someone too close to the situation will miss."

She lifted her chin. "And what exactly have I missed?"

"Did you know it was your mother who got out the Christmas decorations for me to use on the little tree?"

"You must have pressured her. She wouldn't have voluntarily gotten those out. Those were...were our family ornaments, collected over the years."

"Actually, it was her idea. She insisted I decorate it for you. She thought it would make you happy."

No, that wasn't possible. Was it? Reese took a step back. When the back of her knee bumped into the couch, she sat down. What did this mean? Had she been so busy that she'd missed seeing that her mother truly was back to being herself?

"I had no idea it would upset you so much."

"It's just that...that my father always made Christmas such a big affair. It's hard to think of it and not think of him." But she failed to add the most painful part. She couldn't bring herself to admit that her father had left them on Christmas Eve for another woman. And he'd spent their money on that woman...buying her a house and leaving them in debt.

Alex stepped forward and took a seat beside her. "I didn't know."

"My mother didn't mention it?"

"She said that it has been awhile since you two celebrated Christmas, and she thought it was time you both had a good one."

Reese's heart filled with an unexpected joy. "She really said that?"

He nodded. "Otherwise I wouldn't have gone through with decorating the tree without your approval."

If this was okay with her mother, who was she to disapprove? Maybe it hadn't just been her mother who'd been deeply affected by her father's actions. In the past couple of years, Reese had been so busy worrying about keeping a roof over their heads that she hadn't realized how much her father's actions had hurt her. Or how she'd let her father steal the magic of the holiday from her.

Reese turned to Alex. "I'm sorry I was so grinchy about it."

"Grinchy?"

"Yeah, you know the story, *How the Grinch Stole Christmas?*"

"I'm not familiar with it."

"I didn't think there was anyone who didn't know that story. You must have lived a sheltered life."

"I had books, but they were educational."

"Like I said, you lived a sheltered life. Don't worry. I'm sure we can find you a copy somewhere and broaden your horizons."

"My horizons are plenty broad," he protested. "Would you mind if I brought the tree back out here?"

"Suit yourself." She most certainly wasn't the only one used to having her way.

As he strode away, she wondered why it had taken a total stranger from another land to open her eyes and help her see her life more clearly. It was as if she'd been living with tunnel vision these past couple of years, focusing on protecting her mother from further pain and keeping their home.

And though Alex was certainly a nice distraction, she couldn't let herself lose focus now. The Willows was far from being out of debt. In fact, even with Alex's generous fee she still might have to let go of Sandy, the maid and a single mom. The thought pinched at her heart.

With it being Christmas, surely there would be a miracle or something. It wasn't as though she was really a grinch, but if she had to eliminate Sandy's position at Christmastime, the comparison with that fictional character would hit far too close to home—heartless.

"Here we go." Alex strode back into the room.

She noticed how when he entered a room, his presence commanded attention. She wasn't sure what it was about him that gave her that impression. It could be his good looks or his six-foot-plus height. But no. It went beyond that. It was something much more significant, but she just couldn't put her finger on it. Maybe it was the way he carried himself, with a straight spine and level shoulders. Or the way he had that knowing look in his blue eyes. She sighed in frustration, unable to nail down exactly what was so different about him.

Alex paused. "Did you change your mind?"

"Oh, no. I guess I'm more tired than I'd originally thought."

"After I plug in this cord, would you mind turning out the lights? There's nothing like the glow of a Christmas tree."

She got to her feet and moved to the switch.

When the colored bulbs lit up the chubby little tree that to Reese resembled nothing more than a branch, she doused the overhead light. But it wasn't the tree that caught and held her attention. It was the look on Alex's face. For a second, it was the marvel of a little boy staring at a Christmas tree for the first time.

"Isn't your Christmas tree like this?" She was genuinely curious.

He shook his head. "It's quite tall and it's more formal, similar to the one you have downstairs."

"You mean it doesn't have candy canes and little bell and penguin ornaments?"

Again he shook his head. "No. Everything has to be picture-perfect. The way my mother would have wanted it."

A little voice in the back of her mind said to let the comment pass, but she couldn't. She wanted to know more about him. Maybe if she demystified him, he'd have less of a hold on her thoughts.

"Your mother…did you lose her?"

The words hung heavy in the air.

At last, Alex nodded. "She died when I was a teenager. Christmas was her favorite holiday. In fact, Papa still has the—the house decorated like she used to do. On Christmas Eve, for just a moment, it's like she's still there and going to step into the living room at any moment."

"It's good that you have such happy memories to hold on to."

"Enough about me. I'm sure you have special memories of the holidays."

She waved away his comment. "They aren't worth getting into."

She wished she could concentrate on the good times, but her father's betrayal had smeared and practically obliterated them. In her mind, that man was not worth remembering. Not after what he'd done to them. She stuffed the memories to the back of her mind.

This was why she no longer enjoyed the holidays— they dredged up unwanted memories. She wished she had nothing but good memories, like Alex. She envied him.

"I'm going to sleep." Not that she'd close her eyes any time soon. "Would you mind turning out the lights before you go to bed?"

"Not a problem." He smiled at her and her stomach fluttered. "But before you go, there's one other thing."

With nothing but the gentle glow of the little tree filling the room, it was far too romantic. Her gaze returned to his lips. They looked smooth and soft. She wondered what it'd be like to meet up with him under the mistletoe. Realizing she'd hung some downstairs for the bride and groom to indulge in, she wished she'd saved some for up here.

Alex cleared his throat. As her gaze rose to meet his, amusement danced in his eyes. Surely he didn't have a clue what she'd been thinking. Did he?

"What were you saying?" She struggled to do her best to sound normal and not let on that her heart was racing faster than the hooves of the horses who pulled the carriages around Central Park.

"I don't want to embarrass you, but did you know you have a leak in your roof?"

She nodded. "I had it fixed last week. I just haven't gotten around to getting the interior repaired."

"I could take a look at it. If you want."

She shook her head. "You're a paying guest. Not hired help."

"But I am volunteering."

Why did he always have to push? Well, this time he wasn't getting his way. "I don't need your help."

He stared at her long and hard as though trying to get her to change her mind. "Understood. I'll see you tomorrow."

At last she'd gotten through to him. "Good night."

She turned and headed back down the hall. She could sense his gaze following her, but she refused to glance back. He created a mixed-up ball of emotions in her that constantly kept her off kilter.

And what unsettled her the most was the fact that she liked him. No matter how much he pushed and prodded her, beneath it all he was genuinely a nice guy. Although he was awfully tight-lipped about his past and his family. She noticed how every time he started to mention a piece of his life, he clammed up. What was that all about?

Time passed quickly. In no time at all, Alex moved across the hall to the executive suite. He was amazed by how hard

Reese worked every single day, from the time she got up before the sun until she dropped into bed late at night. He soon found himself bored of the internet, even though his leaked letter to the paparazzi had worked as he'd hoped. Now the gossip sites were filled with all sorts of outlandish stories, but the most important part was that they were looking for him. He just had to keep his disguise in place a little longer.

He thought of Reese and how she'd react upon learning he was a prince. Somehow he couldn't imagine she'd treat him any different if she knew the truth. Or was it that he didn't want her to treat him different? He liked their budding friendship—in fact, he liked it very much.

Guilt plagued him for not being more open with her. She'd been kind and generous with him—he wanted to treat her with the same sort of respect. He considered telling her everything, but in the next thought he recalled how deviating from the plan had cost his mother her life.

Alex paced back and forth in his suite. It was best for everyone to keep up the pretense of being a businessman—which he truly was back in Mirraccino. What he needed now was something to keep him busy.

It was still early in the morning when he strode across the hall to Reese's apartment and rapped his knuckles firmly on the dark wood door. No answer. After having lived with her for the past few days, he didn't think anything of trying the doorknob. When it opened, he stepped inside.

"Reese, are you here?"

Again, no answer.

He glanced around, pleased to find that the little tree was still centered on the coffee table and a cottony white cloth with little sparkles had been placed around the base. Maybe at last Reese was starting to find her holiday spirit.

Though the place was clean, it was showing its age. It was very striking how different this apartment was from his polished, well-kept suite. He turned in a circle, taking in the details. The yellowing walls could use a fresh coat of paint. And the ceiling was missing plaster where the roof had leaked.

A thought started to take shape. He might be of royal blood, but that didn't mean he hadn't gotten his hands dirty. Thanks to a very patient maintenance worker who used to be put in charge of him whenever he got in trouble as a youth, he'd learned a lot. Probably a lot more than most people of his status. And it wasn't until now that he realized what a gift it was to have a practical skill set.

He set off to the downstairs in search of Reese. When he couldn't locate her anywhere, he ended up in the kitchen. The chef was there. He was a unique guy, tall and wiry and about Alex's age, maybe a little younger. But his worn face said that there was so much more to his life's story than cooking for pampered guests. Above all that, the guy seemed like an all-around fine fellow.

"Good morning, Bob. Have you seen Reese this morning?"

"Morning. What would you like for breakfast? I can whip you up something in no time. If you want to wait in the dining room, I'll bring it in to you."

"That won't be necessary. I can eat in here." Alex set about getting himself a cup of coffee before Bob could make the offer. "About Reese, have you seen her?"

"She passed through here awhile ago, mumbling something about business to take care of. She wasn't in a talkative mood. Come to think of it, I haven't seen her since. In fact, I'm not used to this place being so utterly quiet."

Bob's last comment stuck with Alex. He never really thought about Reese keeping her staff on duty just for him.

That certainly wasn't necessary. He could fend for himself. After all, he was supposed to be just an ordinary citizen— not royalty. He'd have a word with her later.

"Do you like working here?" Alex took his cup of black coffee and sat down at the marble counter.

"I'm lucky to have this job. Reese helped me out at a really bad time in my life." Bob turned back to the stove. "If it wasn't for Reese, who knows where I would have ended up."

"I take it she's a good boss?"

"The best." Bob turned from the omelet he was preparing and pointed his spatula at Alex. "And I won't stand by and let someone hurt her."

Alex held up his palms innocently. "You don't have to worry about me. I'll be moving on soon."

"Good."

"Now that we have that clear, I was wondering if you might help me with a special project."

Bob wiped his hands off on a towel. "Depends on what you have in mind."

"I have some extra time on my hands and I'd like to put it to good use."

"Well, if you're looking for things to do, you can sight-see or hit the clubs. They don't call it the city that never sleeps for no reason."

Alex shook his head. "I had something else in mind. But I'll need your help."

Bob sat an empty bowl in the sink. After a quick glance at the omelet, he stepped up to the counter. "What exactly do you have in mind?"

CHAPTER SEVEN

"WHAT ARE YOU DOING?"

Reese glared up at Alex, who was standing on a ladder in the corner of the living room. With a chisel in one hand and a hammer in the other, he turned. Was that guilt reflected in his blue eyes?

"I got bored." He lowered the hand tools to the top of the ladder.

She crossed her arms. "So you decided to make a mess of my apartment?"

Her gaze swept across the room, taking in the drop cloths covering everything. Cans and tools sat off to the side. And then her gaze settled back on the culprit. Alex was flashing her a guilty grin like some little boy caught with his hand in the cookie jar. But she refused to let his good looks and dopey grin get to her.

"Alex, explain this. What in the world are you doing?"

"Fixing the ceiling."

She frowned at him. What was this man thinking? Obviously he hadn't been when he made the hole in her ceiling. It would cost a small fortune to repair it—money she didn't have. She'd already made the rounds to the banks. No one was willing to help her refinance The Willows. She was officially tapped out.

In fact, she'd returned home determined to figure out a

way to meet next month's payroll. She really didn't want to let Sandy go before Christmas. Reese would do anything to keep that from happening, but sometimes the best of intentions just weren't enough.

"Alex, do you know what a mess you've created? There's no way that I'll be able to get someone in here to fix it."

"You don't need to hire anyone. I have this under control."

Her neck was getting sore staring up at him. "Would you get down off that ladder so I can talk to you without straining my neck?"

He did as she asked and approached her. He was so tall. So muscular. And as her gaze rose up over his broad chest and shoulders, she realized having him step off the ladder was a big miscalculation on her part.

His navy T-shirt was stretched across his firm chest. Her mouth grew dry. Did he have to look so good? Specks of crumbled plaster covered him, from his short dark hair to the jeans that hung low on his lean waist. She resisted the urge to brush him off—to see if his muscles were as firm as they appeared.

"If you'd give me a chance, I think you'll be impressed with what I can do."

She didn't doubt that she'd be very impressed, but her mind was no longer on the repairs. Her thoughts had tumbled into a far more dangerous territory.

Her gaze settled on his mouth. Was he an experienced kisser? With his sexy looks, he was definitely experienced in a lot more than kissing. The temperature in the room started to climb. When she realized that he was staring back at her, waiting for a response, she struggled to tamp down her raging hormones.

"You need to stop what you're doing. This—this is a

bad idea." She didn't know if the words were meant more for him or for herself.

"Really, I can do this. I used to help—" He glanced down at the carpet. "The guy who fixed up our house when I was a kid. I learned a lot."

She groaned. "When you were a kid? Are you serious?"

"Trust me."

She resisted the urge to roll her eyes and instead glanced back up at the looming hole in her ceiling. A cold draft brushed across her skin. A band of tension tightened across her forehead. She couldn't leave the ceiling in this condition; she'd go broke trying to keep the place warm.

"Seeing as you started this project without my permission, you can't possibly expect me to pay you to do the repairs."

His blue eyes lit up. "I agree. And truthfully, I did try to ask you before starting this, but when you were gone for the day, I thought I'd surprise you."

"Humph…you certainly achieved your goal." She eyed him. "You know I really should toss you to the curb. No one would blame me. Tell me, do you always go around vandalizing people's homes?"

His dark brows drew together. "That's not what I'm doing. And I've never done this for anyone else."

"What makes me so special?" She stared at him, looking for a sign of pity in his eyes. And if she found it, she didn't care what it cost her. She would show him to the door. She didn't do handouts.

His gaze was steady. "The truth is you'd be helping me."

"Helping you?" That wasn't the answer she'd been expecting. Before she could say more, the phone rang. "Don't move. I'll be right back."

She walked away, still trying to wrap her mind around what had gotten into him. She'd bet ten to one odds he didn't know what he was doing. She really ought to bounce him out on his very cute backside...but she needed the money he'd paid to stay here. Being hard up for money really did limit one's options—she hated learning things the hard way.

Of course when she answered the phone and found an impatient creditor at the other end, it did nothing to improve her mood. The man wanted to know why they hadn't received a payment for the past month. After she tap-danced her way into an extension, she walked back into the apartment. Alex was back up on the ladder, making the hole in her ceiling even bigger. She inwardly groaned.

"Do you ever listen to instructions?" She didn't even bother to mask the frustration in her voice.

He glanced down at her and shot her a sheepish grin. "I want to get as much done today as I can."

"And what if I tell you that I want you to stop?"

His gaze searched hers. "Is that what you really want?"

"It doesn't matter what I want. I don't have the money to hire a contractor. I've got creditors calling and wanting to know why they haven't been paid." She pressed her lips tightly together, realizing she'd spoken those words out loud.

"Are things really that bad?"

She shrugged, not meeting his gaze. "I'll turn things around. One way or the other."

"I'm sure you will." He glanced back at the work waiting for him. "In the meantime, I better get back to work, because I don't want to miss dinner."

She cast a hesitant look back at the hole in the ceiling before turning back to him. "You promise you know what you're doing?"

He smiled and crossed his heart. "I promise."

With effort, she resisted the urge to return the smile.

She wanted him to know that she was serious. Was it his sexy accent that made his promise so much easier to swallow? Or was it something more?

"Okay. I have a few things to do before dinner."

She reached the doorway when he said, "You know you don't have to keep Bob around on my account. I can fend for myself."

"This is his job and he's counting on a paycheck. The stubborn man doesn't accept anything that might be construed as charity."

Alex sent her a knowing smile. "Sounds like the pot calling the pot black."

"It's kettle. The pot calling the kettle black."

"So it is. And you, my dear, are the pot."

With a frustrated sigh, she turned her back on Alex and the crater-size hole in the ceiling. She had bigger problems to solve. Like finding a way out of this horrendous financial mess that she'd inherited. The thought of her father and how much trouble he'd brought to her and her mother renewed Reese's determination not to fall for Alex's charm. She needed to keep things simple where men were concerned—especially where Alex was concerned.

Not yet.

Alex groaned and hit the snooze setting on his phone, silencing the loud foghorn sound. He'd been having the most delightful dream and Reese was in it. He'd been holding her close with her generous curves pressing to him. A moan rose in his throat as he desperately tried to recreate the dream.

She'd been gazing up at him with those eyes that could bend him to her will with just a glance. He'd been about to kiss her when the blasted alarm interrupted.

Try as he might, there was no returning to Reese's arms.

He rolled over and stretched. Days had turned into two weeks and his body had adjusted to the time change. He wondered how much longer he'd be here.

For the first time, the thought of packing his bags and catching the first flight back to Mirraccino didn't sound appealing. This chance to be a regular citizen instead of a royal prince was far more appealing than he'd imagined—Reese's face and those luscious lips filled his mind.

The images from his dream followed him to the shower—a cold shower. After all, it was only a dream, a really hot dream, but a dream just the same.

He pulled a pair of jeans from the wicker laundry basket. Reese had generously offered to show him how to do his own laundry. He had much to learn, but he didn't mind. However, when he pulled a T-shirt out of the dryer to fold, he frowned. It was pink. Pink?

He balled it up and tossed it aside. His thoughts turned back to his beautiful hostess. Maybe if he were to tell her the truth about himself he could—what? Ask her to hook up with him? No. Reese wasn't the love 'em and leave 'em type.

He pushed the tormenting thoughts to the back of his mind as he finished up his laundry and sat down at his computer. He typed his name in the search engine. In no time at all, there were thousands of results. Good. He had their attention now. His gaze skimmed down over the top headlines: *With Rising Tensions in Mirraccino, Where Is Prince Alexandro? Is Prince Alexandro on a Secret Mission? The Mirraccino Palace Is Mum about Prince Alexandro's Absence.*

The headlines struck a chord with him. He should be at home, helping his papa. Instead he was here, repairing a hole in the ceiling for a woman whose image taunted him at night while her lush lips teased him by day. Still, he was doing an important function. As long as the press was sniffing out stories about him, his family could function under the radar.

A couple of older photos of him popped up on social networks with new tags. They were of him posing with beautiful women. All of them were strangers to him. He honestly couldn't even recall their names. Once the photos were taken, they'd gone their separate ways. *Then he saw one headline, proclaiming:*

Did the Prince Ditch Duty for Love?

His clenched hand struck the desktop, jarring his computer. No, he didn't. But no one outside of the family would ever know that he was doing his duty—no matter how much it cost him. No matter how much he hated keeping the truth from Reese.

His gaze roamed over the headlines again and he frowned. No one was going to win his heart. He didn't have time for foolish notions of Cupid and hearts. When it came time for him to marry, it would be because it was what was expected of him.

He wouldn't set himself up for the horrendous pain he'd seen his father live through after his mother's death. Or the years of loneliness. It had almost been too much to observe.

Yet Alex couldn't let the headlines get to him. They created the attention he wanted—even if they poked at some soft spots. He supposed under the circumstances he couldn't be choosy about how the swirl of curiosity happened as long as it worked.

Perhaps it was time to feed the press a few more bread crumbs. He wrote an anonymous email that because of his security precautions would be impossible for the paparazzi to trace.

To whom it concerns:
I have inside information about Prince Alexandro Castanavo's whereabouts. For a little extra money I have photos.
But this information will not come cheap. It'll be worth the
hefty price tag. Let's just say the prince is not off doing
diplomatic work. Time is ticking. This offer has gone out
to numerous outlets. First come, first served.

He smiled as he pressed send. That should spark some
interest.

Not about to waste any more time, he set aside his laptop
and headed straight to Reese's apartment to check on the
primer he'd applied to the walls and ceiling. All the while,
his thoughts centered on Reese. He desperately wanted to
be up front with her about everything.

But he knew people weren't always what they seemed
and that sometimes they were put in positions where they
were forced to make choices they might otherwise not
make. This financial crisis Reese was facing was one such
instance where she might do something desperate to bring
in money to keep this place afloat.

And what would be easier than selling the story of a
prince undercover while the crown prince eloped with a
woman he barely knew? But another voice, a much louder
voice inside him, said he was being overly cautious. Reese
was trustworthy. And the time had come to be honest with
her...about everything.

CHAPTER EIGHT

THIS WAS THE answer to her problems.

It had to be.

Reese stood in the inn's office, staring at the paintings she'd completed back before she'd dropped out of school. They'd been viewed by notable figures in the art world and generous offers had been made. Of course, in her infinite wisdom, she'd wanted to hold out, so she'd turned down the offers. She'd dreamed of one day having her own gallery showing. Of people requesting her work by name. But all of that had come to a crashing end one snowy night.

Now her only hope to hang on to the only life she'd ever known came down to selling these paintings. And if she didn't sell them, she'd have to let Sandy go just days before Christmas. The thought made her stomach roll.

Who ever said being the boss was a great thing?

Sometimes it just downright rotten.

And this was most definitely one of those times.

"What's put that frown on your face?"

She glanced up to find Alex leaning casually against the doorjamb. A black T-shirt stretched across his broad chest. The short sleeves strained around his bulging biceps as he crossed his arms. No one had a right to look that good.

When her gaze lifted to his mouth, he smiled. Her stomach did a somersault. What was it about him that had her thinking she should have taken more time with her makeup or at least flat ironed her hair into submission instead of throwing it haphazardly into a ponytail?

She swallowed hard and hoped her voice sounded nonchalant. "I was thinking."

"Must be something serious."

"I—I just figured out a solution to a problem." She moved away from the canvases, hoping Alex wouldn't be too curious.

"That's great—"

"Did you need something?" She shuffled some papers around on her desk to keep from looking at him. "Please don't tell me there's a problem with the apartment."

"Not like you're imagining. I'm almost finished."

"Really?" This good news was music to her ears.

"Yes. But I wanted to talk to you about something."

"Can it wait?" She sent him a pleading look. "I was on my way out the door."

He didn't say anything at first. "Of course it can wait until later."

"Good." She didn't need any more problems right now. "Do you need anything while I'm out?"

"Actually, I do." He stepped up to her desk. "And your offer keeps me from having to call a cab."

She laughed. "Come on. What was that cabbie's name? Freddy?" Alex nodded and she continued to tease him. "I'm sure Freddy would love to give you a ride."

Alex shook his head vehemently. "That is never going to happen. I think he had delusions of being a grand prix driver."

She patted Alex's arm, noticing the steely strength beneath her fingertips. As the zing of awareness arrowed into her chest, the breath caught in her throat. She raised her head and their gazes caught and held. Was he going to kiss her? They'd been doing this dance for so long now that it had become pure torture. The wondering. The imagining.

Her gaze connected with his. Definite interest reflected in them. Would it be so bad giving in this once and seeing if he could kiss as well as she imagined when she was alone in the dark of the night, tossing and turning?

Alex cleared his throat. "Do you have pen and paper?"

"What?" She blinked.

"I need to write you a list."

"Oh. Right."

Then, realizing she was still touching him, she pulled her hand away, immediately noticing how her fingers cooled off. He was definitely hot and in more than one way. And she'd just made a fool of herself. She'd only imagined he was interested in her. Her cheeks warmed as she handed over a pen and notepad.

His gaze was unwavering as he looked at her. "I appreciate you doing me this favor."

He wrote out the short list before reaching into his back pocket and pulling out some cash. He handed both over to her.

"I don't need money. After all, it's my ceiling that you're repairing. The least I can do is pay for the supplies."

"And you wouldn't be paying for those supplies right now if it weren't for my idea to surprise you and start the job without your permission."

She had a feeling that the money was being offered because he felt sorry for her. But he made a valid point. With that thought in mind, she folded the money and slipped it in her pocket.

"I should get going. I have to get the truck loaded up." It wasn't until the words were out of her mouth that she realized she'd said too much.

Alex glanced back at the canvases. "Are those what you need put in the truck?"

"Yes. But I've got it."

He strode over to her paintings. "What are you doing with these?"

How much should she tell him? She found herself eager to get his take on her plan. After all, it wasn't as though she could talk to any of the staff. She didn't want to worry them. And her mother, well, even if she was still at the house, she wouldn't understand. She'd beg Reese to keep the paintings—that they were too precious to part with.

But other lives were counting on her now.

Alex stepped over to the cases that held what she thought were her three best pieces of work. "Do you mind if I take a look?"

She did mind, but she found herself saying, "Go ahead. Just be careful. I can't let anything happen to those."

She had to admit that she really was curious about his reaction to her work. Would he like the pieces? Her stomach shivered in anticipation.

Alex took his time looking over each piece. He made some very observant comments that truly impressed her. If she didn't know better, she'd think that he too was an art student.

"Those are very impressive."

"Do you mean it?"

"Of course." He made direct eye contact with her. "You're quite talented."

Sure, she'd been told her work was good by experts, but there was just something about Alex seeing her work that made her feel exposed. Maybe it was that a stranger's opinions could be swept aside, but Alex's impression of her art would stay with her. For a moment, she wondered when his opinion had begun to mean so much to her.

"Do you still paint?"

She shook her head. "I don't have time for things like that these days."

"This place must keep you busy." He glanced back at the paintings. "Are you planning to sell these?"

"I'm going to speak with some gallery owners about showing them. I'm hoping that they'll fetch a good price. A couple of years ago, I had people interested in them. But back then I had bigger plans. I wanted to keep them and have a showing. But life took a sharp turn before any of that could happen...if it ever would have."

"I am sure it would have."

"Are you an artist?"

He shook his head. "I don't have an artistic bone in my body. I can only appreciate others' work. And you're very good."

"Thank you. At one point in my life I thought I'd have a future in art. I'd been dreaming about it since I was a little girl. But things change."

"You shouldn't give up on your dreams. No one should."

She shook her head, wanting to chase away the *what if*s and the *maybe*s. "That part of my life is over."

"You're young. You have lots of choices ahead of you."

"My mother needs me. I won't just abandon her like... erm...it doesn't matter. I don't even know why we're talking about it. I need to get these in the truck and soon I'll have the money to keep the doors to this place open."

What was taking her so long?

Alex paced the length of the living room. She'd been gone all day. How long did it take to talk to a couple of people? Surely they'd worked all of the details of the sale out by now. After all, he hadn't just been boosting her ego—she really was talented.

Now that he'd made up his mind to be honest with her about himself, he was anxious to get it over with. He doubted she would take the news well at first. She might not even believe him. But hopefully he'd be able to smooth things over. He couldn't imagine what it'd be like to have Reese turn her back on him—not speak to him again. His chest tightened. That couldn't happen.

He retrieved his laptop and settled down on an armchair, hoping to find a distraction. He logged on to his computer, anxious to see what the latest gossip consisted of. As long as it was about him and his fictitious romance and not his brother's real-life romantic disaster, he'd be satisfied.

The sound of a door closing caught his attention. He quickly closed his laptop and got to his feet. "Reese, is that you?"

She stepped into the living room. "Yes."

Her tone was flat and her gaze didn't quite reach his. He couldn't help himself—he had to know. "How did your day go?"

Her eyes were bloodshot and her face was pale. "It doesn't matter. I have some paperwork to do. Is there anything I can get for you?"

"Yes, there is." All thoughts of his need to tell her of his background vanished. Comforting her was his only priority. He attempted to reach out to her, to pull her close, but her cold gaze met his—freezing him out. His arms lowered. "You can talk to me. Tell me what happened."

Her eyes blazed with irritation. "Why do you always have to push? Why can't you leave things alone? First it's the Christmas tree. Then it's my apartment. You can't fix everything."

He took a step back, not expecting that outburst. "I am concerned. I'd like to help if I can."

"Well, you can't. This is my problem. I'll deal with it on my own."

No matter how much she wanted him to walk away, he couldn't. The raw pain in her brown eyes ate at him. Reese was the pillar of strength that everyone in this mansion leaned on. It was time that she had someone she could turn to for support.

"You don't have to do this alone."

"Why do you want to get involved?"

"I'd like to think that we're friends and that you can turn to me with your problems."

"You are my guest and I am the manager of this inn. That's all we are to each other." A coldness threaded through her words.

His voice lowered. "You don't believe that."

"I can't do this now." She turned away.

Acting against his better judgment, he reached out, wrapping his fingers around her forearm. "Don't push me away. Talk to me. Maybe there's something I can do to help."

She turned back, her gaze moving to his fingers. He immediately released her.

She sighed and lifted her chin to him. "I know you're trying to be nice, but don't you understand? You can't help. No one can."

"Something can always be done." He signaled for her to follow him to the couch. "Sit down and tell me what happened. If nothing else, you might feel better after you get it out in the open instead of keeping it bottled up inside."

She glanced around as though looking to see if anyone was close enough to overhear.

"Don't worry, Bob is at the market. And Sandy had to leave early because her little girl got sick and needed to be picked up from day care."

"Oh, no. Is it anything serious?"

"Not from what I could tell. Sandy said the girl hadn't felt well that morning, but she had hoped that whatever it was would pass. Apparently it didn't."

"So we're alone?"

He nodded. "Except for the groundskeeper. But I rarely ever see him inside the mansion. The only time I ever did see him inside was when I first arrived here and he'd dropped by to give your mother a pine cone wreath."

"Yes, Mr. Winston is very good to Mom."

It was good to know that there was someone around watching out for Reese and her mother. But that didn't mean Alex couldn't do his part, too.

"Sounds like Mr. Winston has more than one reason for keeping the grounds looking so nice."

Reese's fine brows drew together, forming a formidable line. And her eyes darkened. What in the world had he said wrong now?

CHAPTER NINE

"THAT'S IMPOSSIBLE."

Reese sat back, stunned by the thought of her mother liking Howard Winston. Her mother was still recovering from the mess after her father's death. Her mother would never let another man into her life, not after the way they'd been betrayed. It wasn't possible. Men weren't to be trusted.

"Are you so sure?" Alex persisted. "I mean, I only saw them together a couple of times, but there was definitely something going on there."

"They're just friends." Reese rushed on, unwilling to give his observation any credence. "Mom would never get involved with another man. Not after...after my father."

She'd almost let it slip that her father was a horrible, lying, conniving man, but she caught herself in time. Airing her family's dirty laundry to a stranger—well, Alex wasn't a stranger any longer. And the truth was she didn't know what he was to her.

Still, she didn't like to talk about her father—with anyone. The man wasn't worth the breath to speak his name. After all, he hadn't even loved them. His own family. He'd scraped off their savings and spent the money on his new woman—the woman he had left her mother for on Christmas Eve. And he'd been such a coward that he'd only left a note. He couldn't face them and admit what he'd done.

The backs of her eyes stung. Why did she still let the memory get her worked up? Two years had passed since her father's betrayal had come to light and her mother had crumbled.

Alex got to his feet. "I didn't mean to upset you. I thought you might be happy about your mother having someone in her life."

"I—I hadn't noticed." She choked the words out around the lump in her throat. "I've had a lot of other things on my mind. This place can take a lot of time and attention."

"Then maybe what you need to do is get out of here."

Her eyes widened. "You mean leave?"

He smiled, hoping to ease the horrified look on her face. "I am not talking about forever. I was thinking more along the lines of an early dinner."

"Oh." Heat flashed in her cheeks. She didn't know why she'd jumped to the wrong conclusion. Then again, maybe she did.

On the ride home, she'd been daydreaming about packing her bags and heading somewhere, anywhere but here. Not that she would ever do it. But sometimes the pressures got to be too much. Just like tomorrow, when she had to tell Sandy that she would have to lay her off. But she would hire Sandy back just as soon as possible—if there was still an inn to employ her.

Alex shifted his weight from one foot to the other. "If you want, we can leave a note for Bob letting him know he can have the evening off."

She shook her head. "I can't afford to splurge."

"Maybe you misunderstood. This is my treat. I think it's time for me to get out of here and check out a bit of

New York City. And who better to show me some of the finest cuisine?"

She arched a brow. "Are you serious?"

He nodded.

He was probably right about her getting out of the house. A little time away and a chance to unwind would have her thinking more clearly. Oh, who was she kidding? There was no way she'd unwind when she knew that she had the horrible task of laying off one of her valued employees, who was more a friend than a worker.

After her father's betrayal, she'd closed herself off, only letting those closest to her in. And the three people who worked for her had gained her trust and friendship. They were a family. They'd filled in when her mother wasn't capable of doing more than caring for herself. They'd been there to support her, to cheer her on, and she couldn't love them more.

Alex shot her a pleading stare. "Surely sharing dinner with me can't be that bad of an idea."

Reese worried her lower lip. She really had no desire to go out, but he was, after all, the paying guest—a guest who'd spent a lot of his time fixing up her private apartment. Giving him a brief tour of Rockefeller Center and dinner was the least she could do.

"I did hear Bob mention that he still needed to run out and buy his girlfriend a Christmas present. I'm sure he wouldn't mind leaving early. I'll give him a call."

"And I'll change out of these work clothes into something presentable."

When he turned away, she noticed how his dark jeans rode low on his trim waist and clung to him in all of the right places. The man was certainly built. She swallowed hard. Any woman would have to be out of her tree to turn his offer down.

She struggled to sound normal. "Um, sure. I'll meet you back here in ten minutes."

He nodded and headed for the steps.

If he was going to dress up, she supposed she should do the same thing. She mentally rummaged through her closet. She didn't own anything special. The best she could do was her little black dress. It was something she kept on hand for hosting weddings.

Some funny feeling inside her told her this dinner was going to be a game changer. They wouldn't be quite the same again. But in the next breath, she assured herself she was making too much of the dinner. After all, what could possibly happen?

What would it take to make her smile?

Alex sneaked a glance at Reese's drawn white face. The lights of the tall Christmas tree reflected in her eyes, but the excitement that had been there when they'd decorated the tree back at the inn was gone. He had to do something to make things better. But what?

She still hadn't opened up to him. Sure, he'd surmised that her plans to sell her paintings today hadn't worked out, but it went deeper than disappointment. He'd been hoping that when he took her out on the town, she'd loosen up and temporarily forget her problems. So far it wasn't working.

"Maybe stopping here was a bad idea." Alex raked his fingers through his short hair.

"No, it wasn't." She reached out and squeezed his hand. She smiled up at him, but the gesture didn't quite reach her eyes. "It's just that I used to come to Rockefeller Center every Christmas with my father. Back then the tree looked ginormous to me."

"I am sorry that it now makes you sad."

She shook her head. "It's not that. It's just that back then things weren't so messed up. At least, I don't think they were. I'd like to think that part of my life was genuine and not riddled with lies."

"What lies?" Had he missed something she said? Impossible. He was captivated by her every word.

She shook her head and turned back to the tree. "It's nothing. Just me rambling on about things that aren't important."

He stepped in front of her. "It sure sounded important to me. And I'd like to understand if you'll tell me."

"Why do you care? I am just your host."

"And my friend," he added quickly. Then he stopped himself before he could say more—things that he, the prince of a far-off land, had no right saying to anyone. His feelings were irrelevant. His duty was to the crown of Mirraccino. That was what he'd been telling himself for years.

She smiled up at him. "You're very sweet. It's surprising that you're not taken yet."

He pressed a hand to his chest. "Who would want to kidnap me?"

She laughed. "Your English is very good, but I'm quickly learning that you aren't as familiar with some of our sayings. What I meant was I'm surprised that you're not in a committed relationship."

His thoughts briefly went to the king and his insistence that Alex formalize the plans to announce his engagement to Catherine, an heiress to a shipping empire. The entire reason for the match was political positioning. Combining her family's ships with the ports of Mirraccino would truly make for a powerful resource and secure Mirraccino's economic future. It didn't matter that he and Catherine didn't have feelings for each other. An advantageous marriage was what was expected of him—his wants and desires did not count.

As dedicated as Alex was to the crown, he'd never been able to visualize a future with Catherine. In fact, they planned to get together after Christmas and discuss their options. His gut told him to end things—to let her get on with her life. He didn't like the thought of her waiting around for him to develop feelings for her that obviously weren't going to appear. And marrying her out of pure duty seemed so cold. But it was what his family wanted—what they expected.

Catherine was beautiful and he did enjoy her company, but there just wasn't an attraction. That spark. Nothing close to what he felt around Reese. Now where had that come from? It wasn't as though he was planning to start anything with Reese. The last thing his family needed was another complication.

He didn't want to think about himself. It was Reese who concerned him. "Who put that sadness in your eyes?"

She swiped at her eyes. "It's no one. I—I mean it's the problems with the inn. I just need a quick influx of cash."

"What can I do to make it better?" He would do anything within his power—aside from risking his nation.

A watery smile lit up her face as she shook her head. "You've already done enough."

"But how?" He was once again confused. "You mean my reservation?"

"No, by being a caring friend."

Before he had a chance to digest her words, she was on tiptoes and leaning forward. Her warm lips pressed to his. The breath caught in his lungs. Sure, he'd fantasized about this—heck, he'd dreamed of this—but he never imagined it could be this amazing.

She was about to pull back when he snaked his arms around her waist and pulled her closer. Her hands became pinned against his chest. The problems of the Mirraccino nation and the crown's expectations of him slipped away as the kiss deepened. When she met him lip to lip and tongue to tongue, no other thoughts registered except one—he was the luckiest man alive. Nothing had ever felt this right.

She worked her hands up over his shoulders. Her fingers raked through his hair, causing the low rumble of a moan to form in the back of his throat. Her body snuggled closer but with their bulky winter garb he was barred from enjoying her voluptuous curves pressed to his.

He nibbled on her full bottom lip, reveling in the swift intake of her breath. She wanted him as much as he wanted her. The only problem was they were standing in the middle of Rockefeller Center—and in front of the Christmas tree, no less. Not exactly the place to get carried away.

Still, he couldn't let her go...not quite yet. He'd been with his share of women, but they'd never touched a part of him deep inside. It was more than physical—not that the physical wasn't great. But there was something more about Reese, and in that moment his brain turned to mush and he couldn't put his finger on exactly why she was different.

A bright flash startled him out of the moment. His eyes sprang open and with great regret he pulled away from her. Immediately the cold air settled in, but his blood was too hot for him to be bothered by the crisp air.

"What's the matter?" Reese asked.

"I—I thought I saw something. I am certain it's nothing."

His gaze scanned the area, searching for the person with the camera. Had the paparazzi tracked him down? Had they snapped a picture of him holding Reese close?

He studied the other couples and families with small children. It could have been any of them. He was making too much of the situation. If it was the paparazzi, he couldn't imagine they'd worry about hiding. He was just being paranoid without his security detail.

When he turned his attention back to Reese, she glanced up at him. Her cheeks had bright pink splotches. He couldn't decide if it was the dipping temperatures or embarrassment. And now that the cold air was filling with white fluffy flakes, his brain was starting to make connections again. He owed her an apology.

Years of being a prince had taught him that there was a time and a place for everything. This was not the time to ravish her luscious lips—he needed to keep things low-key between them. He still had yet to reveal his true identity to her. But he would fix that this evening—no more secrets.

He gave her hand a squeeze. "My apologies. I shouldn't have taken advantage of the moment."

"You didn't." Her gaze lowered. "I'm the one who should be apologizing. I started it."

She had, but he was the one who'd taken it to the next level. When she started walking, he fell in step next to her. Hand in hand, they moved as though they'd been together for years.

She glanced over at him. "Are you still up for going to dinner like we planned?"

"Do you still want to go?"

She nodded.

He was hungry, there was no doubt about that. But food wasn't what he craved. He swallowed hard, trying to keep his thoughts focused on his mission tonight—being honest with Reese without chasing her away.

Big snowflakes drifted lazily to the ground. They quickly covered her hair, reminding him of a snow angel. He'd never seen anyone so beautiful. It was going to be hard to stay focused on his priorities when all he wanted to do was get closer to Reese. If only his life were different....

In that moment, he heard the king's clear, distinct voice in his head. *Your life is one of honor—of duty. You must always think of the kingdom first.*

And that's what he was doing, but each day it was getting harder and harder to live by those rules. He glanced at Reese. Definitely much harder than he'd ever imagined.

CHAPTER TEN

REESE WAS SURPRISED by how much she was enjoying the evening. The trendy restaurant had been mentioned by a few of her guests and she now understood why. It was cozy with soft lighting and a few holiday decorations scattered about. And the tapas menu was simply divine. She loved trying a bit of this and a bit of that.

And thanks to the deteriorating weather, the restaurant was quiet enough to make conversation. Everything was going fine until Alex turned the conversation back to her. After the waiter delivered the coffee and a slice of triple-chocolate cake, Alex studied her over the rim of his cup.

He took a sip of the steamy brew before returning it to the saucer. "Tell me about him?"

Reese's heart clenched. "Who?"

Please don't let him be asking about her father. She never spoke of him…with anyone, including her mother. And she certainly wasn't about to sit here in public and reveal how that man had lied to their faces before betraying her and her mother in the worst way.

Alex leaned forward, propping his elbows on the edge of the table. "I want to know about your ex-boyfriend. The man who broke your heart."

She let out a pent-up breath. Josh was someone she could talk about. It'd taken her time to sort through the pain he'd caused, but in the end, she'd realized his lies were what had hurt her the most—not his absence from her life.

"Josh was someone I met in college. He was a smart dresser with expensive tastes. I was surprised when he offered me a ride home from a party one night. When he dropped me off, he was impressed by my family's mansion—if only I'd known then what I know now. Anyway, he insisted I give him my phone number."

Sympathy reflected in Alex's blue gaze. "He was after your money?"

"Yes. But I was too naive to know it then. I let myself get so caught up in the thought of being in love that I let it slide when things always had to be his way. And when he'd criticize my outfits, I thought it was my fault for being so naive about fashion."

"What a jerk." Alex's jaw flexed.

"When my father died, things changed. Josh transformed into the perfect gentleman. He said all of the right things and even talked of us getting married. He made me feel secure."

The memories washed over her, bringing with them the forgotten embarrassment and pain. She blinked repeatedly. She'd been wrong—recalling her past with Josh hurt more than she'd been willing to admit.

Alex reached across the table and squeezed her hand. In his touch she found reassurance and a strength within herself that she hadn't known was there.

She swallowed down the jagged lump in her throat. "Everything was fine until he learned I wasn't an heiress. In fact, I was in debt. Poorer than a church mouse. I don't know if I'll ever get out of debt before I'm a little old lady."

"You're so much better off without him. He isn't worth your tears."

She ran her fingertips over her cheeks, only then realizing that they were damp. "Once Josh knew I couldn't support him, he stopped coming around and didn't return my calls. But by that point, I was so busy looking after my mother and keeping the bank from taking the house that Josh's absence got pushed to the back of my mind."

"I'm so sorry he hurt you like that—"

"Don't be. It's done and over with. I don't want to talk about him anymore." And she couldn't bear to think of that time in her life—it was truly her darkest hour.

"They say talking about things helps you heal."

"I tend to think that chocolate heals all." She took the last bite of chocolate cake and moaned at its rich taste. "Now it's your turn. Tell me more about yourself."

"Me?" His eyes widened. "I'm boring. Surely you want to talk about something more interesting."

She shook her head. "Fair is fair. I told you about my no-good ex. Now it's your turn to tell me something that I don't already know about you."

He leaned back in his chair as though contemplating what to tell her. Then he glanced around. She followed his gaze, finding the nearby tables empty. Her anticipation grew. He was obviously about to take her into his confidence—what could be so private?

"What if I told you I'm a prince?"

Disappointment popped her excitement. "I'd say you have delusions of grandeur. I thought you were going to be serious."

He leaned forward as though he were going to say more, but her phone chimed. She held up a finger for him to give her a moment as she fished the device out of her purse. "It's my mother. I have to get it."

She got to her feet, grabbed her coat and rushed to the exit, where she'd be able to hear better without the background music. She stepped out into the cold evening air when the chime stopped. Drat. It could be important. She better call back.

The snow was still falling, enveloping everything in a white blanket. Not many people were out in the wintry weather. Those who were had their hoods up and kept their heads low as they moved along the partially cleared sidewalk. Only one man was taking his time and gazing in the various restaurant and store windows. It seemed awfully cold to be strolling around. But to each his own.

The wind kicked up. She turned her back to the biting cold and pulled up the collar on her coat. She'd just retrieved her aunt's number when she heard a man's voice call out. She turned around.

"Hey!" The man who'd been window gazing was now staring at her. "Yeah, you."

Beneath the harsh glare of the street lamps decorated with tinsel, Reese spotted a camera in the man's hands. He lifted the camera and in the next instance a bright flash momentarily blinded her. She blinked repeatedly.

He stepped closer. "What's your name?"

She stepped back. "Excuse me."

Who was this guy? And why had he taken her photo? People on the sidewalk paused and stared at her as though trying to figure out if they should know her. Like a deer in headlights, she froze.

"Come on," the man coaxed. "Give me a pretty smile."

Reese put her hands up to block the man's shot. "I don't know who you are, but leave me alone!"

"How old are you, honey? Twenty? Twenty-two?"

She went to turn back toward the restaurant when she stepped on a patch of ice. Her arms flailed through the snowy air. Her feet slid. Clutching her phone in a death grip as though it could help her, she plunged face-first toward the pavement.

* * *

Alex smiled as he traced Reese's steps to the exit.

The evening had gone better than he'd ever imagined. The tip of his tongue traced over his lower lip as he recalled the sweetness of Reese's touch. She sure could turn a kiss into a full-fledged experience. He just hoped that once he convinced her he was telling her the truth she'd understand, because he wasn't ready to let her go—not yet.

He pushed open the glass door when he saw Reese sway and fall to the ground. The sound of her name caught in his throat. He moved into action as a flash lit up the night—the paparazzi. Right now, his only concern was making sure Reese was okay.

Alex knelt beside her sprawled body. His chest tightened as he waited for her to speak. "Reese, are you okay?"

"I…I don't know. The fall knocked the breath out of me." She turned over on her backside. "My arm hurts, and my knees."

"I'm so sorry." When she started to get up, he pressed a hand to her shoulder. "Sit still for a second and take a couple of breaths."

Alex glanced around, spotting a man with a camera farther down the sidewalk. His gut instinct was to go after the man, but he wouldn't leave Reese. She needed him.

The photographer took a moment to snap another picture before he escaped into the night. Alex was certain that it would end up in the gossip rags that night, but his only concern was Reese.

And this incident was all his fault. He'd gotten caught up in the moment—only thinking of his need to comfort Reese—to be with her. He'd failed to follow any of the safety protocols drilled into him as a kid. He'd gotten so comfortable in his anonymous role that he'd forgotten just how easily things could unravel. Now once again, his rash decision had hurt someone he cared about.

That thought struck him.

He cared about Reese. It was true. But he didn't have time right now to figure out exactly what that meant. Right now he had to determine if she was all right to move. He needed to get them both off this city street. Luckily, with the inclement weather, not that many people were out and about.

"This is my fault." Alex held his hands out to her. "The least I can do is help you up."

"I've got it."

"You need help. You're sitting on a patch of ice." He continued to reach out to her. "Take my hands."

When she went to reach out to him, she gasped.

"What is it?"

"My right arm. I had my phone in my hand and came down on my elbow."

"How about your left arm? Is it all right?"

"I think so."

He gripped her good arm while she held the injured arm to her chest. An urge came over him to scoop her up into his arms and hold her tight, promising that everything would be better, but he knew that could never happen. He'd waited too long. Too much had happened. Things had gotten too out of control.

And now when Reese found out the truth—the whole truth—she'd look at him with an accusing stare. She was hurt because of him. And he couldn't blame her. None of this would have happened if only he had stayed back at the inn. He'd had a plan. A good plan. And he'd abandoned it.

He noticed the grim line of her lips as she cradled the injured arm and he felt lower than a sea urchin. "I am taking you to a hospital."

"I don't need to go. It's just a sprain."

He sent her a disapproving stare. "I insist the doctors have a look at you."

Deciding that her black heels were definitely not to be trusted on the slick sidewalk, he wrapped his arm around her waist. Even though most of the walkway had been cleared, there were still patches of snow and ice. His arm fit nicely around her curves. The heat of her body permeated her clothes and warmed his hand.

At the truck, he paused by the passenger door and opened it for her.

She cast him a hesitant look. "You're going to drive?"

He nodded. "You can't drive with your arm injured. How far to the hospital?"

"It's just a few blocks from here."

"Good." He helped her into the truck and then set out to get her some help.

"I don't understand what that man wanted."

"What did he say to you?"

"He wanted my name and I think my age. If this is some sort of human interest story for the local paper, they have a strange way of conducting themselves."

"Did he mention which paper he works for?"

"I don't even know if he works for a paper. That's just my best guess. When I first spotted him, he was staring in windows. I didn't know what he was up to."

Mentally Alex kicked himself for letting this happen. He was certain that photographer had known who he was and had most likely tracked him from Rockefeller Center to where they'd had dinner. Well, it wouldn't happen again. When he got back to the inn, he would be placing a call to Mirraccino to update the king on the recent turn of events and would request that his security detail be dispatched immediately.

Worry and guilt settled heavily on his shoulders. There was no excuse for his poor behavior. How would he keep Reese from hating him?

In one evening, he'd broken his promise to himself to follow the rules and keep those closest to him safe. He glanced at Reese, who was still holding her arm. He'd failed her in more than one way.

He should have trusted her with the truth about himself before now. But at first he'd worried that she'd sell the information. And then he'd enjoyed his role as plain Alex and selfishly didn't want her treating him differently. Now he'd waited too long.

CHAPTER ELEVEN

WHY WAS HE acting so strangely?

Reese sat on the edge of the emergency-room exam table and studied the drawn lines on Alex's handsome face. She recalled him apologizing and blaming himself for her injury. What was up with that? He hadn't even been outside when she'd slipped.

Why did she have this feeling she was missing something? She was about to ask him when the doctor entered the room.

The gray-haired man in a white coat had a serious expression on his face as he introduced himself and shook her good hand. "The films show you didn't break any bones. However, you have some minor cuts and abrasions. The worst injury is a contusion to your elbow."

Alex's hands clenched as he stood next to her. "How bad is it?"

His worry and anxiety were palpable. Had he never seen anyone get hurt before? If this was how he reacted to scrapes and bruises, she was really glad there was no blood.

The doctor's brow arched as he took in Alex's presence. Reese spoke up. "It's okay. He's my friend."

"All in all, she's lucky. We'll clean her up and give her some anti-inflammatories to help with the swelling. She'll be sore for a day or two, but she'll feel better soon."

Reese detected the whoosh of breath from Alex. She'd swear he was more relieved than she was over the diagnosis. Although the thought of a cast was not one she would have relished when she had to take over the maid duties. How exactly would she have changed linens one-handed? Or managed any of the other tasks?

It seemed to take an eternity until she was released from the hospital. She tried to talk to Alex, but his moodiness wasn't of any comfort. When he did speak, it was only in one-syllable answers. You'd think he was the one who'd been hurt, not her.

It was all his fault.

Reese had been put in harm's way. She'd been hurt. And it was all because he hadn't taken the proper precautions. It wouldn't happen again.

With her snug in bed, Alex moved into action. He had some explaining to do. His papa would not be pleased— not that he could make Alex feel any guiltier than he already did.

While he spoke with the king, Alex scanned the internet trying to locate the photo from this evening, but no matter what he typed in the search engine, nothing popped up. He was certain the man with the camera had been part of the media and not just some fan. So where was the picture?

Alex braced himself for some fictitious story to accompany the photo. He just hoped that it wasn't too scandalous. His family had been through enough with his brother's overnight marriage to a practical stranger.

"You should have listened to me!" The king's voice vibrated the phone. "How badly is the girl injured?"

"She's going to be sore for a while, but there's nothing serious."

"You know that you must make this right. Her injuries

are the result of your poor judgment. You shouldn't have been out in public without your security detail."

"I'll do my best to make it up to her."

"Make sure you do. We don't need her turning to the media with a sob story or worse. We're already dealing with enough here."

He would take care of it. But first he had to be honest with her. He just hoped that with her being so loyal to her mother and her need to hang on to this mansion that had been in her family for generations that she'd be able to understand his loyalty to his family and the crown.

"How are things with Demetrius? Have the issues been resolved?"

"Almost. We need another day or two. Can you make that happen considering everything that just occurred?"

"Yes." That was his duty, no matter what.

Alex raked his fingers through his hair and blew out a long slow breath. "I'll make sure our plan does not unravel because of tonight's incident. I already have a backup plan in motion. I will step things up and take care of Reese at the same time."

"I don't like the sound of this. The last time you had an idea, you snuck out of the palace and took too many risks with your safety. This time I insist you tell me about this backup plan."

Alex rolled out his plan for his papa. He also took into consideration the king's suggestions and made a few adjustments until they were both satisfied.

"What about Catherine?"

The muscles in Alex's neck tightened. "I'll speak with her when I get home."

The logical thing would be to go to Catherine and formalize the marriage that their families were so eager to see take place. But how was he supposed to make a commitment to a woman he didn't love?

His priority now was speaking with Reese. He'd do that first thing in the morning. Somehow he had to make her understand his choices were for the best—for all concerned.

She was, after all, understanding and generous with her employees. These were just two of the qualities that he admired about her. He just hoped she'd extend him the same courtesy.

CHAPTER TWELVE

Beeeep! Beeeep!

Who in the world had their finger stuck on the front-door buzzer?

Reese groaned. She rolled over and opened one eye. It was still dark out. What in the world? Her hazy gaze settled on the green numbers on the clock. It wasn't even 6 a.m. She still had another half hour to sleep. Maybe they'd go away.

Beep. Beep. Beep.

Another groan formed deep in her dry throat. She wasn't expecting anyone. Maybe one of the employees had forgotten their pass card. Wait. No one came in this early.

Well, she wouldn't know what was going on until she answered the door.

She clambered out of bed and grabbed her old blue robe. Her elbow throbbed. There was no way the wrap on her arm would fit easily through the sleeve. Instead she draped the robe over her shoulder while holding her arm to her chest.

Her bare feet padded quietly across the floor. The door to Alex's suite was just down the hall from hers. There were no sounds or light coming from his rooms. Lucky him. He was probably still enjoying a peaceful night's sleep. Whatever had her out of bed at this hour had better be important.

She glanced through the window that ran down each

side of the front door, finding Mr. Winston standing there. What in the world?

"Please come inside." She held the door open for him. "What are you doing here at this hour?"

"I was up early, reading the paper while drinking my coffee, when I stumbled across something you need to see."

"Couldn't this have waited a few more hours?"

"No. In fact, I got here just in time."

"In time for what?" She was thoroughly confused. She really needed a piping-hot cup of coffee to wash away the cobwebs in her mind.

"Read the headline." He held the morning paper out to her. "It'll explain everything."

She accepted the paper and unfolded it. Her eyes immediately met a black-and-white photo of Alex. Her gaze skimmed the headline: Royal Prince Finds Love.

The breath caught in her throat as she read the words once more. Below the headline was a picture of her on the sidewalk with Alex next to her. Her mouth gaped. The photo had been taken last night.

She struggled to make sense of her rambling thoughts. This is why the man on the sidewalk had been questioning her? Alex was a prince?

How could that be true? Alex was royalty? Impossible.

Then their conversation at the restaurant came rushing back to her. She read the headline again. He had been telling her the truth. Alex was an honest-to-goodness prince.

"It's true," she said in astonishment.

"You know about this?" Mr. Winston's gaze searched her face.

She hadn't meant to say the words aloud. "He mentioned something about this last night."

"Do you understand the trouble we're going to have here?" The groundskeeper wrung his hands together. "I already had to escort two reporters off the property and close the gate. Thank goodness your mother isn't here."

It wasn't just her mother who would not approve of the three-ring circus going on in front of the property. Ever since Reese's father had died, the snooty neighbors had stuck their collective noses up in the air. They didn't approve of the inn. They'd even gone out of their way with the local government and business associations to try to block her from opening The Willows. They didn't want their exclusive neighborhood blemished with a bunch of riffraff.

This latest scandal of sorts would only add fuel to a fire that had finally died down to small smoldering embers. And it was all Alex's fault—correction, it was all Prince Alexandro Castanavo's fault.

She glanced toward the window. "Do we need to call the police?"

Mr. Winston rubbed his gloved hands together. "I don't think it'll be necessary at this point. But if that fella you've got staying here decides to stay on, you might have a real problem on your hands. Do you want me toss him out?"

"Um...no. I'll take care of him." She worried her bottom lip as she figured out what to do next. "Until he leaves, can you keep the press off the property?"

"I can try. But they could sneak around back without me knowing."

She tapped the folded newspaper against her thigh. "I'll call Bob and ask if he can come help you. Surely they'll get bored and go away soon."

"I wouldn't count on that. They seem to be rapidly growing in numbers."

"Please do your best. And thank you for helping."

Mr. Winston's face softened. "No need to thank me. I'm just glad I was up early and saw the paper."

She marched up the steps, coming to a stop in front

of Alex's room. She lifted her hand to knock on his door when her robe slipped from her shoulder. The cool early-morning air sent goose bumps rushing down her skin.

What should she say? Why had he kept his identity a secret? What was he doing here at The Willows? The unending questions whirled round in her mind.

Maybe it'd be best if she got dressed before confronting him. It'd also give her a moment to figure out exactly what she was going to say to him. Most importantly, she wondered if he was truly going to come clean about last night.

Reese called Bob and then rushed through the shower. The more she thought about how Alex had duped her, the angrier she got. And to think she'd started to trust him—to open up to him.

Minutes later, she returned to his door. With her good hand, she knocked.

There was no answer.

She added more force to her rapid knock. "Alex, I know you're in there. Wake up!"

There was a crash. A curse.

The door swung open. Alex stood there in a pair of boxers. His short hair was scattered in all directions. "What's wrong? Is it your arm?"

"No." She drew her gaze from his bare chest to meet his confused look.

"Reese, what is it?"

"This. This is what's wrong." She pressed the paper to his bare chest. When the backs of her fingers made contact with his heated skin, a tingling sensation shot up her arm and settled in her chest. She immediately pulled away. Now wasn't the time for her hormones to take control. She had to think clearly.

He grabbed the paper and without even unfolding it to read the headline said, "I can explain this."

"So you know what's in it?"

He nodded. "I planned to explain everything in the morning. Speaking of morning, what are you doing up so early? The sun isn't even up yet."

"The sun may not be up, but that didn't stop the reporters from blocking the sidewalk and spilling out into the road. My neighbors are going to have a royal hissy fit over this one."

It wasn't until the words were out of her mouth that she realized her poor choice of words. She looked at him as he moved to the window facing the road and peered out. He was a royal prince. It was taking a bit for her to wrap her mind around that image. To her he was still Alex, who'd stood on the ladder plastering her ceiling. The same Alex who'd kicked back in her living room enjoying a pizza. And the Alex who'd kissed her last night.

She stared at him. His muscled shoulders were pulled back. His tanned back was straight and his head was held tall. And when he turned to her, his faraway gaze said he was deep in thought. His nose was straight and his jawline squared. He definitely looked like a very sexy Prince Charming.

In that moment, it struck her that she was speaking to an honest-to-goodness prince. Royalty. The accusations and heated words knotted up in her throat.

As though he remembered she was still in the room, his gaze met hers. "Do you mind if I throw on some clothes before we get into this?"

Realizing that she was staring at his very bare, very tempting chest, she nodded and turned away. "I'll meet you downstairs."

She headed for the door without waiting for his answer. She needed to talk to him, but not like this. Once he was dressed, she'd be able to have a serious conversation with him.

When she reached the ground floor, she glanced out the front window, finding Mr. Winston strolling along the perimeter of the property. He was such a good guy. She couldn't imagine letting him and the others go. How could she let them down?

She gave herself a mental shake. She would deal with that problem later. Right now she needed to deal with her guest—the man she'd begun to think of as a friend—the man she'd shared a kiss with the night before. She paced the length of the living room. How long did it take to throw on some clothes?

She walked to the foyer and glanced up the staircase. There was no sign of him. With each passing moment, her irritation rose. Why hadn't he been honest with her? Why all of the dodging and evasiveness?

When he finally stepped into the room, she stopped and met his unwavering gaze. His hair was still damp and a bit unruly. He'd put on a blue sweater and jeans. His feet were still bare. She drew her gaze upward, refusing to be swayed by his good looks and his royal breeding. There was something different about him.

"Your hair, it's lighter."

"I started washing out the temporary hair dye."

She openly stared at him. "There's something else."

"I didn't put in the colored contacts."

Instead of a vibrant blue, his eyes were a blue-gray.

"Is there more?" He'd really thought through his charade. Her gaze skimmed over him, looking for any other changes.

"That's all."

She tilted her chin up. "You owe me an explanation. And it better be good. Real good."

"I meant to tell you—"

"When? After you got me under your spell? After we—" She pressed her fingers to her lips.

She hadn't meant to go down that path. In fact, she hadn't meant to mention the kiss, but she just couldn't forget it. Nor could she dismiss the way his touch filled her stomach with a sense of fluttering butterflies.

"It's not what you're thinking. I'm staying at The Willows because I needed someplace quiet to stay."

"Someplace where you could hide from the press?"

He nodded. "This place is private enough while still being close to the city."

"And this explains why you could afford to rent out the whole place. But why weren't you up front with me?"

"I didn't have a choice—"

"Everyone has a choice. When we started getting closer, I started opening up to you about my past, but you still remained quiet."

"You don't know how many times I wanted to open up to you." He stepped up to her, but she backed away. His gaze pleaded with her. "I really do have a legitimate reason for not telling you the truth. Will you sit down and hear me out?"

She moved to the armchair while he took a seat on the end of the couch. "I'm listening."

Frustration creased Alex's face. "You must believe me when I say the kiss last night was real. And if you deny it, you'll only be lying to yourself."

The memory of his breath tickling her cheek. The gentle scent of his spicy cologne teasing her nose. And then his warm lips had been there, pressing against hers. Alex was right. The kiss had been out of this world.

"You mentioned something about a duty. A duty to do what?" she prompted, trying to keep not only him but also her own thoughts on target.

"To protect my country at all costs."

Reese rubbed the shoulder of her injured arm, trying to ease the dull ache. "Go on."

"I'm sorry about last night with that reporter. You were injured because I didn't follow protocol—again."

"Again?"

He paused as though searching for where to begin. "I was rebellious when I was younger. I hated all of the rules and protocols. I didn't understand their importance. When I was fifteen, I got in an argument with the king before a public outing."

"I'm guessing that was a no-no."

Alex nodded. "I ignored the mandated protocol of staying with the bodyguards at the event and took off into the crowd. With the guards chasing after me, the king and queen were not fully protected. A gunshot by a subversive meant for the king struck—struck my mother."

Reese sat back, stunned by the traumatic event in Alex's childhood. She reached out and squeezed his hand. Sympathy welled up in her for the guilt a fifteen-year-old should never have to experience.

"Before my mother died, she had me make a promise—to take care of Papa. I've kept that promise ever since. It's the very least I could do after what I did."

"Your mother must have loved your father dearly."

"Not always. Theirs was an arranged marriage."

Reese had heard of them existing in some cultures, but she found it startling that people would marry for something other than love. "How did they meet?"

"My grandfather wanted Mirraccino's wine industry to flourish beyond our nation's boundaries. He'd determined the best way to do that was to join forces with one of Italy's major wine producers and distributors. And during one of those meetings, my grandfather was introduced to my mother. It was then and there that my grandfathers came to agreement to merge the families through marriage."

"I can't imagine having to marry someone that you don't love."

"As a royal, one must always do their duty. It's an expectation that starts at birth." Alex shrugged.

"Lucky for your parents it all worked out—"

"Not quite. If only I'd have followed the rules, she… she might still be here."

"You can't blame yourself. You were young and kids don't think before they act."

"I grew up fast that day. I swore I would toe the line and protect my family at all costs—even at the risk of my own safety. I couldn't bear the thought of losing them both."

"And that's why you kept your identity from me—you were protecting your family?"

"I'm here on a most important mission for my country."

"A mission?" Alarm bells rang in her mind. What sort of situation had he gotten her mixed up in?

"If I tell you, do you promise that it'll go no further than you and me?"

She worried her bottom lip. She wanted to know. She needed to know. But what if it was something bad? She eyed up the man she knew as Alex. Her gut told her that he was a good guy, even if he had misled her.

"It'll stay between us."

The lines in his face eased. "My country is a small group of islands in the Mediterranean. It has a strong hold in the shipping industry and wines."

She listened as Alex revealed some of the history of his islands. She was amazed that his small country could have an uprising. When she thought of a sunny island, she thought of peaceful beaches and lazy afternoons. It just showed that she spent too much time wrapped up in her own little part of the world.

After he explained about his brother's impulsive marriage, Alex looked her directly in the eyes. "So you see how my brother's impulsive behavior would be disastrous for our nation."

She wasn't so sure she saw the situation the same as him. "So what you're saying is that you don't believe in love at first sight?"

He shook his head. "No, I don't. I believe in lust and need. But love…well, it grows over time. Like my parents' marriage."

Reese got his message loud and clear. The kiss last night meant nothing. A pain pinged in her chest. She sucked down the feelings of rejection. After all, it was only a kiss. Right now, she needed to hear the rest of Alex's explanation.

"So you think your brother married this girl just so he could have his way with her?" Reese didn't even know his brother, but she wasn't buying that story.

"I didn't say that."

"Sure you did. But something tells me if he looks anything like you that he could have almost any woman he wanted. So why would he offer marriage if he didn't love her?"

Alex paused and stared off into the distance as though he were truly considering her argument. "Maybe you do have a point. Perhaps he was genuinely infatuated with her."

She laughed in frustration and shook her head. "You just won't give in to the fact that your brother might truly love this woman and that your family is trying to tear them apart."

She was about to ask him what he would do if his family tried to come between them, but she stopped herself in time. After all, there wasn't anything for his family to disrupt.

Alex frowned. "It doesn't matter if he loves her or not. He's the crown prince. A wife will be chosen for him. Just as was done for my father and his father."

She wasn't going to argue his brother's case. It was none of her affair. But the pack of reporters outside was a different matter. "Now that you have the press off of your brother's trail, what are you going to do? The press can't camp out on my sidewalk. The neighbors are probably on the phone with the police right now."

"I have a plan, but I need your help."

The little hairs on the back of her neck lifted. "What do you want me to do?"

He held up the paper. "I need you to play the part of my girlfriend."

CHAPTER THIRTEEN

"I COULDN'T BE more serious."

Alex sent her a pleading look that had a way of melting through her resistance. He wanted her to be his pretend girlfriend? Her, Reese Harding, the girlfriend of an honest-to-goodness prince?

The phone started to ring. This was the perfect excuse for her to escape his intense stare. His eyes on her made her heart race and short-circuited her thoughts.

"You've got the wrong woman." She started for the hallway.

"Reese, please wait. Hear me out." There was a weary tone in his voice that stirred her sympathy.

She stopped but didn't turn around. She knew that if she did she'd cave. And she just wasn't ready to give in to him just yet. "I need to get the phone."

"Let the answering machine pick it up. This is important." He cleared his throat. "I know I made a mess of this. I'm truly sorry."

She nodded, letting him know that she'd heard him.

"Will you at least look at me?"

Reese drew in a deep breath. Part of her wanted to keep going out the door and let him know that what he'd done couldn't be forgiven with two little words of apology. But another part of her understood where he was coming from.

He'd been doing what he thought was right and necessary to protect his family. How could she fault him for that?

"I wouldn't ask you to do this if it were not a matter of national security."

Her gaze narrowed in on him, trying to decide if this was the truth or not. "National security? Shouldn't you be talking to some government agency?"

"Not the United States." He got to his feet and moved to stand in front of her. "My country is in trouble."

That's right. He was a prince. Not Alex the repair guy. Not Alex who helped her decorate the Christmas tree. And certainly not Alex the laid-back guy who enjoyed an extra-cheese pizza.

"I don't think I can help you. I run an inn. I'm not an actress. I could never pretend to be a rich debutante or some ritzy character."

"But you have something better than money and a well-known name."

"And what's that?"

"You are a woman of mystery. A woman who has the press waiting to eat out of your hand."

She was really getting confused. "What exactly is it you want me to do? Pose for the cameras?"

"In a way, yes."

She shook her head. "I'm not a model. The black dress that I wore last night and ripped on the pavement was my best dress. You'll have to find someone else."

"That isn't possible."

"Sure you can. This is New York City. The place is crawling with single women. And I'm sure a lot would clamor to be seen on your arm."

"But they're not you—the mystery woman in the photo." He glanced away as though he hadn't meant to blurt that part out. "We could make this a full-fledged business deal."

"A business deal?" She pressed her good hand to her hip. "It's really that important?"

He nodded. "If you were to continue our charade, I would pay off the debt on The Willows."

She stared at him. "You can't be serious. Nothing could be that important."

"Trust me. It's of the utmost importance." He leaned back in the ladder-back chair. "When this situation is behind us, you will own The Willows outright. Maybe then you can go back to art school and follow your dreams."

Reese placed a hand on the archway leading to the foyer to steady herself. Had she truly heard him correctly? Impossible. No one could toss around that much money...except maybe a prince. But what struck her even more was the desperation reflected in his eyes. How could she turn him down with so much at stake?

But did he know what he was asking of her? Did he know that her heart was still bruised by the way he took her feelings so lightly? Did he know that kiss was the most amazing thing to happen to her in a very long time?

Pretending to be his girlfriend would only stir up more unwanted emotions. She shouldn't even consider the idea. It spelled trouble with a capital *T*.

"If I agree, how long will this charade go on for?"

"Not long. Once my brother and the king have the situation settled, the press will find another story to interest them. The paparazzi's attention span is quite short."

"So we're talking a few days?"

"Perhaps longer."

"A week? Or two?"

"Maybe longer." When her mouth gaped open, he added, "No more than a month. At most."

Her gut told her to back out of this agreement as fast as possible—to save herself. But another part of her fancied the idea of dating a prince—even if it was all a show. Above all, she wasn't ready to say goodbye to Alex.

Before she could change her mind, she uttered, "Fine. You have yourself a fake girlfriend."

"There's one more thing you should know."

Her stomach tightened into a knot. "There's more?"

"We need to return to Mirraccino first thing in the morning."

"What?" He couldn't possibly be serious. This was just too much. "But I can't leave. It's Christmastime. I—I don't even have any presents bought for anyone."

He sent her a weary smile, as though relieved. "You can buy your gifts in Mirraccino and I'll make sure they're shipped in time for Christmas."

She frowned at him. "You seem to have an answer for everything."

"This is a once-in-a-lifetime proposition. How can you pass it up?" When she didn't say anything, he added, "If I didn't truly need your help, I wouldn't have asked."

"But what about The Willows? I can't just turn my back on it. And thanks to you, the place will most likely be booked solid through the New Year."

He smiled. "See, I told you things would turn around."

"Don't smile. This isn't good. I don't know how to do everything."

"How about your mother? She could run the inn while you're away."

"My mother? I don't think so."

"Why not? She seems fully capable to me. In fact, she seems to feel a bit left out. She almost glowed when your aunt needed her. Sometimes people need to be needed."

"And you think that she could run this place on her own?" Reese shook her head. "If you'd seen her after my dad died. She was a mess. No, it'd be too much for her."

"I don't think you give her enough credit. Maybe you've been caring for her for so long that you don't even see that she's recovered and ready to take on life if you would just let her."

"And what if something goes wrong and I'm out of the country?"

"Mr. Winston can help her."

Reese's mind replayed how Mr. Winston had always been there, trying to cheer up her mother. And over the past year, he'd made it his mission to bring her a bouquet each day from the flower gardens. She realized that her mother had seemed to spring back to life during that period. Was it possible it had something to do with Mr. Winston?

Her hands balled at her sides as she considered that maybe her mother didn't need her hovering anymore. Maybe it was time her mother stood on her own again.

She tilted her chin up and met Alex's steady gaze. "Tell me what you expect from me in exchange for this all-expenses-paid vacation to some Mediterranean island."

He reached into his pants pocket and pulled out a small black velvet box. "You'll need to wear this."

Reese's heart thumped. She'd always dreamed of the day a man would present her with a diamond ring and ask her to be his wife. What girl didn't at some point in her life? But not like this. She didn't want a fake engagement.

"I can't pretend to be your fiancée."

He gestured to the box in her hand. "Open it before deciding."

She had to admit she was curious to see the contents. The lid creaked open. Inside sat a ring with a large pink teardrop sapphire in the center with diamonds encircling it. The breath caught in Reese's throat. She'd never seen anything so beautiful. Ever.

"Is it real?"

"Most definitely."

"Where did you get it?"

"I had it shipped from Mirraccino. I hope you like it."

At a loss for words, she nodded and continued to stare at the stunning piece of jewelry. She was tempted to slip it on her finger...just to see how it'd look. After all, she'd probably never, ever hold something so precious in her hands again. Talk about your once-in-a-lifetime experiences.

Her gaze lifted to find Alex studying her reaction. She closed the lid and held it out to him. "I can't take this. It's too much. What if I lose it or something?"

"It's perfect for you. And you won't lose it. You're very responsible."

"But people will think that you and I...that we're something we're not."

"That's the point. I need people to talk about us instead of about my family."

As tempted as she was to place the magnificent ring on her finger, she returned the ring box to his hand and wrapped his fingers around it. "We'll be living a lie."

"Why does it have to be a lie? I am giving you this ring. That's a fact. You and I are friends. That's another fact. What stories people make up beyond that is out of our control."

"Still, it'll be a lie of omission."

"And sometimes a little white lie is more important than the truth. If your friend were to ask you if she looks like she put on weight and she has, would you tell her that she's fat?"

"Of course not." It wasn't until the words were out of her mouth that she realized she'd fallen into his trap.

"I just need a little diversion to keep my family safe and the country at peace. Please help me."

How could she turn away? And it wasn't just about

him. It was about the innocent people of his nation, who hadn't signed up for a scandal. Maybe she could help him. Maybe...

"I—I can't give you an answer now." No way was she jumping into this proposition without thinking it through— without the pressure of his pleading stare. "I'll have to think it over and talk to my mother. I'll let you know."

"By tonight."

"What?" He had to be kidding. This was a huge decision for her, to step into the spotlight with a prince and pull off some sort of charade. "I need more time than that. There are things to consider. Arrangements to be made."

"I'm sorry, but this has to happen before someone lets the bat out of the bag—"

"It's cat." When he sent her a puzzled look, she added, "Lets the cat out of the bag."

He sighed. "Someday I'll get all of your sayings straight."

Reese's mind had moved past Alex's loose grasp of idioms. She envisioned escaping the cold and snow to visit a far-off island. And what was even more tempting was being on the arm of the sexiest prince alive.

Some people would think she was crazy to even hesitate. But they hadn't lived the past two years of her life. If they had, they'd be cautious, too.

Still, the thought of jetting off to paradise with Alex made her heart flutter. It'd definitely be the experience of a lifetime. Could she honestly pass up a chance to spend more time with him?

She met his blue eyes. "If I agree to this, and I'm not saying that I will, I'm not lying to people. I won't tell them that you and I...that we're anything more than friends."

"And I wouldn't ask you to."

"Then I'll give you my answer tonight."

She turned and walked away before he could say anything else. She had enough things to consider. She didn't need him adding anything else. Once in the office, she turned off the ringer on the phone. She'd get to the messages shortly. She just needed a moment to breathe.

As she sat there and stared off into space, Alex's words came back to her—he was doing what he must to protect his family and heritage, much like she was trying to protect the patchwork of people whom she now considered her family. They weren't as different as she'd originally thought. The love for those they considered family came first. And this trip would help both of their families.

She really didn't have that much to consider after all. If her mother was able to handle the inn, she would be boarding a plane tomorrow. But when she thought of slipping on that ring and stepping in front of the cameras on Alex's arm, her insides quivered. Thankfully she'd have Alex to lean on. With his dream smile and charming ways, surely he'd be able to distract the paparazzi. He'd have them believing anything he told them.

But what about her? Would she be able to remember that this trip was nothing more than a fantasy and that they were each playing a part? How would she protect her heart from the charming prince?

The big moment had arrived.

A black limousine with diplomatic flags rolled to a stop by the airport entrance.

Alex took a deep breath, wondering if he'd been right to drag Reese into this game with the paparazzi. Still, he couldn't imagine anyone else playing the part of his girlfriend. He had absolutely no desire to hold anyone else's hand or to stare longingly into their eyes—for the media's sake, of course. Oh, who was he trying to bluff? Reese's kisses were as sweet as Mirraccino's juiciest grapes and held a promise of what was to come next.

He glanced over at Reese's now pale face. He hated that their departure had to be made such a public affair. She was wearing the newly repaired little black dress that had done him in the other night when they'd visited Rockefeller Center and he'd at last held her close.

He knew that any attempt to kiss her now would be rebuffed. Reese might have agreed to help him, but things had changed. She even looked at him differently, as though she didn't quite trust him. And he couldn't blame her.

None of this had worked out the way he'd wanted. His gaze slipped to her arm. "How's the arm feeling?"

"What?" She glanced at him with a questioning look.

"The arm—how is it today?"

"Don't start coddling me. My mother did enough of that when she got home yesterday from my aunt's."

He knew to tread lightly around the subject of her mother. Even though all of the staff at The Willows had offered to pitch in extra to help her mother run the place while they were in Mirraccino, Reese was still uncomfortable with the decision. He couldn't tell if it was leaving her mother or if it was letting go of the control she had over the inn, but either way this trip would do her some good. A well-deserved vacation.

"Make sure and tell me if the pain gets worse. We have some of the finest doctors in Mirraccino. They'll see that you're healing properly."

"Did you see all of those reporters and fans out there? Some are even holding signs."

"Don't worry. We have security. Those people won't be able to get to you."

"Is it always like this when you travel?"

"Not this bad. But I had to swirl up sufficient gossip

about my love life to gain the paparazzi's attention." With each passing moment it was getting more difficult to remember what was real and what was fake.

"I'd say it's working." She fidgeted with the hem of her dress. "So do you like all of this fuss?"

"Gaining positive press coverage is part of my duty as prince. A large part of Mirraccino's revenue comes from the tourism industry."

She inhaled a deep breath and lifted her chin to him. "Then let's get this over with."

"But first you will need this." He removed the black velvet box from his pocket and opened it.

She glanced at the ring and then back at his face. There was something in her expression, a tenderness—a question—and in a blink it was gone. Perhaps he'd just imagined it.

She held out her hand for the ring. He could just place it in her palm, but he wanted an excuse to touch her—to recover some of that closeness they'd shared before reality had pulled up the blind on their relationship and left all of the flaws visible under the bright light.

He took her hand in his, noticing how cold her skin was compared to his. Was she truly cold? Or was it a bad case of nerves? Did she also find this moment a little too real?

He slipped the ring on her finger and pushed it over her knuckle. It fit perfectly. And more than that, it looked perfect. He'd picked it out especially for her when this idea had started to take shape. Of course, working with his jeweler back in Mirraccino over the internet had been a bit of a risk, but the ring had turned out better than he'd hoped.

"Perfect."

"What?"

"The ring. It fits perfectly."

She glanced down at her hand, and he wanted to ask

what she was thinking, but he refrained. Was she having second thoughts? With them about to face the press, it was best just to let her be. He didn't want to say anything to upset her further.

When she lifted her gaze to meet his, there was such turmoil in her eyes—such agony. His resolve crumbled, spreading like snowflakes in a blizzard. He couldn't just sit by and not at least try to comfort her. He reached out and pulled her close. Her head willingly came to rest on his shoulder. Her silky hair brushed against his neck and the delicate scent of her floral shampoo teased his senses.

"You don't have to worry. I'll protect you." He meant it with every fiber of his being.

She lifted her head and looked at him. "You'll be my Prince Charming and ride to my rescue?"

"Yes." His gaze dipped to her lips. They were full and berry-red. Like a magnet, they drew him in and his head dipped. His mouth brushed her trembling lips.

It took him every bit of willpower to keep from devouring her lips. She tasted sweet and smelled divine. When she didn't back away, he continued his exploration. He'd never known a kiss could be so intoxicating. She tasted sweeter than the finest Mirraccino light pink Zinfandel.

This act of being a devoted couple was becoming more and more desirable with each fleeting second he held her close. He couldn't imagine ever letting her go. He wanted this kiss to go on and on. And if they hadn't been in the back of a hired car with the paparazzi just a few steps away, he'd have liked to find out where this heated moment would lead.

As it was, he was grateful for the tinted windows. There were certain things he must share with the world. This wasn't one of them. This was a very private moment that had nothing to do with providing cover for his family.

His hand slid up her arm and cradled her neck. Her pulse thumped against his palm, causing his heart to beat out a similar staccato pounding. This moment was something he would never forget. Everything about Reese was unforgettable. How in the world was he going to let her walk away when the time came?

A tap on the car door signaled that everyone was in place for them to make their grand entrance into the airport. Reese jerked back, her eyes wide and round.

"It's okay." Alex gave her arm a reassuring squeeze. "They won't open the door until I signal them."

Her fingers pressed to her now bare lips. They were slightly swollen. And her cheeks had taken on a rosy hue. He smiled, enjoying that he'd been the one to make her look ravished.

"I can't go out there now. I must look a mess."

"You look beautiful."

She reached for her purse. "I need to fix my makeup."

His hand covered hers. "Leave it. You can't improve on perfection."

Her questioning gaze met his and he pulled her hand away from her purse.

"Shall we go?"

"Wait! I—I've never done something like this. What if I make a mistake? What if I say or do the wrong thing?"

"Is that all you are worried about?" His face lifted into a smile. Relief flooded his body.

She nodded and stared at him as though not understanding his reaction.

"You'll do a wonderful job. The paparazzi are already enthralled with you."

"But I don't know how to be a prince's girlfriend."

"You're doing an excellent job." He sent her a certain look, hoping to steady her nerves. "And I don't plan to let you close enough to the press to speak to them. This is more about teasing them and letting them wonder about you and me."

Her shoulders straightened and she blinked away the uncertainty in her eyes. "You really think I can help you do this?"

He nodded. "I wouldn't have asked you otherwise."

She reached for his hand, lacing his fingers with hers. He gave her a reassuring squeeze. "Ready?"

She nodded.

"Don't forget these." He handed her a pair of dark shades and a big black hat with a wide brim to shield her face from the cameras. "Make the paparazzi work for a close-up of you."

"Part of the cat-and-mouse strategy?"

"Exactly."

She settled the glasses on her face, hiding her expressive eyes. Next he handed over the hat, which she angled off to the side. And last, he helped her turn up the collar of her black wool coat.

"There. All set." Alex signaled the driver.

In seconds, the back car door swung open. For the first time, a natural smile pulled at his lips as he faced the cameras. He was proud to have Reese on his arm.

Alex knew it was dangerous to get too comfortable with this arrangement. Soon the final curtain would fall on their show. The thought niggled at him. Was this all just a show? Or was he more invested in this situation than he was willing to admit?

CHAPTER FOURTEEN

SO THIS WAS PARADISE?

Reese stared out the window as the private jet flew over Mirraccino, headed for the private landing strip used by the royal family. Alex's family. She couldn't believe that they'd gone from a gray, snowy day to clear blue skies. The sandy beaches captured her attention. She tried to restrain her awe over the islands' beauty, but she couldn't help herself. As the plane dipped lower, she had an even better view. Never had she seen such picturesque land—from the tropical gardens to the white beaches.

"This place is amazing."

"I'm glad you think so. Just wait until you see it all up close and personal."

She tore her gaze from the window to look at him as panic set in. "But I forgot my camera. My mother is never going to believe this place."

"I have a camera at the palace you can use." He leaned back in his seat. "Now you see part of the reason I want to protect it. The subversives have in mind to rip up the protected land surrounding the beaches and turn it all into exclusive resorts and condos. They can't see that they'll be destroying a national treasure."

"And that's what the revolt is over?"

"No. There's much more to it, but it boils down to a very

unhappy man who has an ax to grind with my papa about something from their childhood. I have never been privy to the details, as the king says that it is not worth repeating. Either way, I've met the man and he's hard, cold and revels in controversy."

"So if this man learns about your brother's marriage, he'll have more ammunition to use against your family."

"Yes. And over the years he has gained a following of troublemakers who think that they can manage the country better than the king and the governing body. But don't worry yourself about it. You have other things to think about. Like enjoying yourself and smiling—a lot."

She should know more about what was expected of her while she was here. "What exactly will I have to do while I'm here?"

"What would you like to do?"

"I'd like to tour the islands, especially the beaches. They look amazing. Maybe go swimming, except I forgot to pack my swimsuit."

"There's something you should know—"

Her body stiffened. "Not more bad news."

"No, nothing like that. I only wanted to warn you that though it is sunny out, the temperature is cool. So swimming in the sea wouldn't be advisable. However, there's a private pool within the palace walls that you're free to use at your leisure. As for clothes, you don't have to worry. I'll have someone stop by with an assortment for you to choose from."

"But I couldn't. I don't have the money."

"It's a perk of the job. You have to look the part of a prince's...um, girlfriend."

She didn't like the thought of taking handouts. But he was right. Her wardrobe was either supercasual, jeans and T-shirts, or business suits for hosting weddings and events.

With her recent lack of a social life, she hadn't needed anything else.

But ever since Alex had dropped into her world, things had changed drastically. In fact, it was just settling into her mind that she would be staying in a palace. An honest-to-goodness palace. This trip had some truly amazing perks—besides the devastatingly handsome guy beside her, who could make her insides melt when his lips pressed to hers.

Her gaze settled on Alex. He leaned back in the leather seat and attached his seat belt as the pilot came over the intercom to instruct them to prepare for landing. This was it. She was about to step into a fairy tale. This would be a story she could tell her children one day—if she ever found that one man she could trust.

Things moved quickly after the plane's wheels touched down. The Mirraccino palace with its enormity and beauty left her speechless, and that didn't happen often. The palace's warm tan, coral and turquoise tones glistened in the sunlight. It reminded her of fine jewelry. Its graceful curves and stunning turrets were regal while reflecting an island flair.

She pointed a finger at the magnificent structure as she struggled to find her voice. "You...you live here?"

His eyes lit up and his lips lifted at the corners. "Yes. I was born here. The whole royal family lives here. In fact, I need to check in on my papa and brother as soon as we get inside. I hope you don't mind."

"Not at all. I know you've been worried about them. It's really nice how close you are with your family."

Alex cleared his throat. "We're just your average family."

She couldn't help but laugh. "Not quite."

Nothing about Alex was average. Not the Learjet they

JENNIFER FAYE

131

flew in on or the magnificent palace he called home. But there was more than just the physical elements of Alex's life that stood out. There was his need to look after her when she got hurt. And his need to fix her apartment.

But then there was the other side of this man—the side that withheld the truth about himself. How did she get past that? And should she even want to? After all, this whole game of charades was temporary. She had to be careful not to forget that this whole trip was nothing more than to benefit the paparazzi.

A man in a dark suit stepped out of the palace. He didn't smile or give any indication that he even saw her. The man's focus was on Alex. Something told her that he wasn't there to retrieve their luggage—not that she had much. She turned a questioning look to Alex.

His demeanor turned stiff and unreadable. "I need to deal with something. If you want to wait inside, I'll be right in."

"No problem." She didn't have to be asked twice. She was eager to see the interior of this amazing palace.

This all has to be a dream.

Reese resisted the urge to pinch herself.

She entered the grand entryway. Her high heels clicked over the marble floor. She craned her neck, taking in the splendor of the walls and high ceiling. She was in awe of the spaciousness and the sheer elegance of the interior, which included a crystal chandelier. And if that wasn't enough to make a girl swoon, standing before her was a man almost as handsome as Alex—in fact, they looked a lot alike. The man filled out a navy suit with the top two buttons of his blue dress shirt undone.

His hair was a deeper shade than Alex's. But it was the man's eyes that held her attention. They were blue, but there was something more—something she couldn't quite define. Perhaps it was loneliness or pain. Whatever it was her heart went out to him.

He spoke in a foreign language.

She held up her hands to stop him. "I'm sorry. I don't understand what you're trying to say."

"No, it is I who am sorry. I forgot that you're American. Welcome to Mirraccino." His voice was deep like Alex's. "I'm Demetrius. You must be Alexandro's friend."

"Ah, yes, I...I'm Reese." She clutched her purse strap tighter. "Alex is talking with someone outside. He'll be right in."

As if on cue, Alex stepped up behind her and placed his hands possessively on her shoulders, as though they belonged together. "Sorry about that. There's a problem down at the port. But nothing that can't be dealt with later. I see I am too late to make the introductions."

Demetrius stepped forward. "This will give me a chance to say this once. Thank you both for everything you've done to keep the paparazzi from making this difficult situation even worse."

Reese wasn't sure what to say to the crown prince. Should she just say *you're welcome?* Or offer her condolences on the dissolution of his marriage?

Alex rode to her rescue when he stepped around her. "Is everything resolved?"

Demetrius's shoulders slumped. "She's gone."

"It's for the best." Alex's matter-of-fact voice startled Reese. "You have a duty to Papa. To the nation. That must always come first."

Demetrius's pained stare met his brother's unflinching gaze. How could Alex be so emotionless? Reese obviously didn't know him as well as she'd thought. She struggled to keep the frown of disapproval from her face.

As it was, the room practically vibrated with emotion.

With bated breath she waited to see if the brothers would come to blows.

Demetrius's hands clenched at his sides. "That's the difference between us, little brother. I don't believe that duty is the be-all and end-all of life."

"And look what that thinking cost you. You look terrible and this whole episode was taxing on Papa."

"Just because you can live without love doesn't mean that I can." Demetrius's eyes narrowed. "And don't think I'm the only one who has his future drawn out for them. You have no more freedom than I do. And we all know that you're the good son who'll marry whoever they choose for you—"

"Enough." Alex's voice held a hard edge. "I know this is a hard time for you, but we have a guest."

Demetrius's gaze moved to Reese. "I'm sorry you had to witness that. Just be glad that you're here doing a job and you didn't actually fall for my brother. He can be heartless at times."

Before she could even think of a response, Demetrius stormed out of the room.

She turned a startled look at Alex. "How could you say that to him? Couldn't you see the pain he's in?"

"He has to remember what's at stake. Living here—" he waved his hands around "—comes with responsibilities others don't think of. My brother can't afford to forget that his decisions affect far more than just himself. He'll get over that woman."

Reese's mouth gaped open. "I was wrong. I'm not the grinch around here. You are."

"What's that supposed to mean?"

"Read the book, you'll find out. And maybe you'll learn a lesson, too."

His forehead wrinkled. "I don't need a child's book to

tell me that there's no room for romance when it comes to the future of this nation."

"And you had to remind your brother of that right now when you can plainly see that he's brokenhearted?"

Alex raked his fingers through his hair. "You're right. I didn't handle it very well."

"That's an understatement." There was one more thing that she had to know. "Is he right? Will a wife be chosen for you?"

Alex's gaze met hers. "My family has plans for me to make an advantageous marriage to a woman from an influential family. We are a small nation and in these uncertain times we can't have enough allies."

Reese's heart sank. "Will you go through with it? Will you marry who they choose?"

He sighed and raked his fingers through his dark hair, scattering the strands. "I don't know. I have more to consider than my happiness. If my marriage can benefit Mirraccino, I must take that into consideration."

All of a sudden this scenario was beginning to sound all too familiar. What was it about men putting everything ahead of love? Did they really think you could sustain a meaningful relationship without it?

She glared at Alex, letting her anger mask her disappointment. "You're just like Josh—"

"What?" Hurt reflected in Alex's eyes. In a blink it was replaced with a hard wall that locked her out. "I can't believe you'd compare me to him."

"Both of you are out to have relationships with women you think can help you. It doesn't matter if you care about them or not. All that matters is what you can get from them."

"That's not true. I'd never lead a woman on."

"True." He definitely wouldn't do that. "You'd tell them up front what you wanted."

Alex reached out to her, but she backed away. "You're tired after our long trip and you're letting my brother get you worked up. We can talk about this later."

He was right. She was getting worked up. But she refused to let another man hurt her—betray her. And the thought of Alex belonging to another woman hurt more than she wanted to admit—even to herself.

"Go after your brother and make things right."

Alex's eyes widened as though he wasn't used to being ordered around. "You're serious?"

"Yes. Go."

"I'll send someone to show you to your room. Later, I'll give you the grand tour."

She nodded her approval. "I need to call my mother and check on things."

Armed with the knowledge that Alex would have a bride chosen for him, she'd have to be careful going forward. She didn't want to get swept up in paradise with a sexy prince and lose her heart. Because in the end, she'd be going back to New York.

Alone.

CHAPTER FIFTEEN

IT WAS JUST the two of them, at last.

Alex stopped next to Reese in front of the glass doors leading to the garden. He hoped a good night's sleep had put her in a better frame of mind. She had to be overcome with exhaustion to accuse him of being anything like her ex-boyfriend. He was nothing like that jerk. He'd never intentionally use a woman. She just didn't understand how things worked when you were born into royalty.

"How are things between you and your brother?" Reese asked, drawing him from his thoughts.

"Getting better. You were right. He really cared about that woman."

They stepped onto the patio and Reese glanced up at him with those big brown eyes. "Does this mean you now believe in love at first sight?"

Alex smiled, amazed by her persistence. "I'll take it under advisement. Perhaps there's more to this love thing than I understand."

She smiled, too, and he had to resist the urge to plant a kiss on her upturned lips. He didn't want to press his luck. At least today she was speaking to him and not glaring at him as though he was the enemy.

They descended the sweeping steps to the edge of the sculpted garden. The sun was high overhead. He enjoyed the fact that she had on a teal dress that he'd personally picked out. When he'd first laid his eyes on it, he'd known it would look spectacular with Reese's long auburn hair.

"You look beautiful."

"Thank you. I don't even want to think how much this dress must have cost you. Did you know that it has a designer label?"

He smiled, enjoying the enthusiasm in her voice. "All that matters is that you like it and you look beautiful in it."

She ducked her head. "I considered not wearing it. It has to be so expensive. I didn't want to do anything to ruin it. But then I realized that I don't own anything suitable to wear here. And I didn't want to embarrass you."

"You could never do that." And he meant every word. He was proud to be seen with a woman who was just as beautiful on the inside as out.

She stopped in front of him and turned. Her shoulders straightened and her chin tilted up. "Tell me about her."

"Who?"

"The woman your family wants you to marry."

He resisted the urge to roll his eyes. "You don't want to hear about Catherine."

"Catherine. That's her name?"

"Yes." He didn't like where this conversation was headed. "There are some flowers over here that I think you'll like."

Reese didn't move. "This Catherine. What does she think of you being in the papers with me?"

"I—I don't know." He hadn't thought about it. Perhaps he should have let her in on the plan, but they'd never made a point of being a part of each other's lives. "We don't talk very often."

"But you're supposed to marry her."

"It's what our families have arranged. It's what is expected of us."

"But neither of you has agreed to the arrangement?"

Was that a glimmer of hope in Reese's eyes? Was she hoping there was room in his life for her?

"Catherine and I have never talked about marriage. We're friends and we spend time together when our families visit."

"Do you love her?"

At last, the question he'd been certain would come up. "Catherine is a wonderful friend. And a very sweet person. But no, I'm not in love with her."

Reese's mouth settled into a firm line as she glanced away, leaving him to wonder about the direction of her thoughts. He'd rather she get it all out in the open, but instead of prodding her, he remained silent. She was at least still here with him. He shouldn't push his luck.

Reese set off down one of the many meandering paths in the sprawling garden. It amazed him how fast she could move while wearing those silver high heels—but boy, was it a sight worth beholding. As she turned a corner, he realized she was getting away. He set off after her.

He'd just caught up to her when she came to an abrupt halt. It was all he could do to keep from running into her. His hands came to rest on her shoulders as he regained his balance. He was just about to ask what she thought she was doing when his gaze settled on the king.

His papa had stopped in front of them. "I didn't know anyone ever took the time to stroll through the gardens."

Alex glanced at Reese's wide-eyed stare and immediately knew that she was intimidated by not only his papa's title but also his booming voice. "I was just showing Reese around."

"There's lots to see. Your mama firmly believed that

it was necessary to pause every day and smell the roses. Your mama knew what was important in life. Sometimes I wonder if she'd approve of my choices, especially with you boys."

Alex was rendered silent, unused to seeing his papa in this state of contemplation concerning his family.

Reese cleared her throat. "I think you've done a great job with Alex. He's kind and thoughtful. You should be proud of him."

"I am." The king's tired face lit up. For a moment, he studied Reese. "Perhaps I am worried for no reason. Now, make sure my son shows you the yellow roses. They were his mama's favorites. If you'll excuse me, I've got to get back to work."

As his papa walked away, Alex was struck by how much his papa still vividly loved his mama. Alex wondered what it must be like to experience such a profound love. But was it worth the risk of ending up alone like his papa—

"Did you hear me?" Reese sent him a puzzled look.

"I'm sorry. What were you saying?"

"I wanted to know which direction led to the roses."

He led her along the wide meandering path edged with low-cut hedges that formed various geometric planting spaces. Each section was planted with just one type of flower, fruit or vegetable. Even though he'd lived here his whole life, he still found the vibrant colors beautiful, but today he only had eyes for Reese.

"With all of these gorgeous flowers, it's like paradise here. You're so lucky."

He looked around the vast garden. He definitely saw it in a different light after living in Reese's world for a few weeks. And though he was blessed financially, Reese was much better off. Her life contained priceless things such as the wonderful relationship she had with her mother, who obviously loved her very much. And even the people who worked for Reese were totally devoted to her.

His guards were devoted to him to the point of laying down their lives to protect him, but it wasn't out of love. It was a duty—an allegiance to a greater good. He wondered what it would be like to have a warm relationship with those around him like Reese had with her staff.

She glanced at him. "You seem to have a lot on your mind."

"I was thinking that until now I've never considered myself lucky. Sure, I appreciate the fact that I lead a privileged life, but sometimes I wake up and wish I had a normal life."

"You can't be serious. You'd really want to give all of this up?"

He shrugged. "Sometimes. When the rules and duties dictate my entire life."

Her forehead wrinkled. "You mean like now, when you had to drop everything and fly to New York?"

"Actually, that's something I'll always be grateful for." He stopped walking and turned to her. "It gave me the opportunity to meet you."

"Are you flirting with me?"

"I don't know. Is it working?"

A hint of a smile pulled at her rosy lips. "What do you think?"

His heart thumped against his ribs. The sun glistened off her auburn hair and her eyes sparkled. He was drawn to her as he was drawn to none other. His fingers stroked her cheek and she leaned ever so slightly into his touch.

His royal duties and the knowledge that Reese would never fit into the king's idea of the proper wife fled his mind. In this moment, the only thing that mattered was the

woman standing before him with longing in her eyes—
such beautiful eyes.

His head dipped down and her soft lips were there meeting his. He moved slowly at first. Like a bird to nectar, he
didn't want to startle her. But when she matched him move
for move, his heart pounded harder. Faster.

An overwhelming need grew in him for more of this—
more of Reese. His arms encircled her waist, pulling her
flush to him. He'd never experienced a kiss so tantalizing,
so sweet. And he'd never wanted someone so much in his
life. Not just physically. Her very presence in his life was
like a smoothing balm, easing away the rough edges. It
was as if he'd donned a pair of glasses and could see things
so much more clearly.

A gentle moan swelled in his throat as her fingers
threaded through his hair. He wanted more, oh, so much
more. He needed to move them out of the garden. Someplace where they wouldn't be under constant supervision
of the security detail—someplace where they could see
where this would lead.

There was the sound of hurried footsteps followed by
someone loudly clearing his throat. Alex knew the sound—
it was time to get back to work. Damn. Why did duty call
at the least inopportune times?

With great reluctance he released Reese. "I must go.
I've been waiting on an important call."

It was as though he could see the walls rising between
them in Reese's eyes. He couldn't blame her for wanting
to come first in someone's life. The men in her life had
relegated her to an afterthought and collateral damage.
She deserved so much better. Not that he was the man to
give her all the love she deserved.

As he walked away, he inwardly groaned. His common

sense and emotions warred with each other. When it came to Reese, she had him reconsidering everything in his life.

Reese was in dangerous territory.

And though she knew that Alex could never have a future with her, she couldn't resist his sultry kisses. Or keep her heart from pounding when his fingers touched hers.

She needed some space—a chance to clear her mind and remember that this was just a show for the press. But there was no time for getting away. There was no chance for her to be alone except at night in her room. They had a job to do—keep the press concentrating on them while his brother pulled himself together and the last of the legal negotiations were handled.

And this morning, Reese and Prince Alexandro were about to have their first press-covered outing. Alex's long, lean fingers threaded through hers as they strolled along the palace drive on their way to tour the nearby village of Portolina. His grip was strong and she drew comfort from it as she was about to be paraded before the cameras.

This public appearance didn't require big sunglasses or hats to hide behind. Instead Reese had selected a pair of dark jeans, a navy blazer and a white blouse. Alex had advised she dress casually. She hoped her choice in clothes would suffice.

Reese gripped Alex's hand tighter. When he glanced her way, her stomach quivered. But it had nothing to do with the reporters waiting for them on the other side of the palace gates. No, the fluttering feeling had everything to do with the man who had her mind utterly confused between her want to continue the kiss from yesterday and her need to protect herself from being hurt when this fairy tale ended.

Alex leaned over and whispered in her ear, "Trust me. You'll be fine."

She let out a pent-up breath and nodded. They approached the gate as it swung wide open. She faced the paparazzi's flashing cameras and smiled brightly.

"When will the formal engagement announcement be released?" shouted a reporter.

"Is there a ball planned to celebrate the impending nuptials?"

"When's the wedding?" chorused a number of voices.

"The palace has no comment." A spokesman stepped forward as planned to field the questions. "Prince Alexandro and Ms. Harding are out for a stroll about the village. If there are any announcements to be made in the future, my office will notify you."

Security cleared the drive for them. Reese wasn't sure her legs would support her—her knees felt like gelatin. As though Alex understood, he moved her hand to the crook of his arm for additional support and then covered it with his other hand.

As they made their way toward the small village, he leaned over and whispered in her ear, "You're doing great. Now they'll never guess your deep dark secret."

She turned to him and arched a questioning brow.

He leaned in again. His minty-fresh breath tickled her neck, sending delicious sensations racing to her core. His voice was low but clear. "That you're a bit grinchy. And that beneath that makeup you're really green."

She laughed and the tension in her body eased. "You looked up the story I told you about."

He nodded and returned her smile. So he really did hear what she said. Her lips parted as her smile intensified.

With the paparazzi trailing behind, Alex gave her a walking tour of Portolina—a small village near the palace. If not for the festive red-and-green decorations, it would not seem like Christmas—at least not the cold, snowy Christmas that Reese was accustomed to in New York.

The stroke of Alex's thumb against the back of her hand sent her pulse racing as she tried to keep her attention focused on this fascinating town. It was teeming with history, from the old structures with their stone-and-mortar walls to the stone walkways. She even found the doorways fascinating, as some were rectangular and others were arched. Beautiful old brass knockers adorned the heavy wood doors. This place definitely had a unique old-world feel to it. She could see why Alex and his family weren't eager to bulldoze this place and modernize it with condos.

Some people rode scooters but most villagers walked. Many of them smiled and waved. Some even came up to Alex—their prince—and greeted him like some returning hero. But most of all, she could feel their gazes on her. Of course, Reese couldn't tell if they were curious about her or the caravan of reporters. She noticed how Alex barely gave the paparazzi much notice. He merely went about his day and she tried following his lead, enjoying the sights and sounds.

The paths he led her on ebbed and flowed through the village, sometimes between buildings and sometimes under passageways. It was so different from her life in New York City. With the camera Alex had lent her, she took dozens of photos—eager to remember every moment of this amazing trip.

They sat down in a coffeehouse that had been closed to the public. Alex lifted her hand and kissed it. "What's bothering you, *bella?*"

Her heart stuttered as she stopped and stared at him. His reference to her with such an endearing term caught her off guard. But before she let herself get caught up in the moment, she reminded herself that this was all an illusion. She pulled her hand away. He was playing his part—acting like the ardent lover. Nothing more.

But if that was the case, why was he doing it when there was no one within hearing distance? Reese could feel her last bit of resolve giving way. And as he once again reached across the café table to her, she didn't shy away. His warm hand engulfed hers reassuringly. She could feel her resistance to his charms crumble even further.

"You can tell me anything." His voice was soft and encouraging.

Glancing around just to make sure they were in fact alone, she lowered her voice and said, "They expect us to get married. This is what I was worried about. They've jumped to the wrong conclusion. I'll have to call my mother and warn her not to believe anything she reads in the paper."

Reese glanced down at the ring causing all of the ruckus. She wiggled her finger, enjoying the way the light danced over the jewels. It truly was the most beautiful ring she'd ever seen.

Alex waved away her worries. "Don't worry about it. Just enjoy yourself." There was a pause and then he added, "You are enjoying yourself, aren't you?"

"Yes. But when this illusion ends, everyone will think it's my fault."

"*Bella,* you worry too much. After all, you are forgetting that I control what information is fed to the press. On my honor, I promise your good name will remain intact."

She wanted to smile and take comfort in his words, but she couldn't. They weren't the words she was longing to hear. She wanted him to say that she mattered to him. That this illusion was real to him. That it wasn't going to end.

After their extensive lunch was served, the waiter brought them espresso to wash it down. Reese, not used to such a large meal, wasn't sure she had room for it.

Alex took a sip of the steaming brew. "I have some meetings this afternoon that I must attend, but feel free to finish touring the village."

"I think I'll do that. I still have my Christmas shopping to do."

"I promise to return as soon as I can."

"Don't rush on my account. I know that you have important issues to attend to."

"Nothing is more important than you." His warm gaze met hers and her insides melted. "You're my guest and I want you to be happy here. I hope the paparazzi's attention has not been too much for you."

"Actually, your staff has done a great job of keeping them at a distance. And I think the people of Portolina are amazingly kind. You're lucky to live here. I'll never forget my visit."

Her heart pinched at the thought of one day waking up and no longer bumping into Alex. She didn't know how someone she'd only met recently could become such an important part of her life.

She brought her thoughts up short. This was ridiculous. She was falling for her own PR scam. They weren't a couple. And he wasn't someone that she should trust, but with each passing day she was finding her mistrust of him sliding away.

Maybe like the Grinch, Alex's heart was starting to grow. Which gave her a great idea for a Christmas present. There was a small bookstore just back a little ways. She would get him a copy of *How the Grinch Stole Christmas*. Perhaps it wasn't too late for him to see life differently.

CHAPTER SIXTEEN

HOW COULD IT BE more than a week since they'd arrived in Mirraccino?

Alex's body tensed as he realized there was no longer a need for Reese to stay—except for the fact that he wasn't ready to let her go yet. He'd spent every available moment with her, and he still hadn't gotten his fill of her. He'd never had this sort of experience with anyone before.

They'd toured Mirraccino's finest vineyards and taken a trip to the bustling port on the other side of the island. The outings allowed her to rest her arm and the bruises time to begin to fade. And best of all, her frosty demeanor had melted beneath the bright sunshine.

He knew as Prince Alexandro, he should end things here and now. But the plain, ordinary Alex didn't want to let go. He couldn't imagine Reese being gone from his life. How did one return to a dull and repetitive life after being shown a bright, sparkling world full of hope?

Alex had made his decision. No matter what the king said, it was simply too soon for Reese to leave. His brother, the crown prince, was simply not in good enough spirits yet to deal with the press. It wouldn't take much for them to notice the crown prince's melancholy expression. He wore it like an old war wound, reminding his whole family of what he'd lost in order to uphold his royal duty.

Thanks to Reese, Alex was starting to believe his brother's feelings for the woman had run much deeper than he'd originally thought. The price of being royal could cut quite deep at times. He was about to pay his own dues when Reese left for the States. He wasn't relishing that impending day. In fact, he refused to think of it today.

Christmas Day had at last arrived and the paparazzi had fled for their own homes, leaving everyone at the palace in peace—at least for one day. And now that the official photos had been taken, the gifts opened and the extravagant lunch served, he had a very special surprise in mind for Reese. He'd been working on it all week and now he was anxious to surprise her.

"I can't believe the size of your Christmas tree." Reese's voice was full of awe as they strolled back to their rooms, which were in two different wings. "It's a good thing I remembered to have you take my picture next to it. My mother never would have believed it was, what— twenty feet tall?"

"I don't know." He smiled over the things that impressed her. "If you want I can inquire."

"No. That's okay. The picture will say it all. You did get the whole tree in the picture, didn't you?"

"Yes. Now I have a question for you." He sensed her expectant look. "After we change clothes, would you join me for a stroll along the beach?"

"I don't know." Her gaze didn't meet his. "I'm kind of tired. It's been a really long day."

He wasn't going to give up that easily. This was far too important—he had a very special surprise for her. "Or is it that you stayed awake all night waiting for Santa?"

There was no hint of a smile on her face. "Something like that."

"I was only teasing you."

"I know." She continued staring at the floor.

His finger lifted her chin. Sadness reflected in her eyes. "Reese, talk to me. I'll make it better."

She shook her head. "You can't. No one can."

His voice softened. "Sometimes talking things over can make a person feel better."

She leaned her back against the closed door and pulled at the short sleeves of her midnight-blue dress. "Do you really care?"

His fingers moved some loose strands of silky hair from her face and tucked them behind her ear. "You know I do. I care very much."

Reese glanced up and down the hall as though to confirm that they truly were alone. This must be more serious than he'd originally thought.

"Why don't we step into your room?" he suggested.

She nodded and turned to open the door. Inside, she approached the bed, where she perched on the edge. With the door closed, no one would bother them. Alex's mind spiraled with all of the intimate possibilities awaiting them. Perhaps this hadn't been such a good idea for a serious talk.

Reese lifted her face. Her shiny eyes and pale face stopped his wayward thoughts in their tracks. He sat down beside her and took her hand in his.

Her voice came out very soft. "I was up last night thinking about how my life has changed since my father died at Christmas two years ago."

The news smacked into Alex, stunning him for a moment. "I had no idea."

"I didn't want to make a big deal of it. It was Christmas Eve, to be exact. He was leaving…leaving me and my mother to meet his longtime lover." She swiped at her eyes. "He didn't even have the nerve to tell us to our faces. He wrote a note. A note! Who writes a note to tell the people that he is supposed to love that their lives were a lie and he doesn't love them and he wants out?"

Alex didn't have a clue what to say. Her rigid back and level shoulders sent keep-away vibes. So he sat there quietly waiting for her to get it all out.

"He hit a patch of black ice and went over an embankment. They say he died on impact. He didn't even have the decency to stick around to say goodbye. There was no time for questions—and no answer to why he'd destroyed our family. It was all over in a heartbeat."

"I'm so sorry he did that to you and your mother."

Reese swiped at her eyes. "At the time, I thought I had Josh to lean on. He was there for the funeral. He was the perfect gentleman, sympathizing with me and my mother." A hollow laugh echoed from her chest. "He had the nerve to condemn my father for his actions. And yet when it came to light that the savings had been drained off and the mansion had been mortgaged to pay for my father's new life, Josh couldn't get out the door fast enough."

Her shoulders drooped as she got the last of the sad story out. It was as though without all of the anger and pain, she deflated.

Instead of words, he turned, drawing her into his arms. She didn't resist. In fact, she leaned into his embrace. Maybe his plan for today wasn't such a good idea after all.

Reese inhaled a shaky breath. "Now you know why I've been so hesitant to trust you—to trust anyone."

Alex lifted her chin with his thumb. When her brown gaze met his, he said, "You can trust me. I promise I won't abandon you and I won't betray you."

He leaned forward, pressing his lips gently against hers in a reassuring kiss. Her bottom lip trembled beneath his. He didn't know how anyone could take her for granted. Reese was everything he'd ever wanted in a woman and more.

She pulled back and gave him a watery smile. "Thank you. I didn't mean to put a damper on the day."

"And if I had known what a tough day this would be for you, I wouldn't have tried to talk you into an outing."

"The truth is, I'll never be able to relax now."

"Are you saying you want to go?" He didn't want her to do anything that she wasn't up for.

She nodded and wiped away the moisture on her cheeks. "Just let me get changed."

"I'll meet you back here in ten minutes."

"Sounds good. Thank you for listening and understanding." The smile that touched her lips this time was genuine, and it warmed a spot in his chest.

On second thought, maybe his plan was just what she needed to push away her not-so-happy past and replace it with new, happy memories. Yes, he liked that idea. Reese deserved to be happy after the way she went out of her way for the people in her life—he wanted to be the one who went out of his way for her.

In that moment, he realized something that he'd been avoiding for a while now. He had feelings for Reese—deep feelings. He knew it was a big risk with his heart. Thoughts of his heartbroken father flashed through his mind. But in the next breath, he envisioned Reese's face.

He didn't have a choice.

Somehow, someway, she'd sneaked past his defenses. He cared for her more than anyone else in his life. But he didn't know what to do with these feelings. He was a prince. There were expectations he must fulfill for the good of the kingdom.

As he headed for his suite, he realized it was time he called Catherine. They needed to meet after the holidays were over. In light of his genuine feelings for Reese, he couldn't let the lingering questions surrounding the anticipated royal engagement drag on.

Although with all that hinged on the engagement, breaking the news to Catherine would have to be handled face-to-face and very carefully.

Reese's mouth gaped.

Gripping the red beach bag hanging over her shoulder and with Alex holding her other hand, she stood on the sand utterly speechless. Her gaze searched his smiling face before she turned back to the towering palm tree all decked out with white twinkle lights. The scene belonged on a postcard. It was picture-perfect…just like Alex in his khaki pants and white shirt with the sleeves rolled up and the collar unbuttoned.

Alex gave her hand a squeeze. "Do you like your surprise?"

"I love it." She nodded and smiled. Her gaze roamed around, trying to take it all in. "Is this all for me?"

His eyes lit up as he gazed at her. "It's my Christmas present to you."

The wall around her heart that had been eroding all week completely crumbled in that moment. She was totally vulnerable to him and she didn't care. "But you've already given me so much that I can never repay."

"That was all about our deal. This, well, this is because I wanted to do something special for you." He shifted his weight from one foot to the other. "And I know how much you enjoy the little lights, so I ordered enough to decorate the bungalow inside and out. Do you like it?"

She nodded vigorously. "No one has ever done anything so thoughtful for me. Thank you."

She lifted up on her tiptoes and without thinking of how

their diverse lives would never mesh, leaned into him and pressed her lips to his. She heard the swift intake of his breath. They'd been building toward this moment since their first kiss at Rockefeller Center. With each touch, look, kiss, she felt a heady need growing within her. The electricity between them had crackled and arced ever since they met. And now beneath the darkening Mediterranean sky, it had the strength of a lightning bolt. Her insides warmed with undeniable anticipation.

She swallowed hard, trying to regain her composure. "Are you going to show me the inside?"

He blinked as though he, too, had been thoroughly distracted by the kiss that promised more to follow. "Um… yes. Lead the way."

She easily made it up the stone steps that meandered up the embankment and led to a wide-open terrace with a white table and matching chairs. An arrangement of red poinsettias was placed in the center of the table, where a burning white candle flickered within a hurricane lamp. She wondered if his attention to details extended to all parts of his life.

She stopped on the terrace and turned to Alex. This night was so romantic, so perfect. Her heart thumped against her ribs. He'd done all of this for her. With every passing moment it was becoming increasingly difficult to remember that she was only playing a part for the sake of his nation's national security.

And then her chest tightened. Her palms grew damp. And she bit down on her lower lip. In that moment, she remembered how much it hurt when happy illusions shattered and reality ran up and smacked her in the face. She'd promised herself she wouldn't set herself up to be hurt like that again. It was just too painful.

Needing to add a dash of reality to this picture-perfect

evening, she asked, "Have you thought about how we're going to end all of this?"

Alex's brow creased. "Why would I think about something like that when we're having such a wonderful time?"

He had a good point, but fear overrode his words. "But eventually you're going to have to tell the press something when I go back to the States without you."

His fingers caressed her cheek. "Just for tonight, forget about the future and enjoy the moment."

She wanted to, more than he knew. But this just wasn't right. They'd gotten caught up in the show they were putting on for the public. In reality, there was another woman in Alex's life.

The sobering reality propelled her away from him—needing a little space to resign herself to the fact that this evening, as beautiful as it was, couldn't happen. If they made love—if she laid her heart on the line—she couldn't bear to walk away from him. As it was, stepping on the plane now would be torture, but to know exactly what she'd be missing would be unbearable.

She stepped up to the rail to gaze out over the ocean as the sun was setting. Pink and purple stretched across the horizon as a big ball of orange sank beneath the sea. The breeze tickled over her skin while the scent of salt filled her nose.

When she heard his footsteps approaching her, she tried to act normal—whatever that amounted to these days. "I've never seen anything so beautiful."

"I have." Alex's hands wrapped around her waist. "And I am holding her."

His compliment made her heart go tap-tap in her chest. She turned in his arms. "I'm sure you've been with much prettier women. What about Catherine? Shouldn't she be the one who is here with you?"

His brows gathered. "No, she shouldn't."

"But you're supposed to marry her."

"Is that what's bothering you?" When she nodded, he added, "Then stop worrying. I've called Catherine."

He did? Her heart took flight. "You told her about me?"

"Yes—"

Reese launched herself at him, smothering his words with a passionate kiss. Excitement and relief pumped through her veins. Her arms wrapped around his neck, pulling him close. There was nothing more she needed to hear. He'd told Catherine that they were together now. How could she have ever doubted him?

Reese hadn't known she could ever be this happy. The rush of feelings inside her was intense and they were fighting to get out. The time had come to quit holding back and trust him with her heart. Because if anyone was a good guy, it was Alex.

She pulled back and looked up at him. "Sometimes fantasies really do come true."

"Yes, they do."

He drew her back to him, the heat of his body permeating her dress. His lips pressed to hers. This time there was no hesitation in his touch. There was a deep need and a passionate desire in the way his mouth moved over hers. It lit a fire within her that mounted in intensity with each passing second.

Someone cleared his throat.

Reese jumped, pulling away from Alex's hold. She didn't know why she'd automatically assumed that they were alone. And that Alex had planned this as a romantic getaway for two.

Heat scorched her cheeks as she turned to face their visitor.

The butler stood at attention. "Sir, we need to know if you would like us to set up the meal inside or out."

Alex glanced at her. "It's your choice. Where would you like to dine?"

"Without the sun, the temps are dipping." She rubbed her arms, which were growing cold without his warmth next to them. "Would you mind if we eat inside?"

"Not at all. Would you like a fire lit?"

She glanced through the glass doors at the stone fireplace. The idea of sitting next to a crackling fire with Alex sounded perfectly romantic. "Yes, please."

Once the butler and small staff set about laying out the meal, Alex approached the fireplace mantel and retrieved a red plush Santa hat. "I think this will help set the mood."

She let him place the hat upon her head. "I guess it depends on what sort of mood you're creating."

"I'll let you wonder about that for now."

She spied another Santa hat on the mantel and decided that the prince needed to have some fun with her. She tossed her beach bag on the couch and raced over to the mantel. With the other Santa hat in hand, she turned to Alex.

A smile lit up his face as he started shaking his head. "No way. I am not wearing that."

"This evening is all your creation. I think that you're more Santa today than I am. I'll be Santa's elf."

He stopped shaking his head as his eyes lit up with definite interest. "My elf, huh? I guess that means that you have to listen to me."

"I don't think so." She backed up but he followed her with a devilish look in his eyes. "Don't go getting any wild ideas."

He grabbed her by the sides and started tickling her. His fingers easily found her sensitive spots. She could barely breathe from all of the laughter. Though his magical fingers had stopped moving, he continued to hold her close. It felt so natural to be in his arms. Her arms draped over his shoulders as she leaned into him, trying to catch her breath.

His gaze met hers. "You know Santa left some packages over there under the tree for you."

She leaned her head to the side to see around his hulking form. "I can't believe I didn't see those before." She glanced back at him. "Are you sure they're for me?"

"I don't know. Were you a good girl this year?"

She nodded.

"Are you sure?"

She nodded again. "Can I open them now?"

"Not quite yet." When she stuck out her bottom lip, he added, "Surely you can wait until after dinner."

"But that's not what I'm pouting about. I only have one gift for you." She pulled away from him to move to the couch and reached in her beach bag. She removed a package all neatly wrapped in white tissue paper with a shiny red bow.

"You didn't have to get me anything."

"That's what makes it special. I wanted to. But I must warn you that it's nothing expensive or impressive."

"Anything you give me will be a thousand times more special than the most expensive wines or sports car."

"A sports car? So that's what you wanted Santa to bring you?"

He reached out for her hand and drew her to him, pulling her down on his lap. "Everything I want is here. You didn't have to get me a gift."

"I would have given it to you this morning at the gift exchange with your family, but I knew your family wouldn't understand the meaning behind it. And I didn't want to do anything that might be misconstrued by your father."

"That you don't have to worry about. Did you notice how well he's taken to you?"

"I know. What was up with that?"

"I told you that you had nothing to worry about by coming here. He really likes you—they all do. Most especially me."

By the glow of the firelight, they enjoyed soup and antipasto. Neither of them was that hungry after the large Christmas luncheon. This light fare was just perfect. And Alex was the perfect date as he kept her smiling and laughing with stories of adventures from his childhood.

"You were quite the daredevil back in the day," Reese surmised as she settled down on the rug and pillows in front of the fireplace. "Something tells me that the adventurous part of you is still lurking in there behind the prim and proper prince."

"You think so." He popped a bottle of Mirraccino's finest sparkling wine and the cork flew across the room. The contents bubbled over the top and he sucked up the overflow before it could make a mess.

"My point is proven." She laughed.

He poured them each a flute of the bubbly golden fluid and then held one out to her. She accepted it with a smile. This whole trip had been amazing and she had no doubt where the evening was headed.

"To the most beautiful woman I have ever known. May all of your wishes come true."

Their glasses clinked and before Reese even held the crystal stemware to her lips, a fluttery feeling filled her stomach. Her gaze met his hungry one. She took a sip of the sweet wine, but she barely noticed it as the cold liquid slid down her dry throat.

"You do know that we're all alone now?" He set aside his glass.

She set her wine next to his. Her gaze slipped down to his lips. They looked quite inviting. "Does this mean that I get my Christmas present now?"

His voice came out unusually deep and gravelly. "That depends on what present you want to unwrap first."

She leaned toward him. "I think I'll start right here."

In the next breath her lips were covering his. When his arms wrapped around her, pulling her close, she could no longer deny that she had fallen for her very own Prince Charming. She loved Alex with every fiber of her being.

His hands encompassed her waist, pulling her to him. She willingly leaned into him. The sudden shift of her weight sent them falling back against the stack of pillows. She met him kiss for kiss, touch for touch. The fire crackled as Alex nuzzled her neck, causing her to laugh. She couldn't remember ever feeling so alive—so in love.

CHAPTER SEVENTEEN

A KNOCK SOUNDED.

Alex woke with a start. He squinted as the bright morning sun peeked in through the windows, catching him in the eyes. He glanced over finding Reese still breathing evenly as she lay snuggled beneath the pile of blankets. His thoughts filled with visions of her being in his arms. It had been the most amazing night of his life.

One kiss had led to another. One touch had led to another. And at last they'd ended up curled in front of the fireplace. He recalled how Reese's face had lit up with happiness. The sparkle in her big brown eyes had been his undoing. Her joy had filled a spot in him that he hadn't even known was empty.

He turned away from her sleeping figure and ran a hand over his hair, trying to will away the fogginess of sleep. This wasn't supposed to have happened. He hadn't meant for them to get in so deeply. Not yet. He still had so much to set straight with his family. And yet he couldn't deny that he cared deeply for Reese.

Another knock had him jumping to his feet. The fire had died out hours ago and a distinct chill hung in the air. He rushed to throw on his discarded and now wrinkled clothes. He moved silently across the hardwood floor to the front door.

His personal assistant stood at the door. The older man's face was creased with lines, but nothing in his very proper demeanor gave way to his thoughts of finding Alex in an awkward moment.

"Good morning, Guido." Alex kept his voice low so as not to wake Reese, since they'd gotten very little sleep. "What can I do for you?"

"I'm sorry to interrupt, sir." He also kept his voice to a whisper. "There's an urgent matter you must deal with at the palace."

Alex's chest tightened. He didn't like the sound of that. Thoughts of his papa's health and his brother's latest fiasco raced through his mind. "What is it?"

"There's another problem with a shipment at the port. I don't know the details. Only that you are requested to come immediately. I have a car waiting for you."

"Thank you. I'll be along soon."

"Yes, sir."

Alex closed the door gently. One of the problems with being a small nation was that the government was much more hands-on. He didn't understand why all of a sudden they were having endless problems at the port. And it didn't help matters that the problems seemed to concern a fleet of cargo ships owned by Catherine's father, who had been less than pleased with the last problem, involving a falsified manifest and a very greedy captain.

Alex didn't even want to guess what the harbormaster had uncovered this time. Dread coursed through his body. Still, there was no way around it. The only thing he could hope was that it was another shipping company.

"Who was at the door?" Reese's sleepy voice was deeper than normal and very sexy.

If only Alex didn't have important matters to tend to, he'd spend a leisurely morning with her. But duty came first.

"It was a message from the palace that my attendance is needed."

Reese's eyes widened. "Is something wrong?"

"Nothing for you to worry about. Just a problem at the port." He slipped on his loafers and collected his things. "Take your time. There is food in the kitchen."

"But our presents. We didn't open them—"

"I'm sorry. There's no time now." He glanced at the fanciful packages beneath the tree. "It'll give us something to look forward to later."

"Unless we get distracted again." Her voice was still deep from sleep.

The sultry sound made him groan with frustration. "We'll get to them...eventually."

Her cheeks beamed a crimson hue, but that didn't stop her from teasing him. "I can't promise you that it'll be any time soon. I have plans for you."

"I'll hold you to your word." He leaned down and gave her a lingering kiss that made it almost painful to tear himself away from her. "I'll send the car back for you, but I have no idea how long I'll be."

How could someone be so unhappy when surrounded by such beauty?

Reese paced back and forth. It wasn't so much that she was unhappy...more like bored. Frustrated. Agitated. There was a whole dictionary full of words to describe her mood.

Sure, her palace suite was beautiful, from the high ceiling with its white, blue and gold polychrome tiles to the huge canopied bed. It was like sleeping in a very elegant museum—in fact, the entire palace was like something people only viewed in glossy magazines. It made her hesitant to touch anything for fear of breaking something.

She strolled over to the large window overlooking the sea. The sun was shining and the water was tranquil, unlike her mind, which could not rest. Her thoughts continually drifted back to Alex, as they had done so often since their very special evening together. Her cheeks warmed at the memory of how sweet and loving he'd been with her. It had been a perfect evening. So then why had Alex been gone the past twenty-four hours?

The only message she'd received from him had come the prior evening, when he'd extended his apologies for missing dinner, claiming he had work to do. The note only made her even more curious about his whereabouts. What was so important? And why couldn't he deliver the message in person?

Unable to spend another lonely moment in her opulent suite, she threw on some old comfy jeans and a pink hoodie with a navy-blue New York logo emblazed over it. The clothes certainly weren't anywhere close to the fancy ones she'd been wearing since she'd arrived in Mirraccino, but she didn't feel a need to put on a show today. Besides, where she was headed there wouldn't be any paparazzi. And if there were, she was in no mood to care.

She headed for the private beach, hoping to clear her head—to figure out where she and Alex went from here. The sun warmed her back and helped her to relax. As for Alex, things there were complicated. It wasn't like being in a relationship with the guy next door. But she couldn't just walk away, either. The other night had drastically changed things. She'd given her heart to him.

A smile tugged at her face as she thought of Alex and how far they'd come. When she'd met him, she hadn't wanted a man in her life. She'd been unhappy, even though she hadn't realized it at the time. She'd had her eyes closed to her mother's progress, but Alex had helped her see things that were right in front of her. She'd learned to trust him and that she didn't have to be in control of everything all of the time. In fact, her daily calls to her mother revealed that The Willows was prospering without Reese's presence.

Her steps were light. It was as if she were tiptoeing along the fluffy white clouds dotting the sky. She was humming a little ditty to herself as she strolled down the beach, and then she spotted Alex. He was dressed in blue slacks and a blue button-up shirt with the sleeves rolled up. The breeze off the sea rustled his dark hair, scattering the strands. She was just about to call out to him when she got close enough to notice someone at his side. A woman. She was much shorter, with long dark hair that shimmered in the sun. They leaned toward each other as they laughed about something.

A sick feeling settled in the pit of Reese's stomach. She took a step backward. So this was why he'd been too busy to see her?

No. Alex wouldn't do something like this to her. He'd promised that she could trust him. And she'd given him her heart.

She dragged in a deep breath, hoping to calm her rising heart rate. She was jumping to conclusions. After all, he wasn't her father. He'd never leave her bed to go to another woman. *Have faith. Alex will make this right.*

Reese leveled her shoulders and forced her feet to move in the direction of the man she loved. She refused to be childish and jealous. There was a simple explanation to this. One that would make her feel foolish for jumping to conclusions. Maybe she was his cousin. Or the woman his brother had married. That must be it. He was comforting the woman and passing along a message from his brother.

"Good morning." Reese forced a smile on her face.

They both turned to her. Alex's brows lifted and the woman's eyes lit up as her gaze moved from Alex to Reese and back again. The woman's painted lips lifted into a smile.

Reese's radar was going off loud and clear, but she insisted on giving Alex a chance. "Beautiful morning, isn't it?"

Alex nodded. "Um…yes, it is." The surprise on his face slid behind a blank wall. "Reese, I would like you to meet Catherine."

"It is good to meet you." The woman's voice was warm and friendly. "You are the one helping, no?"

Catherine's English was tough to understand behind a heavy accent. "Yes…yes, I am."

But there was so much more to their relationship. Why did the woman seem a bit confused? Alex had said he'd told Catherine about her. An uneasy feeling settled in her stomach. She'd once again let her naivety get her into trouble. She should have asked him exactly what he'd told the woman. Because it obviously wasn't that he loved Reese. That much was clear.

Catherine smiled and held out her hand. "I would like us to be friends, no?"

Reese didn't have much choice but to force a smile and extend her hand. The sunshine gleamed off the pink sapphire, reminding her of the heated kiss she'd shared with Alex when he'd given it to her. What would Catherine make of the ring?

She searched the woman's face for some hint of hostility or jealousy, but she didn't detect any. The woman truly appeared to be kind and outgoing. What was Reese missing? Had Alex duped them both?

Not understanding any of this, she turned a questioning look to Alex. But his gaze didn't meet hers. Except for the slight tic in his cheek, there was nothing in his out-ward appearance to let her know that he was uncomfort-able with this meeting.

Oblivious to the undercurrents running between Alex and Reese, Catherine said, "You help Alex with paparazzi, no?" The woman's voice was soft and gentle. When Reese nodded, the woman continued to speak. "You are a good woman. He is lucky to have you."

What could she say to that? Though it killed her to ex-change pleasantries when all she wanted to do was con-front Alex, she uttered, "Thank you."

Alex cleared his throat. "Catherine and I were headed back inside. I have a meeting to attend. Would you care to join us?"

There was no warmth in his voice. No acknowledge-ment that they were anything more than casual acquain-tances. Just the cool politeness of a politician.

"Yes, join us. I want to know about you and New York." Catherine's eyes reflected her sincerity.

With determined reserve, Reese maintained a cool out-ward appearance. "I think I'll stay out here. I'd like to stretch my legs. One can only be cooped up for so long."

Reese turned to Alex and bit back an impolite comment. There was no way she could be rude to Alex in front of this woman. As much as she wanted to dislike Catherine, she couldn't; she appeared to be a genuinely nice person. In another universe, Reese could imagine being fast friends with Catherine. But not here—not today.

Reese could only presume that the woman didn't know what had transpired between her and Alex the other night. And there was no way she would be the one to tell her. That was Alex's problem.

What she had to say to him—and there was a lot—would have to wait. She didn't need this woman knowing what a fool she'd made of herself, falling for a prince far outside her league.

A look of relief crossed Alex's face. "Then we'll leave you to enjoy the day."

He extended his arm to Catherine, who turned to Reese. "Nice to meet you. We talk later."

"Nice to meet you, too." Reese couldn't believe how hard it was to say those words without choking on her own tongue.

She stood there watching the departing couple. Catherine's head momentarily leaned against Alex's arm, as though she knew him well—very well. The thought slashed into Reese's heart. She was the odd man out.

It wasn't until they turned the corner and headed up the steps toward the palace that Reese realized she'd been holding her breath. She was afraid to breathe out—afraid the balled-up emotions inside her would come tumbling out. She blinked repeatedly, clearing her blurring vision. She wanted to believe that this was some sort of nightmare and she'd wake up soon. Because it just couldn't be possible that she'd been duped into being the other woman.

Her stomach lurched. Her hands wrapped around her midsection as she willed away the waves of nausea. After all of the days and nights of wondering how her father's lover could have carried on an affair—now Reese was in those very uncomfortable shoes. And she hated it.

She started walking down the beach with no destination in mind. Her only thought was to get away. Her steps came faster. Throughout the whole drama with her father's death and finding out that he'd siphoned off their savings, she'd had a hard time believing her mother hadn't known anything about it. How could she not?

Looking back on it, there had been so many clues—so many things that didn't add up. She'd ended up harboring angry feelings toward her mother for allowing all of that to happen to them by turning a blind eye to her father's activities. But now Reese had more compassion for the situation her mother had been in. When you love someone, you trust them.

Reese stopped walking, drawing one quick breath after the other. She glanced around, realizing she'd ended up back at the bungalow. She hadn't realized she'd wandered so far down the beach.

Her legs were tired and her face was warm from the sun, but it was the aching loss in her chest that had the backs of her eyes stinging. She refused to dissolve into a puddle of tears. She wouldn't stop living just because she'd once again let herself be duped by a man. The memory of Alex and Catherine arm in arm and with their heads together, laughing, was emblazoned on her memory. How could she have trusted him?

With renewed anger, she started off for the palace. This fairy tale had come to an end. And like Cinderella, it was time to trade in her gowns for a vacuum and a day planner.

She'd reached the bottom of the steps up the cliff when she spotted Alex sitting there. He didn't notice her at first and she paused, not sure she was up for this confrontation. Still, it was best to meet it head-on and get it over with. She didn't want any lingering *what if*s or *should have*s. This would end things cleanly.

Leveling her shoulders, she headed straight for him. When he saw her, he got to his feet and met her halfway. Lines bracketed his eyes and his face looked as though he'd aged a few years. Was he that worried that she'd blow things for him with Catherine? She took a bit of satisfaction in knowing that he was stressed. It was the least he could feel after he'd used her without any thought to her feelings.

"Reese, you had me worried. You didn't tell anyone where you were going."

She crossed her arms and narrowed her gaze on him. "I'm sure you were too busy to be worried about me."

"That's not fair. You know I care."

"Was Catherine the reason you took off after we spent the night together?" *Right after I'd given you my heart. When I'd at last trusted you.*

"No. I told you there was a problem at the port."

Reese crossed her arms and hitched up a hip. "So what's she doing here?"

"She knew I wanted to speak with her, and since a problem had arisen with one of the ships her father owns, she flew in. I knew nothing of her arrival until last evening."

Reese wasn't about to assume anything this time around. "Does Catherine know how you spent the other night?"

V-shaped lines etched between his brows. "Of course she doesn't know. What kind of man do you think I am? I don't go around discussing personal things."

"The kind who likes to keep a woman on the side like a spare suit or an extra pair of shoes." Her voice quavered with anger. "Is that what I am to you?"

"No, of course not." His blue eyes pleaded with her to believe him, but she was too worked up to be swayed so easily. "But you don't understand. I can't just blurt out to Catherine that I have feelings for you."

"Why?"

He glanced down and rubbed the back of his neck. "Because I won't hurt her like that. She deserves better."

Reese heard the words he hadn't spoken, louder and clearer than anything else. He cared about Catherine. Those powerful words blindsided Reese. They knocked into her full force, stealing the breath from her lungs. She stumbled back.

He had real feelings for Catherine.

Reese's teeth sank into her lower lip, holding in a back-lash of anger and a truckload of pain. How stupid could she have been? Catherine oozed money and culture. The woman was a perfect match for a prince. Reese glanced down at her faded jeans and worn sweatshirt. She'd laugh at the comparison, but she was afraid that it'd come out in sobs. She swallowed down her emotions.

"We don't have anything left to say to each other. You should go to her—to your future fiancée."

"You're spinning this out of control. Catherine has nothing to do with you and me."

"Yes, she does. She has everything to do with this. You care about her."

Not me!

A sob caught in the back of her throat. A piercing pain struck her heart, causing a burning sensation at the backs of her eyes. She loved him, but he didn't feel the same way. She clenched her hands, fighting to keep her pain bottled up. She refused to let him see just how deeply he'd hurt her.

"Let me explain. We can work this out—"

"No, we can't." Her nails dug into her palms as she struggled to maintain her composure. "Do you know how much this hurts? It's killing me to stand here. To be so close to you and yet so far away."

He lifted his head and stared up at the blue sky for a moment, as though coming up with a rebuttal. "You don't understand. I do care about her. But I don't love her."

Reese heard the sincerity in his voice and saw the plead-ing look in his eyes. Maybe he hadn't set out to make her the other woman, but that didn't change the fact that three was a crowd. And she wasn't going to stick around to make a further fool of herself.

"I'm leaving."

Alex reached out, grabbing her arm. "Don't leave like this."

She spun around so fast his eyes widened in surprise. "Why not? What reason do I have to stay?" Her throat burned as the raw words came tumbling out. "Did you end things with Catherine? Did you tell your family the marriage is off?"

He held her gaze. "It's not that easy. Her father is very influential. If he pulls his business from Mirraccino, it'll have a devastating ripple effect on the country's economy. But you must know that I have never made any promises to her. It's all a business arrangement—my duty."

"You're forgetting I saw you two together. You aren't strangers."

"You're right. Catherine and I have been friends since we were kids. But I swear it has never gone further than that—"

"Stop." She wasn't going to let his smooth tongue and convincing words confuse her. "The fact is you can't have us both. It's time you choose between your duty and your desires."

She stood there pleading with her eyes for him to choose her—to choose love. But as the strained silence stretched on, her hopes were dashed. She had no choice but to accept that his duty to the crown would always come first. She might have fallen in love with him, but obviously it was a one-way street.

A tear dripped onto her cheek and she quickly dashed it away. "I—I have some packing to do."

She pulled her shoulders back and moved past him with determined steps. It was time to make a hasty exit before she dissolved into a disgusting puddle of self-pity. And she couldn't let that happen. Her heart was already in tattered ruins. The only thing she had left was her pride.

Alex jogged over to stand in front of her. "Give me time to sort things out."

"You can have all of the time in the world. I'm leaving." Then as an afterthought, she slipped off the pink sapphire and tossed it at him. "And I won't be needing this any longer."

She turned and strode up the beach...alone.

CHAPTER EIGHTEEN

ALEX PLACED THE STORYBOOK Reese had given him for Christmas next to his suitcase.

He probably shouldn't have opened it without her. But after she'd left he'd been so lonely without her that he needed a tangible connection.

He stared down at the hardback copy of *How the Grinch Stole Christmas.* Was she sending him a message? Did she really think his heart was three sizes too small? Probably. And he couldn't blame her for thinking so. He'd made a total mess of things.

Since the day she'd left him standing on the beach, he'd barely slept. He couldn't wipe the devastated look on her face from his mind. For all of his trying to stay aloof and objective, he'd fallen head over heels in love with her.

It wasn't until he'd tried explaining his relationship with Catherine and his family's expectations for him to Reese that he realized he'd spent his entire life being the perfect prince and honor bound to the crown. And he just couldn't do it any longer—not at the expense of his love for the one woman who made him want more than his position within the monarchy, the woman who made him believe that without love, he had nothing.

Now the time had come for him to make his needs a priority, even if they didn't coincide with the family's view of an acceptable life for a prince. At last, he fully understood what his brother had gone through with his brief marriage. And from the look of Demetrius, he really did love that woman. Now Alex wondered if his brother would ever have a chance at true happiness.

However, Alex wasn't the crown prince. He wasn't held to such high standards. He'd made his decision and now he didn't have time to waste. After a few phone calls to make the necessary arrangements, Alex went to meet with the king.

Papa was having breakfast with his brother and Catherine. Alex came to a stop at the end of the formal dining table, more certain than ever that he was doing the right thing.

"You're late." The king pointed at a chair. "Join us."

"I don't have time. I have something urgent I must do."

"I would think Catherine's presence would be your priority."

Alex glanced at Catherine. He'd spoken to her last night and explained how he had planned to do his duty, no matter what was asked of him, but somewhere along the way, he'd lost his heart to a beautiful firecracker from New York. And he just couldn't pass up his one chance to be truly happy. Catherine was happy for him. She had a secret of her own. She was in love with someone, too, but she had been reluctant to do anything about it. Now both Catherine and he could be happy.

She nodded at him, as though giving him encouragement to keep going. He hoped someday he, Reese and Catherine could all be friends. But he had to win back Reese's heart first.

"Catherine and I have spoken and we're not getting engaged. Not now. Not ever."

The king's gaze narrowed. "Alexandro, we've discussed

this and it has been decided that you'll marry Catherine. And it's high time that you do it."

Alex shook his head. "From now on, I'll be making my own decisions about who I marry." He made direct eye contact with the king. "I'll not let you bully me into giving up the woman that I love like you did with Demetrius."

The king's fork clattered against the plate. "I did no such thing. Your brother and that woman decided to part ways of their own accord."

Alex didn't believe it. Demetrius was too distraught to have dumped his wife. But when Alex turned to his twin, his brother nodded his head.

"It's true. Papa didn't split us up."

The king sat back and crossed his arms. Alex wasn't about to give up. This was far too important—Reese was far too important.

Alex continued to stand at attention the way he used to do when he was young and in a world of trouble. "You should also know that I'm not going to drop everything in my life to cover for the latest scandal to strike the family. I have my own life to lead. And my priority is seeking the forgiveness of the woman I love. I've put my duty ahead of her since the day I met her. Now it's time that she comes first."

His brother's mouth gaped. Too bad he hadn't been able to make such a bold move. But the crown prince didn't have as many options.

Everyone grew quiet, waiting for the king's reaction. What would he say? Alex didn't honestly know. The breath caught in his throat as he waited, hoping the king wouldn't disown him.

His papa made direct eye contact with him. "I've done a lot of thinking these past few weeks. Though there are legitimate reasons for a strategic marriage, perhaps there's another way to strike up the necessary allegiances. Who am I to deny my sons a chance to know love like your mother and I shared?"

Alex had to be certain he'd heard the king correctly. "You approve of Reese."

The king's silver head nodded. "When you are in New York, make sure you invite your new princess to the palace for the winter ball. It will be the perfect place to properly introduce her to everyone."

Alex truly liked the idea of escorting Reese to the ball. He just hoped she would find it in her heart to forgive him. "I'll most definitely invite her."

Alex didn't spare any time making his way to the private airstrip. With the king's blessing, he knew that he could now have his family and the woman he loved—if she would forgive him.

CHAPTER NINETEEN

THIS HAS TO WORK.

Alex stared blindly out the car window. Large, fluffy snowflakes fell, limiting visibility. Aside from the snow, his return to New York City was so different than his last visit. This time he was surrounded by his security detail and instead of a wild taxi ride he was settled in the comfortable backseat of a black town car with diplomatic tags. There was no looking over his shoulder. This time it didn't matter who knew he was in town.

His only goal for being here was to win back Reese's trust—her love.

The car tires crunched over the snow. He glanced out the window at the passing houses. They were getting close. His gut tightened. Normally when he had an important speech, he'd make notes and settle most of what he'd say ahead of time. This time, he didn't know what he'd say. He didn't even know if he'd get past the front door.

The car tires spun a bit as the car eased into the driveway. Alex pulled on his leather gloves. Before the car pulled to a full stop, Alex had the back door open. He took the porch steps two at a time.

His foot had just touched the porch when the door swung open. It was Reese. Her long hair was swept back in a smooth ponytail. Her bangs fell smoothly over her forehead.

Her eyes widened as she took in his appearance. "What are you doing here?"

He might have been prepared for the winter weather, but he wasn't prepared for the hard edge in her voice.

"Hello, Reese. You forgot your Christmas presents."

Her eyes grew round. "You flew all the way here to give me some presents?"

"And I thought we should talk—"

"No. Take your presents and go away. We said everything that needed to be said." She waved him away. When he didn't move, she added, "We were a publicity stunt. Nothing more. Now go home to Catherine."

He refused to be deterred. One way or another, she'd hear him out. "I am here on a matter of great importance."

"That's too bad. I'm on my way out. I don't have time to talk."

"Then let me give you a ride." He moved aside so she could see his hired car. Other women he'd met would swoon at this opportunity. But Reese wasn't other women. She wouldn't be easily swayed. But she was most definitely worth the effort.

When he sensed she was about to turn him down, he added, "Either let me take you or expect to see me waiting here when you return."

"You wouldn't."

He arched a brow. There was hardly a thing he wouldn't do to win her back.

She sighed and rolled her eyes. "Fine. If this is what it takes to get rid of you, let's get it over with."

Her pointed words stabbed at his chest. He knew he'd hurt her, but he'd been hoping with time that she would have become more reasonable—more understanding. So much for that wishful thinking. He would have to do a lot of pleading if he was ever going to get her to forgive him.

And he wasn't well versed in apologies. Good thing he was a quick learner.

He waved away the driver, getting the door for her himself. Reese was one of the strongest people he knew. She'd held together her family after her father's betrayal. Not everyone could do that. Now he had to hope that she had enough compassion in her heart for him—to realize that he'd learned from his mistakes.

Reese gave the driver a Manhattan address before turning to Alex. "I hope you really do have something important on your mind. Otherwise you're wasting both our time."

"Trust me. This is very important." She arched a disbelieving brow at him, but he didn't let that deter him. "Do you mind me asking where we're headed?"

"An art school. I've enrolled and this is the first class of the semester. I'm working on my graphic art."

"But what about The Willows? How do you have time to do everything?"

She leaned her head back against the black leather upholstery and stared up at the ceiling. "When I got back from Mirraccino, I found that you were right." Her face contorted into a frown as she made the admission. "I'd been hovering over my mother too much. While I was gone, she handled this place. She regained her footing."

"That's great news. And now you can follow your dreams."

Reese nodded. "It seems my mother and Mr.—erm, Howard are officially dating, too."

"And how does that make you feel?"

She shrugged. "Happy, I guess. After all, it isn't like she owed anything to the memory of my father. So if Howard makes her happy, I'm good with that. Now what brings you here?"

He removed an official invitation with the royal seal from the inner pocket of his black wool coat. He held it out to her. When their fingers brushed, a jolt rushed up his arm and settled in his chest. She quickly pulled back.

He cleared his throat. "Before you open that, I have a few things to say."

She glanced out the window into the snowy afternoon. "Make it quick. We're almost there."

"Reese, I want you to know how sorry I am for not being more up front about my situation with Catherine. I had mentioned you to her on the phone, but I didn't bring up that we were intimately involved. I wasn't sure of Catherine's feelings and didn't want to announce that I wasn't going through with the engagement over the phone."

Reese nailed him with an astonished stare. "So it was better to keep your fiancée in the dark?"

"She was never my fiancée. Not like you're thinking. I never proposed to her. I never loved her. We are friends. Nothing more. In fact, when I told her that you and I were involved, she told me that she was happy to be released from the arrangement because she had fallen in love with someone."

Reese's brows rose. "You're serious."

"Yes. Catherine was as relieved as I was to call off the marriage."

"I bet your family didn't take it well."

"The king respected my decision."

Reese twisted around to look at him face-to-face. "You're really serious? You stood up and told everyone about us?"

"Yes, I did. I realized that I'd let my sense of duty take over my life. I told them that I wouldn't be on call twenty-four-seven to cover up any scandals. You had to come first."

Her eyes opened wide. "You really said that?"

He nodded, reaching out to take her hands in his. "Please believe me. I know I messed up in the past, but I won't let that happen again. No more secrets."

His gaze probed hers, looking for some sign that he was getting through to her. But in a blink her surprise slid behind a solid wall of indifference. Was he wrong about her? Didn't she feel the same as him?

Before he could think of something else to say to convince her to give him another chance, the car pulled to a stop in front of a building.

She grabbed her backpack from the seat. "This is where I get out."

"Can I wait for you? We can talk some more. I know we can work this out."

"No. You've said what you've come here to say. Now please go."

She got out of the car and closed the door with a resounding thud. His chest ached as he watched her walk away. He raked his fingers through his hair and pulled on the short strands as he fought off the urge to go after her.

What had she just done?

Panic clutched Reese's chest. She rushed over to the building, heedless of the coating of snow on the sidewalk. She yanked open the door of the arts building and hustled inside with no real destination in mind. It wasn't until she was away from the wall of windows and out of sight of the car that she stopped and leaned against the wall. It was then that she let out a pent-up breath.

Had she lost her mind?

Had she really just turned down an honest-to-goodness prince?

But it wasn't a royal prince that she loved. It was plain Alex—a living, breathing, imperfect human—the same person who'd hurt her. Alex just happened to come with an impressive title and hung his coat in an amazing palace. But those physical things weren't enough to sway her decision.

The backs of her eyes stung and she blinked, refusing to give in to tears. He'd said all of the right things. Why couldn't she let down her guard? Why couldn't she give him another chance?

She glanced at the large metal clock on the far wall. She had five minutes until her class started. She'd been hoping that going back to school would fill the empty spot in her life—help her forget—but nothing could wipe away the memories of Alex.

Part of her wanted to run back out the door and into his arms. The other part of her said it just wasn't right. Something was missing.

She glanced down at the envelope he'd handed her in the car. Her name was scrolled over the front of the heavy parchment. The royal seal of Mirraccino was stamped onto the back. Curiosity poked at her.

Her finger slipped into the opening in the flap and she ripped along the fold. Inside was an invitation that read:

King Ferdinando of Mirraccino formally invites you to the Royal Winter Ball. The grand fete will take place at the royal palace on Saturday, the seventh of March at six o'clock. The honor of your presence is requested.

Reese stared at the invitation for a moment, stunned that she was holding an invitation to a royal ball. A deep, weary sigh passed her lips. When she went to put the invitation in her purse, it slipped from her fingers and fluttered to the floor.

She bent over to snatch it up when she noticed some handwriting on the back of the invite. She pulled it closer.

Reese, I love you with every fiber of my being. Please be my princess at the ball.
Alex

He loved her!

Those were the words she'd been waiting to hear.

Her lips lifted and her heart pounded. In that moment, the pieces all fell into place. She loved him and he loved her.

In the next breath, the smile slipped from her lips. She'd sent him away. Was it too late? Was he gone for good?

She took off running for the door. He had to be there. He couldn't have left yet.

Please let him still be here.

Practically knocking over a couple of young guys coming through the door, she yelled an apology over her shoulder and kept moving. She stepped onto the sidewalk and stopped.

The black town car was gone. For the first time ever, Alex had finally done as she'd asked. Why now? Tears pricked her eyes.

And then she saw it. The black town car. That had to be the one. It was approaching the end of the block and had on its turn signal.

She had to stop him. Not worrying about the ice or snow, she set off running after the car. She couldn't give up. She was so close to having the man she loved.

The car came to a stop at the intersection. She called out to Alex, not that he would hear her. Then the brake lights went out and the car surged forward. Reese's chest burned as she called out one last time to him.

Then the bright brake lights flashed on and Alex emerged from the back. He sent her a questioning look before he set off toward her with open arms. She rushed toward him with the intention of never leaving his embrace.

After he held her for a moment, he took a step back so they could make eye contact. "I don't understand. What changed your mind?"

"You did."

"But how? When you got out of the car, you were so certain."

She held up the invitation. "What you wrote here said everything I needed to know."

His eyes closed as he sighed. "I was so worried about apologizing that I totally forgot to tell you the most important part. Reese, since I've known you my heart has grown three sizes because it's so full of love for you. I promise I'll tell you every day for the rest of our lives."

She smiled up at him. "Why don't you start now?"

"I love you."

"I love you, too."

EPILOGUE

Two months later...

PRINCE ALEXANDRO CASTANAVO stared across the hallway at Reese. He'd never seen anyone so beautiful. She stole his breath away. And the best part was she was beautiful inside and out. After they'd spent the past couple of weeks at the palace, no one in Mirraccino could deny that Reese would make a generous and kind princess.

Tonight's ball was for the residents of Mirraccino. With it being between growing seasons, this was the nation's chance to celebrate the past year and the royal family's chance to mingle with the citizens—to bring the island together.

And it was Alex's chance to introduce them to the queen of his heart. They were going to love her as much as he did—well, maybe not that much, but pretty close.

He approached and offered his arm to her. She smiled up at him and his heart thumped. How had he ended up being the luckiest man alive?

"May I escort you into the ballroom?"

Reese grabbed the skirt of her royal-blue-and-silver gown and curtsied. Her eyes sparkled with mischief.

"Why yes, Your Highness."

"You know, I like the sound of that." He couldn't help but

tease her back and he put on a serious expression. "Perhaps I'll have you address me as Your Highness all the time."

Reese's mouth gaped. "You wouldn't."

He smiled. "I'm teasing you. I love you the way you are, strong and feisty. I'd never try to change that about you."

Before he could say more, they were summoned inside the ballroom to be announced.

"His Royal Highness, Prince Alexandro Castanavo, and Her Ladyship, Miss Reese Harding."

Before they could be ushered into the crowd, Alex held up his hand, pausing the procession. "If you all will allow me a moment, I have something very special to share."

A hush fell over the crowded room. He fished a black velvet box from his pocket. He was surprised the box had any material left after he'd looked inside at least a couple hundred times trying to decide if it was the right ring for Reese. In the end, he couldn't imagine her with any other ring.

He dropped to one knee and heard Reese's swift intake of breath. He lifted his head and smiled at her, hoping to reassure her. Still, she sent him a wide-eyed gaze.

He took her now trembling hand in his and he realized that perhaps his idea to share this very special moment with everyone he cared about had been a miscalculation. But he was on bended knee now and the room was so quiet that he could hear the beating of his own heart.

"Reese, would you do me the honor of being my princess today and for all of the days of my life?"

Her eyes sparkled with tears of joy as she vigorously nodded. "Yes, I will."

He stood tall and removed the ring from the box. His hands weren't too steady as he slipped the five-carat pink sapphire surrounded by sixty-four diamond side stones onto her finger.

"You kept it." She held up her hand to look at it.

"I thought the ring had a special meaning for us. You aren't disappointed, are you?"

She held up her hand to admire the engagement ring. "I love it!" Her warm gaze moved to him. "But not as much as I love you."

* * * * *

LET'S TALK
Romance

For exclusive extracts, competitions
and special offers, find us online:

- **f** facebook.com/millsandboon
- **🐦** @MillsandBoon
- **📷** @MillsandBoonUK

Get in touch on 01413 063232

For all the latest titles coming soon, visit
millsandboon.co.uk/nextmonth

MILLS & BOON

THE HEART OF ROMANCE

A ROMANCE FOR EVERY READER

MODERN

Prepare to be swept off your feet by sophisticated, sexy and seductive heroes, in some of the world's most glamourous and roman locations, where power and passion collide.

HISTORICAL

Escape with historical heroes from time gone by. Whether your passion for wicked Regency Rakes, muscled Vikings or rugged Highlanders, a the romance of the past.

MEDICAL

Set your pulse racing with dedicated, delectable doctors in the high-pre sure world of medicine, where emotions run high and passion, comfor love are the best medicine.

True Love

Celebrate true love with tender stories of heartfelt romance, from the rush of falling in love to the joy a new baby can bring, and a focus on emotional heart of a relationship.

Desire

Indulge in secrets and scandal, intense drama and plenty of sizzling ho action with powerful and passionate heroes who have it all: wealth, sta good looks…everything but the right woman.

HEROES

Experience all the excitement of a gripping thriller, with an intense ro mance at its heart. Resourceful, true-to-life women and strong, fearless face danger and desire - a killer combination!

To see which titles are coming soon, please visit
millsandboon.co.uk/nextmonth

JOIN US ON SOCIAL MEDIA!

Stay up to date with our latest releases, author news and gossip, special offers and discounts, and all the behind-the-scenes action from Mills & Boon...

 @millsandboon

 @millsandboonuk

 facebook.com/millsandboon

 @millsandboonuk

It might just be true love...